SHADOW CALL

Also by AdriAnne Strickland & Michael Miller

Shadow Run

SHADOW

ADRIANNE STRICKLAND &
MICHAEL MILLER

CALL

Delacorte Press

Text copyright © 2018 by Michael Miller and AdriAnne Strickland

All rights reserved. Published in the United States by Delacorte Press, an imprint of Random House Children's Books, a division of Penguin Random House LLC, New York.

Delacorte Press is a registered trademark and the colophon is a trademark of Penguin Random House LLC.

Visit us on the Web! GetUnderlined.com

Educators and librarians, for a variety of teaching tools, visit us at RHTeachersLibrarians.com

Library of Congress Cataloging-in-Publication Data
Names: Strickland, AdriAnne, author. | Miller, Michael, author.
Title: Shadow call / AdriAnne Strickland & Michael Miller.
Description: First edition. | New York : Delacorte Press, [2018] | Sequel to: Shadow run. | Summary: Now sharing the responsibilities of captaining the *Kaitan* with Nev, Qole sets out to stop an evil plan.
Identifiers: LCCN 2016059251 | ISBN 978-0-399-55257-1 (hc) | ISBN 978-0-399-55258-8 (ebook)
Subjects: | CYAC: Science fiction. | Princes—Fiction. | Families—Fiction. | Adventure and adventurers—Fiction. | Space ships—Fiction.
Classification: LCC PZ7.S91658 Sh 2018 | DDC [Fic]—dc23

The text of this book is set in 12-point Bembo.

Printed in the United States of America
10 9 8 7 6 5 4 3 2 1
First Edition

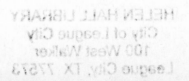

To Margaret. I can write of joy because of you.

—**Michael**

To all the Pamelas and Daniels in my life.

—**AdriAnne**

Prelude

THIS NIGHT WAS MINE.

The party was in full swing: the gossip buzzed along my skin, the music thrummed through the soles of my towering heels, and the crowd flowed around me like a river of colorful silks and gems, bending to me.

The ballroom itself was the crown jewel of the palace: a transparent crystalline floor, slowly darkening bell-shaped walls, and the blackness above, where a scale holo-map of our star system hovered and sparkled in the air. Directly under the image of Luvos, my homeworld, in the heart of the palace that overlooked our capital city, I stood. I was the center of it all, everything and everyone in my orbit.

But I had a mission. Heathran Belarius had arrived and was in my sights. I snatched a glittering goblet from a passing platter and downed the contents, which lent me extra fire. Not that I felt like I needed it, particularly. Not even the heir to the galaxy's most powerful family would be able to withstand my charm, despite how forbidding he looked in his dark purple suit and gold cravat, which perfectly offset his near-black skin. His flat eyes scanned the crowd, seeking . . .

Someone stepped in front of me, cutting off my view of Heathran in the scintillating crowd. The words of dismissal rose on my tongue, ready to be bared.

"Marsius!" I said instead as I recognized my little brother. "I was about to greet Heathran. We have very important business to discuss."

The dismissal sheathed in my words didn't escape him, and he made a face. "You never discuss important business. You probably want to talk about clothes or the latest gossip vid or"—his face distorted further—"*kissing* or something."

"Or something," I said as patiently as I could manage, suppressing the desire to put my hands around his throat and squeeze. Amazing how an eleven-year-old could try to be so belittling to his superiors. "And since you've made your distaste for such topics plain, why don't you run along and leave me to it?" Tousling his brown hair, I looked over his head to find Heathran slowly migrating from where he'd stood near the ballroom entrance. He wasn't getting much farther from me, but he wasn't getting any closer, either.

"Because you *should* be discussing important business," Marsius said, dodging out from under my hand and drawing my eyes back to him once again.

I tried not to grind my teeth in impatience. Tonight was for smiling. "Oh? And I suppose you're here to tell me what that is. Let me guess," I said, giving him a taste of his own belittling medicine. "Now that I'm heiress, you'll want more sweets at dinner, and your favorite team to be declared the unending victors—"

"Sol," Marsius interrupted with a frustrated jerk of his head, "just because I'm younger than you doesn't mean I'm stupid. And I know you're not stupid either, even though you act like it most of the time." He hurried on after my eyes involuntarily widened, misreading my surprise for anger, most likely. "Which is why I've been trying to talk to you for weeks. I have a plan."

"For how to get more cake on the menu?" I asked dismissively, trying to move around him.

He planted himself in front of me once again, a miniature version of all the men in dress suits who'd been trying to force my attention to *their* plans, of late. "I can help you. We can help each other. I know that you don't really want to be heiress, that you didn't want Nev to be exiled." His voice grew ragged over the name. *Of course.* This was about Nev, our older brother and mutual grievance. "I think we need Nev back. I know I can convince him to return, but Father won't listen to me."

I sighed. Clearly, Marsius didn't grasp the severity of the situation. "Nev forced Father to disinherit and exile him. Our brother betrayed us for a commoner girl, and you know exactly how many soldiers and Bladeguards he killed in the process. And our family has been an absolute disaster since he was exiled. You think I don't pay attention to important business, hm?" I asked, flicking him lightly on his silver cravat, which seemed too grand for his lanky neck. "Well, our finances have taken a dive, our research into Shadow has stalled, and everyone is moping about like you."

"But what are you doing to elevate it?"

"*Alleviate* it, you mean?" I asked, smirking as he flushed. He

3

might want to play at being an adult, but there was nothing like an older sister to remind him he wasn't one. I tossed my shining golden curls. "By being a pleasant diversion. How do you like my party?" I didn't wait for him to answer; his expression was answer enough. "Don't fret, Marsius. I promise to talk to Father about Nev."

Despite my not specifying *when,* he brightened. "Really? I can—"

"You can enjoy yourself, like other kids your age are doing."

"But—"

"You can help, I know. You'll help by leaving me in peace right now." It sounded churlish, but I was out of patience. Before Marsius could make even more of a scene, I stepped around him, and bumped right into someone else. A broad chest blocked my view, another dark suit. I wanted to run them through with my smile . . . and then my sharpness melted entirely.

"Father!"

"Solara," he said, giving me a nod. "Marsius."

There was no mistaking the dismissal in how he said my little brother's name, and no avoiding it for Marsius. He bowed his head and dodged off through the crowd, sending me one last pleading look. I didn't acknowledge it. Too bad Father hadn't dismissed me with him. I could have gone straight for Heathran, who was drifting away from me, now that he'd seen who was speaking to me.

Nothing killed the potential for romance like a father—and a king, no less.

Father stood, regarding me for a moment, taking in the daring cut of my dress with a disapproving twitch of his eyelid. His own suit was the model of a Dracorte king's, darkest of blues, subtly embossed with our family emblem at the cuffs, less subtly layered in silver embroidery and military medals that no doubt indicated something grand about his person. The ensemble looked as stiff and uncompromising as he was, though the sharpness of his Dracorte-silver eyes looked dull from the pressure of recent events.

He surprised me by holding out his hand. "Will you honor me with a dance?"

He hadn't paid any attention to me yet this evening, never mind that this was the party celebrating that he'd declared me his heiress. Perhaps he was too busy silently mourning his previous heir.

And perhaps he was right to.

I stilled the thrill of both anticipation and apprehension that came with Father's attention, and took his hand. "The honor is mine."

"We need to talk." Of course, he wouldn't want to simply dance with his daughter. He was here because he wanted something, just like everyone else. The music and our choreographed motions would cover any disturbance between us.

"If this is about that peace accord you wanted me to study, please, spare me. I'll get to it soon." Actually, I already knew it back to front, but even if I'd wanted to tell him that, he likely wouldn't have believed me. I hadn't exactly cultivated the image of studious daughter.

Father led me into the first couple steps of the dance. For a flaring, astonishing second, I wished he would just move with me to the music and keep his mouth shut, and not only because I knew I wouldn't like whatever he was going to say. He was a skilled dancer, and I could almost imagine enjoying myself. But the feeling, and any chance of that happening, passed.

"It's about your Rendering, and your Flight," he said. "You need to complete these important rites of passage for anyone to truly take you seriously as heiress."

That was *almost* enough to make both my feet and my smile slip. I hadn't expected him to want me to pass the test of the Rendering at all, or complete a Flight—a solo mission to bring something of value back to the family—quite so quickly. "I had some thoughts on where I could go on my Flight to improve diplomatic ties with our family, but—"

"That wouldn't be to Embra, would it?" Father said flatly, with a sardonic lift of one brow.

Embra was the Belarius homeworld. Heathran's. Father thought I wanted to use an honored family tradition in order to go *flirt*. He was taking me as seriously as Marsius was.

I carried on, ignoring both him and my white-hot flash of rage. "But surely you don't expect me to complete the *Rendering*. Nev did that when he was eight!"

He spun me in a circle. "All the more reason you should be able to admirably undergo it at age eighteen."

I laughed as I came back to him, though I wished I could scream. "You expect *me,* in these heels, to stand around with weights on my shoulders for an entire night in front of an audience just to prove I can?"

"It's to prove your dedication to—"

"I know the symbolism," I snapped, my cheerful façade breaking for just a moment. "And I know my dedication to my family and my subjects can be demonstrated in other ways." I couldn't help a smirk. "Have Marsius stand in for me. He's young and resilient."

No one else would have noticed, but Father missed a beat. "You can't be serious. You would allow your little brother to accept your burden?"

"It's called a joke, Father dear," I said, rolling my eyes. "Must every moment be serious unto death?"

Father's face was a perfect mask for the dancers around us. "I'm disheartened to see that being made heiress has done nothing for your sense of responsibility or decorum."

My hand clenched sharply in his. I wasn't sure what I wanted to do more, tear away or crush his fingers. Would that I could do either without causing a scene.

Father shot me a disapproving look at what he probably perceived as a childish show of emotion. "However, I can't say as I'm surprised. Which is why I've just come from speaking with Gavros."

Whatever they'd spoken of, then, it couldn't be good. "Gavros . . ." I acted as though I couldn't quite place the name. "Gavros Dracorte? The general? Some second cousin or another of yours?"

"He's a royal of the finest breeding, and of the highest military distinction. Qualities which will make him an excellent match."

Match. The word was like a punch to the stomach. "For whom?" I asked, even though I knew.

"For you, of course. Don't be obtuse."

It took everything I had not to come to a halt, to let him lead me in a few more steps. To follow like an animal to the slaughter. "But he's *old*." Gavros was younger than Father by a score of years, but he was still over twice my age.

"He is hale and in his prime, with an unparalleled grasp of strategy. You'll find his intellectual prowess stimulating," Father insisted in that tone of his, as if he could direct gravity to weigh more heavily upon me. "Anyway, you knew long ago that your eventual royal partner wouldn't be someone you've flirted with at a party." His eyes flicked in Heathran's direction.

"And you can never pollute the Dracorte name with another royal line. Not even one that some may see as superior to ours."

I didn't bother telling him that I agreed. I took a deep breath and murmured quietly, "That's why I never intend to marry."

Father paused for less than a beat this time, as if he was ready for combat. "You will put the stability of the entire system at risk for a childish whim?" Weighty or not, his voice was still calm. Rather, it was *my* hand that twitched in his again. *Childish whim?* Hadn't Nev been the one to give up the throne over an infatuation, putting us all in this position in the first place? "Solara, we are talking about the fate of our family, not a game."

True. The game was up.

"Perhaps you're right." My vision glossed in tears, and I lifted my lids enough so that only Father might see them, looking entirely vulnerable despite how he might hate it. I kept my voice low. "I'm not ready for this, *especially* not marriage. Nev had his whole life to prepare for rule, to accept the responsibility. I thought I would have more time to adjust."

But Father hadn't given me any time.

"We're not talking about *him*," Father growled under his breath, sending me into another spin that was a little too fast.

"Why aren't we?" I'd promised Marsius, after all. It was just happening sooner than I'd expected. "Everyone thinks Nev should be here instead of me, only no one is saying it aloud." I held Father's eyes as he led me in a complex series of steps, and he blinked first. I'd watched him stare down my brothers more times than I could count, but he'd never managed the same with me. "If you believe I'm not cut out for ruling, then just say so."

"*Nevarian*"—he had a difficult time saying the name—"is

a traitor to the throne. *Your* throne, someday, even though you seem not to care much about it. I don't want to hear his name again." This lapse in Nev's duty was a failure to be taken so seriously it couldn't even be discussed, not childishness, as he saw my own shortcomings. Even as a disappointment, Nev had done better than I, in Father's eyes. "He is no longer our concern."

Father sounded like he meant it, but my older brother still had worth to many here, not the least of whom were Mother and Marsius. Many people still looked to him, idolized him, even in his absence, even after all the damage he'd done to our capital, Dracorva.

No one would take me seriously as his replacement. I cast a glance at the farthest planet in the model of our system, its sun a faint spark at the distant edge of the ceiling, nearly lost in darkness, where Nev was spending his exile with his common girl.

"Erratic, irresponsible notions such as these are all the more reason for you to make haste in marrying," Father continued. "Gavros will be able to support you, guide you in decisions—"

Rule for you, make you into a figurehead.

"I refuse to marry him, or anyone." My voice turned to steel, slicing through the lecture and making Father blink and miss another step. "And you can't make me."

He stared for a long moment. I could see the flash of desperation, as brief as the twitch of my hand, in his eyes. Our family was in peril, and yet he viewed *me*, a young woman assuming the throne alone, as its greatest danger. In that moment, if there was a way he could have forced me to marry, I knew he would have.

And I hated him for it.

"You yourself just conceded that you aren't ready for this

responsibility," Father said slowly, "and yet you refuse my solution. What exactly are you proposing?"

"If I need help, there is one person who has trained for this from birth—if no longer to rule, then to advise me as *I* rule, from behind the throne. His failures will be hidden in my shadow, and his strengths will become mine. We need to go to Alaxak." My voice didn't waver now. "That will be my Flight. And"—I swallowed—"I promise I'll complete the Rendering afterward."

Father only had to see Nev again and he would understand. No doubt he believed Nev to be an unforgivable traitor. But perhaps not before he would at least *try* to treat with him. *Try* to see him differently, despite his past behavior—the same courtesy he refused to extend to me.

When he met Mother's eyes across the ballroom, I knew then that he would do it. Mother missed Nev. Underneath all her layers of prim and proper, she was completely sentimental at heart. Father missed him too, but the difference was that she'd admit it.

The music swelled. Despite losing Heathran for the moment, the night was indeed mine.

1

QOLE

I WAS HOME. NOT ONLY WAS I IN MY CAPTAIN'S QUARTERS ON THE *Kaitan,* but the ship was docked on Alaxak, in my village harbor, Gamut. I stretched on the furs of my bunk, still drowsy from my afternoon nap after a furious Shadow-fishing schedule had kept us up all night. I wasn't ready to be awake, but a knock at the door sent me sitting up.

"Hey?" I answered.

I knew who it would be before I heard his voice. "It's me."

"Hi," I said as Nev entered without waiting.

Ancestors, but the sight of him still took my breath away, even with how easily he slipped in that door these days, even with the scraggly beard he now wore as a partial disguise against casual observers. The startling silver-gray eyes, so bright they nearly glowed, the sculpted face, the perfect waves of light brown hair my fingers itched to touch. The fact that all these features came from *very* particular bloodlines didn't seem to bother me anymore. Not much, anyway.

I stood up as he entered, and before I knew what was happening, his arms were around me, and he was crushing me to his chest.

Whoa. I still wasn't used to this. And, Great Collapse, he was strong.

"I missed you," he breathed into my hair.

I let out a strangled laugh. "You saw me all day—er, night. And you're also squeezing the air from my lungs."

"Sorry." He loosened his hold but didn't let me go, perching his chin on the top of my head. "And I was *around* you. It's not the same."

"Well, we can't exactly be doing *this* in the middle of a Shadow run. We might as well fly straight into a star."

Nev's arms slipped away from me. Maybe he'd sensed my stiffness. I didn't mind his presence here—in fact, part of me wanted it to be a more permanent arrangement. But the tension from the previous run was still too fresh in my mind.

Instead of talking about any of that, he said, "Come out with me."

I blinked at him. "Where?"

"There's a bonfire on the beach tonight." He playfully tugged my arm toward the door. "You know, you led me to believe this place was dreadfully boring—and I thought it was too, when I was here by myself. But I now know that I was just never invited to where the real fun was."

I sighed. "I don't go to these things often myself. I mean, I'm invited, but . . ."

Not many people wanted me around. Everyone knew what happened to people in my family. It happened to other families too, even on other planets near concentrations of

Shadow, but my family was one of the oldest on Alaxak, our Shadow grounds the biggest. Now only Arjan and I were left of the Uvgamuts. We were like missiles ready to explode.

Not so fun at parties.

That didn't stop Nev. "All the more reason for you to come," he said.

Somehow, I let him drag me out the door and off the ship. "Wait, the rest of your disguise," I said as we headed down the ramp that stretched to the dock.

His new beard wasn't enough to mask him, though it helped. He paused to slip in the flat brown contacts and bite down on a capsule, both of which he always carried with him now. His features altered in seconds, almost like they were shifting slightly on his face, and then we were good to go.

The walk down to the beach was freezing, crystalline, stunning. I'd seen it many times, but alongside Nev, an outsider, I viewed it with new eyes. The night sky was black velvet glittering with gems, with a sash of shimmering, colorful light across the expanse—the far-off molecular clouds. The two moons shone like spotlights. Our breath fogged the air as we stared up at it all, walking hand in hand and trying not to trip over rocks, chunks of ice, or driftwood on the path from the dock down to the beach. Gamut itself was a collection of softly glowing orbs beyond the shore, as were the lights of various starships along the dock.

The ocean was a humming whoosh in our ears, and for a second, I didn't know if I'd ever been anywhere more perfectly beautiful. In that moment, I forgot everything that was bothering me.

Until Nev finally brought it up.

"I know today—last night—was difficult. I know the crew hasn't entirely accepted me, especially Arjan, and since he's your brother, you might find that particularly troubling." He spoke quickly, as if to get it all out before I could stop him— deny it, even though there was nothing to deny. He and Arjan had been at each other's throats the entire run. "But we *can* do this," Nev finished.

This. That little word held so much. And I got the feeling that Nev had intended it to. What was *this*? Nev, living and working on my ship, my planet? The two of us together, not just as captain and crew, but as something more? Building a future we could both share, despite coming from completely different places?

I wasn't even quite sure what that future would look like. I didn't know if I could share the responsibilities of captaining the *Kaitan* with Nev, or if he could give up all remnants of his old life to accept them. Even if we could, would we make our union more official? I'd never let myself consider something like marriage before. I never thought I'd live long enough.

I still didn't know if I would, but for some reason, the threat of death was no longer enough to keep me from toying with the possibilities.

"I didn't bring you out here to talk about that, though," he said, helping me over a particularly large driftwood log, pale as bone in the night. No one usually helped me step over things; he only got away with it because he was holding my hand. Still, I somehow liked it. Which meant my brain was definitely turning into a puddle of sickly sweet goop.

"So what *do* you want to talk about?"

"Anything. We haven't had much time for simple con- versation with so much outside interference." As if our cop- ing with his exile and fishing for Shadow were only *outside interference*—but in the darkness, I caught Nev's grin, which let me know he was joking. "Why, Miss Uvgamut, courtship usually involves getting to know one another, flirtatious banter, flattery, starlit walks . . ."

I tried to suppress my own grin. "Is that what this is—courtship?" Nev looked at me so seriously for a moment that my cheeks grew warmer than should have been possible out here. I went on quickly. "Well, whoever wrote your courtship manuals probably didn't plan for it to be below freezing. Or for giant logs and pebble beaches in place of crystal floors and hand-tailored gowns," I teased, as he struggled up onto another log that was waist-high. The bonfire winked at us in the distance from beyond it.

"Oh, I don't think any Dracorvan courtship manual would have covered someone like you. You're one of a kind, I'm afraid." He stuck his hand down for me, but I ignored it and vaulted up onto the log instead.

"Is this the flattery part of the flirtatious banter?"

Nev laughed loudly, his unrestrained amusement ringing all around us, and I realized I loved that sound.

His hands slid along my arms, top to bottom. It didn't matter that I was buried in layers of fur-lined leather; his touch made me shiver. "I can't believe I ever thought flattery would work on you," he said. "Remember when we first met? You told me if I sucked up any harder, you'd think you were in a vacuum."

Now I couldn't keep from grinning. "Who knows, maybe it did work."

"Should I try again, then?" He cleared his throat theatrically and swept his hand to his heart. "You fly a ship better than a Bladeguard wields a Disruption Blade, and you lead your crew like a seasoned general—"

My own laugh rang out now. "Ancestors, no. Stop!"

"So then let's get to know each other instead."

I looked away as his eyes grew more intense again. Unlike him, I didn't magically have the right words for these types of situations. "Nev, I think it's safe to say we know each other."

He shrugged. "I know what you sound like when you're afraid. I know what you look like when you think you're about to die." Before everything could get too serious, he added, "What I *don't* know is what your favorite color is."

I was about to answer something teasing, until I thought about it for a second. "You know, I'm not entirely sure. Wait, yes, I am. It's the cloudy silvery-blue of glacial runoff. You?"

"Somewhat similar to yours, actually: aquamarine, because it reminds me of Luvos's sky and oceans." At the mention of his home planet—the home he could never see again—my smile dropped away. Nev noticed, and his own smile quickly filled in for mine. "Moving on. Hm, you'll probably throw me off this log if I ask what your favorite flower is."

"Hey, don't assume I don't like flowers," I said with mock indignation, then seized his shoulders and threw him off the log. Unfortunately, Nev was too fast and dragged me with him. We both went tumbling in sand that was part windblown snow and crusty ice.

Nev took advantage of our tumble and pinned my shoulders to the ground, leaning on top of me while he was at it. The stars sparkled in his hair. My breath caught, and not just because of his weight on my chest. It didn't matter that his eyes were dull, his nose was a bit crooked, and his jaw, cheekbones, and brow looked off. Whatever it was inside that made him shone out like a sun and drew me in like nothing else could.

"This is where I'm supposed to compliment your beauty and try to kiss you," he said, his words warm, foggy caresses on my cheeks. "But because you're you and I'm me . . ." He sprinkled snow on my neck, where it trickled down the back of my fur hood.

I squeaked and threw him off me. He sat up, but he was laughing so hard he couldn't stand.

"Now I know what you sound like when you squeak," he said, gasping. "See, learning new things."

I tossed a handful of snow at his face. While he was busy trying to block, then spitting and wiping his eyes, I rolled to my feet and stuck out a hand, for him this time.

"Mr. Dracorte," I said in the finest courtly tone I could muster, which was probably laughable. Instead of laughing, he blinked at me in surprise. *Mr.* sounded so strange with *Dracorte,* but I wasn't about to call him *Prince* or *Your Highness.* I didn't think he would want me to, either. "Might you escort me to the bonfire?"

He grinned and took my hand. After I pulled him to his feet, he kept hold of it. I looked at him, feeling suddenly shy. "It's a snow-whisper. My favorite flower. They don't look like much, just these tiny, pale pink blossoms, but they actually bloom on snow. You can even find them in Gamut in early spring."

His voice was low. "I would very much like to find some with you, when the time comes. But for now . . ."

The bonfire was a massive orange beacon, beckoning us through the darkness between the waves and the shore. I could hear the thrumming of music even at a distance. Some bonfires were the quieter kind, with mingling and conversation. Some, like this one, were for only one purpose. The silhouettes of heavily clad figures leapt and spun—so different from the confined forms of the royal dances that I'd suffered through on Luvos, but no less skillful. Pounding, whipping feet kicked up sand in time to a powerful drumbeat backed by a half-dozen other instruments and a singer with a lovely, smoky voice.

Nev leaned close, his breath a husky murmur in my ear that made me buzz. "I want to dance with you."

I didn't—couldn't—resist as we drew near and the music took hold of us. Nev swept me up in his arms, sending us into something like a skipping waltz, but looser, freer. I was still terrible at it, but I threw my head back and laughed, my hair spilling out of my hood. Fire and the shadows of other dancers spun in the night. I couldn't tell who they were, and I didn't care. Mostly, all I could see was Nev's flame-glowing face, which didn't even look strange to me anymore.

He bent his head and kissed my cheek, then neck, trying to nuzzle deeper into the layers. His lips were chilly, but I'd never felt so warm. *Definitely* different from how we'd danced before. Even here, in the darkness, I was suddenly conscious of who might be watching us. Sure enough, somebody whooped, but it didn't matter.

Nev pulled away for a second, his eyes glowing even behind his contacts in the firelight. Then, finally, he kissed me on the lips, first softly, then deeply, his tongue joining mine and carrying on the dance. My heart, my body, and the very air pounded with the beat. My head spun, but it felt like the entire planet was shifting around us.

The motion of his lips paused, his mouth alongside my face, his breath panting. "Qole." He swallowed, started again, and my pulse leapt, as if attached to his words by a string. "Qole, I think I lo—"

A harsh beeping shredded what he was about to say, wrenching both our eyes open. It was coming from our comms, from Nev's on his wrist and mine clipped to the inside of my coat.

Nev opened the line before I could.

"What?" he snapped.

"Sorry to disturb you, *Your Highness*." My older brother's tone made me wince. "But Basra has just informed me that there's a spike in Shadow activity. I know working for a living might be an unfamiliar concept for you, but it's time to fish."

I cut in before Nev could say something to irritate Arjan further. "Thanks for letting us know. Prep the ship. We'll be right there."

———

Death was headed straight for us once again.

"Arjan, look out!" I shouted into the comm.

I could see his skiff against the bright, rainbow hues of the molecular clouds through the viewport ringing my captain's station on the much bigger *Kaitan*. My brother was towing a glowing net between his ship and ours while banking around other asteroids and debris. Except he hadn't seen the giant rock whirling straight for our net.

The net was only meant to hold Shadow, the energy source we were trying to harvest. Not asteroids. Never mind the damage that would cause to our new net—but the tension of the impact would draw Arjan's skiff and the *Kaitan* together, as if we were weights at the end of a string, flinging us into each other.

Arjan cursed and barrel-rolled, twisting the cables around each other and collapsing the surface area of the shimmering mag-field. But not fast enough. The cables still glanced off the asteroid. The *Kaitan* shuddered, and his skiff lurched violently.

He barely managed to straighten out in time before colliding head-on with yet another asteroid.

Just another day fishing for Shadow in the Alaxak Asteroid Sea.

"Sorry. I assumed he'd seen it, or I would have shot it," Eton said from his perch up in the weapons turret.

"Great Collapse, Arjan," I said, "that was too close. Watch your blind spot!"

"Captain, word choice," Basra warned off-comm from his station below me, visible through the grating under my feet. The gender-fluid, slightly slouched twenty-five-year-old beneath me was not only the best trader in the galaxy and so knew how to read people like infopads, but he was also Arjan's boyfriend. Or girlfriend, depending. His appearance and expression were neutral at the moment, only his eyes sharp in his handsome, coppery face.

It was too late to take back my words.

"Yeah, well"—my brother's voice was bitter, cracking, furious—"that's a little hard when I'm *missing an eye.*"

Sure enough, the asteroid had been on his left, on the side where he now wore a leather eye patch to cover the empty socket. I usually tried to position the *Kaitan* so the mag-field net wasn't on his left, but sometimes it was simply impossible.

"I offered to be his spotter," Nev muttered from the co-pilot station. That console had never been used until now, except by me as a child when I'd watch my father fly. I didn't turn to look at him, trying to keep my focus. I wasn't used to having company up here.

My hand tightened on the throttle. Nev's past—a royal among us commoners—made it difficult for some of the crew to accept him. Maybe, in some ways, for me too. And somehow it was even harder to accept him here in the copilot's chair than it was in my captain's quarters. Our differences were easier to ignore behind closed doors, without an audience.

For Arjan, having anyone in the skiff, helping him fly, would have been much worse: an admission. My brother couldn't fly nearly as well now. He was putting us all at risk. I'd been trying to give him time to adjust, but I couldn't deny it anymore.

I eased off the throttle, making our course less deadly and forcing Arjan, on the other side of the net, to slow with me.

I hoped Nev would keep quiet, but he added, more loudly, "Maybe next time, you'll let me—"

"I don't need your help, *Prince,*" Arjan hissed through the comm. "Don't you think you've done enough already, hey?"

I tensed. Nev's guilt over what had happened was huge, as was his desire for forgiveness, his hope that he was one of us now.

The word *prince* made it clear that he was not. Not forgiven, not one of us.

"Nev doesn't have to be the key," Basra said crisply from below. "You know I can help you. Bionic replacements are—"

"Astronomically expensive," Arjan shot right back. "I don't feel like being indebted to any more rich people, unlike some of us."

Both Basra and I sat back in unison. I wondered if he felt as stung as I did. Basra wasn't just a *rich person.* He was also deeply in love with Arjan.

I felt stung for a different reason. Yes, I'd used some of Nev's remaining funds to rebuild the *Kaitan.* Not only had I repaired all the damage we'd taken and installed a new mag-field net, but I'd upgraded the ship's electronics, weapon systems, and containment hold.

The latter was now strong enough to contain a large amount of Shadow until it could be pumped off. This way, we didn't need a loader—someone who had to risk their life near-constantly by filling smaller canisters with a substance that could drive them mad or burn them to ash in a heartbeat. Nev was probably happy to pay for that, since I'd first hired him on as our loader, back before we knew he was a prince. Before everything had fallen apart.

But it wasn't like I'd just accepted his charity. He was the reason the ship was in shambles in the first place, and part of the reason Arjan was missing an eye. He owed us, not the other way around.

And yet Arjan refused to accept anything from him or anyone else.

"Just get the damned bionic eye, Arjan, so you can stop nearly killing us."

Great Collapse. Leave it to Telu to speak the truth nobody else wanted to. Our hacker, my childhood friend, sat at a station near Basra's, her eyes focused on her feeds, alert for any drones she would have to reroute. The spike of black hair slashing her face and the stark lines of the tattoo around one eye made her look as sharp as she was.

"How about you stop being a bitch—" Arjan began.

"How about," Eton snarled through the comm, "I shut you all up with a few plasma missiles?" We had those now, thanks to Nev. Even Eton, my huge surly weapons tech, grudgingly appreciated *those* upgrades. Still, he couldn't keep from adding, "Or maybe we can all agree to just launch Nev out of the airlock, and I shoot *him* instead."

"All right, pack her up," I said. "Get back to the ship, Arjan."

"What?" Arjan demanded. "No, we need to finish this run. We still need to make our *own* money, remember?"

"If you guys are going to bicker like children, we're going

home. Children can't make Shadow runs. You act like this, we'll *actually* die, not just *nearly* die."

"But—"

"Now," I snarled.

Only the roar of his engines answered me. The skiff shot forward, and I had to lay on the throttle myself to keep up.

"Arjan!"

"I can't hear you!" he called. "Comm is cutting out."

That was a steaming pile of scat, and he knew it. It would serve him right if I didn't keep up and let him reach the end of his tether to come to a neck-whipping halt, but I didn't want to hurt our equipment. There was no way I'd be willing to ask Nev to buy us a *second* net.

Maybe its destruction would be unavoidable, because Arjan was heading right for an even denser cluster of asteroids, interwoven with thick bands of Shadow that flowed in a glittering purple-black river against the brightness of the molecular clouds in the background. Both Basra and Telu swore beneath me. A run like that would have been tough in the old days. Now, as much as I hated to admit it, it would be nigh impossible.

"Yeah, I know," I said in response.

"Qole," Nev said, his tone calm but edged with concern. "That won't only be difficult for Arjan. Remember to let me help you. You're not alone."

The problem was, even back when Nev hadn't been up here, I hadn't felt alone. I'd *had* help; it just wasn't of the human variety.

I sensed it, as Arjan careened toward the rivers of Shadow in his skiff: the ripple, as if he'd reached out to touch it. My brother had been avoiding any blatant use of Shadow longer than I had, but now his need to prove himself seemed to be overcoming his fear of the substance and what it could do to us. His very rational fear.

Despite that, it called to me—or at least to the Shadow already inside me, lining my bones and veins like soot after generations of my people's exposure. I wanted to answer. But that was why Nev was here. With his support, I wasn't supposed to purposefully draw on large amounts of it *or* ignore it, because either extreme seemed to trigger hallucinations and bone-deep weariness or violent mood swings. But it was a fine line to walk, especially if that line traversed an asteroid field.

My hands tightened on the controls, my focus sharpening.

"Qole . . . ," Nev repeated.

"You're a decent pilot, Nev, but you're not this good," I said through gritted teeth.

"I don't have to be. I just have to help *you* be good enough."

"I'm going to use it if I have to, Nev. I can't let him kill himself."

"You won't have to," Telu said. "I can hack his controls, force him to return." She spoke over the comm, not caring that Arjan could hear.

I shook my head, even though she wasn't looking up at me. "That could get him killed, we're already too deep in the asteroid field. He needs full control. Eton, be ready to blast the net apart if it catches and he's in trouble."

"Roger," Eton responded, "though I might not be able to get it in time."

"Idiot," Basra murmured. "If he doesn't die, I believe *I* may kill him."

"Get in line," I said.

But Arjan didn't die. The skiff rolled and dipped, pivoted

and rose. He wasn't just threading a needle; he was threading a dozen at the same time. He must be using so much Shadow, his eye would be fully black with it by now.

What he was doing was amazing, and yet keeping up with him in the *Kaitan* was even harder. The skiff was far smaller and more maneuverable. I heard the roar of photon blasts as Eton shot debris out of my way, while I did my best to dodge the bigger asteroids. Nev was my backup, his hands sure and swift on the controls, adding thrust where I needed it and giving me an extra pair of eyes. He watched readouts I couldn't pay attention to and made minor adjustments to avoid collisions that wouldn't have been fatal but would have caused damage.

"Large one, fast approaching, bearing one-three-seven—*blasted hell!*" Nev shouted, as I barely reacted in time. The surface of the asteroid came so close to the viewport I could have counted the craters in its surface before it went whizzing by.

I ground my teeth. I could still do this without . . .

Then I saw the drone, breaking away from the other side of the asteroid where it had been clinging. It must have been powered down so Telu couldn't detect its signal, but I'd gotten too close to its defense field.

Drones didn't like that. Without a hacker, there wasn't much to do but run as fast as you could. Attacking a drone would lead more than just that one to retaliate, since they responded to destructive threats by beaming alert signals to their companions. Not even their masters could reprogram that function, not since the know-how to do so was lost in the Great Collapse. Hundreds of thousands of drones interlaced the systems, and they could theoretically overwhelm any fleet. But we had a hacker.

Telu cursed. "Sneaky bastard!" And then to me, she said, "On it."

But not even Telu could hack its programming fast enough and send it on another course of action. The drone, three times the size of the *Kaitan,* launched straight for us.

Everyone cursed then. Tentacles waving, plasma-rimmed maw gaping, the drone lashed out at our ship. Without thinking, I threw the *Kaitan* into a maneuver that kept us from being rent in half, and heard Arjan shout over the comms.

Right. He was attached to us, and I'd sent him whipping. We usually only encountered dangerous drones with advanced warning and full maneuverability—as in, *without* the skiff deployed. I couldn't move without taking Arjan into account during Shadow runs either, but unlike asteroids, this drone wouldn't stick to a simple trajectory that we could both predict.

"Sorry, Cap, this is weird," Telu said through gritted teeth. "Its programming isn't responding like normal. It's almost like . . . Just gimme one more second."

Nev wasn't enough. Even together, we would never be good enough. Blackness flickered at the edges of my vision. It wasn't the darkness of space outside, but the darkness within me.

Everything was suddenly sharper, clearer, moving more slowly. I dodged the next five asteroids and the drone, and kept in line with Arjan with ease, dancing and skimming around everything like light over the ocean's surface, all without tangling our net. If Arjan had threaded a dozen needles with the skiff, I was weaving an entire tapestry with the *Kaitan.* Eton didn't even have to fire.

In the seconds that could have just as easily spelled our deaths, Telu had time to hack and reprogram the drone, and it went shooting off into the blackness. For a moment, all of us, even Arjan, just breathed.

"Qole . . . ," Nev began.

"Don't. Just don't. Not now."

"Okay," he said, and I could feel him turning back to his feeds. "But after."

At least now we all knew there would *be* an after.

——

By the time Arjan strode onto the bridge with a triumphant grin on his face, our new containment hold was filled to bursting with Shadow. Not that it improved my mood. All of us were waiting for him on the bridge, in fact, in a line like a firing squad.

He was much healthier than he had been even a couple of weeks ago, standing tall and looking more filled out, only fading pink scars lacing his tawny skin where there had once been angry red wounds. But his eye . . . that would never heal without help. His black hair, once shoulder length, was chopped short and spiky to keep it out of the eye patch.

His grin fell when he saw the looks on all our faces. "Oh, come on."

He especially avoided Basra's gaze, but with a stubborn set to his mouth. He'd known Basra would be furious but had acted anyway. Maybe even *because* it would infuriate Basra. Arjan wasn't only resentful because Basra was rich, but because Arjan hadn't known he was, not while they shared the same ship as crew, or even after they started sharing the same bunk.

Basra glanced at me, as if saying, *After you.*

I tried to keep my voice level without much success. "You disobeyed a direct order and put the rest of us in jeopardy—"

Arjan's eye narrowed a fraction. "I couldn't hear you clearly."

"Like hell you couldn't!" I snarled at him, unable to resist stamping my foot while I was at it. "We just had those systems replaced. Don't you *dare* lie to me."

"Never mind that you're lying to yourself."

Before I could ask him what *that* was supposed to mean, Telu said, "The comm channels were as clear as deep space, Arjan. I would know, since that's part of *my job* to monitor them."

He shot her a look reminiscent of the obscenity he'd spat at her earlier, then said, "What's the big deal anyway? I pulled off the run, *and* outmaneuvered a drone."

I broke our formation to march right up to him, jabbing a finger in his chest. "No, *you* didn't. *Shadow* did."

He shrugged. "Yeah, so what? It's our blasted curse, so why not use it to our advantage while we can, at least?"

Curse was one thing he had right. My father and mother had gone mad and died in their early forties. My oldest brother, Onai, had followed them at twenty-five. Arjan was twenty-one and I was seventeen. At the rate we'd been going . . . who knew?

"*Why not?* Are you serious, Arjan?"

"Maybe you can pretend you don't need it anymore, but tell me how else I could have done that, how else I could keep doing what I've always done." *With only one eye,* he didn't add, but we all heard it. His anger took on a desperate note, and he tossed his head at Nev. "Just because you're using him as a crutch, he's not going to be mine."

My breath hissed in between my teeth. "Oh, so instead you want to use the thing that will *kill* you?"

28

"I'd rather be dead than a Dracorte pawn for another second. What is he doing here, anyway?" He gestured violently at Nev this time. "He's a royal! These are *his family's* drones, in case you've forgotten. He doesn't belong on this ship with us. He grew up in a blasted palace with everything he could have ever wanted, with servants feeding him off gold platters and armies shielding him from any real danger."

Nev would never defend himself, but Telu snorted. "He doesn't have any of that anymore. Remember, he helped the rest of us rip his palace half apart to get *you* out of there."

"I was *there* because of him," Arjan spat back. And, unfortunately, my brother had been too out of it to see what Nev had done, what he had sacrificed, to help rescue him. Being told something and experiencing it were two very different things.

But Telu knew. "Still, he gave it all up. For us."

"No, he gave it all up because his father, the king, exiled him on pain of death," Eton said, casting his disapproving scowl in Nev's direction, this time . . . but not before glancing at me.

Not that again. I was so sick of Eton's attempts to tear down Nev in front of me to make himself look . . . what? Stronger? More loyal? The better protector of the crew?

Telu turned on Eton with her own ferocious glare. "Nev chose us before that, and you know it! That's *why* he was exiled—"

"He's just playing at being a Shadow fisherman!" Arjan said, his voice rising over everyone's. "This is a game to him, not life. This is *my* life. And I'm in control of it."

"You're *out* of control," I said quietly into the silence that followed.

"Speak for yourself," he snapped. "How are your eyes?"

"I don't—"

29

Arjan got right in my face, towering over me and staring me down with his one eye. "How black did they turn? And *don't you dare lie to me,*" he mocked.

I flinched away. He had never spoken like this to me before. It was usually *me* cowing *him.* Basra watched him warily, while Telu and Eton seemed just as surprised as I was, freezing in place.

"You forced me to do it," I said, my voice coming out faster, higher-pitched. For a second, I sounded like his little sister instead of his captain.

"Hey," Nev said sharply, stepping up beside Arjan.

Arjan's own brown eye flashed black, as dark as his eye patch, and he spoke to Nev without even turning his head. "*Do not* touch me."

After a glance at me, Nev took a step back.

"We're both dead, Qole, one way or another," my brother murmured, his voice softer now. "It's just how we die that matters."

He turned and walked off the bridge before I could answer. Not that I had an answer for him.

"I'll try to talk to him, though I wouldn't rate my chances at success very high," Basra said, stalking after him. "Good thing I have a gambling problem."

I stared after them both in silence. We were all gambling with something or another: Shadow, these ships, our lives, the people we loved. In this situation, I myself had gambled on Arjan and lost. Control of my crew had slipped away, at least briefly. We'd already been through so much that something like this could fracture us. I could spot the signs of it happening, but I was too stunned by Arjan to stop it in its tracks.

I glanced at Nev, then away again. He wanted to talk, but

my hands were shaking. All I could think about was how Arjan had looked at me, what he'd said.

We're both dead . . . one way or another.

Eton and Telu started to slip away without speaking to each other, and I deliberately turned away from Eton so he couldn't catch my gaze. The lines were drawn: Telu on Nev's side, Eton with Arjan, and me trying to stay as neutral as Basra, somehow in the middle.

But just as Basra couldn't truly be neutral when it came to Arjan, I couldn't be, either, when it came to my brother, or . . .

"Nev." I hadn't spoken. It was Telu from her station, her voice raised to a pitch of worry, a comm at her ear.

"What's wrong?"

"I'm picking up a signal. Ships—a lot of them—have arrived in Alaxak's airspace."

"Whose?" Nev demanded, his voice rising with my sudden surge of adrenaline. The lines of the *Kaitan* grew hard and sharp around me.

"Your family's—the Dracortes. It's a delegation from Luvos. The king and queen—your sister too—they're asking for you." Nev's eyes flew wide as he looked at me. "They want you to meet them. Immediately."

II

NEV

THE VIEW OF ALAXAK OUT THE AIRLOCK WAS IMPOSSIBLY BRIGHT IN THE light of its sun, an answering call to the endless stars around us. The beauty was heart-stopping; it put all the jewels of the royal houses to shame. I was briefly reminded of the equally heart-stopping walk I had taken with Qole earlier, but the happiness of that moment felt bitter now. I looked at the remains of the portal floating between me and the planet: steel girders, black stone, and inky alloy shards in the rough shape of two monoliths—the broken intergalactic portals of a past civilization. That matched my mood more aptly: something wondrous now cold, ruined, and empty.

"Are you sure this is a good idea?" Qole's voice was measured, but I knew she was worried.

"The portal ruins are a lovely and historic place to wait, and I'll be fine in this suit." I tried to keep my tone light, but

I wasn't fooling her any more than she was me. *Any rational human being would be worried.* I tightened the straps of my Disruption Blades over my outfit, whose lightweight material could handle the vacuum of space and wouldn't impede my motions if it came to a fight, though it wasn't intended for extensive stays off-ship.

Qole's eyes were virtually black in the stark shadows cast by the *Kaitan*'s lights. "I didn't mean your drop point, exactly. Do you have to go at all?"

I sighed. "What else can I do?" It felt strange to utter those words; I was used to a world of options at my disposal. "The message clearly stated that they just want to talk. You don't say no to my family, even if it's just a polite request."

"You *have* said no in the past, and there's always an alternative." When she wasn't being so fatalistic about her own future, she could be decidedly optimistic. "You could meet on neutral ground. Or at the very least, let the *Kaitan* take you."

"And put you and the entire crew at equal risk? Not a chance. You've done enough for me, Qole."

She shook her head. "I just want to know you're doing this because you believe it's the best choice, not because ..." She hesitated.

Because no one but you really wants me here?

At least, I desperately hoped she still did.

"I want what's best for everyone." I tapped my wrist feed. "Telu, go ahead and reactivate the tracker." I had attempted to deactivate the tracking system in the device shortly after being exiled, only to discover that Telu had already logged in and done so. Her technological omnipresence was annoying, humbling, and quite useful.

I didn't get a response, but the wrist feed flashed red, then green, emitting a low beep. Just like that, I was back online, across the systems. Alerts were no doubt going off on the ships in orbit, and in private status updates, security offices, and high-level feeds across the systems. The exiled Prince Nevarian was back on the map.

When I looked up, Qole was closer than I had expected. I could almost feel the warmth of her through my suit, and something inside me lurched. She didn't say anything, didn't try to dissuade me from what I was doing, didn't reassure me. We were simply together.

Qole wasn't beautiful the way royals were—refined, symmetrical, and inviting—but she was beautiful. Her features were strong, her full lips quick to smile or scowl, her face as real as the life she lived. Fierce, vibrant, and breathtaking—you were invited at your own risk. It was a risk I would always take.

A few strands of her dark hair fell free of her braid and across her cheek. I raised my hand to brush them away but paused when the comm inside the airlock blared.

"Captain, time for us to get out of sight!" Eton bellowed.

Qole took a step back, toward the inner airlock doors. "Nev ... remember, we're willing to do what it takes to keep you safe."

I wanted to say I would do anything, *anything* to keep her safe, as well. That I cared for her. That I loved her. But no words came out of my mouth, and she turned, whisked back onto the bridge by the opening and closing hiss of doors.

I believed what she'd said. Knowing Qole made it impossible to dismiss her words as anything other than true, but I doubted that all of her—*my*—crewmates felt the same way. Basra and Telu didn't seem to mind me, maybe even liked me, but Eton was a perpetually uncompromising mountain, and Arjan flat-out hated me—a perfectly reasonable position, given the circumstances, but no more enjoyable for it. Would *they* help me if I needed it?

I donned my helmet and looked out over the portal, floating like the picked-over bones of some giant, long-extinct space behemoth. Once a marvel of human innovation, one we'd never rediscovered, and now a primitive docking station for a shuttle to pick me up. Qole's antique of a ship was a bustling hub of technology, life, and even warmth in comparison. As much as my family might desire my presence for whatever purpose, leaving here was the last thing I wanted to do. Still, when the outer airlock doors opened, I pushed myself out into the cold void.

———

It was strange to be back on a ship that didn't shudder and lurch when flying. The shuttles of the elite lacked the power and maneuverability that the *Kaitan* possessed, but a great many resources were devoted to not disturbing the delicate constitutions of the appropriately wealthy. That, and I doubted the pilot was being nearly as swift and aggressive in navigating as Qole usually was.

I sat in a comfortable seat in the back, sandwiched between two royal guards. They were armored and armed, and we had exchanged no words from the moment the shuttle's airlock doors had opened.

Despite all this, they were oddly reassuring. If violence had been intended, there would be at least one Bladeguard present. The elite of the elite, Bladeguards were warriors, spies, and assassins wielding Disruption Blades, weapons capable of bypassing energy shields and disabling electronics.

The only Bladeguard on board was me. I shifted in my seat, readjusting the sheathed, twin Disruption Blades on my lap to be more comfortable. The guards hadn't confiscated them, which was strange. While it reinforced the idea that this was just a friendly chat, the reassurance soured into worry. None of this made sense. I'd been exiled. For good reason. Why parley now?

The viewport in front of the pilot suddenly flared with sunlight as we rose out of the shadow of one of Alaxak's moons. There, gleaming and framed by blackness, flanked by cruisers and destroyers, was the *Luvos Sunrise*.

Composed of sweeping arcs, decorated in intricate patterns designed to reflect the beauties of space, the *Luvos Sunrise* was for royalty only. It wasn't particularly maneuverable, but it was one of the fastest, most heavily armored cruisers in the systems, and was capable of sustaining itself for nearly an age. Of course, another family had built it for us, but that was seldom mentioned. We had a reputation to maintain.

A reputation I had turned into a giant, smoking crater.

I had only a few seconds to appreciate the sight before the *Luvos Sunrise* filled our viewport, growing rapidly larger until the docking bay became an open rectangle of golden light. We docked with no audible noise, nor sense of pressurization or gravitational change. My guards stood and flanked the shuttle door on both sides without saying a word; it unfolded seconds later, forming the staircase for my disembarkation into the hangar.

A full complement of guards awaited me at the bottom of the steps, and I nodded at their commander as I descended, mag-linking my blades to my hips once again. "Good evening, Commander Pierce." I recognized him from the Academy; we had trained together more than once.

"Good evening." The commander's tone was perfectly neutral, and he saluted me crisply. "Follow me, sir."

Ah, no royal honorific. He turned and started walking briskly, and I fell into step just beside him.

"Congratulations." I doubted he wanted to talk, but I was curious. "The last time I saw you, you weren't a lieutenant yet."

"Most of my officers and friends were murdered," Commander Pierce bit out. "I had an unexpected promotion."

Unifier's name, of course. Me. I kept it a secret from everyone, even Qole, but I could still see the faces of the people I had shot or run through with my weapons when I closed my eyes.

"I'm sorry," I replied quietly. No matter that I had killed those people while fighting against the torture of innocents, I had still killed them. We passed the rest of the walk in silence.

I had seen it all before. The carpeted hallways, the hearth fires defying the reality of space, the rare white hardwood from Luvos's forests, the silver filigree and engravings—everything to establish that this was the ship of Dracorte royalty: rulers of the system, right hand of the galactic empire, and champions of the Unifier. Many times before, I had approached the doors to the royal chambers, so similar to those at home, and had them thrown open to reveal my family on the other side. I had always gone striding through, full of purpose, knowing my place in the world.

Now I walked through calmly, but the only thing I knew for certain was that everything had changed, and I suspected it was about to do so again.

I stopped and took stock.

"Your Majesty." I didn't think he would want me calling him Father. I bowed deeply in greeting. King Thelarus Dracorte was a tall, imposing man, with closely cropped hair and beard. There was more gray in his beard than last time, and exhaustion under his eyes.

"Mother." I bowed again, just as deeply. Queen Ysandrei Dracorte, stately, beautiful, and calm in every situation. She was the mirror to Father in so many ways, and in this case, I saw the telltale signs of profound distress just as clearly as in him, and they cut even deeper.

"Sister." I bowed less deeply, resisting the temptation to throw her a rueful grimace. Solara and I had never been close, but the last time we had seen one another, she had been instrumental in saving Qole. While she was considered by many to be the most beautiful and active social butterfly in the system, I was beginning to realize there was much more to her than met the eye. It struck me as unfortunate that I was learning about this now, as we might have become true friends otherwise.

I straightened my spine. The last person was standing alone, behind my family, clad completely in black. The synthetics were so skintight that his impressively muscled body could have just as well been naked. The material covered his face, so he looked like nothing more than a statue. The handle of a Disruption Blade could be seen over his shoulder. He was a Bladeguard, a bodyguard, that much was certain, but something coiled inside me, an animal instinct recognizing another as a threat. Where was Devrak Hansen, my friend and mentor? His many duties did not always allow him to be present, but surely, as head of security, he would have been here for something as important as this.

The man didn't hesitate to approach me. Without a word, he held out his hands—for my blades, I realized. Of course a traitor wouldn't be allowed in the presence of the king and queen with them, whether or not I was their son. I unlinked them and passed them over. The Bladeguard snapped them into place at his own hips.

We waited in silence, and while it was only a few seconds, it was an eternity from the perspective of royal protocol. *They don't know what to say.* I tried to see myself through their eyes—tired, same as they, but sporting an untrimmed beard and a dirtier version of my traveling overcoat, combined with a hodgepodge of clothes I had adopted on Alaxak. Here he was, the disreputable son, once the hope of a domain stretching across space, now dressed like a vagrant and reappearing from the half-frozen planet below.

"How is Marsius?" I wanted to ask *where* my little brother was, but I knew they wouldn't have wanted him here. And as much as I wanted to see him, I understood it would have been too hard on him.

And the less exposure to the traitor, the better, no doubt.

"As well as can be expected," Father said, his voice giving away nothing.

Mother took a sudden breath, making up her mind. "Nevarian . . . are *you* all right?"

I hadn't expected that. Moisture watered my vision for a second.

Father helped dispel it. "Is *he* all right?" he asked incredulously, his voice sharp and hard as a Disruption Blade. "Nevarian, the question is, do you care if the rest of your family is all right? How the systems are? Or do you only care for your own interests?"

Father was wasting no time on pleasantries. This was to be a fun family time after all. Anger boiled behind my eyes and coursed into the sinews of my hand, tempting me to form fists. There were so many things I could say. So many tactics in argumentation I had been taught, that I could throw in his face, but I'd already learned that he knew these better than I. Instead, I remembered Qole, who spoke of what mattered, not what won her an argument.

"I care very much." This time my hands did form fists, but not because of anger. "Not a day goes by that I don't try to learn what is happening in the systems, that I don't lose sleep nights for wondering what I have done to everyone and everything I love."

"Then *how could you turn your back on us?*" Thelarus almost choked, yelling the words.

The shock of Father losing his composure made my own evaporate. "I *didn't!*" My entire body spasmed, both hands punching at the ground. "I love you! All of you! Father, Mother, Marsius, Solara. *My family.* I love our people. I would die for them. I would die for *you!* I would be glad to, and it would be the simplest, easiest choice I could make. You raised me to defend what I love." My voice graveled, emotion overriding any sense of thought, any articulation. "And I love Qole too. So what was I supposed to do?"

My gaze dropped as my vision blurred. Silence descended once again, and I looked up, drawing in a ragged breath. "Father." If he didn't respond, he didn't reject being called that, at least. "Mother. You raised me. Taught me. Made me. Everything good in me is in you. And I have never known more surely that I acted in the right way than when I defended Arjan from being murdered simply for our own advancement."

"He's right, you know." Solara's voice was warm and husky, as soothing as honey. Everyone looked at her in surprise. She was usually trying to be clever or happily trivial, so none of us were used to her seriousness now. Her eyes were grave, and she descended the few steps from the dais upon which my parents stood to come to my side, placing one hand gently on my cheek.

"You did make him this way." She smiled at me slightly and mouthed the words that only I could see. *Reach out to them.* She turned to our parents. "Did any of us ever doubt that Nev believed our family the greatest? That he was the most idealistic, the most passionate? If you teach an animal to be a guardian, how can you be surprised at what happens when we threaten what it loves?"

A hint of a smile crossed my lips despite myself. "Thanks for the flattering description, Sol."

But it seemed to be working. My parents weren't arguing. Solara walked back to them as I composed myself. *Reach out to them. Right.*

"Why are you here?" I asked with a weary shake of my head. "I'm exiled, disinherited, and I've been nothing but a thorn in your side. If you're here to judge me, I will submit. Because I will never support our family's endeavors if we continue to pose a danger to innocents."

Father sighed, and his shoulders shifted. "Nev . . ." For the first time in months, he sounded like my parent again, not the ruler of Luvos.

Mother finished his sentence. "*Power is always dangerous to those who have none, and you cannot effect change without power.* He knows, Thelarus. I'm just not sure he accepts. Nev, we're here because we miss you, the family is unstable, and Solara can't bear the burden of rule alone."

"And yet she refuses to marry," Thelarus interjected.

Solara shrugged helplessly, her expression chagrined. Of course she would have rejected such a thing, if whomever Father had chosen hadn't suited her tastes. I recalled the time

Mother had wished her to don a particular gown for an event. Not only had Solara refused, I'd found the gown cut into thin strips under her bed after Mother had insisted she wear it. Perhaps it was wise, I thought wryly, that Father hadn't tried to force her on this—not for the family's sake, but for her potential betrothed's.

"We hoped something else could be worked out," Mother finished, obviously having learned her lesson from the gown.

I narrowed my eyes. "And where do I come in?"

Father grimaced. "We need someone we can trust, and I suppose we want to know if you can still be loyal to me, to us, when I was not entirely loyal to you."

I was struck dumb. I wasn't sure I'd ever heard Father admit any true wrongdoing in my entire life.

"Understand." He held my gaze. "All I would change would be my decision to withhold truth from you from the outset, to keep you uninvolved. Someday you will be faced with the choice of surrendering your ideals to save your subjects, and then you will know sacrifice." He raised his hand to forestall any objection. "Understand also: you are still disinherited for your betrayal. But perhaps things could be different, with regard to your exile. I do not entirely know the way forward, but I do know that I must put aside my pride if, indeed, our family and our beliefs are to survive the coming storm. What say you? Can you do that in return? For me?"

"What would it entail?" I asked, my voice wary, but I couldn't help the dizzying joy that rose in my chest at the thought of seeing my home again.

"I know we will never see eye to eye. Because of that, I could never leave control of the system to you, your betrayal aside. But you have training and knowledge that Solara lacks.

What we all hope is that you could advise your sister, perhaps even help her rule from behind the throne, when the time comes. She has the will to rule, no doubt," Thelarus said, shooting her a glance, "and possesses the steel that is necessary in a leader, but you could be the experienced hand that helps guide it. She will have the ultimate say, but you could be her voice of reason."

Solara's face went still, and I couldn't tell what she was thinking. But she wouldn't have been here if she hadn't agreed with the plan.

I could barely breathe or move myself, to keep from hoping. "Would I have to leave Alaxak? Leave . . . Qole?"

"From time to time, I imagine, but not permanently. The beauty of this arrangement is that you can still support your sister while pursuing . . . other interests . . . outside the public eye, if that's what it will take for you to do your duty." Thelarus's lips twisted in disapproval. "You, of course, will remain officially disinherited, and your sister will be the face of Dracorte leadership, but such a situation could be for the best. You have strengths that she needs, and, unless I am *entirely* mistaken about you, I thought you might appreciate the chance to redeem yourself. To help your family, even though you turned your back on us."

Disapproval or not, the fact that he could acknowledge my perspective as a strength was light-years beyond where we'd been before. I couldn't stop it now—hope, love for this man, these women, rose within me like a sun, practically blinding me with its light.

Qole would hate this plan. It would strike her as a betrayal, but maybe I could convince her otherwise. Just as she hadn't belonged on Luvos, I didn't entirely belong on Alaxak, and she knew it. Perhaps I could serve the purpose I was meant to fulfill, but without truly leaving her. Help both her *and* my family, something that I'd grown to think was impossible.

It still might be impossible. I kneeled, head bowed, feeling slightly unsteady. My next words were careful; I knew I stood on a knife's edge, and I wanted them to listen, to understand the fullness of everything I felt. "Are we not meant to be the power that protects the weak? Let me do that for you. I will serve Dracorva, and gladly, if it is for that."

I *had* to protect Qole, Arjan, and Telu, and even Eton and Basra, from becoming casualties of my family designs. And yet, as it was now, I was largely useless to them. What if, this way, I could not only protect them but be of much greater use to many more people?

Solara choked back a sob. "Oh, just say you'll come back to us, Nev. We all miss you. We need to be a family." She held out her arms to all of us.

I had spent most of my life preaching to anyone who would listen about my family, but after my time on the *Kaitan,* that word had evolved. I'd imagined, at times, how different things would be if I had experienced such closeness as I saw between the crew. Now I stood to see Mother walking to me, arms outstretched.

A dam I hadn't known existed burst, flooding me with relief. Tears filled my eyes as I found myself enfolded in her embrace, and even Father, as reserved as anyone I'd known, reached out to squeeze my shoulder. His grip was strong, unshakable.

It lasted only a moment, but as we pulled away, I felt so much lighter I wanted to laugh. The Bladeguard, kneeling beside us in reverence at our private moment, stood as my parents stepped back.

The blades at his hips whispered out as he did so. By the time I registered it, it was too late. They stabbed neatly upward—straight through the chests of Thelarus and Ysandrei Dracorte.

Their gasps lingered in my ears as they crumpled. With a wet sound, he withdrew them in almost the same instant.

A complete lack of understanding hit me, a thousand conflicting thoughts exploding like a dying ship. My parents sagged forward and I tried to catch them, only managing to break their falls. Then my training sputtered to life and I lunged at the Bladeguard. Droplets of blood scattered as he flipped the blades around with whistling speed and handed them to me hilt first, which my reaching hands mindlessly accepted. I barely registered that they were my weapons.

But he didn't attack. He didn't even unsheathe his own blade. He retreated, dodging around Solara and out through a door that had slid open behind the dais to reveal a hallway beyond. An emergency escape route for my family, ironically.

I couldn't even think of pursuing. Dropping to the ground by my parents, I gathered them to me. *Breathe.*

I was managing; Father was not. His mouth was open, his eyes sightless as he lay on his back. Mother was crumpled like a shattered vase, blood pooling around her. *Stasis.* I needed stasis. Stop the blood loss. Freeze them, prevent their tissue from dying. They could be revived. There had to be help, the best medical care in the galaxy, right here, on this ship. Solara wasn't moving; she must have been in shock. Hopeless as it was, I started to rise, to run for the door, to scream for help, when I heard the faintest sound from the queen.

"Nev ..."

I clawed at her, turning her over, putting pressure on the wound. "Mother, I'm getting help."

Her mouth quirked in a smile, and she ignored what I said. Her lips quivered, and I could barely hear her as she formed the words "We love you. The sundering is coming, and your heart will save us."

Her breath caught, sighed out of her, then ceased.

"Solara," I cried, "help me!"

But Solara backed away, steadily holding my disbelieving gaze until she turned and stepped through the doorway, after the assassin. Her own eyes were flat, devoid of anything other than assessment. "Why?"

She didn't look back, and the door slid shut.

Distantly, I heard explosions rocking the ship. But I hardly noticed as I kneeled on the bloody throne room floor, alone, with my mother's head in my lap.

III

QOLE

"Firing back up," I gasped, when a dozen streaks of white light flared and headed for the *Luvos Sunrise*. Someone had killed Nev's parents, the Dracorte king and queen, and maybe even his sister, and now they were finishing the job by blowing up the entire ship. I only knew that Nev was still alive because I could hear him breathing.

I knew, because I'd heard everything through the comm in his wrist feed, which Telu had hacked to transmit back to the *Kaitan*. The *Kaitan* was in orbit around Alaxak, hovering with our engines down and our signals muted from casual observers.

He wouldn't be breathing for long if those missiles hit their mark.

So many. Never mind the mysterious blasts that had already rocked the royal cruiser from within; this was a rain of death even for a ship that size, especially since their energy shields weren't up. "Why aren't they defending themselves?"

"Their whole central mainframe is on lockdown," Telu said. "Somebody hacked the whole system, crippled it. And those initial explosions probably didn't help—they likely targeted the shield generators since I'm not getting even the slightest response there."

I threw us into full throttle before I entirely knew what I was doing. But it was the only thing I could do.

"Um, should we be going *toward* the fiery inferno?" Eton's voice came over the comm from the weapons turret.

Before I could say anything, Arjan bounded onto the bridge behind me. "What are you doing, Qole?"

"I have to," I said, without looking at him. "I have to try."

"He's as good as dead!" My brother came alongside me and threw his hands at the viewport, where the Dracorte entourage was now pulling away, leaving blooms of fire in the blackness where the *Luvos Sunrise* was foundering.

"We don't know that," I said. I couldn't hear Nev anymore, but the roar of the *Kaitan*'s engines might have been masking any sound he was making. "Telu, patch me through to Nev so he'll hear me, if he can."

"Captain," Basra said, in the brief silence that followed while Telu worked, "I'm getting some very . . . disturbing . . . ripples across all my feeds. Something big is happening, and I don't mean here."

If it was disturbing to Basra, it had to be cataclysmic. But right now, I couldn't deal with anything except the giant exploding ship in front of us. "Later. Telu?"

"Done!"

"Nev?" I asked hesitantly, unable to imagine what I would do if only more silence answered me.

"Hi, Qole." His voice came back, broken, dazed, and empty. He must have just been sitting quietly, not moving.

My relief didn't last long. "What are you doing?" I snapped. "Ancestors, you need to go!"

"My parents . . . Solara—"

"I know, but tell me you're running for an escape pod."

I heard a rustling on the other end. He was shifting now, at least. "I can feel the explosions. They're shaking the entire ship. I don't think I'll make it. I don't even know if—"

"*Nevarian Dracorte,*" I practically shouted. "You get off your ass and run faster than you ever have, *now.* That is an order from your captain."

"Qole, I—"

"So help me, Nev," I hissed, "I am flying to help you, and if you aren't ready when I get there, then we're probably all dead." I was playing dirty, but I couldn't have cared less.

He sucked his breath in on the other end. "Okay. I'm going."

The fire grew in the viewport. Ripples of it snaked and curled across the darkness, waving like tentacles, a monster of flame entwining the *Luvos Sunrise.*

"What do you expect we'll be able to do against *that?*" Eton hollered.

"I'm not sure," I said through gritted teeth. "Just be ready, all of you."

"Qole." Arjan was the one who sounded dazed now. "You'll risk us all, for *him?*"

"We did the same for you. It's all about how you die, right?" I said with a short laugh. "Anyway, I'm not planning on dying." I closed my eyes and inhaled. When I opened them, a film of darkness coated my vision. "Not yet."

Shadow. I could feel it humming in my veins, buzzing

along my skin, filling my muscles, sharpening my sight. I hadn't called forth this much of it since we had barely escaped Dracorva with our lives. I could feel even more, a lot more, packing the *Kaitan*'s containment hold like a held breath, waiting to come rushing out at my signal.

"Nev, are you running?" I asked.

"Fast . . . as . . . I . . . can," he panted over the comm. I could hear the strain behind his words.

"Do you need Telu to locate an exit?"

"No, I—*blasted hell.*" A distant roar rumbled in the background behind his curse.

"What?" I nearly screeched. I could see so much—individual tendrils of fire, small pieces of debris, and even dust dissipating into space from the *Luvos Sunrise*. I dodged everything coming at us, as if it were all moving in slow motion. But I couldn't see what Nev was seeing, and it was enough to make me want to panic. "Telu, do you have eyes on him?"

"No, Cap, I'm trying to get in, but the ship's cameras are routed through the mainframe, and I can't—"

"I'm fine," Nev gasped, his voice breaking through Telu's response. "That hallway was . . . compromised. Changing routes."

We were close enough to the royal ship now to practically count the cracks through the viewport, to feel the heat on our faces. Craters marred the once-sleek surface, and gas and water from leaking lines, along with fire, were glittering like atmospheric clouds around it. It was a huge, burning planetoid. "Where are you headed?"

He was running again. "Escape pods . . . fourteenth floor . . . sector E—"

"Where is *that*? I don't have the blasted schematics in front of me!"

50

Good thing Nev knew his ships. "Port . . . stern . . . about midway . . . next to a huge vent. If it's still there."

I rocketed the *Kaitan* around the starboard stern, headed for the port side. There, I saw a massive vent, and several huge round openings, sealed with retractable doors—launch tubes.

"Almost . . . there," Nev groaned.

There was a hum that sounded like a door opening, and I didn't wait to ask. "Are you in an escape pod?"

"Closed and sealed. Buckling myself in."

Just then, a new shock wave of explosions began erupting along the hull of the *Luvos Sunrise*. Something must have triggered a chain reaction, because they weren't stopping.

"Nev, launch now!"

There was a pause where I heard only his breathing. It lasted a mere second, but a lifetime could have passed. "It's . . . it's not working."

"All primary systems are down, but there should be a manual override," I insisted.

"I *know*, and it's not launching."

"Telu?" I said, unable to keep the desperation out of my voice.

"Been working on it for the last few minutes," she muttered. Her fingers were flying along her various screens and infopads. "They tried to wipe the system. I can only get low-level responses, which would be enough if I could . . . Got it!"

"Go, Nev, hit it!"

There was a rush of air blasting into space from one of the launch tubes—the portal had opened. But . . . there was no escape pod. The wave of explosions was still headed our way, almost like a retracting ripple, closing in, constricting around us.

"Why hasn't it launched yet?" I shouted at no one in particular.

"I don't know!" Telu shouted back, her voice loud from beneath me and over the comm. "It should have!"

"I think something physical is blocking it," Nev said, breathing hard. "There was a grinding, then nothing." He paused, and his silence was a weight on my chest, like *I* couldn't speak, or breathe. "I think I'm stuck."

The fire was almost upon us, all around us. The *Sunrise* was nearly as bright as its namesake.

"No . . ." I started.

"Qole, this might be it. I just want to tell you—"

"No!" I cried again. And then there wasn't fire surrounding us. There was Shadow. Everything I could pull from the containment hold and direct at the *Luvos Sunrise*.

Shadow was the fire's opposite: where the flames were frenetic and brilliant orange, Shadow was liquid smooth and black. The only glow it had was a purplish cast with occasional bursts of white. In a sense, it was still like fighting fire with fire, since Shadow was just as deadly. No, even deadlier.

More powerful.

"Qole," Nev tried again, "whatever happens, my—"

"Sorry, I'm sort of busy." My voice wasn't harsh. More like it was coming from far away, somewhere outside my body. Maybe because a large part of my focus *was* outside my body, with something else—first in the containment hold, then pouring through the maglock and back out into space in a dense black mist.

I raised my arm, and a wave of Shadow coiled in response. I threw it at the *Sunrise,* where it ate into the hull, then spread. The blackness carved out a half sphere bigger than the *Kaitan* around Nev's escape pod, as easily as a hand scooping up fresh snow. Deadly though the substance was, I controlled it, directed it away from Nev and toward the collapsing inferno.

It was just another energy shield, in a sense. One that devoured everything else. When the flames encountered my barrier, the darkness swallowed them. I tried not to think about what—or *who*—else it might be devouring in the ship.

At the very least, it ate through whatever was trapping the escape pod and generated an immense amount of heat and pressure. The pod fired out of its launch tube like a missile.

That was for the best, because I couldn't hold the Shadow barrier any longer and the *Luvos Sunrise* took that opportunity to dissolve into its constituent parts, with even more fire and explosions than there had already been. Many chunks of metal and pieces of scrap rocketed outward like missiles, not just the escape pod.

I tried to reach for the controls, but I froze when I saw my skin peeling back from my fingers, flaking away into the air and leaving only bone. I blinked, and my hand was back to normal.

That split-second hesitation nearly cost us our lives. A sheet of metal plating whirled like a deadly saw blade straight for us, large enough to cleave the bridge from the ship. Eton unloaded a string of photon rockets into it, blasting it into smaller, but still-deadly chunks, while Arjan seized the controls and dove the *Kaitan* out of the way. Everyone was yelling curses at the same time.

"I thought you didn't want to die!" Arjan shouted at me, dodging a few more flying pieces of the *Luvos Sunrise,* which grew more scattered as he took us farther away. "You waiting for an invitation to your funeral or something?"

"No, I—" I gasped, clenching my fingers into fists, not wanting to see them coming apart again. "I'm sorry. The Shadow—I was hallucinating."

Arjan's eyes widened. "Are you still?"

I shook myself and reached for the controls. "It doesn't matter."

There was only brotherly concern in his voice now. "Of course it—"

"Where's Nev?" I interrupted, and Arjan reluctantly moved out of the way.

Telu answered immediately, despite having just been swearing up a violent storm along with everyone else. "He isn't responding. The comm in his wrist feed has gone dead. But the pod is still intact, from what I can see," she added quickly.

I ignored my heart as it tried to skip several beats, pinching in my chest. There were a number of reasons his comm could have gone out. That didn't mean anything for certain. But it did pose a problem. "How are we going to dock with him if we can't communicate?"

"Um." She chuckled nervously. "Docking won't be an issue, since the momentum of his pod fired him into the gravitational pull of Alaxak's atmosphere. He's, uh, in the process of landing."

"Do you mean *crash*-landing?"

"Not necessarily," she said, at the same time Eton said "Probably."

Telu scowled. "*No*, he'll be fine if his parachute deploys. Even if he's experiencing electrical and mechanical failure, it should still activate. As long as the chute mechanism took no direct damage, it should automatically sense the correct air pressure—"

"That's a whole lot of *should* and *if*," Eton growled. "Let's add another: he *should* survive *if* he still has oxygen and life support. Why isn't he responding?"

"Like I said, his comm is down."

"And why is his comm down?"

"What, do you *want* him to be dead?" Telu cried.

"Shut up!" I shouted, interrupting their argument. "Telu, direct me."

She rattled off Nev's coordinates, which were changing rapidly by the second. I had to lay on all speed to catch up. The *Kaitan* shook around us under the strain, while the pod itself was already like a meteor, flame streaking behind it as it plummeted through the nighttime darkness of the Alaxan atmosphere. I kept pace alongside, *well* off to the side, to avoid getting in the way of the chute.

If it deployed.

"Come on, come on," I muttered to myself, my eyes riveted to Nev's slash of light across the glowing curve of the horizon. The flames abruptly sputtered out like a torch without fuel, and white streams took their place as the pod began to cut through the clouds. "Telu, when should the chute deploy?"

"Um . . ." I could practically hear the rapid fire of her gaze as it shot along her screens. "If I pulled up the manual for the correct model, it should be . . . about . . . *now.*"

Everyone fell silent as we all found a viewport or a feed that showed the descent of Nev's pod, slicing through the night sky. Everyone's breath was held. And continued to hold.

Nothing.

"Come on, come on, come on," I began to chant again. And then I closed my eyes for a second, spoke to the darkness behind my lids. Shadow had helped me with so many things, but I couldn't think of a way it might now. I only had a mindless plea: *Please, please, please.*

I felt something, a fluttering at the edge of my senses, in the direction of the escape pod. Then a voice I'd never heard, like the hiss of air out an airlock, spoke in a whisper in my ear: "Yes."

My eyes flew open right as the chute deployed. It whipped and thrashed in the air behind the pod, and then the canvas unfolded in a rippling crack. The sudden resistance yanked the pod back violently before letting it fall, more slowly, toward the planet's surface.

Telu let out a shout of triumph. Basra sighed in relief. Eton grunted from up in the turret, and Arjan's hands flexed on the edge of the dash. I was still too stunned, by both the voice and the seeming result of it, to react.

"What now?" Arjan demanded, noticing my silence, my blank stare, with worry in his tone.

"Nothing," I said quickly. First, visual hallucinations, which I'd already experienced before . . . but now auditory hallucinations? Voices? I'd had feelings or thoughts in my head that didn't seem like my own, but never spoken words. This was new, and it was not good, because it meant the Shadow poisoning—and the madness that went with it—was getting worse. But maybe using so much Shadow and going mad would be worth it, if Nev was still alive.

"He still might not be alive," Eton said from the turret, as if reading my thoughts.

"Eton, shut the hell up," Telu bit out.

"I actually second that," Basra murmured.

It was nice to know that at least half of the crew cared if Nev lived or died.

It didn't take long for the escape pod to hit the ocean, sending up a giant plume of water and slush ice into the darkness of the night. The parachute wilted like a blossom around it, collapsing into the gentle rollers. I set the *Kaitan* down next to the pod, directed a spotlight at it, and then sat there. I wanted to move from my captain's chair, but I couldn't—both because I needed to control the ship and because my legs wouldn't work.

"Well, *someone* needs to see if he's alive," Telu said into yet another silence. "What if the door is stuck?"

But the door wasn't stuck. It ejected from the top of the pod. It spun once in the air and landed with a splash. By then, Nev had already poked his head out, and I'd already covered my mouth with my hands, gasping as if I hadn't breathed since the first missiles had flown at the *Luvos Sunrise*. I didn't even try to stop the tears that flooded my eyes.

He's alive, he's alive. Ancestors, he's alive . . .

I managed to get myself under control enough to keep the ship steady while Eton tossed a line out to the escape pod and dragged Nev on board, soaked in freezing water. But as soon as I saw him, still breathing if pale and bloodstained under the bridge lights, the tears came again and nothing could keep me from hurling myself at him, my arms wrapping around him in something like a death grip.

I didn't even loosen my hold when the disembodied voice spoke again: "Yes."

Nev was holding me just as tightly, but he felt wooden. "My parents . . . ," he said again. The words caught in his throat.

Of course he wouldn't be able to appreciate being alive after what he'd just witnessed. Which meant I couldn't tell him at what cost I had gotten him out alive—the cost of the voice. He would only feel worse. I held him tighter.

"What happened?" I breathed into his neck. "I heard parts, but we had no visual. And then we lost all connection."

"That was because I smashed my wrist feed in the pod before it launched."

"Why?" Pulling away to give him a bewildered look, I noticed that the rest of the crew was staring at us, but I had a hard time caring. "We thought maybe . . ." I swallowed, still unable to imagine him dead even now that I knew he was alive. "I didn't know what to expect."

"I had to." Nev's gaze floated off over my shoulder, staring. "The tracker . . . Solara has to think I died on board. If she could do this to our parents, to me, to get what she wants, who knows what she'll do to all of you if she realizes I'm still here?"

"Solara?" I said, uncomprehending at first. "Wait, *she* did this?"

Nev shook his head, and yet he confirmed my disbelieving words. "She did it all. She didn't wield the blades herself, but she might as well have."

"But she helped us in Dracorva! Why would she go to all that trouble only to do this? She could have just killed you then."

"No, she couldn't. First, she had to ruin my reputation in the eyes of our citizens, and my parents. *That's* what she helped me do so she could be named heiress before . . . before she . . ." He choked on a despairing laugh. "Unifier save us, but she's the queen now."

"That's what she wanted? But she never gave any hint of that, ever." I glanced around, making sure I wasn't the only one who had been completely fooled.

Eton shook his head, eyes wide, while Arjan's mouth was open in shock. Telu had never met Solara, so she looked understandably baffled by the sudden turn in the conversation. Basra pursed his lips thoughtfully.

"Well, this changes things," he murmured. If anything, he sounded vaguely impressed, as if someone else had made a clever trade before he'd thought of it.

"There's much more to her than meets the eye," Nev said, as if repeating a joke that wasn't funny. "This latest stage of her plan was apparently all to avoid having to share power through marriage. Or with me."

It was my turn to shake my head. "Heiress or not, there's no way anyone is going to let her rule after this! She—"

"She framed me, Qole." Nev's voice was flat, lifeless. He lifted his hands to stare at them, as if even he saw the blood there. "Everyone will believe that I was the one who murdered our parents, because no one will question her claims after what I've done. And now she'll inherit the throne—*has* inherited the throne, in all but name," he amended.

"But . . . ," I stammered, "but she blew up their ship for no good reason, other than to kill you. No one is going to believe any story she comes up with."

"Oh," Nev said with a ghost of his usual smile, "somehow I doubt that very much."

———

The vid arrived a few hours later, in the still-dark morning, broadcasted across the inter-systems network. Solara had clearly been busy, since there was no possible way she was back on Luvos yet. She was working in transit.

We'd barely had time to return to Gamut's harbor and eat our first meal in a long while. It was an attempt to regroup— Nev tried to pretend like he hadn't been hollowed out and somehow left standing, while I tried to pretend I couldn't hear the occasional whisper in my ear or see bits of skin start to fly away from the backs of my hands. None of the rest of the crew really knew what to say. What did you say to a friend who had just seen his parents murdered before his eyes?

None of us were very hungry, but somehow we weren't tired, either. Maybe because we could sense what was coming.

We sat in the ship's messroom, gathered around the table to eat one of Eton's latest creations: fried fish of some sort, with a flaky crust and delicate spices, piled with sautéed seaweed. The guy really did cook as well as he could shoot.

When the emergency broadcast began, playing automatically across all vid feeds, we all stopped eating. Nev went entirely still.

Solara appeared on the messroom screen, her dazzling blond hair falling in a glinting waterfall over one shoulder, her skin as radiant as sunlit snow, her lips as red as drops of blood. Her gown was also red, encrusted with enough gold embroidery that she shouldn't have been able to hold herself upright. Her eyes, however, weren't red, even though the moisture in them seemed to hint that she'd been crying. Through the liquid sheen, the sharp silver-gray irises flashed back at us.

A monster glinting under the water's surface. A psychopath dressed as a grieving young princess.

"I have news of the greatest tragedy ever to befall the Dracorte family," she began in a solemn tone. "My indecorous haste in making this announcement, even as I flee for my life to the safety of Luvos, is an attempt to put to rest the rumors that must already be spreading. Approximately three and a half hours ago, my parents—King Thelarus and Queen Ysandrei— were murdered, assassinated by none other than their son and my brother, Nevarian Dracorte."

On the table, Nev's hands squeezed so tightly around his fork that he bent it in half.

Solara's features softened, and her eyes somehow grew wider, more vulnerable. *Ancestors, she's good.* "Many of you might be wondering how this could be possible. I wouldn't have been able to believe it myself if I hadn't witnessed it firsthand. As you know, Nevarian committed treason barely a month ago, compromising the safety of our planet and very citadel, and so my father and mother had no choice but to exile him.

"Still, we wished to believe the best of him, that he would someday be able to return to us. This made my royal parents particularly vulnerable to his pleas. At Nevarian's bequest, the king and queen decided to take a journey, on which I was to accompany them, to the most far-flung planet in our system, Alaxak, for the purpose of making peace. I chose to view their decision as a willingness to forgive rather than a sign of weakness. If only I had argued more rigorously against it, perhaps I could have averted this tragedy."

Her lips trembled, but her voice didn't. "As soon as my brother boarded our ship, I grew even more apprehensive. The comm channels went down and security feeds stopped recording. We were cut off. I know now that this was because Nevarian had once again employed the hacker who so recently compromised our citadel security, using her to infiltrate the ship's network and block all outgoing signals—"

"*Hey*," Telu said, "I did not! I mean, I could have, but that's a flaming load of scat!"

"—which allowed my brother the freedom to put his deceitful plot into motion undetected," Solara continued. "If my parents had been more cautious, less willfully ignorant of what he was capable of, then perhaps he wouldn't have succeeded in planting high-energy explosives on board with the help of only a few other disloyal, murderous subjects. He set these explosives to detonate when he met with the king and queen, providing a distraction for when he . . . when he—" She paused, as if she couldn't go on. "Well, I cannot put into words something so horrible that it can only be seen to be believed. Unfortunately, all that remains as evidence of this heinous crime is a vid that I recorded myself when I realized something was terribly amiss."

The picture cut to a shot of Nev approaching his parents, arms raised, then to his parents gasping with twin blades through their chests, and then to Nev holding his bloody swords, his parents' bodies falling into him. It had obviously been edited heavily, but it still looked bad for him. Very bad.

And yet, if anyone knew Nev half as well as I did, they'd know the look on his face in the vid wasn't murderous. It was one of horrified shock.

It was the expression he wore now, since he wasn't able to turn away fast enough before rewatching the deaths of his parents. I put a hand on his knee as he turned to the wall, his jaw clenched, shoulders shaking. I wished I could comfort him in some other way, but I knew nothing I said right now would make this better. And besides, the broadcast wasn't over.

The feed cut back to Solara, who looked even more disturbingly *undisturbed*. She was putting on a good act, but next to the real thing, there was no comparison. "My bodyguards barely fought off my brother and got me off the ship, on an escape pod whose manual override function let us escape the hacker's lockdown and flee to safety."

Telu snorted. "Does she mean the manual override that she'd overridden in order to *keep* the escape pods from escaping?"

"The *Luvos Sunrise* attempted to fire upon us with artillery that would soon have overwhelmed us without a response. There was only one thing we could do." She bowed her golden head, as if it pained her to say it. "We completed what Nevarian himself had already begun with his explosives, but at least we ensured that he would pay for his crimes. We shot down the *Luvos Sunrise*. There were no survivors. Inquiries will of course be made, and a full investigation launched. The logs from the ships that accompanied the *Luvos Sunrise* will provide information—"

"That she totally fabricated, I'm sure," Telu snapped.

"—to help piece together everything that happened. Many lives were lost, but at least such a noble sacrifice permitted the execution of the worst traitor our family has ever seen: that of my brother-no-longer, Nevarian Dracorte."

Eton scoffed. "Well, that's *definitely* not true."

Solara squared her shoulders, as if adjusting the weight of a heavy burden. "It is with great solemnity that I must now accept the Throne of Luvos far earlier than intended. My coronation will occur shortly after my arrival home. In the meantime, there is justice to dispense."

"What, is she going to try to kill him twice?" Arjan said.

Nev was shaking his head. "This is not good," he murmured.

"What?" I asked, blinking at him.

He didn't answer, but Solara did. "Alaxak's role in my brother's treason has gone unaddressed long enough. Nevarian has paid for my parents' murder with his life, but Alaxak must also answer for the deaths of their sovereigns—and the deaths of so many innocents. Their time as a planet on the fringes of society, divorced from Dracorte law and justice, has come to an end."

"Oh, blasted hell," Arjan said.

Oh no . . .

"I will appoint a new governor of Alaxak—a position that has too long gone unfilled—and they will soon arrive with a much stronger contingent of law enforcement officers than the planet has ever seen. Not only will this force continue to guard our drone network in the region, but they will keep order, and also oversee our new Shadow operation."

"What?" The word came out of my mouth before I could help it, my own fork falling from numb fingers.

"Shadow operation?" Arjan demanded.

As if she'd heard him, Solara elaborated. "With our new bioengineered fuel, combining Shadow and algae, my family now has the ability to produce the most revolutionary new energy source in the systems, for the benefit of all. And yet, with Alaxak's history of . . . disobedience—"

"You mean history of being *used,*" Telu growled, slamming the table with her fist.

"—we must take firmer control over our primary source of Shadow, lest it be threatened. From this day forth, the Dracorte family is laying rightful claim to the rich Shadow grounds in and around the Alaxak Asteroid Sea."

"Rightful?" Arjan hissed through his teeth.

"Those. Are. Ours," I ground out. Both my brother's and my gazes were riveted to the screen, as if we could somehow get through to her.

"The people of Alaxak will be compensated accordingly," Solara said, her tone gracious, "and given jobs as they so desire on our new state-of-the-line Shadow rigs. The harvesting of Shadow on such an industrial scale will be controlled, safe, and profitable to all." Almost as an afterthought, she added, "Traditional means of harvesting are too dangerous and therefore prohibited, for everyone's own good."

In those few words, I saw everything—my operation, my way of life, my people—collapsing.

She smiled tremulously, though it never reached her eyes. "Justice doesn't have to be harsh, and can remain in keeping with the late king's and queen's . . . gentler . . . sensibilities. This way, the Dracortes will take steps to guarantee our security, and in return, Alaxak will no longer be a lawless den fit to harbor criminals. It will be a place of prosperity, safety, and stability."

And cultural annihilation. She'd left that part out.

Solara frowned slightly, her tone reluctant. "Failure to comply with the implementation of this new system would leave us with no choice but to respond with far stricter measures, with the Dracorte military might at our disposal. Such justice would be the least that the late king and queen would truly deserve."

She took a deep breath. "Now it is time for us, and all of Luvos, to mourn. It is with great sorrow that I assume this heavy mantle at our dear sovereigns' passing. The burden of rule is immense, but I won't let my beloved parents, our noble legacy and lineage, nor our glorious system down. In the Unifier's name, this I swear."

The screen went black. We all stared—and then jumped when a plate hit the wall and shattered, spraying food and bits of thick plastic everywhere.

I expected it to have been Arjan or Telu, or even Eton—someone with a temper—but it was Nev's arm that was left extended over the table, *his* gasping breaths that filled the silence.

"If that isn't enough," Basra said calmly, almost mock-cheerfully, into the awkward silence, "the feeds are already exploding with her praise—*beauty, strength, and poise in the face of tragedy.*" He tossed his infopad down on the table. "She undeniably knows how to play the game better than I ever could have guessed, and that's saying something."

"Sink them—Dracorte Industries." We all looked at Arjan, who'd spoken up coldly, matter-of-factly. He pointed at Nev, his eye narrowed. "You warned his family not to mess with us, Bas. This definitely qualifies. You own so much of their resources and products, and you nearly did it once. So do it again. Wreck them financially."

So *now* he wanted Basra's help. I supposed this was more important than a bionic eye or ship upgrades. Not that I'd yet seen much indication that Arjan had forgiven Basra for lying about his identity for so long, and I hoped that wouldn't make Basra less inclined to help us.

"I can't." Basra's mouth twisted in distaste. "And before you ask why not, it's because I *don't* own much of theirs anymore." He glanced at his infopad. "Or any of it, as of about three hours ago. I tried to warn you as we were approaching the *Luvos Sunrise,* but there were admittedly more pressing matters to attend to."

Nev shook his head, but he still sounded dazed, breathless. "How is that possible? The Dracortes can't just buy back what you own without your permission—we couldn't afford it, anyway."

That was my basic grasp, as well, of the power that Basra held over them in his inherited role as the investor, Hersius Kartolus the Thirteenth, though I obviously didn't understand everything about the situation. These were forces so far over my head that I'd never had reason to consider them much before, and yet now they were coming down *on* our heads, ready to crush us.

"Well, Solara isn't playing by the rules, because she forcibly orchestrated a buyback by placing those resources under government control," Basra said, "and, in so doing, escaped my influence over her." He leaned back and folded his arms across his stomach. "The money to do so came from a loan by the Treznor-Nirmana family."

"Treznor-Nirmana?" Nev asked incredulously. "We're too far in debt to them already!"

It was true—the Dracortes being so indebted to the equally royal Treznor-Nirmanas was what had made his family so desperate for any advancement. Desperate enough to kidnap Arjan and me and torture us for what they could gain from us.

Basra shrugged. "They were the lesser of two evils, perhaps. I'd be flattered under other circumstances, and pleased to be considerably richer. At least the trade didn't go off without a hitch. King Makar Treznor-Nirmana opposed loaning Solara more money, and so he and his council are at odds right now. He might even be on the verge of being deposed, if he hasn't been already."

Nev grabbed his hair. "What good does *that* do us? Whoever leads them, they'll still practically own my family! What does Solara think she's doing?"

"Hey," Arjan snapped. "Isn't anything bad for your family good for us?"

"In this case, Nev's right—it wasn't much good for either of us," Basra said. "Treznor instability aside, this makes us sort of even, and yet Solara is still the one with the rather large navy. Not only that, but by seizing ownership of the Shadow grounds and placing the market under government control, she's effectively keeping me from turning around and buying up all their Shadow—which would have been my next move." He sighed. "Now I truly am just another *rich person.*"

With that, he looked sideways at Arjan, his expression almost sulky. So he had definitely been stung by my brother's comment, and tension was obviously still high between them. But we had a vastly bigger problem than who had offended whom—unless, of course, the offended party was one Solara

Dracorte, psychopathic princess and soon-to-be queen of our system.

She was precisely our problem.

"Then ... then we're screwed," Telu said. Her voice was higher, more afraid, than I usually ever heard it. "She'll come in and take everything from us."

A force as strong as gravity tugged on me, but in the opposite direction, dragging me upright. It was my own gravity—the energy that kept me moving, breathing, fighting. There was no way, *no way* I was just going to sit by while this happened. "No," I said, standing above everyone. "She won't."

"And just how are you going to stop her?" Eton demanded. "You can't do anything against a force like hers. We tricked the Dracortes before, but it was a surprise attack—they weren't ready. We wouldn't stand a farmer's chance against a Bladeguard if we faced her on the field of battle with an army at her back."

But I wasn't looking at him, or hearing him. All I could see was Arjan and Telu, staring at me with the faint beginnings of hope, Basra with curiosity, and Nev ... Nev, I didn't look at either, because he started to shake his head.

And all I could hear was the whisper in my ear that came from no lips I could see moving: "Yes."

"She won't, because I won't let her," I said. "None of us will. And I don't just mean this crew." I strode away from the table before they could argue. "Get ready, we're going to Chorda. We need to talk to some fishermen."

IV

NEV

IN WANTING TO HEAD TO CHORDA, QOLE EVIDENTLY MEANT TO TALK TO *everyone* on Alaxak who could be reached. Chorda was the nominal seat of government—nominal because Alaxak had carried on quite well after the last governor died and the next appointee kept finding reasons to delay arrival. Finally, everyone agreed remote decisions were quite all right.

It was also the largest gathering place, where the de facto leaders of other areas apparently came together to make consensus-based decisions.

I didn't imagine we were flying out immediately—word of a gathering had to spread, after all—so I excused myself from the table to go to the ship's head. I never made it there, sliding down along the wall of the corridor to sit on the grating, my head leaned back, eyes closed.

I had been to Chorda once, when I first arrived on Alaxak

and started my search for someone like Qole. Arriving there had led me to here. I would be coming full circle.

Except now everything was in tatters. I had tried to help Qole, tried to give up on my family, tried to give myself back to them ... for all the good any of it had done. Now my parents were dead, Solara would be queen, and the people of Alaxak were going to lose their entire way of life.

If not their *lives* if they tried to resist.

My mind ran over what the clergy of the Unifier had told me about loss, what I believed, and it all dissolved in front of what I was feeling. Everyone being united right now didn't seem all that much of a comfort, or a guide.

The Church had never talked about your sister not only betraying you, but having your parents assassinated. I knew the blood was on her hands, but I wanted to blame the Bladeguard who had done it. I couldn't reconcile what had happened with what I had known of Solara—fun, frivolous, quick to laugh, and even quicker to grow bored. I had seen her as my one ally on Luvos, the person who had risked everything to help me save Qole.

Only if I thought hard could I remember incidents like the shredded gown that now struck me as suspect. Solara had never cried over anyone else's pain, or when one of her pets had died, despite appearing to dote upon them. At such times, I would occasionally catch that same assessing look in her eyes that she'd given me as I cradled our dead mother. Specifically, I recalled a beautiful caged bird in her quarters whose wings kept breaking, supposedly when it flapped too violently against the bars. But now I doubted the cause, never mind the many times Solara had made splints for the poor creature.

I also remembered a pale, trembling companion of hers,

whose arm had been horrifically sliced. Solara had insisted it was an accident, that they were pretending to be Bladeguards with a pair of ceremonial swords they'd lifted out of a display. The odd thing was that there had been *two* cuts. The girl hadn't argued before being rushed to the med bay. In fact, she'd hardly said a word—something I'd attributed to shock but now guessed was pure fear.

These things had occurred only when Solara was young, so they were dim in my memory, nearly forgotten. She must have grown more careful, calculated, since then. She'd put her cheerful, trivial mask in place, hiding her true, dangerous, *sick* self behind witty banter and subtle manipulation.

And now my little brother, Marsius, was alone with her. I almost couldn't stomach the thought. Nor this:

If I had been so wrong about her, what else was I wrong about?

"You keeping it together?"

I had secretly hoped Qole would find me and we could speak privately. I wanted to ask her how she had moved on after her family had died, one by one. How she had dealt with day-to-day life when everything felt surreal, pointless, and unavoidably mundane. How I wanted reality to reflect how broken I was, but instead, gravity, light, and everyone else just carried along as they always had.

However, it wasn't Qole who loomed over me. It was Eton, his broad face impassive. I knew he didn't like me, and I couldn't blame him. *I* didn't much like me right now.

I took a deep breath. "Everything normal is still . . . normal. We still have to prep the ship, talk to one another, do the same things we do every day." I looked up at him. "How do you do it?"

"Do what?" Eton frowned, the lines on his face making the question seem more like a threat. I imagined he would look menacing even while giggling and flying a kite.

I rested my arms across my knees. *Function at all* was what I wanted to say. "Sleep. Eat. At some point, your life fell apart. Does it get better, or are you . . . is it always like this inside?"

Eton folded into a cross-legged position, surprising me by how sudden and seamless the motion was. "Why the hell do you think my life fell apart?" Something in the flatness of his voice was more disconcerting than his usual crabbiness.

I now knew he was one of the luminaries who had trained at the Royal Academy years before me, earning a place through sheer skill, despite not being royal. One day he'd simply disappeared. Since putting together who he was, I'd tried to quietly unearth what had happened, to no avail. Whatever it had been, his reputation was deserved, as he was a mountain of muscle that moved more gracefully than anyone had a right to.

I didn't think it would be wise to tell him he'd been my subject of study. "I can't imagine you'd be here if it hadn't," I said instead.

His eyes narrowed, but he didn't argue. "I was a mercenary before this."

That still didn't explain his exit from Dracorva but was nonetheless fascinating. There were countless mercenary groups in the systems, many acting as proxy armies for the families. Some were a league apart, virtual factions unto themselves. It was the perfect place for someone of Eton's talents to vanish.

"I saw plenty of death, but at one point I . . ." He trailed off, rubbing his thumb and forefinger, as if considering the mote of an emotion that was getting the better of him. "I killed a girl about Qole's age. I left after that, and when I met Qole, she reminded me of her. Being here gives me purpose." Eton's voice gained more of an edge. "And no, it doesn't get easier. What you learn is you have to hold on to something stronger. Figure out what you'll fight for no matter the cost, and then don't let go of that. That's it. That's all you get, Prince."

I tried for a laugh, and winced at the sound. "'Prince' no longer. I thought it was my destiny as such to create a better existence for people—*that* was my cause worth fighting for. Rather neat how none of it is true anymore."

"Destiny is bullshit." Eton grunted. "You don't get to live in the future, and you aren't in the past. All you get is right now."

I frowned. "Oh? What do you think I should be doing right now?"

"You can pull yourself together and be useful to this crew." His eyes bored into mine. The ship bucked on a few sudden waves as he stood, never losing balance. There must have been a storm coming in. Fitting. "If your being here helps us, then we're good. If you're more useful gone, then you're gone."

"A threat. Goodness. I was starting to think we were having a real conversation."

To my surprise, something like warmth flickered in Eton's eyes. "I'm sorry about your family," he said. "But I can't help with that. I can help with this one, though."

I nodded as he walked away, message received.

———

It took a week to activate some sort of communication chain that existed between the towns and villages of Alaxak, and to give folks time to wrap up any fishing runs and off-load the Shadow in their holds. Somehow, Qole and I managed not to talk about anything other than logistics. Perhaps it was more by design than the chaos of the moment, at least on my part. She wouldn't have wanted to hear what I had to say, nor did I want to say it. And maybe I wouldn't have to, because I suspected someone else would say it for me.

The question was, would she listen?

On the designated date that had been set, we landed in the ocean without the hiss and explosion of steam that was typical after the heat of atmospheric reentry. Qole had flown in-atmosphere to conserve fuel, and put us down on the water outside Chorda.

Despite Alaxak being in the grip of an ice age and technically classified as a "frozen" planet, the period was warming. All that meant was that the temperatures had risen enough so that the equatorial band was no longer covered in ice, allowing vegetation and animal life to start creeping in. Humans had arrived in the middle of this process—thousands of years ago, well before the Great Collapse—and some, now known as native Alaxans, had decided that the climate could be considered survivable.

Other villages and towns dotted the coast, and Chorda was the largest of these, situated near a rare equatorial forest. The *Kaitan Heritage* taxied toward the cliffs. They rose above us, high, jagged outcroppings reaching out into the ocean like the canines of a carnivore.

Oddly, we taxied into the bay adjacent to the one to which our coordinates directed us. Qole muttered something about this dock being a lot quieter. We exited as a group, down the cargo ramp of the *Kaitan* into the deep evening. It was definitely quiet. There wasn't another ship in sight. I wondered if no one had bothered to come, if this was a useless effort. The gust of wind that hit had rain in it, misting me with a sheen of moisture noticeably warmer than Gamut's.

"Ugh, give me a real winter anytime instead of this muck." Telu shivered and lifted the ruff of her jacket.

"The first time I came here I thought Chorda was frigid," I remarked, looking around us. I'd practically been a different person then. I'd even looked like one.

Stairs, weathered to a degree that made me believe they had been cut before Shadow fishing was the way of life, climbed steeply up the cliff. When we reached the top, the steps dropped down again immediately. In front of us lay an old caldera, a giant valley ringed by cliffs, forming another harbor to the sea. The stone walls that protected us from the wind also created favorable conditions for tall deciduous trees to take hold. The green spread was broken by the twinkling lights of warehouses, the cannery tower, and the larger dock where madness was unfolding.

"Looks like everyone got the message," Basra murmured, staring down. What might have been a typically peaceful, if industrious, scene was a riot of glowing contrails, flaring thrusters, and thundering turbines. Alaxan vessel standards were as nonexistent as air traffic control, and ships of every size, type, and make were jockeying for position to land in port.

Some freighters had skiffs attached to every surface, huge spools of mag-cables connected to each one. Some were tiny, gnatlike, retrofitted fighters with tiny scoops to capture Shadow. Still others were obvious amalgamations of two entirely different ships for purposes I couldn't imagine. The variety and inventiveness of the modifications were unending. There were roughly eight hundred Shadow-fishing ships on Alaxak, total, and it looked as if the bulk of them had come.

"Most everyone is here," Arjan said in a wondering tone, as if he had never seen this either.

"Good," Qole replied grimly. "Let's find out how angry they are."

———

"Pretty angry!" Telu yelled over the roaring hubbub of the gathering hall. The converted warehouse, lit with the eerie glare of Shadow lamps and furnaces, was a far cry from the royal meeting chambers and corporate boardrooms that represented my political experience. If the variety of ships outside had been a revelation, it was nothing compared to the characters milling around us by the hundreds. Most were captains, Qole told me, since not every crewmember would fit. Weathered and rugged, they wore custom leathers or well-patched synthetics and sported a variety of tools I had never imagined, let alone seen. Several of them were missing hands or limbs, or had suffered some accident that caused them to make do with rough prostheses. Modern medicine could have aided any of them, could they only access or afford it. I suddenly understood Arjan and his disdain for anything more than an eye patch a bit better. And for royals.

As if reading my thoughts, Telu muttered, "Good thing you're dead, hey?"

Not only was I supposed to be dead, I'd disguised myself as heavily as possible, leaving nothing that would hint at royalty. I fit right in.

At a glance, citizens of my home planet would have deemed everyone here dangerous and uncivilized, instead of competent and independent, as I knew them to be. Part of me wondered if my family would have felt differently about exploiting these people if they had ever experienced life on Alaxak—a thought that became buried under a cavalcade of other painful reminders. *Now is not the time. Just don't think about them.*

"What are those?" I asked quietly, nodding toward the middle of the gathering hall, where approximately thirty waist-high black cylinders stood in a ring.

"Those are the talking stumps," Telu helpfully supplied, and then fell silent as she scanned the teeming space.

"Stumps? As in tree stumps?" I frowned. "Those are thicker than any trees I've seen on the planet."

She glanced up at me through a shock of hair. "Been over the entire planet, hey?"

I looked for a snappy comeback but couldn't muster one. "Point."

Telu looked at me again, concern flickering across her face. Then she sighed. "They're petrified. There's one for each village representative."

I looked around, trying to spot someone in the crowd who carried with them the telltale air of a politician. "Where are they? And who elects them?"

"They elect themselves whenever they feel like it. If you have something to say, and you feel you can represent a village with your stance, you go up to a stump," Telu replied, lowering herself into a crouch on the floor, as though settling in for a long wait. "If enough people disagree with you, they can come up with a different representative instead."

I shook my head. "I never read any of this in our records on Alaxak. What if people are unhappy about a decision that gets made when they aren't here?"

"Should have been here, then, shouldn't they?" Arjan interjected, and then fell silent as someone in the crowd approached us.

Tall and solidly built, he wore an overcoat covered in buckles that reached down to his knees, and a pair of goggles strapped to the top of his head. Like many others there, he was obviously a pilot, likely of a Shadow-fishing vessel. Most curiously, his hair was streaked with gray; older Shadow fishermen weren't exactly unheard of, but they were much less common.

Telu stood up abruptly, tension radiating off her in waves. Jaw clenched, she exchanged glances with Qole.

He stopped a few feet away and nodded at her. "Telu, it's good to see you looking so well."

The normally verbose Telu stared at him for a moment. Finally, she said, "Thanks. I hope you're here to fight the scat that the Dracortes are raining down upon us." She kept her tone neutral, but her words were clipped, precise.

He made a noncommittal gesture. "I have been made aware of . . . details that perhaps not everyone has. I'm about to share them with everyone, and I'm glad you've come to hear me out—as family should."

He then nodded at Qole in casual acknowledgment, never mind that it was she who had called this gathering. She only returned his gaze steadily until he left.

"Family?" I murmured.

"Uncle. Dad's side," Telu said shortly.

Qole's gaze and mine finally met, her look confirming everything I needed to know.

Telu's father had been an alcoholic, and worse, abusive to his family. Qole had helped Telu frame her father for shooting down a drone, one of the few offenses that caused the offworlder peace officers on Alaxak to enforce the law. Telu's father was still in prison, as far as I knew. Qole had told me the story in confidence, but she had never mentioned any other of Telu's family. I would have thought any kin would have stepped up to help Telu first, but apparently not.

Her uncle, however, was the first to enter the circle. He raised his hand at a black stump, which acted as a lectern. Qole nudged Arjan, and they both slid forward through the crowd as the man began to speak. I stayed with the others. Eton, Basra, and I were offworlders who wouldn't have much say here, and Telu looked as though she didn't want to get near her uncle.

"Friends and family!" he intoned, his voice sonorous and carrying easily to the far reaches of the warehouse. "We know why we are here. Great changes are coming, and our people are in danger." He paused, his gaze sweeping the crowd, and I could have sworn it lingered on our little group. "My name is Hiat Uvmathun, and I have more news. I believe that if we act wisely, remembering the good decisions made at each stump in the past, we will endure as we always have."

His next words captured my attention. "We don't know for sure why this is happening. My attempts to find out who was involved with the *Luvos Sunrise*—who this mysterious hacker is who apparently aided their now-dead traitor prince—have been unsuccessful." His gaze definitely lingered for a split second on Telu. "But we do know the royal Dracorte family is in political upheaval, which has resulted in one of the less offensive offspring ascending to the throne."

I was pretty sure we all made a sort of choking sound. *Less offensive?* Perhaps he didn't understand Solara's venom in that vid, or else . . . I was beginning to suspect that maybe he understood my sister all too well, because, like her, he could see the gain in other people's suffering. Or, in his case, the benefit of risking nothing.

That didn't mean he wasn't smart, but I didn't have to like

it, or him. At least he was keeping Telu's involvement a secret. Probably only so he wouldn't be implicated by association.

"Is he your father's younger brother?" I muttered to Telu, as Hiat let his words sink in.

She nodded, her eyes fixed on her uncle with a combination of outrage and horror.

"Interesting. Rubion was my father's too." The man who'd taken Arjan's eye.

"Maybe they're predisposed to be dicks," Telu grated back. But I got from her what I'd wanted to see—that spark, that sharpness.

Basra flashed a grin, and Eton grunted, his mouth twitching in an attempt not to smile. I wasn't sure how the latter felt about Hiat's perspective, but at least there was that.

Hiat cleared his throat and continued as the murmuring rose to a volume he deemed ripe for smothering. "Now, the Dracortes are putting new policies for Shadow fishing into place, ones that promise to change everything. Immediately after the broadcast, I reached out to Dracorte family authorities to learn the details of their proposal." He paused, making sure he had everyone's attention. I wasn't surprised by what came next. "They intend to take a more active approach in dealing with us, but contrary to what some have said, they are not stopping us from fishing Shadow. Instead, they intend to supply us with freighters from which we can harvest Shadow, and a standardized rate for our catch."

This was a tactic that Solara had no doubt consciously employed: coming across as strong and decisive to both our system and the other families', someone not to be crossed, while quietly appealing to select Alaxans with benevolent offers. Part of me hoped someone would see through it.

"You mean we're going to be their slaves, hey?" A wiry

fellow, with black hair that came almost to his waist, materialized at another stump. "Or a bunch of loaders in their Shadow holds, at best! My name is Wul Uvnuk, and I don't want to trade our Shadow for scat."

"This proposal involves neither slavery nor scat. We will be paid, and the intent is to prevent anyone's overexposure to Shadow ever again," Hiat countered smoothly. "Isn't *that* what we want? Work, pay, and health for our families in the future?"

"How in the frozen sea do they expect giant *freighters* to fish for Shadow?" The new speaker was a woman in her midthirties, her hair twisted into multiple short braids that stuck out in every direction. Streaks of purple had been dyed in the black, and the overall effect was more space pirate than a Shadow-fishing captain. More noticeable, both her legs ended at the knees. She rolled up to a stump on a wheeled conveyance that had obviously been reclaimed from some other use, and she did it with a confidence that hinted at years of practice.

"My name is Jerra Uvthiak," she continued, "and I would remind everyone that we have been one of the primary sources of Shadow for the Dracortes because we can fly where no one else dares."

Hiat was unperturbed. "The family claims that they can do as they say, and they certainly have the means. And, consider"—he spread his hands—"if they are wrong, they will need us regardless. If they are right, we will no longer be only an exotic commodity to the systems, but a critical one."

And so it went. Hiat was calm, reasoned, and persuasive. One by one, people approached the stumps, identifying themselves by name and place, filled with questions. Telu's uncle answered them, gently correcting in some cases and encouraging in others. One by one, the objections died down, and the angry murmur of the crowd with it.

And I began to relax. I knew I shouldn't, and I felt a sting of shame along with relief. But if there was a chance, no matter how unappealing the means, that this didn't have to come to an unwinnable fight, then it was the better option.

Finally, Hiat placed both hands on the black surface before him, raising his voice. "As captain of one of the highest-producing operations on the planet, I have no more to gain than any of you, and much to lose." I highly doubted either was the case. If he had been in touch with my sister's representatives, which seemed likely, he'd been promised a lot for his support. "But we must be wise, ready to adapt to change, and unafraid of a new future. I call on everyone present to agree with my decision—that we send Queen Solara a statement of our cooperation in starting a new chapter between our peoples."

Telu's breath hissed in between her teeth as she leaned in to whisper furiously at me. "If there's no more disagreement with him at the stumps, it will go to a general vote. But probably no one wants to argue against those who've spoken so far, since the speakers all have popular support. Everyone will just *give up* everything we have because *he* won't fight for it!"

Basra leaned toward us and said in a low, steady murmur, "Having already shot Nev's uncle in the face, I could continue the pattern here."

For an absurd moment, I wanted to laugh. But none of this was funny.

"My name is Qole Uvgamut." My head jerked up at the sound of her voice. It didn't so much fill the space as roll over us, strong, devoid of uncertainty. "And you are making a terrible mistake."

Qole stood at the last remaining stump, her back ramrod straight. She was the youngest, by far, of everyone else in the circle, and she looked small in comparison to Hiat, standing directly across from her. She was staring right at him.

I felt more dread than surprise. I'd hoped that if Qole hadn't found the fishermen willing to fight, that she would back away. Regroup. Reassess the situation and realize it was impossible.

I should have known better.

Hiat smiled. "Only the young speak with such certainty. Come, is she really the representative for Gamut?"

"I'm the one who approached the stump, aren't I?"

"It is not your place to speak when a question has been placed to the people," Hiat admonished, and I grimaced. He'd obviously baited her in an effort to make her look inexperienced; I had seen a thousand meetings run by others using the same tactics.

Qole flushed, glancing around. But then Arjan materialized behind her with crossed arms, and I noticed other familiar faces from the docks of Gamut. Telu shoved forward to stand with her, and several others from Gamut began to migrate in that direction. Eton and Basra stayed with me, and it was our silence that Qole needed in this case, anyway—even though I wanted to shout for her to stop.

Quiet settled over the crowd. No one spoke to challenge Qole.

"I," she started again, her voice regaining strength. "I am Qole Uvgamut, also captain of one of the highest-producing fishing operations on the planet, and I oppose your decision on the following grounds."

"You might be a skilled captain, but what do you know of the systems?" Hiat shot back—and the struggle for who had the greater authority had begun. "Have you traveled to other planets as I have? Have you faced the—"

"You *will* be quiet until I am done." Pure fury simmered

in Qole's voice. Hiat swallowed, the words dying in his throat. Her anger alone would have sufficed to shut him up, but I wondered if blackness had crept into her eyes that I hadn't spotted.

"What I have experienced is hardly the question," Qole continued. "We all know what we, the people of Alaxak, have experienced. Hundreds of years, generations upon generations of offworlders coming to us with promises of riches, of new wealth. If we only give up our ways and let them teach us theirs—promises that have, without a single exception, led to our suffering and loss."

I winced. Many nodded.

"And now, it's not even a matter of misplaced trust. This 'deal' is rotten on the surface, blatant thievery. This is *not* to our benefit. In the best light, Solara is stealing our birthright and *letting* us buy back into it as employees, under the guise of generosity. She is just one more queen in a long line of power-hungry rulers intent on taking what is ours simply because she has the force." Qole pointed toward the high ceiling, and a shiver ran down my spine. She was working the crowd without even thinking about it. I could see it in their faces; they believed her. I believed her.

"But even if we want to reject her terms, as you said, she has the power to force us," Hiat said, still reasonable. "Why let it come to that? We are not the head of a mighty system. We do not have a navy."

"But we *can* fight. You were asking earlier who had embarrassed the royals and drawn their attention. Well, we did."

Qole had no sooner finished her sentence than Telu dropped her backpack and unzipped it. She reached inside, and a hologram flashed to life above us, overwhelmingly large. In a

84

split instant, we were transported back to Luvos, on the *Kaitan,* diving toward the swarm of defending starfighters. Telu nearly cackled with glee as the stunned audience watched the video feeds that the ship's monitors had recorded. Every face glowed in awe of the impossible flight Qole had taken us on. Drones, fighters, and the spires of the Dracorva citadel flashed around us in staccato succession, and then were gone.

Qole didn't give them a chance to react, to question. "They took us. They experimented on us." She pointed behind her, and Arjan lifted his eye patch, eliciting gasps of outrage. His own expression was one of grim satisfaction. "They were going to kill us. And we fought back, and we won. By the ancestors, we won."

Neatly done. Qole had taken what could have been a liability, almost a scandal, and turned it to her rousing advantage in the space of a few seconds.

"That was one ship. One crew. In their capital." Qole let that sink in. "Now imagine what all of us can do. So yes, I do believe we can fight back. We must. That is why I challenge your decision, Hiat, with my own—the decision that the people of Alaxak should continue our way of life, and our method of trade, as we have always done."

I had grown up among the decision makers of the systems, and I knew a leader being born when I saw one.

That didn't mean this was good.

Jerra smiled ferociously, her eyes glinting. "I support Captain Uvgamut. Remember, when there is a competing decision, Captain Uvmathun," she said, using the same patronizing tone on Telu's uncle that he'd just used with Qole, "the tradition is to give the people three days to deliberate before we all vote."

My heart started to pound, and I missed the ensuing conversation as I made my way through the crowd, unseeing, to escape into the night air beyond.

———

Unfamiliar with my surroundings, I simply set one foot in front of the other, trying to clear my head. The town was nearly deserted with everyone inside, and in a few moments, after I had walked only several blocks, the street abruptly stopped, dropping into the bay quietly lapping at my feet. The cloudy night had become pitch-black, but indistinct reflections and the metallic clank of ships resting in the water told me that the dock was nearby. No doubt Hiat had claimed one of these premium piers himself.

I sat down on the ledge, looking out into the darkness, soaking in the night and hoping it would calm me down. I didn't like anything that was about to happen, and in a twisted repeat of everything playing through my mind the past week, I didn't see how I could be useful.

"Don't jump."

I started at the voice, turning to see Eton materializing out of the darkness. *I must be really out of it if someone can sneak up on me like that.*

"Jump? No, but you almost scared me off the edge. You're entirely too large to be so quiet anyway. Isn't there a size limitation on sneaking or something?"

Satisfaction glinted in his eyes. "So you're still alive in there."

"Apparently so. If irritation means I'm alive, at any rate. What do you need?"

"I saw you slip out, and I wondered what you were thinking." Eton, his voice casual, walked up to the edge and stared out into the darkness as well, as though he could see beyond the harbor.

"Just how much of your time do you spend watching me?"

"Enough to make sure I'm doing my job."

I nodded. "Fair enough."

We listened to the water lap until I couldn't take it any longer. "It's impossible, you know," I said, louder than I had intended.

"No kidding," Eton grunted, never looking at me.

"Alaxak can't fight my sister. It can't fight the Dracorte military, and it's important enough economically that my family won't just give up on a rebellion. They'll crush it." I gathered a handful of dirt and flung it uselessly into the dark. "It's going to be a slaughter. You were in the Academy; you know what I'm talking about."

Eton looked down at me, arms crossed. "So, what are our assets?"

I blinked at him. He was using the kind of language you might use before a training exercise, and the familiar thought patterns awakened, as though jolted by an external charge.

I shook my head. "Not many. Willing fighters, probably, which count for something, but only up to a point. Distance from Luvos, and maybe an alliance with or defection to another system, if there were time to arrange it, but there's not, and honestly, I doubt the Belarius or Xiaolan families would cross the Dracortes like that, and if they did, that might open the door for the Treznor-Nirmanas to swoop in and corner the Shadow market. And no one else would want to fight my sister. Ugh." I knuckled the ground just thinking about it.

"You're not an asset?" Eton raised his eyebrows. I knew he wasn't trying to be friendly. He was wondering how I could be useful to Qole. Problem was, I couldn't see how.

I spread my hands. "That's the best joke so far. They don't need a Bladeguard; they need a fleet. I've got some money left, but I could literally be swimming in currency like Basra and it's not like it would do any good because *there isn't any time*." I ran my fingers through my hair, clutching at it as I did. "I'm not bragging when I say I've been trained to fight difficult battles, but I wasn't trained to be omnipotent. We need resources, a bargaining chip, something to buy time and find other options to keep our new queen from getting exactly what she wants."

Eton persisted. "But you're the prince."

"No, my menacing friend, I *was* the prince. Now I'm the disgraced, banished, *ex*-prince, who is useless, not to mention supposedly dead." I felt myself begin to gather steam. I should have probably been quieter or more circumspect, but for some reason, it felt satisfying to enumerate everything terrible. "And good thing too, because if Solara knew I was alive, she would consume us with fire. At best, I might start a civil war, incite a rebellion, and still watch Alaxak burn. And then she'd crush the rebellion and we'd all die, or Treznor-Nirmana would interrupt the fight and mop up the remains. Not to mention what fighting would do to Qole even before that point. Using Shadow like that would kill her ahead of any of us. It's all. Just. Bad."

"All right, you've convinced me." One-handed, Eton bent and casually picked up a rock roughly the size of my head and threw it out into the darkness. Instead of a splash, something metallic caved in. "Fighting is a stupid idea. So the only real option is to not fight, right?"

I nodded. "But Qole is going to convince everyone otherwise. She almost convinced me. Being around her is kind of like being in the grip of some gravitational current—everything changes."

"Then listen to me." Eton grabbed my shoulder and pulled me to my feet as easily as if I were another rock. He brought his face close to mine, his voice growing quieter. "That means that Qole needs to change her mind. And I know better than anyone that doing that for her is almost impossible. But." The word was heavy in the air as he paused. His grip fell away. "You and I both know that Qole cares about you . . . well, a lot. She'll listen to you. So talk to her. Convince her."

And here it was, how I could be useful. What I had been avoiding and dreading all along—that it would fall to me to tell Qole the last thing she wanted to hear, the words that could make her despise me, undo everything that I'd been trying to build with her. I'd ruined my relationship with my family by telling them the harsh truth, and yet now I hesitated when it came to Qole. Even after everything I'd lost, I felt I had even more to lose, with her.

My hesitation was cowardice.

Eton looked angry now. Even if he was using me—and he was right to—such an admission must have cost him. But he took a step away, crossing his arms instead of pulverizing me. "Make sure Qole loses to Hiat. If we're going to keep her safe, then you need to make her give up."

PROCESSIONAL

SOLARA

THE MUSIC AS I WALKED DOWN THE AISLE SOUNDED LIKE RELEASE. It was a sigh escaping my soul. I didn't make a peep myself, because this was, after all, a solemn occasion.

Even so, I wanted to snatch the liquid silver crown from the Unifier Bishop as he lifted it as slowly as a crane raising a spire atop a newly completed tower, and then even more slowly lowered it on my head. The red jewels—blood tears, they were called—glinted in the equally solemn lighting. They would be the brightest thing adorning me, aside from my hair, which tumbled in a gilded cascade down my back. I didn't wear red or gold, the colors I preferred. I wore the white of mourning.

After all, even though I wanted to grin with the fierceness of a rising sun, this wasn't cause for celebration. The only reason for my coronation was that my parents were dead. No one liked to mention Nevarian in my presence, but I wasn't a fool. They mourned him too.

People could mourn him all they liked. They just couldn't miss him as a living, breathing threat to both our family and my freedom.

I closed my eyes as I felt the weight on my brow. The crown hadn't gone unnoticed after I'd commissioned it and returned to Luvos. Practically the first thing Devrak, my head of family security and self-appointed babysitter, had said to me when he saw it a few days ago was, "Don't you think you should have chosen blue, Your Highness? The Dracorte colors are *blue* and silver."

"I like red," I'd said, keeping my voice serene, like a queen's should be. "Don't fret, I'll pair it with plenty of blue gowns."

His eyes were lined with grief. "Your parents would have preferred—"

My parents, and their preferences, could rot. They'd not only tried to ensure I would live out the rest of my days in captivity, but their gentle hand in dealing with our enemies had nearly brought about the ruin of the Dracortes. "It symbolizes the blood and tears that I'm willing to shed for our great family."

"It's a wonder you *aren't* crying," he'd murmured. "How are you holding it together so well? Your poise is . . . commendable."

I wasn't sure if that was quite the word he wanted to say.

"I didn't say it would *necessarily* be *my* blood or tears." I touched his cheek, my hand pale against his dark skin. "Ruling well requires every level of sacrifice, my own and others', to keep us strong. Something Nevarian and my dear mother and father didn't understand." I let my voice drop in an approximation of sorrow. "Perhaps if they had, they would still be alive. Oh, and Devrak?"

"Yes, Your Highness?"

"From now on, call me *Your Majesty*. Might as well get accustomed to it."

Devrak had blinked at me, as if seeing me for the first time. Which was true, really. He wouldn't have noticed me before, the girl I had been. Dracorte princesses weren't meant to be noticed, unless it was for their witty repartee or their latest fashion. And I had played my role well. I was nothing if not a loyal member of the family.

Now, with the crown settled on my brow, I couldn't help but smile, solemn occasion or no.

They will all see me soon enough.

When I turned around to face the crowd at my back—thousands of royals and dignitaries from across families and systems—I felt more on display than ever before, but the crown on my head was a comfort. It was a key.

In the middle of a ceremony filled with pomp and tradition, I suddenly remembered one of Nev's earlier birthdays, a casual occasion for once, when our parents had taken us to visit Dracorva's menagerie.

The officials had closed the park for us that sunny afternoon, and while Nev was obsessed with the larger beasts with huge teeth and claws—and was the center of attention himself, of course—I gravitated to the shadowy grottos that held sealed aquariums. In one, I found a feathered serpent called a volassa. It couldn't fly, but it could bunch its coils, spread the feathered membranes along either side of its body, and glide with startling speed at one's jugular. It was the most venomous creature in the entire system.

I looked at it, and it looked back at me with bloodred eyes. I felt *seen*.

And then I jumped when Nev came alongside me and knocked on the glass. "Why are you in here, Sol? There are way more interesting creatures outside."

The serpent looked at him then, with the seething, acidic hatred that one could only possess for people tapping on your aquarium every day. The look that said, *Someday, this lid will open, and then the screaming will commence in earnest.*

The memory was appropriate, since the temple walls around me now were transparent, falling like water to the river far below. I could see the Dracorte citadel across the city, standing even taller. People thought these shining glass structures could contain me, or worse, that I happily fit within—a pretty bird in a cage, a less interesting creature than my brother. They had assumed such my entire life, tap-tap-tapping on my walls and smiling to see a reflection smile back at them, to hear me laugh at their jokes and then respond with my own. They couldn't sense my burning hatred, nor the way my eyes went to their necks.

But now, my lid was open, through the circular crown on my head. And soon they wouldn't be laughing.

The Unifier Bishop had been talking for some time. I'd hardly heard what he said in his boring monotone, only echoing the words I was required to say. But his next line caught my full attention: "And do you hereby swear to do all in your power, granted by the Unifier, to keep this family great?"

My true, silent response was redder than the jewels of my crown. The words were blood on my hands, but also that beating in my veins: *I already have.*

I said aloud, "I swear it."

Devrak wasn't the only one who tried to correct my behavior, who didn't yet understand "the new me," as the fashion vids liked to caption someone who'd merely given themselves a makeover—as if a face, let alone makeup, showed what truly lay underneath.

While I mingled with the many guests in the temple's reception area after the coronation, several of my own generals approached me, Gavros Dracorte among them. I wondered if he'd been aware that my father had wished for us to marry, or if he would understand why I would soon send him away—the better to never see him again.

"A word, Your Majesty." At least *he* was learning my new title fast enough. He was military, so I supposed he had an acute regard for rank. Tall and sturdy in his dress uniform, Dracorte-silver eyes set in a handsome face, he gestured to the side of the hall, where there was a secluded alcove. I followed, resisting a sigh. Men in suits were still diverting me from my goal . . . but not for long.

Once we were separated from the crowd, out of earshot of others, the next person to speak was a woman. General Talia, if I recalled correctly. She was one of the few who'd managed to exceed Dracorte expectations of women and climb to such heights usually reserved for men—by men, of course—despite not being royalty herself. "We've become aware that you've ordered one of our carriers stationed near Aaltos to head for Alaxak. I'm afraid you can't technically give such an order—"

I laughed, as if it were a joke. "Your carrier? Do you own it?"

"No, Your Majesty, but—"

"Well, I do. So I can order it where I please." I tried to walk past them, but Gavros stepped in front of me. He had silver at his temples, too. I met his eyes, and he took a step back.

I also had silver in my hair, in the form of a crown, and mine meant more than his.

"Apologies, Your Majesty," he said, his tone steady, despite his retreat, "but the Dracorte king or queen isn't the commander of the military by default."

"What are you talking about?" I said, feeling an unwelcome ripple of uncertainty in my new queenly serenity. "My father was, *his* father was."

"Yes, and they all passed the trial of the Dracorte Forging to earn the right to command the military. You'll still have control of your forces, of course, but it should be in consultation with a commander, who will best interpret how to fulfill your wishes."

Dracorte Forging. Another ridiculous family ritual meant to keep someone like me in a cage. Nev had sometimes complained about the hoops he had to jump through. But he hadn't understood. Complaining didn't help. You had to jump through—or dodge—all of them until that final hoop was a crown. And then all the rest could burn.

I had done just that, and I'd be damned before I even considered another test of my abilities. And I would be damned before I let someone like Gavros try to argue where I put my fleet.

"And this 'Forging' will no doubt be some needlessly archaic, strenuous, and complicated ritual to prove I'm capable of leading a military, specifically designed to favor a certain type of desiccated relic with a skill set belonging to a bygone era?"

"Um, actually, Your Majesty—"

"I'm not interested, and as queen and sovereign of the Dracorte family, I hereby declare it unnecessary, a subject worthy of mentioning no longer."

"But—"

"Did you mistake me?" I moved closer to Gavros and murmured in his ear like a beloved might. "Get out of my way before I make you regret ever setting one foot in front of the other."

He hastily stepped aside, and I swept past him. I couldn't help smirking as I strode away.

Finally. The path to my goal was clear.

Or not. Back in the crowd, I spotted Heathran through a group of royal offspring, aloof, as usual . . . except for the girl at his side.

Daiyen Xiaolan. I couldn't believe she had the gall to move on Heathran here, at *my* coronation, after I'd made it abundantly apparent to anyone who had eyes that I was interested in him. I had to pause to take a deep breath, reassure myself. Like many individuals who didn't realize it yet, she was subject to my will. And it was my will that *they* weren't going to happen.

It didn't matter if she was the heiress of an entirely different family and system that technically wasn't answerable to mine. Or that Heathran, who might well have an opinion on the matter, was the heir to a family arguably greater than mine, who had invented the faster-than-light drive that kept us all connected and thus under their thumbs. He was the future head of the empire that we ostensibly bowed to, but the Xiaolan family, with this little budding royal romance, wasn't going to usurp *my* family as Belarius's right hand.

"Heathran, darling."

With the thrill that came with displaying brazen familiarity in public, I stepped right up to him and brushed his cheek with a royal kiss of greeting. Light flashed behind my closed lids from the direction of the media cameras. I couldn't blame them. We made quite the pair: me, pale and golden in my white gown, him in a black suit that was only a shade darker than his inky skin. An iridescent purple stone the size of my thumb pinned the white cravat at his neck—the white worn as a gesture of mourning for me. Otherwise, the Belarius colors were purple and gold.

My movements forced Daiyen to step back, and it didn't hurt that she would be in the pictures too. People would only see me, standing between Belarius and Xiaolan. She was decked out in full Xiaolan colors, a floor-length gown of alternating links of green and bronze, like scintillating chain mail. The ensemble looked lovely with her tawny skin tone and long black hair, but I reveled in the fact that I complemented Heathran rather better.

I used to amuse myself by thinking that the metallic counterparts of our family colors illustrated where we stood in the galaxy: Belarius gold and purple, Dracorte silver and blue, Xiaolan bronze and green, Nirmana copper and turquoise, Treznor chrome and charcoal. The other royal families didn't quite rate on this scale: orange and yellow for Enterio, which was really a co-op of smaller independent systems led by a family that could barely be considered royal; and white and teal for Orbit, which was a corporation first, family second, and proud of it.

But then Treznor and Nirmana had combined to become a family with power to rival Belarius, and changed their colors to platinum and black. I'd grown less amused by the thought.

Treznor-Nirmana was still a worthy threat to us, but less of one now. Makar, their king, was nowhere in sight in the crowded hall. Some would perhaps view that as a slight to me, but others would know it for the truth: his standing within his own family was precarious at best, laughable at worst, and all because he'd opposed me.

It was time for Princess Daiyen to learn the danger of crossing my path.

"Daiyen, you're here in Dracorva alone again. I would sympathize, but I know it's a powerful Xiaolan statement. I *so* admire how you're above it all—the romance, the entanglements, the gossip—showing interest in no one. It paints a rather forbidding picture. Not that you couldn't turn heads if you ever *wanted* to, of course."

Daiyen's face tightened at the implication that she wasn't interested in Heathran, nor he in her. The broader assumption was entirely untrue too, since I knew from my spy network that she'd recently engaged in a relationship with a young woman on her planet, Genlai, and a man before that. But, for once, the secrecy of Xiaolan was working against them.

I sighed in Heathran's direction. "I don't have the same fortitude. I've been ever so lonely."

"There have been rumors that you *haven't* been alone," Daiyen said with a hard smile, "but those are just vicious, of course, since you are in mourning, after all."

Point for me and a point for her. My own smile could have cut the marble pillar next to us.

"I hardly think it's appropriate to bring such rumors up, then." Heathran's surprisingly soft voice—one expected something more resonant from someone so tall and broad-shouldered—was chiding and as humorless as usual.

I frowned. "Would that the timing was appropriate for such fun, because that would mean my parents were still alive. Why, this will be the first Dracorte coronation with no true celebration . . . but it is a privilege to honor them so," I added, reminding Daiyen that I was a queen, while she was still a princess. Now for some intimidation. "It's been ever so busy with the ordering of a completely new star fleet from our friends the Treznors . . ."

An inaudible vibration at the comm in my ear caught my focus.

"Oh, if you'll be so kind as to excuse me." I wanted to continue, to deal her a few more solid blows, but I couldn't ignore this. Still, I curtsied slightly—very slightly—to Daiyen and stood on tiptoe to kiss Heathran's cheek in farewell, my lips lingering longer than strictly necessary. My mother would have been scandalized.

Heathran, on the other hand, had heat in his eyes as I pulled away. I counted that a major victory. Any spark with that one was as challenging—and as rewarding—as lighting a fire in an icy wasteland.

Maybe that was how Nev had felt with Qole.

I brushed the thought aside as I slipped through the crowd. Now was not the time to try to relate to my dead brother, since I didn't actually *care* about Heathran beyond thwarting Daiyen and squeezing from him what I needed, and especially not since *I* had killed Nev.

I found myself in front of a small side chamber, flanked in floor-to-ceiling fountains. The pious frequented such rooms to pray in solitude to the Unifier, but they were often empty here, in this temple, since royals usually put their piety on full display.

I smiled poignantly at anyone who saw me enter. I supposed it wouldn't hurt to have them think the new queen was so virtuous as to offer her devotion in seclusion on her coronation day. But I still hoped Heathran wouldn't think I'd dashed away from him to go pray. Not terribly seductive, that.

I lowered my voice to a purr once I'd closed the door behind me and activated the holo function of my comm. "Suvis, dear, you're going to frighten people in that outfit here."

A man appeared out of thin air—or at least his hologram, but his presence was no less for it. He was the opposite of the soft, soothing atmosphere of the room. His black, skintight suit of armor drew the light to him and consumed it. His body practically spelled out violence with its angles and wiry grace. It didn't help that his face was fully covered in a mask.

It wasn't that I minded his attire. It showed off his figure nicely, albeit not leaving much to the imagination, and its intimidation factor was useful. But his employment in my services—and behind closed and carefully guarded doors—was still a secret from the average guest at this event. Speaking to him, even like this, was a risk I didn't like taking in public.

My hand ran down his arm. Even if I couldn't feel it, I saw his muscles respond to my touch, trying to press into me. His suit was synced to my comm, my touch activating microsensors in the fabric. He could feel me, if I couldn't feel him.

I was fine with that.

"My love—" he began, his voice low and rough, the opposite of Heathran's.

"Shh, remember, don't say that out loud where someone might hear," I said gently. Gentleness was the key with this one, despite the viciousness he could unleash at the crook of a finger.

"I know, and I know I'm taking a risk in contacting you. But I had to give you the news immediately."

Something in his tone knocked the purr right out of my own. "What is it?"

"I've received word from one of our contacts here on Alaxak. Your brother is alive."

"What?"

"He somehow survived the destruction of the *Luvos Sunrise.*"

I exhaled. *Qole.* It had to have been her, but I didn't want to admit, not even in front of Suvis, that there was someone capable of making me truly nervous, and that she was also someone I badly needed. For a moment, I wished I'd kept her in Dracorva when I'd had the chance. But then, Nev wouldn't have taken such drastic measures to save her and get himself disinherited. I'd even helped him along, pitting him and Father against each other as best I could, lying to one about the actions and motivations of the other. "What can we do about this, and how quickly?"

"My contact said he can get me within easy range of your brother, but he had some stipulations, protections he requires for certain people after we establish ourselves on the planet. . . ."

"Whatever. Promise him anything. Just end this as soon as possible. *No one* can hear Nevarian is still alive."

"Yes, my lo—Your Majesty." He bowed, then hesitated for a second.

I knew what he wanted. I tucked up to him, pressing my chest against his—or at least the projected image of it—and sliding my hand over his cheek in the same liquid motion. Good thing he needed the mask to feel me, since his face wasn't as impressive as the rest of him. It wasn't grotesque, just composed of thick scars layered over already homely, pale features. The mask was definitely an improvement.

I kissed his lips with all the gentleness I could muster, which was considerable, mostly since I couldn't feel them. That was the only time I would kiss him.

Suvis's hard shoulders relaxed for just a second as he sighed, and then he was out of sight, cutting the connection so quickly that I nearly staggered. I counted to one hundred after that, then slipped out the door.

Devrak was standing on the other side.

I jumped, inwardly cursing myself. Outwardly, I put a hand to my chest and tittered. "Goodness, you startled me."

Devrak was not as darkly handsome and stern as Heathran, nor quite as homely and easily charmed as Suvis. He was somewhere in the middle, a hard one to read and manipulate, especially romantically, since he'd lost his wife and daughter in an accident some years ago and was absurdly devoted to their memory. I imagined he thought of himself as more like a father figure to me, and he was, unfortunately, a good deal cleverer than the other two men.

He folded his arms. "I detected an encrypted comm from Suvis. You shouldn't be so careless as to risk being eavesdropped upon alone in such . . . intimate quarters . . . with your personal guard."

Yes, he was sharp. Usually, no one could keep track of Suvis.

"One becomes intimate with only the Unifier in those quarters, and you only know it was him because you were spying on me." I smiled sweetly, but inside, my gut was twisting. There was no way he could have heard about Nev and kept such a straight face. I hoped. "In other words, it's none of your business."

"Solara, your safety and reputation *are* my business. You know I don't trust that man. Speaking of which—"

I cut him off before he could ask where Suvis was. "Come now, you're just worried he might replace you someday as head of security."

Devrak's jaw tightened, but he soldiered on. "When you chose him as captain of your guard, I held my tongue. He's a good fighter, one of the best Bladeguards I've ever seen. But his stability—"

"He *did* get me off the *Luvos Sunrise.*" I knew all about Suvis's instability, so I didn't need to hear more. "You didn't."

Devrak's face went blank, worse than if I'd stabbed him. It was as if he *wanted* to have gone down with the king and queen. Idiot man and his idiot honor. He was still useful alive, if only to lend me credibility—a legend in his own right. Not that I didn't enjoy twisting the knife a bit, especially if it distracted him.

"Maybe your parents would still be alive if I had been," he said quietly.

"What could you have done, Devrak?" I asked wearily. "You couldn't have killed Nev. It's better he died this way."

"Perhaps, yes."

I resisted a sigh of relief. He definitely didn't know about Nev, not if he could say those words with such true grief.

He swallowed. "Still, you know I would have been there if—"

"Yes, yes, if Father hadn't sent you on a mission right before." A trifling errand that I had indirectly encouraged. It wouldn't have done to have Devrak aboard the *Luvos Sunrise* for what I'd had planned. He would have sensed something was amiss. "The point is, I'm *glad* to still have you." I put a hand on his chest, and for a split second, he twitched, as if maybe to block an attack. Great Collapse, the man was paranoid. For a good reason, I supposed. "Marsius is glad to still have you, as well."

I hoped mentioning my little brother would lend me a compassionate air, but his dark eyes only grew harder. "About Marsius: He's grieving, Solara. His whole family took a trip and only you came back. He's eleven years old, for Unifier's sake. He needs you."

"I've been too busy," I said quickly. The truth was, I couldn't stand seeing him. He looked so sad, and it made some part of me wish I hadn't caused it. I needed to stay away from him.

Or maybe *he* needed to go.

I brightened. "I spoke to our generals earlier. They've impressed upon me the need for a commander in chief of the military. Marsius has it in him. I think he should go to Aaltos immediately for training."

Aaltos was the planet where we conducted military training for the masses. The Royal Academy on Luvos was only for Dracortes and those qualified to become Bladeguards, but Aaltos had a fine academy as well, and also housed the bulk of our generals—especially those who hadn't accompanied me to Alaxak and who weren't in my pocket from either devotion, careful blackmail, or a generous payoff from the Dracorte treasury under the guise of one of my philanthropic donations to charity. See how *they* liked being saddled with a mopey child. They wanted their official commander in chief, after all. And Marsius had said he wanted to help.

This trip to Aaltos not only would stall those generals wanting to cause me trouble and give my little brother something to occupy his time for the next few years instead of crying, but it could keep Devrak away long enough for me to wrap up affairs on Alaxak.

"I'll need you to escort him. Tell Gavros and Talia"—the generals my father had most trusted—"that they are to go to Aaltos, as well, and that they are personally responsible for his training."

Devrak blinked. "They won't like being shoved aside like that."

"*Nothing* is more important than the education of their

future commander, my sole remaining brother. It's the highest honor. And if they suggest otherwise, they'll regret it."

"But who will advise you in military matters? Who will command our forces in their absence?"

"General Illia Faetora." She was pretty much the only other high-ranking woman in the Dracorte military. I approved of Talia in theory; I just didn't like the company she kept.

"But, Your Majesty, favoritism like this will cause a rift in the chain of command, brew resentment, and as far as Marsius goes—"

"He *needs* this, Devrak," I interrupted. "And I need a commander in chief. A man for the people, though, to bring our military together. Marsius might be a prince, but the Aaltos-trained generals are the best-equipped to prepare him for such a role."

"Why send General Gavros Dracorte with him, then?" Devrak asked cleverly. "Your father's cousin trained at the Royal Academy."

"Marsius needs family, of course, to look out for him. It's not up for debate. Place him under their tutelage, make sure he's settled, and report back." My tone was firm.

"I shouldn't leave you—"

"Remember what happened last time you didn't accompany royal family members away from Dracorva?" Another twist of the knife; another blank look of agony. "Do this, Devrak. I'll be safe here."

Before he could try to bring up Suvis's absence again, I left him to go back to the party. Perhaps it wasn't a *party,* but refreshments were circulating, laughter was rising, and aside from Nev's still being alive—temporarily—everything was falling into place. Why couldn't I have a little fun at my own coronation?

V

QOLE

AFTER ANOTHER DAY OF DEBATING THAT INVOLVED YELLING, POSTURING, and even the occasional outburst of laughter, I ended up outside the warehouse in the late evening. Many of the arguments either had already been decided in my favor, or else were just going in circles as Hiat scrambled to hold his ground. But he couldn't. I would see to it.

I hated that man. I'd hated him as a child, growing up with Telu as a best friend. His smiles were all wrong, especially when he turned them on his niece, who had yet another black eye or split lip, gifts from her father. She wasn't worth challenging his brother, in Hiat's eyes. Telu and I had had to take matters into our own hands, as young girls. I would never have had respect or love for him after that, but now ... His own planet, his own people weren't worth it. And for that, I would happily bring *him* down, whatever it took.

I breathed deeply in the muggy night. It was still chilly, but the humidity made the air thick and cloying. I wanted to be back in the sharp clarity of colder temperatures. The sooner this was done, the better—but everyone had another day to decide.

I walked down to the water with the excuse of checking on the *Kaitan*. Really, I was looking for Nev. He'd been so quiet, understandably so with everything that had happened to him barely over a week ago, but . . . he steadied me. In the past month, I hadn't even realized how much he'd been helping to keep the Shadow inside me at bay, until it wasn't contained any longer.

Even as I walked, the ground shivered a little, and I kept seeing things out of the corner of my eye in the night. I didn't even bother looking. If I did turn, nothing would be there. Besides, I didn't actually want to find something that only I could see. At least I no longer heard the voice speaking distinct words in my ear. There was only a distant murmur, a faint whisper, that I could almost pretend was the sound of the sea.

I didn't know how long that would last, though. And with Nev's feeling distant ever since the *Luvos Sunrise,* I wasn't sure if I could do this alone. I didn't want to.

I spotted something that for a second looked like a hallucinatory shape in the darkness, a shadowy outline against the water, but then it resolved itself into a human figure, standing alone.

"Nev?"

He started, turning. "Hi."

It was probably a good thing Nev had made himself scarce lately. His disguise was solid, but I still didn't want anyone asking too many questions about my newest crewmember. At least everyone in Gamut had been used to seeing him around for the past month, and hopefully nobody would match up his timeline with the traitorous royal who had supposedly been sheltering on Alaxak. The Dracortes' embarrassment and suppression of those details was definitely working in our favor, and no one seemed to have fully connected their prince with us—I'd acted oblivious when asked about that. Most people here weren't in the habit of staring too closely at strangers, anyway, especially not to look for someone who was supposed to be dead.

"I've hardly seen you," I said, despite all the reasons it was good that I hadn't.

"I'm sorry, I . . . I've needed some time alone." He took a deep breath. "Fighting Solara isn't a good idea."

That wasn't what I'd been expecting to hear, and my feet jerked me to a halt before I could tell them to. "What?"

He took a short step toward me, as if in entreaty. "I used the wrong words. You *can't* fight her. At least," he amended, "you can't fight her and win."

I felt winded, as if he'd hit me in the stomach. "How can you say that? After everything we've been through?"

"Qole." He sounded as pained as if I'd hit him back. "If this is the last thing you want to hear, believe me, it's the last thing I want to say. That doesn't mean it's not true. We've done the impossible together, all of us. But there was at least some path to victory, some concept of how, if everything went perfectly, maybe we could succeed. That doesn't even exist here." He paused as his voice rose, then shook his head. When his volume dropped, his tone was no less intense. "You may fight back as hard as you will, but Solara can simply speak the wrong words in her sleep and turn all of Alaxak to ash. Just like that. It wouldn't even be a divot in daily expenditure."

It wasn't that I doubted what he was saying; this just didn't

108

sound like him. The Nev I knew would never encourage me to give up.

There was something else. Something was wrong.

I stared at him for a moment, considering, then took three careful steps toward him. I stopped when we were almost touching, and I could feel his body brush against mine, our eyes only inches apart. His eyes widened, and his breath came faster, warm on my face. His response wasn't out of longing; he looked like a cornered animal. "Nev," I said quietly. "What's the real reason for this?"

He blinked. "Er . . . the real reason I think this is impossible? Maybe because it is?"

"No. You look terrified. I've seen you fly into death more calmly than this."

He stared at me, mute, then looked away. I put a hand on his cheek and turned him gently back to face me. He swallowed as he met my eyes.

"Tell me." I dropped my hand, but my tone was insistent. "The truth."

He let out a breath then. "I *am* terrified. That you'd feel betrayed, that you'd think I was just another royal despite what we've been through. But also . . ." His gaze dropped, but only for a second, and then it was back up and almost feverish. His hands gripped my shoulders.

"You'll kill yourself." He choked out those first words, then went on in a rush. "The only way you can fight back is with Shadow. But we both know it'll use you up. Drive you insane. Destroy you." His fingers tightened, as if they sought for purchase. As if he could hold me back. "I can't . . . I can't lose you too."

His hands fell away, and his face twisted. And that was when the rest of the truth came pouring out.

"They're dead, Qole," he said like a gasp. "So many people are dead because of me, because of my best intentions . . . and even because of *their* best intentions. You risk too much, for an impossible outcome. You can't ask me to be party to watching my sister destroy your planet, to watching *you* die. You can't." He was nearly babbling. "I can't. They're dead. They're dead, Qole."

My heart squeezed in my chest, and it was a chain reaction, my throat tightening, pressure building behind my eyes. I had known he was in pain, but I hadn't known how much until now. His words were like blood from an open wound . . . but I didn't know how to stanch it.

Or I did, but I simply couldn't do it. Wouldn't. To do so would be to violate everything I believed in about my home planet and people.

I put my hand on his shoulder, feeling him shake under my fingers. For a moment, we were silent as he gasped and struggled to regain control. When his sobbing subsided, he stared out at the invisible ocean.

"Nothing I can say will make you feel better, but I'm so sorry about your parents," I said finally, softly. "When I lost mine, Arjan helped me keep my world together. If it weren't for him, and his encouraging me to captain the *Kaitan,* I would be dead or worse right now. I had to believe in something other than my pain. You can too." I squeezed his shoulder. "I wish I could do what you want, but this is *my* purpose."

My hand dropped, because there wasn't anything else I could say or do to comfort him. I could only make it worse, but it was the only choice I could make. *Mine.* "No matter what happens, this isn't your fault. You might think you're responsible for making me leave Alaxak, and for what happened after. Or for making me believe that things should change.

That we should fight for a better future, even if it's dangerous, because the alternative is more so. But my choices are my own. I chose to leave Alaxak with you to try to save what was left of my family. I chose to save my brother in Dracorva. I chose to save you from the *Luvos Sunrise*. And I *choose* to save my people now. I don't know if I can, but even if I die trying, it's an easy choice."

I walked away after that, because I couldn't stand seeing how much more I might have hurt him.

————

I should have stayed. Because then maybe I could have stopped him.

I only napped for a few hours, which took us into the next day. The last day—the day that a decision could be made. When I reached the meeting hall from my quarters on the *Kaitan,* I found the discussion in a lull. Hundreds of other captains had retreated permanently to their ships, awaiting a resolution in comfort, but hundreds had stayed to debate. Of those, not many had gotten much sleep, by the looks of it. Arjan, Telu, and Jerra, who'd done a lot of the arguing on my behalf, appeared tired but resolute, and maybe even grimly optimistic. It seemed the argument was almost over. Maybe we could even wrap this up sooner rather than later, if everyone could agree there wasn't anything left to discuss.

Not that there weren't even greater—astronomical—challenges ahead, but at least we would be meeting them head-on, not surrendering.

And then I heard his voice. "Excuse me."

He wasn't talking to me. He was much calmer than he had been, his voice projecting to the entire meeting hall. I spun, apprehension surging in my belly, and saw Nev standing in the center of the stumps. Everyone turned: Hiat and Jerra, Arjan and Telu, Basra and Eton, all the regional representatives ... and hundreds of the most opinionated, influential captains. Everyone important.

I wished the hall were emptier. I wished he weren't going to say what I suddenly knew he was going to say. I wished now that he *weren't* here.

"I am a member of Captain Qole Uvgamut's crew, and like you, I know she is a courageous, strong, and passionate woman. However, I have something to add to her thoughts on the situation. May I speak?"

The word *however* had never filled me with such dread. I wanted to shake my head. Instead I held my breath and glanced around.

Hiat was the first to nod. Of course he would. He'd heard the *however* just as I had, knew that it could hurt my position. The other representatives nodded, some reluctantly, some curious. Even Jerra wheeled closer to hear, her eyes narrowed in suspicion.

"I'm not from Alaxak," Nev began, not taking a position at any stump, as if to illustrate this, "so my name and where I'm from aren't important. I won't pretend to be risking as much as you, or to even fully understand what's at stake. I *do* understand the nature of the threat, though. Perhaps, as an offworlder who has seen the Dracortes in action, I can lend some valuable perspective to this situation."

He spun in a circle, encompassing all present. He was so calm, even though my heart felt like it was breaking. "You have what, a fleet of hundreds, mismatched and outmoded? The Dracortes have thousands of ships at their disposal. *Thou-*

sands. Top-of-the-line starfighters, shining new from Xiaolan factories, exceptionally maneuverable, and seemingly infinite in number. Massive Treznor destroyers, equipped with tractor beams, EMP pulsars, and a missile artillery second to none. They have orbital bombardment stations, weapons you won't even see before they burn Chorda from the face of the planet."

He paused to let this all sink in, then once again held everyone's collective gaze in that way he had. "If you give their queen a reason, she will bring these forces to bear on you. I have heard stories of her, too numerous and detailed to be mere rumor. Even as princess, she was pettily cruel, constantly deceitful, and utterly without mercy. As a queen, she will take *everything* from you, not just some of it, if you defy her. To resist, you need to still have something left to defend."

This was worse than being hit in the stomach. I felt gutted. It was hard to breathe, but I did anyway, then cleared my throat, which was almost too tight to speak. "Don't let him scare you."

"And why shouldn't we?" Hiat asked in that reasonable tone that made me want to rip his face off.

"Because." I held Nev's gaze. It was just the two of us, seeing each other now across the room. Everyone else might as well have vanished. "He can't be trusted."

His eyes widened, as if I'd slapped him.

"But he—"

I didn't let Hiat speak. "He's from Luvos. The Dracorte homeworld." There were hisses of breath. Eton was from Luvos too, of course, but I didn't mention that. They only needed to hate *one* person enough to disregard everything he'd said. "I hoped he wouldn't let his loyalties get in the way of *our* decision, but apparently he can't help but take advantage of us."

"I'm not trying to—" Nev began.

I interrupted him just as I had Hiat. The fear he'd sparked couldn't be fed, or else it would spread like wildfire. Like before, I had to fight fire with fire—betrayal with betrayal.

"As an outsider, he's worse than those of us who would rather surrender." I flicked a glance at Hiat in disdain, and then turned the full force on Nev. Nausea boiled in my stomach, but I made the words as hard and sharp as icicles. "He has nothing to lose, in telling us to give up everything we have. It's only *his* gain for us to capitulate to *his* side. Cowardice is weak, but taking advantage is sick." I took a deep breath. "And I am ashamed I ever let him onto my ship, into our world. He doesn't belong."

Now Nev looked like I'd gutted *him*. His eyes were blank and staring as he dragged a hand over his mouth. It was a mouth I had been kissing with more and more frequency lately. This was like the opposite of kissing, using lips and tongue to take away love. In return, his lips only told of shock and anguish.

So much the better. Or at least that was what I tried to tell myself. He couldn't respond this way, and I'd broken his calm air of authority. If only those in the crowd knew that such self-possession came from his being a Dracorte prince, the supposedly dead one mixed up in all this . . . but I wouldn't take it that far. Because then they would tear him to shreds.

"Qole . . . ," he said, sounding winded.

"That's *Captain Uvgamut* to you."

He swallowed, then nodded, regaining some of his composure, though his eyes still revealed the pain behind the mask. "Captain Uvgamut, where I come from doesn't change the concerns I've raised. You can't fight the Dracortes and win. They have too much power."

Hiat wasn't the only one nodding along with him. There was nothing else for it. Only one way to convince them now.

"Yeah?" I said, my own calm washing over me, deepening inside. My body felt like an ocean surface before a storm. My skin tingled, tight with anticipation. "Well, I know something they don't have, and we do: Our resources. Our strength. Our *Shadow*."

At those words, the Shadow lamps winked out through the entire hall, plunging us into gloom. I felt a surge in the darkness—the darkness in the warehouse, in my eyes, in my blood and bones, as I summoned that Shadow to me.

Before anyone could gasp, a purple corona burst into life above my head, coalescing into a ball of liquid energy. The strange light flickered over the dozens of faces, making them both horrible and beautiful at once. Maybe I looked the same to them.

Or maybe only horrible.

I lifted my hand, and they gasped then. My fingers touched the purple-black flames and flaring white sparks for a brief moment—but long enough to char someone's arm right off. And yet when I dropped my hand, it was whole. I'd felt only a warm tingle.

"They try to burn us? We'll burn *them*."

Then, that hissing auditory hallucination, whispering in my ear: "No."

No one in the meeting hall had spoken. With a flash and a loud pop, I lost my hold on the wild energy. The globe of light vanished and the Shadow lamps flickered back to life.

Everyone stared. I did too—at what no one else could see.

Nev probably knew why I hadn't done this yet. Cracks fractured my vision, crawling along the walls, carving the faces around me. My world started falling apart, if only in my head.

It had to stay in my head. No one could know.

"We have the strength to fight them with the very thing

they would try to take from us," I said, forcing my tone level, strong, even though I felt like whimpering. I made myself smile, standing tall and steady, ignoring the shivers trying to rack my limbs. I looked around at the disbelieving, frightened faces, pretending they weren't disintegrating.

That was the other reason I hadn't demonstrated my power yet. It would make people afraid, unless they could trust I wouldn't come to pieces and unleash such a force on them.

"You might wonder if I can sustain this, but do you see me faltering?" I asked before Nev or Hiat could think to. I spoke through the sparks crackling in my eyes, the admonishing voice in my ears, the flesh peeling off bodies—mine and everyone else's. "I have burned soldiers and ships with this strength, *our* strength, and I will continue to do so. Even if it kills me, I will take as many of *them* down as I can, before I go."

Nev watched me, despairing, and I stared right back. I delivered the final blow. "The only people who need to fear me are the Dracortes."

It didn't take long for the cheering to erupt. Arjan started it, Jerra right behind him. It rose to a roar that vibrated the warehouse walls. Telu clapped in support, while somehow looking as worried as I'd ever seen her. Basra only watched, considering and processing as usual, while everyone whooped and hollered around him. I couldn't spot Eton. Nev turned for the exit, brushing past Hiat, who was staring at me with something bordering on awe.

I had won this little battle, but I didn't know what else I had lost. And I just hoped I would survive long enough for the war.

VI

NEV

IF I HAD THOUGHT I WASN'T FEELING ENOUGH EMOTION, A SINGLE GIANT bell rang inside me now, repeating the same thought, the same feeling, over and over.

You are lost.

Part of me wanted to feel angry at her for using me, throwing me aside as she had, but I couldn't. I simply felt empty. I wanted to rebuke myself for being melodramatic, but as I made my way out of the meeting hall, avoiding the gaze of anyone I knew, the thought only grew stronger. Events were unfolding exactly as they would, regardless of what I tried. In a twisted symmetry, doing what I thought was right alienated those close to me. Except, this time, instead of my family, it was Qole.

Maybe she could do it. When freeing Arjan, I had seen her use her Shadow affinity to turn an entire platoon of soldiers into ash in seconds, and Qole herself didn't seem sure where the outer limits of her abilities lay. But in doing so, she had almost destroyed herself. This time, if anything, using Shadow seemed to have made her stronger, more resolute. And yet I doubted that.

I knew the length she would go to for the people she loved, but I simply didn't see how it was possible. If I was right, Qole was holding herself together through sheer determination, a thought that made my chest tighten. She would deliver herself to oblivion in defense of Alaxak. If I was wrong, I had just alienated her, and no doubt the crew. Most likely for good. And in all probability Qole would still die, only at Solara's hand. It was a lose-lose situation.

I stopped in the middle of the street. I had nowhere to go. It wasn't the *Kaitan* that had become my home after Luvos, but Qole. She was my sanctuary. And now I had lost her too. No choices presented themselves. So much for Eton's advice.

His voice called out behind me. "Nev."

I started walking again. I didn't want to talk to him, or anyone else for that matter. "Didn't work, Eton. Unless you were just trying to get Qole to hate me, in which case, well done."

"Nev, you need to come with me." Eton's tone carried an urgency that made me pause. "I think I've found something that will help Qole."

━━━

Eton didn't say much more as we headed deeper into the industrial quarters of Chorda, and I was too depleted to ask. The warehouses became less dilapidated, the buildings a little taller; some of them looked like they were designed to be employee quarters, or even offices. *This must be where the governor will soon work.* When he came, the dark windows would be lit by busy bureaucrats.

Presuming it wasn't just turned to ash.

Eton, reading the signs above the doorways we were passing, stopped and doubled back. I almost ran into him, but he didn't notice as he wiped the grime off the engraving on the entry plate. An old vacuum-powered mechanism powered the door instead of the more modern maglock doors, and his hand revealed the letters to say *Dracorte Mining Ind.*

Mining. In past generations, my family had profited handsomely from the minerals the drones harvested from the planet. The drones were left over from the Great Collapse, and we had lost all higher-level control over them, but we were the only family with direct and consistent access to their temporary programming. Evidently, when we had cared about the minerals produced from Alaxak, some of the operations had been based from Chorda itself.

Eton pressed on the control switch, and the door hissed open in stuttering increments. A series of questions ran through my head, but he was obviously intent on showing me, and I was happy for the silence, so I followed numbly. I stepped after him into the blackness inside.

Eton stopped, his bulk dimly illuminated by the light of the street outside. "We're here," he announced.

I looked around. "So I see. Now what?"

He turned, and his eyes sent an icy trickle down my spine. "Now you help Qole. I found a way for you to be useful." He walked past me, back outside, and the door slid shut.

All light disappeared. There was a whine in the darkness, and I hurled myself into a rolling dive.

I would have been dead if not for ingrained muscle

memory from endless training. The telltale sound of a charging photon weapon lasted only a fraction of a second, but the reaction to it had been drilled into my subconscious. Blue energy flared and a hissing blast cracked against the pavement where I had been standing.

The momentary light had given me a glimpse of a figure, standing by the door where we had entered. *An assassination.*

I continued to act on autopilot, as if this were another test at the Academy and not a matter of life and death. I dodged to the side, spinning out of my overcoat as I did, throwing it as if it would stop the photon blasts that riddled it with three holes.

It didn't, but it landed on its target, and I launched myself at the noise in a flying kick. It was risky at best, but any attempt to run in a dark and unknown environment would be doomed. I could only hope that between speed and my overcoat on the attacker's head, I could connect the kick, ending the fight.

The kick connected, but it ended nothing. Hitting my attacker felt like hitting a brick wall, and I crashed to the ground, winding myself. I dimly heard the blaster skittering across the floor, and my satisfaction was short-lived as something hard, metallic, and glowing with a strip of white light slammed point-down next to my chest. *Disruption Blade.* I rolled directly into it as violently as I could, felt it rip out of the attacker's grasp, and continued my roll, reaching for the sword in the darkness. I misjudged, and it skittered out of my grasp, warm blood oozing out of my palm where I had touched it.

The lights came on.

It was a giant space, at least two stories tall, entirely empty except for what looked like the ruins of a drone. Its mining cables lay lifeless, pieces of the hull removed where maintenance or salvage had been conducted.

When I turned, I saw my parents' murderer standing in front of me, one hand still on the sensor that had activated the lights. He was completely still, not even breathing hard from our exchange. A small photon blaster lay some distance to the side, and his Disruption Blade, a long, single-edged affair, was on the ground between us.

I rose to my feet, experimentally making a fist. The cut was deep, but my hand was functional.

My darker reveries had already led me here many times. It wasn't Solara I dwelled on hurting; it was him. Fighting the person who had killed my parents, breaking him down, making him feel pain, rage, regret. Exacting revenge. Redeeming my failures.

But rage wasn't infusing me head to toe, as I had imagined. The empty ache inside me expanded, and I wanted to engulf this man in it. I attacked, sprinting past the weapons on the floor. My bare hands would be more than enough, enough to hurt and break.

We met in a flurry of strikes, trapping and deflecting in equal measure, satisfaction settling into me as I recognized the style. He was Academy trained, and that meant there was little he knew that I didn't. I might not have been the best at striking, but I was good, and once I got him to the ground my grappling was second to none. This was familiar territory. I would win.

My thought process was shattered by an elbow to the cheek. I staggered backward, and he advanced steadily, giving no reprieve. His style changed drastically, becoming angular, aggressive, his elbows and knees punishing me each time I attempted a hold. I shifted tactics, changed distances, but the damage became more and more lopsided. Even without the typical insectoid Bladeguard armor, his muscular frame shrugged off my hits as if they were made of air.

I'm being deconstructed, I thought muzzily, working to keep my guard up as I staggered back. The next thing I saw was a knee, coming into my field of view. *That's hard to do* was the last thing to flicker through my brain.

———

I woke up choking. The last time I had done that, it had been Eton who had his arms around my neck, so it was fitting that he had led me here this time around.

Unlike last time, however, my attacker wasn't trying to render me unconscious. His hand grabbed a handful of my hair and twisted my head in the direction of the drone.

"Tell me what your father told you about the drones." The voice was rough, as though his vocal cords had suffered damage at one point. The hold on my neck loosened the barest fraction, but it wouldn't have made any difference anyway. The room was still swimming, and my limbs weren't really responding properly. I took several ragged breaths.

"Next time, reconsider the *shoot first, interrogate later* method. You can't always rely on bad aim." Apparently, my sarcastic bone wasn't broken. Yet.

He hit me in the face. "You could still have talked without your legs. Again, what do you know about the drones?"

"I wouldn't consider screaming as talking, but all right." I spat out some blood. "Why don't you ask Solara? She has access to more data now than I ever did." I pawed at his arm ineffectually, trying to get it between him and my neck. The cut on my hand throbbed, pushed open, but I persisted stubbornly.

"Maybe." The assassin moved his Disruption Blade into view. "But we need to know if your father told you anything else. Anything about their function. So I will cut off parts of you until I'm convinced you're telling the truth."

"That seems reasonable," I gasped. "I'll tell you what I know." I pushed on the elbow around my neck with every scrap of strength I had left, curling my body back in the same moment. Slick with blood from my palm, I slid out of his grasp and kicked him away, scrabbling backward. "We don't understand how they function, as *everyone* damn well knows. Why does that matter?"

He rose over me, blade held out to the side. "It matters, because everything will open."

He was making increasingly less sense, and I was out of time. My training told me I should have a plan.

I found I didn't care. I still wasn't as angry as I should have been. Hurting him, what little I had, had delivered no satisfaction. Qole, Arjan, Basra, Telu, Eton . . . they would continue on without me, and all evidence indicated that my absence would be more useful rather than less. Especially in Eton's case. I still would have preferred to hit the assassin until he stopped breathing, but my body was giving up, the blows to my head taking their toll. I closed my eyes, retreating from the pain, and imagined Qole under the moonlight, laughing.

I heard the whistle of a blade coming down.

VII

QOLE

AFTER MY SHOW OF SHADOW, IT DIDN'T TAKE MUCH LONGER FOR THEM to decide. The various regional representatives could reach their conclusion at any time on the final day, and so there was only another hour or so of working out the details.

Details that mostly concerned what a refusal of Solara's terms might look like.

When we all gathered around the black talking stumps for the final time, I felt a thrill go through me. It was somehow anticipation, determination, dread, all folded into one.

Nev. I couldn't think about Nev.

Since Hiat had begun the meeting and called for a vote, it was his place to close it. "All those in favor of my proposal to cooperate with Queen Solara?"

No hands stirred. The air felt heavy, dust motes hanging in

the light of the Shadow lamps. It was day, but only cracks of sunlight shone at the edges of the warehouse.

"Those decided to oppose Queen Solara?"

The heaviness lifted, as did my heart. Hands shot up all around the circle, along with my own. Arjan nudged me from behind in congratulations; Telu squeezed my arm. Jerra grinned at me from across the circle, and the others nodded their approval. The eyes that met mine were proud, and I had to blink against the sting in my own.

. . . And against the sparks and cracks in my vision.

Because of those, it took me a second to notice that Hiat's hand had gone up with the others'—that he hadn't raised it in support of his own proposal. Maybe he just knew to follow the tide. Or maybe I had really won him over.

Jerra adjusted her wheelchair, squaring herself with the talking stump. "I have an additional proposal to make."

"Ancestors, haven't we been here long enough?" someone in the crowd grumbled. The warehouse was packed with captains—over five hundred of us. It seemed almost everyone had turned out for this decision. *Almost* everyone.

Nev, Eton, and Basra were nowhere in sight. Nev's absence didn't surprise me, but having the others around would have been nice. Then again, maybe it was better that I didn't appear to be under the influence of any offworlders. Maybe I *didn't* actually need them. Nev, especially.

My heart lurched inside, swooping like an injured vessel in flight.

Jerra waited for the murmur to die down, then tossed her purple-streaked, spiky head. "We won't be here much longer, since I imagine this decision will be quick." She paused as all attention focused on her. "For the duration of our resistance, and as long as we see no reason to reconvene and vote otherwise before then, I propose that Qole Uvgamut be the primary decision maker for the fishermen of Alaxak, provided she gives a fair ear to the regional representatives' council. That way, we don't have to do *this* every single time a problem arises."

For a second, there was a silence like a frozen lake, weighty, smooth, and impenetrable. *I* didn't even know what to think. But then the ice cracked—someone chuckled, another snorted, and others murmured in agreement.

"All decided?" Jerra raised her hand.

As before, every representative's hand rose. Not immediately or in unison; Hiat's nearly last. But they rose.

I exhaled and remembered that my vote counted too. My own hand lifted.

Somehow, I was now the provisional leader of Alaxak. Before I could wonder how the blasted hell *this* had happened, there was a beep at my comm. It was the signal my crew and I used for emergencies.

As people began to chatter excitedly and mill in the meeting hall, I put a hand to my ear. "What?"

"Captain, Basra. A rather large ship, Dracorte by the looks of it, just showed up in orbit around Alaxak. Their signals are masked, or else I would have noticed them sooner." That was why Basra wasn't here. He was on the *Kaitan* monitoring the comms. Doing his job. "An advance shuttle, stealth-grade, just landed in the center of Chorda. I would bet they're headed right for you—and that they're armed."

It was a solid bet if Basra was making it. Sure enough, before I could even respond, there was a thunderous banging against the warehouse doors. Everyone froze, falling silent, hundreds of us turning as one to look at the entrance.

"Keep monitoring the situation," I whispered to Basra, "and get ready. I'll get back to the *Kaitan* as soon as possible. We need to stop that ship before it can attack."

"Captain, I'm not sure we can—"

The doors blew inward, interrupting our comm. I closed the channel and blinked against the weak sunlight as my eyes made out the new arrivals.

A squadron stood framed in the entryway. Two dozen or so troops wore Dracorte military fatigues and body armor and wielded photon rifles. Another member of the party had that strange segmented armor and almost casually carried a sword gleaming with a white stripe of energy. A Bladeguard.

Worse, what looked like a metal spider, twice as tall as a human and bristling with gun and rocket barrels, crouched behind all of them, weapons trained on us. It was a mechbot and, aside from the Bladeguards, was more formidable than all the troops combined. I'd only heard stories about them. They were usually reserved for activities like invading planets and meeting armies on land. They were too destructive in palaces or cities that one wished to inhabit afterward.

These guys obviously didn't care too much about Chorda. Where in the blazes was Eton? We could have used him right about now.

Hundreds of us versus two dozen soldiers, a Bladeguard, and a mechbot. We might as well be outnumbered.

I bit off a curse and muttered to Arjan, "You have your two knives, right?" He was skilled in knife fighting, at least as these things were considered on Alaxak, and he didn't usually travel unarmed.

"Four," he said under his breath.

I already knew Telu had her infopads. "Telu, take cover

and try to bring down their comms to make sure word of this doesn't reach their fleet." She inhaled sharply at the mention of *fleet*. "Second priority is to get the mechbot's artillery offline."

If I couldn't simply take it down from here. As Telu began to slip away through the crowd, I tried to dredge up the Shadow inside me, but my vision shuddered so violently, I had to close my eyes and clutch my stomach to keep from vomiting. Useless was what I would be, if I fainted or died—or worse, if I came apart at the seams and went mad. Silently cursing Nev for forcing me to display such power earlier, I swallowed and shoved the Shadow back down. I would have to make do with standard weapons.

I had only a single dagger strapped to my belt, along with a plasma pistol that had once belonged to Nev, an XR-Something that could blast through the hull of a ship. It should suffice for the mechbot.

The Bladeguard stepped forward, clearly the leader of the bunch, his voice carrying into the huge space. "This is a cease-and-disperse order from Artur Rexius, the newly appointed governor of Alaxak, given in the name of Our Majesty, Queen Solara Ysandrei Rezanna Verasia Dracorte."

I leaned toward Arjan, pitching my voice as low as possible. "Do you think you can distract the Bladeguard long enough for me to get by him?"

I felt more than saw Arjan's nod at my shoulder. I glanced at him to see blackness already seeping into the corner of his eye. For once, I wished I could do the same. I felt nearly helpless without it. Powerless to protect my brother, my crew.

"You are meeting without permission on government property," the Bladeguard continued as troops began to file in around him, fanning to the edges of the warehouse.

"Get away from him after that," I breathed quietly to Arjan. "Don't let him close."

"I think it's him who'll have to worry."

I couldn't waste any more words; I could only hope my brother's bravado wouldn't get him killed by a Bladeguard. Unholstering both the pistol and the dagger at my hip, I held them both low at my side and pretended to listen to what the Bladeguard was saying.

"Everyone line up outside now. Once we check your papers, you will be allowed to leave on your ships. You'll only receive a warning in your files. Further unauthorized meetings will incur heavy fines and possible confinement."

"How sweet of you," Jerra snapped, her voice cutting the air. She was the first to speak directly to him. Afterward, she glanced at me, and I gave her the barest nod.

"Excuse me?" the Bladeguard said, his voice low. "Are you challenging my authority here?"

In response, Jerra pivoted in her chair and uppercut one of the troops standing next to her in the crotch. He folded like a dead sapling in a gale. She relieved him of his photon rifle in nearly the same motion, then deftly cracked the back of his head with the butt, under the base of his helmet. He fell limp.

Everything happened at once after that.

The mechbot hummed and whirred as it locked onto multiple targets. The Bladeguard sprang toward Jerra, only to have to leap back when one of Arjan's daggers streaked out and nearly took him in the neck. He batted it aside and lunged toward Arjan instead. Fishermen and soldiers alike exploded into motion.

I had no time myself to watch what was happening around me. I couldn't try to spot Telu in the chaos to see if she was succeeding at her task. I couldn't make sure Arjan avoided the Disruption Blade.

I had to make it to the mechbot. Especially since it started firing.

I dodged behind a tussle involving Dracorte troops. At least, for now, the mechbot didn't seem to be firing into its own men. It was using precision, and several fishermen fell. Its rapid-fire photon blasts were as slender as fingers— glowing fingers that left sizzling holes in your chest when they poked you.

Behind the troops, I swiped the safety off on my plasma pistol with a fingerprint. A heavy hand fell over the top of mine as I did, trying to crush my bones between his grip and the gun.

I flicked a glance at my attacker long enough to be sure it was a soldier, then brought my other hand up, plunging the dagger into his neck. Blood sprayed my cheek as I wrenched it out.

I raised the pistol and aimed.

"Qole, behind you!" Arjan called.

I barely threw myself down fast enough before the Disruption Blade came whistling over my head. I flipped around to see the Bladeguard standing above me, his blade whipping back into position, ready to come down.

Arjan was on him before it could, daggers in either hand. He parried the blow, and then another that was turned on him. Another. The white light of the Disruption Blade streaked the dimness in a blurring flurry, and yet Arjan matched every blow. I'd never seen him move so fast.

His eye was completely black.

Even so, he couldn't keep it up. Not against a Bladeguard, someone who'd trained to fight most of their life. Not with one eye. Not with knives. First one knife went spinning away. And then the other. He planted the third—his last—into the Bladeguard's armpit, in the chink between plates of armor. A pity it wasn't the man's sword arm. He raised his blade, just as the black drained from Arjan's eye and the blood from his face.

And just as I raised my pistol.

Arjan's gaze flicked to me in desperate hope, but the Bladeguard saw and pivoted, Disruption Blade carving the air in the same fluid motion, straight toward my hand. The sword connected with the barrel of my gun a split second after I pulled the trigger.

But the sword didn't stop the blast. Neither did the Bladeguard's armor, or his chest, or the roof above him. The white burst of plasma left a head-sized hole through everything between me and the stars. It might not have been too much to hope that it hit one of the Dracorte ships in orbit.

Maybe the pistol was worth whatever astronomical amount Nev had paid for it. Or maybe it was a waste, since half of the Disruption Blade—the half I'd parted from the hilt with my shot—was now fused to it in a melted lump, completely blocking the barrel. If I fired it now, I might as well be pointing it at myself.

Still, it had bought us our lives, whatever those were worth.

Only seconds after the Bladeguard collapsed in a sizzling heap next to me, Arjan hauled me to my feet, tearing the thing out of my hand in the same motion. "Ancestors, Qole. Are you all right?"

I smelled ozone, cooked meat, blood, and I tried not to gag as I nodded.

I didn't so much care about myself as everyone else. Now that I knew Arjan was all right, I quickly scanned the warehouse. We seemed to be winning based on our sheer numbers alone. But there were bodies on the ground, many that didn't wear Dracorte fatigues. And more were falling as the mechbot kept firing.

"We have to stop that thing, Arjan," I gasped, lurching toward it. I slipped in something, and I didn't look down to see what it was. I didn't want to know.

Arjan caught my arm and hauled me back. "With what? Our bare hands?"

Wul, the long-haired representative who had supported me at the stumps, dodged forward, trying to get close to the mechbot with a plasma grenade. It took the thing half a second to readjust its target and shoot three photon blasts through his head, chest, and stomach.

A horrible cry caught in my throat. I had to stop this. Even if it meant using Shadow to destroy it—and maybe myself. "We need to do *some*—"

That something cut off my shout with the force of cannon fire and sent the mechbot staggering drunkenly. It *was* a cannon, I realized, when I saw the charred debris that had been made of one of its appendages. The mechbot clanked and rattled as it pivoted, now uneven on its spider legs, to face the new threat, but another few massive blasts scattered the entire thing into flying, flaming chunks.

I knew only one person who wielded plasma cannons like one would a rifle. I staggered out of the warehouse into the smoke-hazed sunlight. I almost expected Eton to be grinning at me behind his energy shield and over the steaming barrels of Verta, his lovingly named pair of cannons on swiveling mechanical arms, strapped to his body by a heavy harness. He usually enjoyed using the contraption to such an extent, even to kill, but his face this time was stone.

Before I could thank him, or say anything at all, he dove

into the fray inside. In less than thirty seconds, it was over. Eton and Verta, together, were more deadly than a mechbot.

———

The final tally was grisly, if not the very worst I'd feared. All twenty-four Dracorte soldiers—twenty-five, including the Bladeguard—were down, dead or dying. We'd lost forty-one out of several hundred, and dozens were injured, bad burns from photon rifles marring legs and arms.

Forty-one dead. Captain Wul, a regional representative. Captain Puya, a woman I'd known since I was a child, who'd been friendly with my mother. Another captain from Gamut, as well as a young man named Mati—a crewmember of Hiat's, who'd tried to flirt with me a couple years ago, before Eton had nearly knocked him out. Gone.

I hated to think it, but it was a shame most of the deceased were captains. A few first mates might be able to take over flying those ships, but not all of them had the necessary skills. We would need every pilot we had.

Jerra was alive and unscathed, and so was Hiat . . . of course. Arjan was nicked and scratched, bleeding in a few places, but otherwise fine, thank the ancestors, and Telu surfaced from the shadows, uninjured, gripping her infopads and blinking tears out of her eyes, from the smoke or the carnage, I wasn't sure.

Her voice was steady, if as grim as the death around her. "Thanks to our little adventure on Luvos, I had standard Dracorte comm frequencies programmed in. Overwhelmed them with identical frequencies from all the vessels in the harbor, so they'll just get garbage. I doubt they'll think it's a malfunction, knowing what I can do."

"Dracortes?" someone said.

None of us had time to mourn, or to argue. "If your ship has adequate weapons systems and is bigger than a skiff," I said, "and if you're conscious enough to fly, man your posts and follow me." That would limit our numbers significantly, but I couldn't send valuable captains to an inevitable death. "See to any injuries after we've lifted off. Crews who lost their captains, stay and tend to the wounded, if you don't think you can pilot. Captains without battle-worthy ships, comm the medic in Chorda, as well as anyone else you know from your villages. Warn them. Dracorte forces are in orbit. We have to do whatever we can to stop them before they think to retaliate."

"Qole—" Eton started, in that protective tone he used whenever he thought he could keep me from doing something stupid.

"*Not now,* Eton," I snapped.

I thought someone else might argue, but then Arjan said, "I'll get the ship ready for takeoff," and Telu was saying, "I'll get to masking our signals."

Right on their heels, Jerra added, "Why don't we approach from the planet's shadow, with the Alaxak Asteroid Sea behind us? We'll lose time, but with our signals hidden, they won't see us until we unload everything we have on them. What are their numbers?"

Even bleeding, Arjan was already jogging back to the ship. I commed Basra to check. "One full battle carrier," I repeated.

The word sank like a rock into the sudden silence. A battle carrier. It was like an armada rolled into a single ship—way, *way* bigger and more heavily armored than a destroyer, with equal destructive power. Not to mention the *other* ships they had docked and transported.

"He estimates a fleet of at least a hundred starfighters with the battle carrier," I added.

Hiat whistled. "With only a few hundred of us—even five hundred, if we can rally that many—we'd be lucky just to take out the starfighters."

Jerra snorted. "We're Shadow-fishing captains. I'd like to see a puffed-up prig from some *academy* fly one tenth the maneuvers we can."

"Well, fine, so we beat the starfighters, but then that battle carrier will be left to chew us to pieces. Better throw everything at them. And I mean *everything,* unlike here."

She glared up at him. "Your crewmember's life wasn't enough?"

Hiat stared levelly at me. "That's not what I meant."

I knew what he meant. Shadow. He'd noticed that I'd avoided using it. "Don't worry about *my* willingness to fight," I responded, my dark tone communicating all that my words implied. "I'm ready to take that battle carrier down with me, if I have to."

"Don't be ridiculous," Eton growled. He shoved between us, his cannons forcing Hiat to step back. "Even if you managed, what would everyone else do after *that*? The Dracortes aren't going to let a rebellion go. More battle carriers will follow."

I'd appreciated his help earlier against the mechbot, more than I could ever tell him, but I *didn't* need it, now.

"Eton, back off. Everyone, get to your ships. We'll convene at the coordinates Jerra gives us. But first . . . Hiat."

"Yes?" he asked warily.

"Take ten ships, whoever is ready the fastest, and go to the cannery. Load up on Shadow. I'm going to need it."

Hiat flashed a grin at me, and for a second, I could see Telu's razor sharpness in his eyes. "Will do."

Everyone scattered then, racing for the main dock. Many—

too many—stayed behind to take care of the wounded. I knew we wouldn't have every ship in Chorda—Wul's and Puya's among those that would stay—but I hoped we would still have the numbers to make a difference.

As chaos consumed the port, I was thankful I'd docked in the next bay over, even if it meant a dash up and down an endless flight of stone steps. Arjan was long gone. Telu was already moving, typing at her infopads as she went, barely looking where she was going.

I turned to follow her, and a huge hand caught my arm.

"I swear, Eton—"

"It's about Nev."

The tone of his voice made my breath catch, and I flipped around to face him. "What? Where is he?"

"I caught him. He was trading himself for your safety. His life for yours."

I felt like my stomach had been ripped out, and everything else had followed it, spilling out beneath me. My knees shook and threatened to buckle. I wanted to puke. "No."

Eton nodded, his face the same stone I'd seen before. Nev had stood in front of a hall of my fellow Alaxans and argued on behalf of our mutual enemy, all because he didn't want to see me die, and this was his last resort. He'd tried to sacrifice himself in order to put my life ahead of what was right.

At least I hoped, with every desperate scrap of hope I had left to my name, that it had only been an attempt.

"Where is he?" I ground out, my voice ragged, my heart razor shards of ice in my chest, my throat. Tears spiked in my eyes. "Don't tell me . . ."

He shook his head. "Qole . . ." His own eyes were pained as he looked at me.

Oh, ancestors, no . . . no, no, no.

If I thought what I'd been feeling before was bad, it was nothing, nothing to what I felt now. I covered my mouth, as if I could stop the keening whine that escaped, and then my ears, as if I could block what he was about to say:

"Solara's contact was also an assassin, not just the messenger. I was suspicious of what Nev was up to, so I'd followed him. I tried to save him, for you, but the assassin closed the deal before I could stop it. He's . . . he's gone, Qole."

I wasn't covering my ears anymore—my hands were fists in my hair—but Eton's voice was half drowned out in a roar like rapids that were carrying me away.

No, no, no. My vision swam. Alaxak had melted. It was a place of tears. Death.

"I had to tell you, Qole." Eton's voice again. "I knew you would want to know, but I'm sorry about the timing."

I didn't know how I was supposed to move forward. Flying was the last thing I wanted to do. I wanted to fall to the earth, crumble to ash, let Shadow consume even my bones. A sob wrenched out of me as I gasped and tried to breathe. I wasn't seeing, only staring. It might as well have been my blood pooling on the ground. Distantly, I heard Eton say, "I don't think you can pilot in this state, much less lead a battle. . . ."

But then the unfocused lump in my vision gradually solidified.

It was a body. Wul's body. His family, his friends, his crew, would be fighting or working, even if he was dead.

"I—I have to keep going, Eton," I stammered, my voice faint, far away.

"His last wish was to see you safe." Eton's hand brushed my arm, jarring me back to myself more forcibly than the body had. "You can't throw your life away like this. Not when *he* wanted better for you. He traded his life for yours—don't waste that gift."

His words were like cold water on my face, not blinding me—waking me up. I blinked at him in shock. He was using Nev's love, Nev's *death,* to manipulate me?

The horrible, tearing lump in my chest and throat turned bitter and frozen. I gestured wildly, shaking my head in disgust, tears streaming. "Don't you think Alaxak wants better too? *Needs* better? You expect me just to abandon them? Trade thousands and thousands of lives for my own?" I seized onto that hard, cold core inside me like a pillar, wrapped myself around it. It was ice lining my spine, making it strong, keeping me standing. "Well, I won't. And you—*and* Nev—are wrong to think I ever would. And you're cowards to try to make me. *Cowards!*"

Spit landed on Eton's chest with my cry. I squared my shoulders, trying to calm my breathing. *Don't think. Just move.*

"Get out of my way," I said, my voice ice to match my insides. "And you'd better be on the ship right behind me, or don't bother ever coming back."

I stormed past him and threw my fury into the stairs. Anger was good. It could fuel me. I had to get to the *Kaitan,* and then she would carry me in her arms, keep me away from that crushing despair, that consuming darkness. Or maybe deliver me to it once and for all. I just had to reach the fleet. Whatever happened there, happened.

Don't think. Don't think. Don't think.

Just move.

VIII

NEV

MY EYES SNAPPED OPEN. I HAD BLACKED OUT, BUT THERE WAS NO Disruption Blade in my chest. Instead, one of the most impressive duels I had ever seen was unfolding before me.

Blades cutting, thrusting, and parrying faster than I could follow, two fighters moved in a blur so flowing it felt choreographed. The assassin was as skilled armed as he had been unarmed: aggressive, strong, each strike aimed with brutal intent.

Incredibly, his opponent was better. I recognized the muted greens of the royal Xiaolan guard, and given his size I assumed he was male, but otherwise he was a mystery. His blade was shorter, slightly broader, and he wielded it with one hand instead of two. His movements were measured and easy despite the pace of their combat, like a high-tension spring put under pressure before it snapped back.

And snap back he did. His blade flicked high, then low,

changing the angles of attack constantly. First one scratch, then another, appeared in the assassin's suit. Droplets of blood flickered out from their fight, and the momentum began to shift.

It was, I reflected stupidly, somewhat like the fight I had just experienced, except in reverse.

As my thoughts came back, I glanced around and spotted the photon blaster, still lying where it had fallen. Pain radiated out from my muscles, but I forced myself into action, staggering to my feet and snatching up the weapon.

I didn't go unnoticed. A small cylinder dropped from the grip of the assassin's Disruption Blade, and he dove backward as it did. A flash of light and a bang rendered me deaf, smoke filling the space. I tracked the path he might have taken, firing several shots I was certain wouldn't hit their mark.

"He's gone." The second Bladeguard appeared at my elbow, his voice modulated into a monotone by his helmet. "We should leave."

I started, several seconds too late. "Wonderful. Thank you." Stepping back a few paces, I kept my grip on the photon blaster. "While I'm quite predisposed to like you, you'll understand if caution trumps first impressions. Who are you?"

The reflective faceplate flickered then folded away, and I was staring into the face of Devrak Hansen, head of security for the Dracorte family.

■

I sighed deeply as the painkillers took hold and the throbbing subsided. "Thank you."

"Thank me when we're done talking." Devrak busied himself putting away a medi-kit that was small but comprehensive.

The speed with which he repacked it suggested a thorough familiarity with the contents. He was no longer armored in his Xiaolan disguise, and the new suit that he had donned was a full-body affair. The armor looked thinner than what Bladeguards typically wore, but the vitals were reinforced, and I noticed various mag-couplings at the joints whose purpose I couldn't immediately discern. I felt certain that Devrak was well armed beyond even the Disruption Blade on his hip.

I had never seen such a suit, much less seen him in it. I sighed; everyone seemed to have their secrets.

"Is this a safe house?" I asked. We were in a small prefab housing unit tucked away in the forest, the cliffs of Chorda rising up nearby. It was utilitarian but surprisingly cozy given the wooden furniture and stove, which was warming me now. "I had no idea the family had a safe house on Alaxak."

"I suppose it's theirs, in a sense, as I possess it for their purposes only. Ostensibly, it belongs to a lower-level dignitary in the governor's office. Who shall, incidentally, be arriving before long." Devrak offered me a hot cup of tàs, which I clutched like a lifeline. Slightly bitter and herbal, it was the favored drink of my family. I had learned it was too expensive for most, causing me to avoid it out of guilt. But oh, how I'd missed it.

He settled himself in the chair opposite from me, moving with no apparent stiffness after his recent exertions. I felt an unworthy twinge of resentment. He held his own cup— water—with careful indifference, waiting, I knew, for me to break the silence. I had a thousand questions but wasn't sure where to start, so I observed him.

He was an elegantly austere man, his dark skin contrasted by the streaks of white in a precisely trimmed goatee. Devrak was many things: the head of security and intelligence, former headmaster of the Royal Academy on Luvos, and respected Blademaster. But his most important role had been as my father's friend. Part of my earliest memories, he had long guarded both my family and their interests.

All my family, for better or worse—including Solara.

"How is Marsius?" That was, I supposed, both the simplest and most pressing question I had for him.

His eyes softened. "Your brother is well, away from Solara. He misses you."

"How did you even get here in time? Weren't you just at a coronation a few days ago? It should have taken you a week, five days at least."

"I took a shortcut through the Outer Fringe, and even then I didn't know if I would make it in time. Suvis was already in the area, and I wasn't sure how soon he would make his move."

"The *Outer Fringe?*" It was mostly a drone traffic lane that ships avoided like a plague. "Devrak, the sheer number of drones out there would have made the journey near-suicide, and that's not to mention the pirates, the slavers, and the other nightmarish accounts I find hard to believe, but I nonetheless wouldn't disregard entirely."

Here there be monsters, as the ancient maps used to say.

He stared at me levelly. "It was worth it."

I noticed how deep the lines in his face were, how sunken the eyes. The man had aged years since I had last seen him even just a month ago, as if grief were eating at him.

"I'm sorry," I murmured. The words turned the taste of my tàs even more bitter.

"As am I." Devrak sat up a little straighter. "There are no apologies that can suffice. I profoundly misunderstood your sister. I saw how she inspired worship in some, how extensive her information network was, of course. But she used it for such trivial gossip and vanity that I never sifted out the immediate danger. My failure is abject."

I wanted to comfort him, but he would know my words were hollow. Both of us had failed, and we knew it.

"So is mine." I stared at the bottom of my cup. "To think, I felt she was the only person I could trust at home—other than Marsius, of course, but he's only a child." I glanced back up. "How do you know *I* didn't do what she accused? How do you know I'm not the one who is a murderer?"

Devrak shook his head. "The evidence is entirely contrary. I found your sister's shoe in the hangar where you freed the prisoners, so I knew she was complicit in your escape, and was not entirely the vapid socialite she claimed to be. The vid she showed of your parents' assassination was clearly edited. Coupled with what I know of you as a person, I was never in doubt. Trust someone to act in their nature, not according to expectations. The more you understand a person, the more reliable they are, even if they're not what they seem—a lesson I had to relearn in your sister's case. I was quite overjoyed to discover she had sent her attack dog to kill you, as that meant you were still alive."

I smiled. It felt good to hear Devrak analyzing again, reducing everything to interlocking components. That slight uplift in spirits took my mind back to the *Kaitan,* and to Qole. My smile disappeared. Feeling good didn't seem like something I deserved.

"But why? Why come find me?" I asked bitterly. "Here I am alive. So what?"

"I found you because it is in *my* nature to serve and protect this system and its rightful rulers."

"But—"

"You are now my king," he said without hesitation, "and you are the only one who can stop Solara." He leaned forward, and I fought the desire to shrink back.

"I'm not the king. Solara is the queen, and I'm an exiled, disinherited murderer." *I would be as rejected there as I am here,* I wanted to say. "I see no point in your quest to find me, Devrak. My return from the dead would start a bloody civil war, and we would ultimately be slaughtered. Or you could bring me to comfortable exile with another sympathetic family, but it wouldn't be long before someone discovered where I was and attempted to assassinate me. For Unifier's sake, I'm on *Alaxak,* and I was just betrayed and nearly assassinated by someone I thought was a friend. Well," I amended, "at least not an enemy." I threw my hands in the air, my black mood seeping into my voice. "Every path for me ends in assassination. Besides, who knows? Solara might be a better ruler than me anyway. She wouldn't be the first competent psychopath on the throne."

Devrak splashed his water in my face. For a wild second, I thought he was trying to blind me in order to attack. Once again, I saw Father holding his sword to my chest, Solara backing away after the assassin, Eton leaving me in darkness. Lurching out of the chair blindly, I kicked out and shoved myself back, rolling on the floor into a defensive crouch.

Fingers interlaced, Devrak regarded me from his seat, an eyebrow crooked. "Are you quite done?"

I stood up, shaking, brushing the water off my face. "We're not in the Academy, Devrak. Things don't work the same way here, and you can't make everything a lesson."

"Everything *is* a lesson, unless you know everything. You don't, I'm afraid, and you're being a poor student." Anger laced the older man's words. "Please listen to me carefully. Solara is already taking steps that are leading to a massive destabilization.

War is not far behind. The consequences of her actions are irrelevant to her; all she cares about is securing more power for herself. She is violently crushing any dissent, and the governor she is sending to oversee Alaxak is a perfectly loathsome specimen. And there are other, more disturbing things afoot."

"You think I don't know this?" I snapped. "When will people realize that knowing something is bad doesn't mean you have the power to do anything about it?"

"You have let your grief disembowel you. There is nothing you can do about the pain, but you can do everything in your power—which is still considerable—to protect others." Devrak's insight was as deft as his bladework, and I fell silent. He was kneeling at my side before I could register it, his dark brown eyes, flecked with gold, boring into mine. "If you only love something enough to defend it only when you can win, that is no love at all."

The words took my breath away as they hit home, at once eye-opening and achingly familiar. *Qole.* She was the only other person who talked to me this way. As though what was more important were the choices I made, rather than the immediate results. And now, to have heard the same thing from the two people I admired most . . . it was an experience akin to waking up to a startling vista I had nearly forgotten.

"Moreover, you haven't even examined your options," Devrak continued, his keen gaze no doubt detecting my shift in expression. "Half the generals chafe under Solara's rule, and would embrace you if you take the Forging. They're mostly on Aaltos, where Marsius is by your sister's order. She thinks I'm there with him. These generals are keeping Marsius safe and my true whereabouts a secret. And it's not only them you might sway to your cause. There are other families whose support you could gather."

I stared back at him, my mind spinning.

"Nevarian," Devrak pressed, "you are a prince, and you should be a king. How you feel about that is irrelevant, because the fact is that you now have a level of power and influence of which billions can only dream. I know you are grieving, but circumstances have given you the ability—nay, the *duty* to effect change, *not* the luxury of inaction."

He was right. Just because I didn't want this power did not mean I should not use it to do the best I could, to the best of my ability. It *was* a duty, a burden, that I thought I'd set aside forever, but now it was time to pick it back up. It was frightening, honestly, bearing such responsibility in the face of overwhelming odds. Knowing the risks, the losses we would take, the people who would die, even if we won.

I thought of Qole, holding herself together at the meeting hall, not only facing down Hiat but challenging the will of a queen, with merely her crew arrayed behind her. Her defiance was courage, and I drew on that. "All right."

Devrak stood and stepped back, the lines on his face easing. "You will come with me to Aaltos?"

I nodded. "I suppose if I don't have the decency to be assassinated, I can't simply fade away."

Devrak's answering smile was as brilliant as a sunrise. "Then I am yours to command."

Grim determination settled into my bones. "First, we need to find Qole. I have to tell her."

"What are you going to do about Eton?" Devrak was already in motion, gathering what we needed to depart.

"I don't know. This isn't the first time he's tried to kill me, and I'd be happy to never see him again. But I don't really know how Qole is going to react to any of this."

Eton aside, I was about to declare myself king. I tried to

imagine the look on her face, and didn't like any of the possibilities.

"Eton wasn't always that fanatical. But I don't know if he can be reasoned with any longer." Devrak's tone was thoughtful, and it occurred to me that if anybody would know about Eton's past, it would be him. "Having connections to such men as Suvis is reckless at best, psychotic at worst."

"Somehow, that doesn't surprise me that Eton might be acquainted with my parents' murderer."

Devrak stopped. "That was who killed the king and queen?" I nodded. "I suspected as much, but to hear it confirmed ... Nevarian, this man Suvis is extremely well trained, well positioned, and also pursuing an agenda I don't entirely understand. I'm not even sure Solara does. He's not ... right ... for lack of a better word."

Devrak had dealt with royals, warriors, and politicians across the moral spectrum. To see him so unsettled made me feel the same.

But before I could ask more about Suvis, or tell him about the assassin's strange questions regarding my family's drones, the distinct sounds of ion and photon blasts echoed through the walls from the cliffs around us, growing in frequency with every passing second. Both of us were through the door and outside in an instant.

"Firefight," I breathed.

The sounds came from the direction of the meeting hall. *Qole.*

———

I wasn't prepared for the sight that greeted me at the meeting hall. The structure was damaged; part of the roof had simply vanished. Charred and mutilated bodies, almost all of whom I recognized, littered the ground. The rich, heavy scent of blood hung in the air, and in conjunction with the smell of ozone from the aftermath of ion weapons and burnt synthetics it almost made me gag. The hulking ruin of a mechbot gave testimony to what had happened, and my blood ran cold. I couldn't imagine anyone would survive being trapped in a warehouse with one of those.

But no one living was there any longer. No Qole. I sensed the vibration in the ground first, and then the entire building began to shake. Girders creaked in protest as the air filled with a steadily building roar.

I ran outside to see hundreds of Shadow-fishing vessels erupt from the harbor, engines ablaze, rocketing into the atmosphere. I stared, trying to catch sight of the *Kaitan* ... in vain.

Devrak tried to raise the *Kaitan* on his wrist-comm as we ran to where he had docked his ship, but was equally unsuccessful. I knew there were myriad reasons that might be the case: Qole and the crew might be busy on other channels, there might have been an error in the comm-relay system, it might have been overloaded with other messages—or they were under attack.

The slaughtered fishermen in the meeting hall were the stark reminder that no one was safe, that anyone on the crew could be hurt or gone.

Gravel sprayed around my feet as I slid to a stop. Six uniformed peace officers, no doubt part of the advance team sent by the new governor, were jogging across the street in front of us, rifles up, clearly in a hurry. Their armor was dirtied and pocked with blasts; they had been in combat.

Devrak never slowed. With one hand, he unsheathed his blade, and it glowed to life with a whine. The other hand flicked four glowing disks into the middle of the group with a whine that matched his Disruption Blade. Their trajectories bent in midair, connecting to the nearest photon rifles with a metallic ring. Electricity arced and streaked between each disk, tendrils of energy licking weapon and soldiers alike.

Two rifles shut down, their indicators winking out. Two breached with sharp flashes that left their owners clutching their arms in agony, and the last pair of functioning weapons were brought to bear much too late.

The easy grace with which Devrak moved through them was terrifying. He passed each one as if it were an Academy demonstration, his blade dipping down, cutting across, rolling over and thrusting with a minimum of effort. Only in his finishing strikes did a sudden ferocity display itself, unleashing with deadly power. His left hand held a plasma pistol; anyone who remained moving was dispatched with a single well-placed shot.

He turned in a circle at the end, surveying the area, which was when I noticed the group of locals staring at us. They were a good-sized crowd, armed with industrial tools and a variety of more functional weaponry. Alaxak, it seemed, had wasted no time in forming a militia.

Devrak nodded at them. "Good day. There will be more, I'm sure. I suggest you scavenge the weapons and armor here and then set up guard stations throughout the city. Nev, with me, if you please." He uncharacteristically used my shortened name, no doubt to keep up my disguise for a little longer. His friendly tone—and his extreme display of force, in service of Alaxak—was enough to keep the crowd from trying to stop us.

Devrak led me to the public starport in Chorda, a series of blastpads designed to dock with the transports and freighters that brought people and trade from off-planet. Most vessels on Alaxak typically docked on water, since most of the planet was ocean, but ships in the rest of the systems needed land. Chorda was the only starport on the planet. There were signs of a struggle there as well, but it had evidently moved on, and now all that remained were the rows of abandoned shuttles.

Devrak headed toward a series of small private vessels intended for governance busywork. I was surprised—I would have thought he'd been in a Xiaolan starfighter.

"I'll fly," he informed me on his way up the ladder to the cockpit. "Get on the comms and see if you can raise the *Kaitan* with your identifier."

I couldn't, but I didn't need to. Soon after takeoff, skirting an asteroid, we found Qole's ship hunkered behind one of Alaxak's moons.

We also found the entire mismatched fleet of fishermen with her, hundreds of them, comms and engines quiet in the shadows. I saw what they were doing—using the interference of the moon and its debris to mask their signals and to sneak up on the governor's forces. They still had a short wait before they could move. Good—I had time to talk to Qole.

Suddenly, I felt nervous. She had been so angry at me when I last saw her; I knew I'd never be forgiven. And how was I going to talk to her about Eton, whom she considered adopted family?

Breathe. I realized the person who had constantly repeated that calming refrain was sitting right next to me, and some measure of strength crept back into my bones.

Our welcoming party when we docked with the *Kaitan* was not friendly. We stepped onto the bridge to find the entire crew arrayed in a semicircle around the airlock, bristling with weapons. The sweeping viewport silhouetted them, the blackness of space a stark backdrop accenting their grim expressions. Seeing them as an outsider might, it occurred to me that they were a distinctly menacing outfit.

Basra eyed Devrak heavily—and for that matter, so did Eton. I hadn't thought the burly man capable of growing pale, his eyes fixed with an intensity I couldn't place. He definitely recognized my instructor. And Basra knew it, glancing between the two as if something might happen.

Several things clicked for me at once. Somehow, Basra must have known who Eton was, about his past. I'd thought that it was a remarkable coincidence that they had both ended up on the *Kaitan*. Clearly, the extraordinary captain had factored into Basra's reasoning, and the fact that such a ship afforded someone of his remarkable position anonymity. But with Eton on board, a weapons master who had been a legend in his own right, he would have some of the best protection available. To a calculating mind, it was a perfect place for a base of operations. Funny that Basra's relationship with Arjan, the person here who'd ended up mattering most to him, had been a total accident.

That was the type of thing one couldn't control. My eyes went back to Qole, who looked utterly stricken.

"I thought it had to be a trick, but ... it *is* you," Qole breathed, relief washing over her face, her voice disbelieving. She lowered her weapon, though no one else followed suit.

"In the flesh," I confirmed, confused.

"But ... Eton saw you." She glanced at him. His expression was stony now. "He said you gave yourself up, an assassin ..."

151

She paused, blinking back tears. I had rarely seen her so off-balance in front of the crew.

Realization dawned on me, and I felt stupid for not putting it together sooner. Eton had cleverly used most of the truth to avoid any uncomfortable conversations about figurative daggers in literal backs. He'd told her I was dead.

I had to get Qole away from him before she put the pieces together herself. Not that I wouldn't have necessarily minded seeing Eton torched to a pile of ash, but if the governor's forces were any indication, he was more useful alive. We needed all the help we could get.

"I'm fine. I got away, with the help of Devrak. He's an ally." Qole and Arjan had both met him before, but the others hadn't—at least, not in my presence. Eton was obviously a different story. "Qole, I need to speak with you in private immediately. It's important."

She nodded, visibly pulling herself back together. "My quarters. Arjan, you have the bridge. Keep us next to any interference you can find. Basra, stay in touch with the other captains." Her voice gained strength as she spoke. "Telu, get back to finding a way to get past the jam they're putting out on long-range comms. And Eton, you and Devrak can keep one another company in the hold until I find out what's going on." She pointed a finger to the floor, indicating they should head down to the cargo level. She obviously didn't want Devrak on the bridge—she didn't trust him. But really, it was the man she'd set to guard him that she shouldn't be trusting.

She didn't wait for anyone to respond, and I hurried after her.

"Nev, I thought you were dead," Qole repeated as I closed the door to her quarters. "That you gave yourself up for me, that Solara assassinated you."

I shook my head. "She tried. And if it hadn't been for Devrak, I would be dead. But, Qole, I—"

"How could you?" she interrupted before I could finish. Her voice was pitched low, and it was husky with the effort of keeping it under control. Fury permeated her words. "First, what you did to me in the meeting hall, and now this? Even if you didn't think Solara would send an assassin and that she would just take you prisoner, or that you would somehow outsmart her in the end—whatever it was, I don't care! Don't you know how reckless that was? How much danger that put you in, letting her know where you are—how much danger that still puts us *all* in?"

I had hoped that Qole, after thinking I was dead, would have forgotten most of her anger after I'd misguidedly tried to turn the fishermen's vote against her. But she was still angry at me not only for that, but also for supposedly endangering the crew with my attempt to turn myself over to Solara. Meanwhile, protecting the crew was my goal, with every breath I took.

"You can't be serious," I replied, staring at her. "You are. I barely survived to make it back to you, and you're *mad* at me for it?" A scowl crept across my face. "Well, you know, I'm kind of mad myself."

"No, I'm angry you left in the first place," Qole retorted. "You didn't tell me, or anyone, what you were planning. One minute you were a member of my crew, and the next you decide to abandon us."

A stab of anger ran through me, and the empty ache that

153

had been eating at me receded a little. It felt good, shockingly good, to feel something else, and I let it grow.

"Me, abandon you? You threw me under the grav-lifts back there in the meeting hall! I assumed I wouldn't be back on the crew after that. You all but said I murder babies at night for sport." I waved my hands in the air. " 'Let's not listen to the monstrous offworlder! He's just talking sense, for a change!' You know, things haven't turned out very well for anyone, but it hasn't been for *my* lack of loyalty to the crew." I bit off the words. "So if that's why you're angry, I guess you'll have to be angry."

Qole sighed in frustration. "No, that's not what I meant. I . . ."

"Well, then what? If you're mad at me for putting us at risk by letting Solara know I was alive, then you should know—"

"No!" Once again, she cut me off before I could say what needed to be said. "I mean yes, but . . . Damn it." Her voice caught, and she took another deep breath. "Nev, I thought you had given yourself up. Left us . . . and I don't just mean the crew. I couldn't believe you would just throw away . . ." She stopped talking again, and my breath caught as I waited for her to continue. Throw away what?

But she changed her mind, backtracking. "You have to know I wasn't kicking you off the crew. I had to say what I said in the meeting hall in order to keep everything we've built here alive. It might make you mad, and you might disagree, but that's not me pushing you away. There's a difference."

"I know." My anger dissipated. "I wasn't truly turning on you at the meeting, either. I was trying to help you. But I failed," I said, before she could tell me I had. "And I'm here to make up for it."

Qole shook her head, and something halfway between a

laugh and a sob hitched in her throat. "We kind of implode at this. Shoving each other away, thinking it's for the best. A fine pair we make . . . but I'm so glad you're back. *You're alive.*"

Pair. Back. However much we "imploded" at this, we were on the same side again, here, together, on the *Kaitan*. At least for now.

I didn't respond, her last words lingering. She met my gaze fully, directly, and the world contracted to just the warm brown of her eyes.

Something let loose inside me. It wasn't conscious thought that made me step forward. Conscious thought would have said this wasn't the time, or that it was a bad idea. But I moved to her, and she didn't move away, our arms wrapping around one another as tightly as though we were saving each other from a hull breach. Her body folded against me, and nothing had ever felt more right.

Our mouths found one another, and her hands were in my hair, insistent, and I pulled her to me tighter, lifting her against me, losing myself to the wildfire.

We paused, foreheads against each other's, gasping. Qole brushed a few strands of hair from her face and gave a shaky laugh. "I propose a decision that we work together. Because I still have to stop your sister."

"Funny you should mention, as I might be able to lend a hand." For the first time, what I was about to say didn't fill me with dread. I would be of use again, able to help Qole. Here, in this moment, that desire overwhelmed any other considera- tion. "I'm going to challenge Solara's claims."

She pulled back, her eyes searching my face. "Wait, *what*? I thought that was impossible. Everyone thinks you killed your parents."

"Devrak doesn't think so, and he believes that Solara is

sowing enough discontent that I can sway support in my favor, both in the family and out." It felt good to say. It felt good to feel, and know I was making choices, even if they might be impossible ones. Eton's earlier plan to stop Qole had *sounded* right, but it hadn't *felt* right. And yet, it helped, in this case, that it wasn't necessarily a choice between instinct and logic. "Considering he's the head of our intelligence, he's the one person I might trust to know what he's talking about."

Qole's face hardened. "Did he have anything to do with what happened with Arjan in Dracorva . . . ?"

"No," I said quickly. "My father kept that side of the research hidden even from Devrak. He knew he wouldn't agree." Even so, I couldn't imagine how Qole or Arjan would ever trust a Dracorte again. If they didn't trust me now, would they trust me when I declared myself king of the people who had tortured them?

"I see." Qole disentangled herself from me, straightening out her jacket. I couldn't tell what she was thinking until she looked up with a bright light in her eyes. "That just might change everything."

I felt a little trickle of ice form in my stomach. She was right; it would. And not all of it would be for the better.

If my face showed any doubt, she didn't notice, her mind on other things. "Despite it all, I would have loved to see the expression on your sister's face when she found out you were alive and kicking."

Right, of course. Her kiss had nearly driven the whole point of this conversation from my mind, but now I had to tell her before we faced the crew again.

"Yes, about that." I steeled myself. "There's something you should know. About Eton."

Qole slammed open the door to her quarters and strode out, eyes black.

I could feel it radiating from her, not just the anger, but Shadow, a palpable field that made the hairs on the back of my neck stand up. If I'd been hoping to calm her down beforehand, I'd failed. The last time I had seen Qole like this, she had threatened to throw Eton out of the airlock. Now I was afraid she actually might do it. Or worse. He was hardly my favorite person in the systems, but Qole would regret it, and, if I was being charitable, he didn't deserve to die by the hand of the person he had been trying to protect. After all, we'd *both* done distasteful things in service of that goal.

And, if I was being less charitable and more utilitarian, we needed him in the weapons turret for whatever was to come.

"Qole," I started, just before we reached the hold. I reached for her shoulder, but she batted my hand away without turning.

"Don't," she snapped. "He tried to get you killed, and lied to me. I'm done putting up with him trying to make decisions for me. I'm the *captain*." She paused as raised voices reached us through the door to the hold. Apparently, Devrak and Eton also had some vehemence to go around.

"I don't give a good melting piece of scrap about the systems or royals. It can all burn," Eton snarled. "No, better, I would prefer that it burn. Its time has come."

"The man I knew would not have betrayed someone who trusted him." Devrak's voice was quieter, but it was hard and brittle as chipped stone.

We walked out onto the catwalk that ringed the hold. Below us, surrounded by the green streaks of accumulated space scum, Devrak and Eton were squared off within a few feet of one another. Devrak stood straight, disappointment and anger in his eyes. Eton, his utilitarian combat gear at distinct odds with Devrak's sleek armor, looked oddly defensive, if furious, his shoulders hunched.

"The *prince* is an idiot who believed the lies he was fed," he replied, his voice grating. "Now I've learned to be as ruthless as royals, but to use it to defend innocent people against their games. You should be on my side."

"Was that a game you were playing with Nevarian and Suvis?"

"You know how royals are! It's okay to sacrifice regular citizens' lives for the greater good, as long as they're unknowns, but nobility—oh no. They're worth more." He stabbed his fingers at Devrak. "It's a game I learned from the best, same as you. Pick your cause and win, no matter the cost. If I could give myself up to accomplish the same end, I would. But if that royal wreck can save Qole, then he's damn well going to, if I have to drag him to it. Even if it takes his life."

"The lesson," Devrak said sadly, "was not victory at any cost. The lesson was, *is,* the right action at any cost."

"I listened to that. I listened so well! And it becomes the same damn thing. Now they're both dead," Eton shouted, inches away from Devrak.

Neither Qole nor I were dead, so they had to be talking about someone else. Eton not only knew Devrak, but they had a history.

Apparently it was significant.

All expression left Devrak's face. "And who do you blame for that?"

"Blame?" Eton suddenly began to pace. "Don't worry. I know it's my fault. But it's my fault because I listened. I listened to the lies, and you can damn well bet I won't again." He lifted his leg high and stomped down on an empty storage container, crumbling the entire corner of it like a refreshment can, muscles bulging. I winced. "They killed her, Devrak," Eton continued, "and she had nothing to do with it."

Her? Was this the girl he'd admitted killing during his time as a mercenary? But no, he'd done that *after* leaving Dracorva.

"Eton." Devrak paused, searching for words. "As bad as you feel, you can well imagine that I feel worse. And any failure in her death lies with me, not you."

I had no clue whom they meant, but somehow interrupting to ask didn't seem polite.

Eton's shoulders heaved as he stood, only breathing, visibly trying to wrestle himself under control.

"You cannot let your quest for redemption twist you into what you hate," Devrak added quietly. "Into someone like Suvis."

"So what if I use him? He's made himself into a tool. Solara's pet."

"I've taken your measure both in and outside the arenas. You're better than that."

Eton's face contorted in disdain. "I've left everything in that place. There is not a bolt of that with me now."

With a slight shift in his balance, Devrak changed position and his fist darted out to Eton's face. Eton blocked it without thinking, countering with his own strike, which Devrak trapped and reversed.

After that, I couldn't follow their movements, they were so fast. For several seconds, they shifted across the floor, their arms flowing and folding around one another like vines. I wondered if I hadn't simply been lucky the first time I had fought with Eton—one of many moments with him involving airlocks. It occurred to me that he was genuinely bad for my health.

The two fighters stopped, and Devrak disengaged, bowing slightly. "It would seem you have not left everything behind. If you've kept that, there are other skills you have that would be useful to people. To help them."

Eton shrugged. "I'm helping this crew."

"No, you're not." Qole's voice echoed strangely in the hold, louder than it should have. She jumped over the railing, landing on her feet easily despite the drop, and stalked to Eton. She was a fraction of his size in height and width, but he took a step back.

"Qole . . ."

"Shut up. You have disrespected me from the first day on this ship. You have disobeyed my orders and challenged my decisions, both of which have endangered this crew and my command. But I put up with it, I put up with you. You know why?" Qole's voice could have cut through the hull. "Because I told myself that *you were a good person.*"

For the first time since I'd met him, Eton looked defeated.

"You believe you can dictate the lives of others to get what you want? You think you left the royals behind? The lies, the backstabbing, the dirty deals? No. You are exactly like the worst of them."

Eton's face went white. Qole reached up and grabbed the lapels of his combat shirt, effortlessly pulling him to her eye level. There was a long pause, and when Qole spoke, her voice was quiet, hard.

"Listen to me. Because I think you do care about the outcome of this battle, I'm still going to put you in the turret. You *will* do your job. And when we are done . . . we will continue this conversation."

The ship comm beeped, and Basra's voice cut into the

tense standoff, the urgency in it so unusual it arrested us more effectively than a warning klaxon. "Captain, you need to come to the bridge. The fleet isn't trying to land on Alaxak. They are maneuvering bombardment platforms into orbit."

———

Given her abilities, it was easy to forget that Qole hadn't necessarily studied military technology. We were now getting a grim education from the bridge of the *Kaitan*.

Through the viewport, I could barely pick out a silver speck glistening on the dark side of Alaxak. At that distance, it looked innocent, peaceful even. The infopad that Telu had silently passed to Qole as she'd made her way onto the bridge was what told the true story.

"It was inevitable that word would eventually get out about our resistance in Chorda, and as soon as I picked up on the chatter, Basra got weirded out by the new positioning of *this*," Telu explained. "We thought it was just a freighter, hauling whatever crap the governor might have wanted with him. They've been blocking long-range comms, and no one has really been able to get a good scan on the ships. Hiat has probably the best sensors, and this is the readout I got from him." Her slim fingers deftly highlighted the dots in question. "We amplified a vid feed. Here." She flicked her hand, and the image scaled up dramatically.

"A Model 218 Orbital Peace Platform," Devrak said gravely. "Laser or photon based."

"Peace Platform?" Telu glanced up at him. "You have a real sick sense of humor, pal."

"Thank Treznor-Nirmana. They make and name them."

"It has a few starfighters stationed around it, but otherwise, how good are its defenses?" Arjan asked, refusing to look at Devrak. He focused on the readouts from the copilot's chair.

"It doesn't have any." Eton's voice was more subdued than I would have thought possible. *Good.*

"By the time these are deployed, the area is supposed to be clear," Devrak said. "They're intended to help with atmospheric invasion or planetary pacification. The battle carrier and its starfighters will be the only thing protecting it."

"She's positioning it over Chorda," Qole breathed, and she looked up at me, certainty on her face. "She'll hold the place hostage until we obey. Telu, comm the city immediately. They need to evacuate."

I shook my head, the weight of attempting to fight my family's military might settling on me. I shouldn't have been surprised. Solara hadn't left anything to chance up until now, and it made sense that she had come not simply with force, but overwhelming force. She intended to break the will of Alaxak.

The energy on the bridge changed. It wasn't Shadow; it was the gravity in Qole's voice. "To your stations. Basra, comm the rest of the captains. We can't let that platform get into place. Nev, help Telu in trying to compromise its systems. Devrak, you're here to give me advice. The rest of you know what to do." She was in her captain's seat as she spoke, the *Kaitan* coming to life under her touch. "Solara is going to use it to threaten us into submission if we don't take it out."

"No," Devrak said sadly. "She intends to simply subdue you." He pointed his finger at the nearest video feed. "This is how she responds to resistance."

The platform was shaped like a disk, white with streamlined edges. Our family crest spun lazily as the platform rotated around a tall spire that extended from the top and bottom. The spire flashed silver in the reflected sunlight, a brightness that was steadily eclipsed by a glow from within. It grew more and more intense before a final flash announced that the charge cycle was complete. Golden beams streamed to the surface below. They would have been beautiful if they hadn't heralded death.

We were too far away to do anything about it.

"Comm them! Comm the surface!" Qole shouted, and the bridge filled with panicked chatter as everyone attempted to reach someone, anyone, anywhere, to warn them of what was about to happen. It was a futile gesture. Our long-range communications were still effectively blocked by the fleet.

Only Telu, with her head start and skill, was fast enough to use the QUIN and reach some of the major settlements on the surface. Some responded, communities that were already informed of the governor's imminent arrival. But her contacts in Chorda winked out of existence a few moments later.

"Ancestors, look," Arjan said, horrified. He had brought up some of the video feeds in Chorda, used to broadcast visual weather conditions. Lances of golden energy reached down to the ground, disappeared, and reappeared again a fraction of a second later in another location. Behind them, smoking craters and molten rubble remained. Structures that withstood a direct blast glowed red-hot, or began to list and melt moments later, tiny figures bursting out of them, only to be vaporized by another golden beam.

Chorda was being decimated, and all we could do was watch.

IX

SHADOW FILLED MY EYES AS I LOOKED DOWN AT ALAXAK. MY SKIN, every cell in my body, felt stretched tight with it. The black film across my vision shaded the flares of death and destruction in the viewport surrounding my captain's chair, but they didn't mute the bone-deep horror sounding at my core. Or the rage that rose from it like an all-consuming fire that burned long after the golden beams stopped striking Chorda. The attack lasted for only a minute or so, but it felt unending.

Ancestors. How many had died? How much damage had been done to the oldest settlement on Alaxak, where my people had first set down on our mostly frozen planet millennia ago? I almost couldn't fathom it—what I had seen from space or on the surface feeds. But I knew, with sudden bright clarity, what needed to be done.

They would burn my planet? Then I would burn them down.

"Get ready," I said over the inter-ship comm, addressing our fleet. "Everyone in position."

The ships outside reacted like my crew already had, hurrying into the new formations that we'd decided upon as we'd waited. Jerra and Hiat, whom I'd made squadron leaders, led groups equal to my own—we each had about a hundred ships following us. All ten vessels that had reloaded with Shadow were with me.

Jerra's voice sounded strained over the comms. "We still have to hold. Just for a few more minutes until the moon's shadow brings us a bit closer in orbit, or else they'll notice us too early and blow us to bits before we can even reach them."

"I know." I did, even though my fingers clenched on the throttle. To have to wait to strike back was almost too much for me to bear. My jaw creaked under the strain of my clenched teeth, trying to hold in a sob, or maybe a scream.

Everyone else seemed to be doing the same, just breathing. Breathing through the pain. Eton had bounded for the weapons turret, as if glad to be the one doing the shooting instead of being in my line of sight. Basra and Telu were already at their usual stations below. Nev and Devrak had followed me to the bridge, while Arjan assumed the copilot's station.

"Wait," Nev said. At first I thought he meant that he wanted that spot, but then he shook himself, blinking, like he was coming out of a stupor. He looked out at the enemy fleet. His family's fleet. "Qole, you can't go up against that battle carrier."

"I've taken down a destroyer before," I said with far more chilly confidence than I felt. "This can't be much different."

"It *is* different, and you were *inside* that Treznor destroyer you disabled and . . ." *You used Shadow,* he probably wanted to say, but didn't. Maybe because he didn't want to give me any ideas. "You won't get anywhere near a battle carrier. It will annihilate you, all of you. Even if you get the jump on them."

"I don't care. I need to get to that orbital platform, anyway, before they decide to use it again to annihilate my *planet.* It doesn't have the defenses the battle carrier does, anyway."

"And I'm saying you won't make it there, either." He paused, and his eyes widened. "Unless . . . Devrak and I need to get on that ship. Don't engage with the carrier at all, and don't get near it until we send word. And if we don't get back to you . . . well then, none of us will have to worry about anything for much longer."

Because then we'd be dead, I imagined.

"Your Highness," Devrak said, "what's your plan?"

"We need to take control of the battle carrier," Nev said.

Telu barked a laugh.

Devrak's eyebrows rose. "I'm assuming not by force, with just the two of us."

Nev shook his head. "If we can't convince one of our captains, how can we convince a planet full of our generals?"

I didn't know quite what he meant by that, but Devrak pursed his lips, as if weighing some risk. "Of course I have the rank, but . . ."

Basra's voice came from below us. "If you need money to help your cause, I hear I'm richer than the Great Unifier, or so the rumors say."

Devrak's lips now formed a line, as if the thought of bribery was distasteful. "I don't need money to pull rank. Our military isn't composed of mercenaries. It's that Solara can't know I'm here if I'm going to keep helping Nev in certain covert ways."

Nev looked through the grating beneath his feet to the crew stations below us. "Telu, can you actually do what Solara accused you of? Hack an entire vessel and keep at least its QUIN from sending inter-system messages?"

"Yeah, but it might take me a—"

"Do it now." Nev glanced at me. "With your permission, of course, Captain."

Since Telu wouldn't need to disrupt our signals once we launched our attack—which would happen almost as soon as Nev and Devrak left the ship—she'd have the time, presuming I could keep us alive. And this might be the best chance for us *all* to survive. I nodded. "Do it, Telu."

"I mean, it could take me *days*," Telu snapped, glaring up through her slash of hair. "To be any faster, I would need ... Wait, did you say you have the rank to take command of that battle carrier, Mr. Whatever-Your-Title-Is—Devrak?"

Devrak nodded seriously, despite the informality of her tone.

"Then you have access codes to the QUIN hub that it's linked to. Give them to me."

I thought the head of Nev's family's security would balk more at a rebel hacker demanding he hand over top-secret information that he probably usually guarded with his life, but all he did was glance at Nev.

Nev nodded.

Devrak turned back to Telu. "The QUIN hub with which it communicates is number QL54, and the code that should get you inside is DH13A07M84 ..." The string of numbers and letters carried on, followed by a second verification code.

I lost track, but Telu's fingers were flying. "I assume you know how to cover your tracks. Otherwise I may as well comm the battle carrier from here and announce my presence for them to report to Solara."

Telu scoffed. "Of course I do. No one will know how I got in. Especially since I'm going to reboot the system."

Devrak blinked. "The entire hub? That will make several dozen carriers and destroyers go dark."

"Exactly. For a few minutes, at least. They won't know where the problem is until they realize this one is unreachable. And then they still won't know why. I'll erase this carrier's particle configuration from the launch sequence. Afterward, its quantum link will be disrupted, and it'll only have local comm capability."

Devrak smiled faintly. "The likeliest conclusion they'll come to is that it was destroyed."

"However it works, can we get on with it?" My voice wasn't angry; it was dead. "We're nearly as close as we're going to get undetected."

I barely spared Nev a glance as I turned back to my station. He was alive, but any joy I'd felt upon discovering that had been burned to ash—a shooting star, trailing to dust. *I* was ash, like so much of the surface of Alaxak.

But then I felt hands on my shoulders. Nev's head bent beside mine, his temple pressing into my own. He smelled like sweat, blood, and everything I'd ever wanted, but now couldn't have.

"Fly safe. I'll see you soon." He said the words like he might a prayer. Then he pressed his lips to my cheek.

My own lips tingled, even though he hadn't kissed them, my skin coming alive at his touch. Now was not the time. I needed to be clearheaded, functional . . . mechanical . . . to do what I had to do. But if I was about to die anyway, or if Nev was, then what did it matter if I let myself feel something impossible for just a moment, in spite of it all?

I reached up, squeezing Nev's fingers. He readjusted his grip, his hand coming hard around mine, and for a second we just sat there, holding each other, hands clasped, heads bowed. I closed my eyes against the pricking tears and felt the warmth in my chest rise like blown embers. It wasn't the ice of determination or the heat of rage. No purpose, no function. It was just . . . there, soft and glowing.

For a second, I just let myself love Nev.

But then I had to let go.

When Nev finally straightened, he met my eyes behind their black sheen. "Don't . . ." I knew what he wanted to say. *Don't use Shadow.* And it was something I couldn't promise him. "We'll get through this. Just stay alive. Please." And then he was gone, ducking through the airlock doors and into the docked shuttle. Devrak followed him with a respectful nod to me.

As I watched him go, knowing this might be the last time I would ever see him, the warmth peaked in my chest, burning with such intensity I nearly gasped. With all the Shadow heightening my senses, it felt almost like physical pain.

"Yes." The voice in my ear made me jump in my seat. If I was hearing it already, that didn't bode well. I glanced around, blinking, both looking for anything visually wrong and to make sure Arjan hadn't noticed. Everything, including my skin, was in place, and Arjan was scanning the feeds.

"Open. Embrace." The voice again.

I'd heard those words before, if not so clearly enunciated. They'd been more feelings than anything. In my darkest moment, they'd come to give me hope that maybe Shadow wouldn't drive me mad ... but they hadn't really helped. At least maybe this time, the hallucinations would stay as only harmless, nonsensical sounds. That was the most I could hope for now.

Ignoring the voice, I said, "Jerra, Hiat, you and your forces keep the starfighters busy, and *stay away* from that battle carrier." It should have felt weird to call a pack of fishermen our *forces,* but I did it without thinking. "I'm going for the platform."

"You don't think more of us should help you?" Hiat asked.

"When I'm done with it, there won't be anything left to shoot."

We broke our holding patterns then, once Nev had a good head start on us. Engines and lights flared to life, and our three squadrons went jetting out from behind the moon.

———

The battle carrier noticed us first, the massive photon guns lining its port-side edge turning on us in unison. Scores of starfighters immediately regrouped and swarmed like a hive.

None of us fishing captains had a true squadron leader, no one directing us, and that was what made us better than them. We faced each other, the battle carrier looking as huge as a moon behind the starfighters, with the platform seeming much smaller behind—deceptively tiny and innocent, from this perspective.

Nev and Devrak's little shuttle flew between us all. I suddenly wondered if they had any guns or shields, or if their vessel was as defenseless as it looked.

As if he felt vulnerable, Nev asked, "Telu?"

"Check, got it. Hub rebooting in three, two, one ... Done."

There was no change in the battle carrier. Maybe across the galaxy it had seemed to wink out of existence, along with many other ships elsewhere, but here it was just as large and deadly as ever.

Devrak's voice rang out over the inter-ship comm—a channel that the Dracortes could pick up. "Hailing captain of the DFS *Endeavor,* this is Devrak Hansen, head of royal security. Hold your fire. I repeat, hold your fire."

There was a silence. The starfighters kept gunning for us. The first photon blasts streaked white through the blackness. The fishing vessels around me began to tuck and spin out of the way and to return fire. They were fishing vessels no longer.

A voice responded over the comm with the clipped accent of Luvos, the Dracorte home planet. "Sir, if it is indeed you, I am unable to confirm it with your biometric signal. We can't get a read. We would verify your location and mission with Command, but the QUIN—"

"Is down, yes, and that is because I took it down," Devrak said, his voice smooth and authoritative. "And you can't get a read because the hull of my ship is scrambling my biometric signal. This operation is top secret and of the utmost urgency. Our emergency alert code is EA994634 and my personal identification code is C0021DH." These were different from those he'd given Telu—apparently he had various codes for the degrees of secrecy. "I command you, and Governor Rexius, to *cease fire.*"

Fishermen threaded the sky like they were flying a Shadow run, spiraling around missiles and starfighters alike. The enemy was definitely having trouble hitting any of us, even in our clunkier ships. I barrel-rolled and dove myself, ducking under a group of them and blasting out on the other side, headed straight for the platform.

All the starfighters were still firing. At least the battle carrier hadn't opened up on us ... yet.

"Sir, I beg your pardon," the voice on the other end of the comm said, "but you might be impersonating—"

"Before you choose to risk disobeying a direct order from a superior officer, at least get a look at my face first. We're docking." Devrak's shuttle, like his voice, didn't hesitate, flying straight for one of the battle carrier's open bays, indifferent to the several dozen cannons and missile launchers aimed right at it.

A throat cleared. "As we can detect no explosive devices on your vessel, you are permitted to dock. Sir." The voice sounded nervous now.

I didn't have time to see how that would play out—especially when they realized Nev was onboard. The starfighters were engaging my group as they realized we were trying to push through. Several were on my tail alone. But I would reach the platform ahead of them.

Or at least Shadow would.

I gathered it from the holds of the ships around me, as easily as drawing in a deep breath. A black cloud coiled in front of the *Kaitan,* moving in step with us, ready to lash out at the monstrous, glowing weapon of destruction spinning above my planet.

"What are you doing?" a voice said. A familiar one.

"Nev?" I said, blinking in surprise and narrowly dodging a plasma missile.

"What?" Nev said over the comm-link between only the shuttle and the *Kaitan.* "We're disembarking; I can't really talk now."

"I thought I heard—never mind." *Ancestors.* I could have sworn that was Nev. Obviously I was wrong. That the auditory hallucinations had used a familiar voice to say something was more than they'd ever done before. They were getting worse.

Arjan cast me a sideways glance, but I ignored him, re-focusing on the Shadow in my grasp, on my goal. It didn't matter whose voice it was; it was an illusion, and it wouldn't stop me.

Almost as if the enemy could sense what was coming, their captain's voice blared out over the inter-ship comm. "Cease fire, cease fire, cease fire!"

He must have seen and recognized Devrak.

The starfighters immediately pulled up and withdrew toward the battle carrier, leaving the fishermen to regroup. The wing of someone's vessel in Jerra's crew was smoking and diffusing sparks, but it was the only damage I could see. The remains of several starfighters floated in the black. Despite that, the battle carrier's guns abandoned their targets, the barrels retracting into the gleaming white hull.

I didn't withdraw. With a furious hiss and a jerk of my hand, I sent Shadow crashing toward the platform like a vicious ocean breaker. Purplish, gleaming blackness slammed into the massive white disk. For a second, the wave of Shadow seemed to break against it, scattering into glittering sparks . . . until I realized the glitter was really part of the platform dissolving beneath it. And then the fire started. Brilliant orange cracks appeared across the rest of its surface, like the cracks that were splitting my vision—except these were actually there. Silent explosions bloomed against the black. In mere seconds, it seemed, the platform was only dissipating tendrils of flame and sparkles of light that vanished into the backdrop of stars.

Everything was equally quiet to my ears, except for the voice:

"NO."

And then I realized things weren't quiet at all. Telu and Arjan were whooping, Eton was cursing under his breath, and Nev—the real Nev—was shouting at me. "Stand down, *stand down*, Qole!"

I looked around in surprise—and saw the skin of my left arm tear away in ribbons. My muscles unraveled like string behind it, my nerves like glowing filament, dancing in the air above the wet glisten of white bone. I couldn't help it. I caught at my arm, trying to gather it back together, and let loose a terrified scream.

Arjan flew out of his copilot's seat and was at my side in an instant. "Qole, what's wrong?"

"My arm . . ." I looked at it. It was whole under my fingers.

My brother's face was creased with concern. "Your arm is fine."

"You shouldn't have done that." Nev's voice, again. The comm wasn't active.

"Shut up!" I growled.

My brother blinked at me, looking shocked and hurt. He took a step back.

"No, not you." But that was the wrong thing for me to say.

"Then who?" he asked, quiet. His eye flicked down and back up. I didn't need to follow his gaze to know that Basra and Telu were likely out of their stations and looking up at me too.

"No one. It was no one. I'm fine." The words sounded hollow and shaken, even to me. *I* was shaking.

The real Nev saved me from having to say anything else, his voice coming loud and clear over the comm. "If the various representatives of Alaxak want to meet on the *Kaitan* for a minute, I have an announcement to make. We're safe, but I have more to say than that, and I can't imagine you want to meet on the carrier."

Jerra's voice came back, hard and cold. "And who the hell are you?"

Right. Not everyone knew his voice as well as I did.

"I am Nevarian Thelarus Axandar Rubion Dracorte—your ally, and the rightful king of the Dracorte system." It was the first time he had used his full name since his father had disowned him. The first time he had reclaimed his lineage.

The name hit me like a punch to the stomach.

The roar of too many voices trying to speak at once overtook the comms.

———

Of course, when he'd said he would challenge his sister's claims, he meant more than her accusations of regicide. He also meant her claim to the throne. I'd been too distracted to realize that.

Hours later, I hardly felt less distracted. The voice was murmuring unintelligibly in my ear, the *Kaitan* occasionally tried to crack apart, my skin was defying gravity and flying away, and I was trying to suppress full-body shivers and to stay on my feet without looking like I was trying. On top of all that, a dozen new arrivals crowded around the table in the *Kaitan's* messroom, plugging the space around the table and stepping on each other's toes on the plate-metal flooring, along with my usual crew—including one newly declared king.

And through it all, I couldn't help wondering: What did this mean for us—Nev and me? I felt selfish, petty, idiotic, to even think it when so many bigger parts and pieces were moving around us, when I might not even live beyond tomorrow, but I couldn't help it. We'd kissed after he'd found me on the *Kaitan,* but did that mean he still thought of us as having . . . whatever we'd had? It might not have been much to speak of, but all that might be impossible now. Every daydream I'd ever wandered into with the two of us together on Alaxak was now just that—a fantasy. At least, he certainly wasn't going to be my copilot on Shadow runs anymore.

But then, he *was* a king. Which meant he might be able to decide a few things for himself. Why couldn't he choose *me,* a new future?

Despite everything, the thought made my stomach flip.

Before heading to the battle carrier, he'd taken his contacts out and popped his face back into its usual shape. Even Jerra seemed a little dazzled by his appearance, fidgeting and repositioning her wheelchair against the table several times rather than meet his silver-gray eyes. He still had the beard and his mishmash of clothes—I was glad he hadn't borrowed any Dracorte regalia from the battle carrier, since it wouldn't have gone over well in this crowd.

Because, beautiful as he was, most of them probably would have been happy to gut him.

Before anyone could try, I explained that Nev had been the one to subdue the carrier without a fight and call for the cease-fire, with Devrak's help. I also explained that he'd been a loyal member of my crew for over a month and a half, and while he had been the one to bring us to Dracorva in the first place, he'd then returned to Alaxak with us after he'd realized his family wanted to use us, challenging his father and getting exiled in the process.

"And you just hid him, without telling anyone?" Jerra's voice was stung, angry, and I couldn't help grimacing.

"He would have been assassinated otherwise—his sister

tried, a week and a half ago, on the *Luvos Sunrise,* and again, less than a day ago."

"Maybe you should have let him die, if he's been the one to bring this upon us." Hiat looked truly distressed at what Chorda had suffered, but I didn't feel an ounce of pity for him.

"And what good would he have been to us dead? He helped *stop* this, Hiat. You were the one who wanted to bargain with the Dracorte queen, and now you see what she's capable of." Before he could argue that this wouldn't have happened if we *had* bargained with her, I added, "We all voted to oppose her, because a bargain with her would have been a lie. It would have been subjugation."

Luckily, there were enough nods around the table that Hiat kept his mouth shut.

"Well, what does *he* get out of this?" Arjan folded his arms and turned to Nev. "First, you wanted us to give up, but now you want to fight? Why?"

Nev took a deep breath. "Because now I think we can win. I can rally support and challenge Solara's claim to the throne. Devrak informed me that many of our generals will come to our side if I declare myself king."

"Do you want what your sister wants, *King*?" It sounded worse than *Prince* on my brother's tongue. Worse than an insult. "To rule the system, to rule *us*?"

"No," Nev said calmly, unruffled, despite momentarily looking as exhausted as he probably was, about as close to death as he had recently been. "In fact, I don't want Alaxak at all. I'd just ask, politely"—he glanced around, silvery eyes flashing—"if I can borrow the planet for a time. In exchange, after I wrest power from my sister, I will grant Alaxak complete autonomy . . . including over your Shadow grounds."

Already his tone had changed. Gone was the deferential

crewman. His ingrained authority, the years spent learning how to rule others, rang in his voice.

"Borrow it how?" Jerra asked, a suspicious eyebrow raised. His good looks had flustered her, but she wasn't close to being cowed now, either by his eyes or by his tone. Even though Nev wasn't my enemy—far from it—I wanted to hug her, for a second.

"I'll need a new base of operations in the Dracorte system, preferably one as far from Luvos as possible. Alaxak is exactly that. It's also conveniently lacking any infrastructure controlled by my sister. Instead of needing to overthrow anybody, I have allies . . . if you'll accept me as one."

Arjan wasn't satisfied. "Allies who will benefit *you* after your victory, no doubt, since an ally would grant you exclusive trade rights to Shadow?" He must have been picking up this stuff from Basra.

"With fair prices, higher than you've ever seen. And in return I'll lend you military protection until such time as you can build your own military and protect yourselves, if you wish."

"You *grant* us what should already be ours by right," Jerra said. "What else do we get?"

Nev pointed unerringly at the wall. "How about that battle carrier?"

Even Arjan gaped at that. It wasn't only as big as a small moon; it was worth one.

"It stays," Nev continued, "to protect Alaxak from further threat while I'm gone. You can keep it, with a skeleton crew of ours to teach you how to run it, as long as the QUIN remains offline for the duration of your resistance. The rest of the crew will go planet-side with you and help clean up the damage they caused—including Governor Rexius."

"And just where are *you* going?" Jerra demanded.

Nev smiled at her, though it was as sharp as a knife. "To get more ships, and an army to fly them. I will not let my sister win, and believe me when I say that I have a plan."

My own voice rose, as calm and controlled as I could make it. "And if we don't agree to this?"

I had to ask. For the people who followed me. Even for myself.

Nev met my eyes. It was a gaze I could lean into, steady myself upon, believe in. "If you don't, I'll still leave to fight my sister and declare your autonomy if I win. Of course, I would rather have the honor of your presence at my side as I did." He meant to include everyone, but his eyes remained locked on me as he said it. My stomach flipped again. "My chances of success increase with your help."

"With our *help* or our subservience?" Arjan snapped.

"I will respect you as equals." Nev abruptly hinged at the waist, bowing about forty-five degrees, his hand to his heart. I didn't know enough about courtly bows, but it looked as if it were to a peer.

Arjan nodded, with a mixture of embarrassment and approval, and looked away.

Like the others, I had one last question. "What will you do about Eton?"

Nev's eyes drifted to where Eton stood against the door with his arms folded. The big man suddenly looked like he was trying to make himself smaller. At another time, it might have been funny.

"He's complicit in an attempt on my life, and royal assassination is punishable only by death, according to Dracorte law." Nev paused. "But it was only an attempt, and it occurred on Alaxak, while both he and I were your crewmembers, Captain Uvgamut." By which he meant, I guessed, that he was no longer my crewmember. He wasn't subject to me anymore, just like I wasn't to him—if his next words didn't make it clear enough. "In my first act as king and as your ally . . . I leave his fate in your hands."

Everyone looked at me, and I nodded, a little impressed myself, despite everything.

Eton's face was more tense, not less. I glanced at him only long enough to catch a glimpse.

Everyone was waiting now. I wished this could have been done privately, but I supposed I'd brought it on by testing Nev.

"You're off my ship," I said quietly to Eton. My voice carried in the silence. I didn't look at him, but it was only too obvious whom I meant. "Off Alaxak, if you know what's good for you. If I see you again, I'll kill you myself."

I didn't see Eton leave, but I heard the messroom door slide open and shut. He would probably catch a shuttle to the battle carrier, and maybe stay there. Or maybe he would wander off somewhere else, to some other distant planet. Maybe rejoin the band of ruthless mercenaries he used to be a part of, who were too cutthroat for him to even tell me much about.

I told myself not to care. This was what I had been chosen for—to make decisions on behalf of all of us, not to wallow in my personal grief. I suddenly understood the weight on Nev a little better, the authority in his voice that refused to bow to the pressure. I cleared my throat, made my own voice firm. "I accept your deal, Dracorte." It was probably the first time an Alaxan had used that name without scorn. "We're allies."

There were grim nods around the table. In other circumstances, there might have been cheers for our position to have changed so abruptly for the better. But no one, including me, could forget that Chorda was smoldering and scarred beneath us. I didn't know how much damage had been done, how many lives had been lost ... and I wasn't going to find out firsthand.

"Well then, if you'll excuse me, I have an army to raise." Nev leaned on the table, muscles cording in his forearms. He would have looked nonchalant except for his knowing gaze as he glanced at me. An answering warmth rose in my chest that I couldn't suppress. "Captain Uvgamut, would you please accompany me to represent Alaxak?" He gave me a sheepish smile. "Among other things, I might also need a ride to Aaltos."

INTERLUDE

SOLARA

THROUGH THE HOLODESK FEEDS IN MY NEWLY INSTALLED OFFICE ON THE *Volassa,* the super-destroyer I'd renamed to become my new mode of interstellar transport in lieu of the *Luvos Sunrise,* I watched, over and over, the targeted area on the surface of Alaxak light up like a city coming alive at night. A touch of my finger, confirming the order, had done that. *That* was power. It had nearly made me giggle at the time.

Three days later, it didn't even inspire a smile, but it was still the only thing that made me feel better about what had happened *after:* a Peace Platform and full battle carrier, destroyed, and still another few days before I could mobilize the ships and the funds to retaliate. Nev, still alive, after Suvis had failed to kill him. A new, possibly Xiaolan-backed supporter of Nev—or at least someone *wanted* me to think it was the

Xiaolans. Drones, misbehaving in small pockets all across the systems, with no rhyme or reason. Heathran, sounding reserved in our long-distance missives. Not that that was anything but ordinary from him, but I'd been hoping for extraordinary.

At least I might be able to do something about Heathran, upon arrival.

The *Volassa* was carrying me to Embra, the home planet of the Belarius family, where the leaders of all the systems, mostly royals, gathered on occasion as the Kings' Council—an archaic name I took issue with—to make group decisions that would affect the galactic empire. Belarius the Elder, addressed as such in their system, oversaw the council as its head, and so was arguably a king of kings.

Good thing I was a queen.

Heathran was his heir. Prince of princes. Heirs weren't always invited to attend the Kings' Council, but I would at least be in the same palace as he was in their capital city, Tenérus, in one day's time. Surely our paths would cross.

A message flashed on one of my floating holoscreens, from King Makar Treznor-Nirmana. There was one king who wouldn't be in attendance. I almost couldn't wait to open the recording.

His rich voice filled my office—cordial, this time, though I'd heard it hit almost every note on the emotional scale. He was an eccentric one, which was perhaps part of an elaborate image that was as carefully cultivated as the Xiaolans'... except it had played right into my hands.

"I would have seen you at your coronation or the upcoming Kings' Council," he said. "However, since I am under house arrest—excuse me, house *rest*—after a medi-evaluation deemed me mentally unstable and thus unable to perform my duties as king, a member of the Treznor-Nirmana council will take my place. This peace and solitude is giving me plenty of time to contemplate how to best congratulate you on your ascension. Be sure, you will be hearing from me soon."

I could already hear it lurking in his voice: that jovial tone was just a mask for something dark and dangerous. Maybe it was because he was speaking my language, but that *did* make me smile.

——

When I arrived on Embra the next day, I didn't have much time to find Heathran before the Kings' Council began, and he unfortunately wasn't in attendance to divert me from the tedium—or from the infuriating business on Alaxak.

All I had were a bunch of hard-eyed kings and queens. There was Queen Shanyi Xiaolan, dressed to kill, perhaps literally, with a full cape made of feathers that looked as sharp as knives, her spiky crown supporting the nearly perfect sphere of her black hair. The Enterio "king," which was an elected position and so barely deserving of the title, screamed new money in his garish orange ensemble. The head of Orbit—she preferred *chief executive* to *queen*—a severe woman with white hair pulled back into a tight bun, wore a suit made of rare white melori fur and studded with teal gems. Only Belarius the Elder, seated at the head of the table, wore a truly plain suit, so deep a purple it was nearly black, and a simple gold circlet on his dark brow—downright austere for this group.

I myself wore an understated sheath made from cloth of gold, belted at the waist with silver-linked blood tears to match my crown, with a blue velvet stole over my shoulders. I *had* told Devrak I would pair some blue with my new crown, after all. The dress I'd chosen for Heathran, since I knew it would suit his tastes.

Lord Khala Treznor-Nirmana was the representative in King Makar's place, sitting to my left. Before, he'd always been a temporary stand-in for Makar when the king didn't feel like attending social events. He wasn't the Treznor-Nirmana heir, merely the king's nephew. This time, Khala looked like he was making himself comfortable both in his seat at the table and in his shimmering platinum-threaded suit, subdued only by a black cravat.

Not that recent developments meant Makar would declare him, or anyone, his heir. He had no children and hadn't given any indication of favoring a possible successor yet, which was another great source of resentment from within the family.

I leaned toward Khala and asked in a low murmur, "How is your poor, dear uncle, Lord Khala?"

He gave me a small smile. His expressions were usually thin and too shiny, much like his face, but this one was genuine. The sympathetic sigh was not. "Still resting, I'm afraid. The strain of rule—it was simply too much for him."

Makar had made it even easier for me to take advantage of their family hostilities when he refused something so obvious as to loan me money so I could forcibly buy out Hersius Kartolus's investment in our industries. It was obvious because the Dracortes would be so deeply indebted to their family that we would have a hard time ever being free of them.

Makar, irritatingly, had seen the less obvious: that freedom from Hersius Kartolus was the best move I could have possibly made, whatever the cost. And he didn't want what was best for me, even at the expense of greater leverage over us—leverage that he wisely assumed would not be permanent.

After that, it had taken only the politest speculation about the king's instability and questions about a curious footnote in the Treznor-Nirmana family accords regarding mental conditions impacting one's ability to rule, before Khala had called for the medi-evaluation—administered by a *very* well paid professional, no doubt.

Makar knew it had been me. But that didn't matter. He was indefinitely indisposed.

"And how fares the rebellion on that ice planet of yours?" Queen Shanyi spoke from across the table. Even though her voice was politely disinterested, her dark, black-lined eyes were as knifelike as the feathers of her cape. "I hear you lost a few Xiaolan starfighters. Do let us know if you need more built."

She knew I'd lost a lot more than that. I gave her a gracious nod, while inside I simmered.

Belarius the Elder cleared his throat, saving us from further interaction. The council was in session, so I leaned back, settling in for a long, dry discussion of supply routes and trade arrangements. The sprawling oval table, with a surface of mirror-black when it wasn't activated, would alight with a touch to project a holographic map of the systems in the air above it.

I should have hoped for boredom. Instead, I was immediately bombarded with an angry list of grievances.

"—three settlements in the Enterio system *destroyed* with no provocation by your drones—"

"—planetary supply lines were disrupted because we had to avoid a cluster of them that had gathered for no apparent purpose. We expect full compensation for the delays—"

"—and then they *resumed* mining in places they hadn't touched for years. An entire city had to be evacuated—"

"—your father never would have allowed this to happen—"

Almost everybody spoke out against me with reservations and complaints and flagrant accusations of subterfuge, all except Khala, and likely only because I'd just done him a large favor. Queen Shanyi summed it up nicely.

"Your drones, Queen Solara, are out of control," she said with a cold, imperious nod. "I suggest you take care of it immediately."

For a moment, panic flared inside me. I wanted to break down, sob that I didn't really know what I was doing. It was what had worked in the past when I was in a tight spot. I knew what they thought of me—what everyone thought of me. Harmless and pretty, easy to bully. I'd maintained such an image for so long, despite my decisive public response to my parents' assassination. But if I didn't make them respect me now, they would take liberties elsewhere. I had a fine line to walk.

"Your Majesties," I said, taking a long, steadying breath. "You are unfortunately incorrect that my father would never have allowed these things to happen. My investigations have led me to believe that, in his duplicity, my late brother was behind inciting the malfunction of our drone network, culminating in an attack on our very home." It was a complete fabrication, of course, but let my formerly beloved father and brother fall a little lower—lower than dead, even—in their eyes, and make them doubt my legitimacy less. "Of course, any malfunction in the drone network is incredibly dangerous, and could lead to untold damages." I let my eyes linger on the Enterio "king." *Your markets and safety are in my hands.*

I paused, mustering more concern into my voice. "That is why I intend to stop this. I have already dispatched aid and reparations to the settlements that have been damaged and appointed a crack team of hackers working around the clock to remove the malicious code Nevarian spread. Give me one month, and I will have the situation completely in hand."

One by one, they agreed to give me time. I had painted myself into a corner, but one slightly larger than they had first given me.

Now I needed to get out of it.

━━━

Afterward, I let myself wander the wide halls of the Belarius palace, accompanied by only a few of my Home Guard, who hung back far enough to be unobtrusive. It was wise of them. If they had come near me, I would have been tempted to snatch a decorative gold spear from where it was affixed to a marble column and run them through.

Belarius architecture and finery had none of the embellishments that the Dracortes favored. It was as if their attire and buildings with their refined simplicity in design, coupled with the most expensive materials in the systems, didn't deign to need such frills. If Dracorva's cityscape brought to mind white lace fluttering in a breeze, Tenérus's was the finest cloth of gold, but bolts and bolts of it, in blunt, towering stacks—as if to say since it was obvious they had it, they didn't need to do anything with it.

The truth of the matter was, the Dracorte family was nearly bankrupt, which would make dealing with those drones problematic. Unlike with the rebellion, blunt force wouldn't help. Even if we could attack them, it'd ruin the family to do so. Our drones still mined and harvested a large share of our copious raw materials and resources. They were at times frustrating, since the technology to fully reprogram them—or to even power them off—had been lost in the Great Collapse, but until now, we'd managed. Nothing like this had ever happened before. Their programming hadn't changed or malfunctioned in hundreds of years. Why now?

I couldn't do much without funds, especially from under the collective Treznor-Nirmana thumb. They themselves would probably be happy to lend me more, until I choked to death on debt. Rather, I needed someone who didn't want to watch the Dracorte downfall with glee, someone sympathetic, and above all, generous.

The old Hersius Kartolus, the Twelfth, would have been an ideal source of capital, independent from royal bickering. But this new Hersius, the Thirteenth, happened to be an insane young man, or even woman on occasion, or so I'd heard, who happened to be in love with Qole's brother. Whom we'd tortured. An unfortunate piece of luck, that.

My heels clicked more sharply, echoing in the marble hall and betraying my mood. What I really wanted to do was stomp and scream. Maybe throw a priceless vase or two.

And yet, I reminded myself with a calming breath, perhaps what my family had done would be worthwhile in the long run. We were about to offer up Shadow to the galaxy as a revolutionary new fuel, and our research into the energy's startling effects on humans had resumed. Arjan had helped us make great strides in that sector. Now all we needed to do was secure our Shadow grounds, and for that, I just needed the money to deploy the fleet.

A massive influx of revenue *was* coming from Shadow, and yet not soon enough, not with the drones acting as they were and not with the rebellion on Alaxak. What I needed, in the meantime, was . . .

. . . leaning against a marble pillar before me, after I turned a corner.

The timing would have been perfect—it was the exact moment I'd been hoping to "fortuitously" stumble upon, except that the object of my attention, Heathran, was standing with Daiyen Xiaolan and another girl.

My gaze homed in on Daiyen like a plasma missile. My smile felt as sharp as my heels as I strolled up. I barely glanced at the other girl standing with them, only enough to register features and dark coloring that matched Heathran's—his younger sister, seventeen or so, probably only there to keep up appearances.

"Why, there you are!" I exclaimed brightly. Too brightly, like a solar flare. Heathran's sister—Shadia was her name— suppressed a flinch. "I was wondering where you'd both gotten off to while the rest of us were meeting."

Daiyen flicked her chilly gaze, as dark and pointed as her mother's, at the sleek black wrist feed coiled around her arm like a serpent—Xiaolan-design, of course—and she smiled. "Mother informs me that was quite the riot in there. Elder even had to call for order." She managed to say the Belarius title in a slyly teasing way, as if she were on familiar terms with the most powerful man in the systems.

I wanted to grit my teeth. Hinting at Heathran's father's disapproval was a solid blow, not that she would even understand entirely why. I didn't need or even want the Elder's endorsement as a potential match for Heathran. I had no intention of marrying his son. Ever. And yet if he disliked me, or worse, found me an unfit ruler, there was no way he would allow Heathran to loan me what I needed, whether or not I managed to charm the latter into *thinking* there was something between us.

"If only you could have been there." I made myself sigh regretfully. "It's difficult being the youngest on the council. I just feel like people my age, as you are, have such a clearer view of the systems."

Sometimes I longed to say what truly lay under all the niceties of speech, but then, this was more fun. A subtle war game played with pretty words.

"We were just . . . ," Heathran began, but then he hesitated. Good. He didn't like any assumptions that might be made about this little gathering.

Surprisingly, Shadia spoke up, less intimidated than I'd initially thought. Perhaps she wished to change the subject for her brother's sake. Or maybe Daiyen's. "I'm terribly sorry to hear the news about your mother. And father," she added belatedly.

I blinked at her, because she clearly meant it. And then I remembered: the girl had lost her mother—as had Heathran—to assassination. It had happened so long ago, ten years or more, that I almost never thought about it, but it had obviously left an impression on the girl. Enough so that *my* mother's death was more prominent in her mind than my father's, though it was usually the opposite for those expressing their sympathies.

But then, her mother would have been on the council had she still been alive, because Belarius kings and queens shared power equally as spouses—it was even expected of them. Xiaolan didn't: their society was matriarchal, and the queen took only a consort. Makar's Nirmana wife and queen could have theoretically been at the meeting if he had been himself, but she usually preferred to stay out of the public eye. Much like my own mother, she was happy—no, *expected*—to let her husband take over most major decisions, a common attitude in both Nirmana and Dracorte cultures.

Which was why I never planned to marry.

"Thank you, Shadia, dear. It's good to see you again," I

said warmly, but my tone didn't entirely couch the dismissal in my words.

She took her cue, ducking her head in a slight curtsy befitting one royal to another, though it was a touch deferential. "I was just leaving. I'm afraid my studies can't wait."

Belarius equality between the sexes or no, she was still forced to study, as a princess. I nearly shuddered at the thought, and then basked in the assurance that nobody in my family, man or woman, could tell me what to do ever again. Amazing, the difference a crown made.

Daiyen's eyes narrowed a fraction at the girl's departure. "You must be so busy yourself, as a new queen," she said, turning my own line of attack back on me. "You must have more important things to be doing than indulging us with your company, what with your drone problems and rebellion and all." She smiled sympathetically.

She *really* should have stayed home. Because a plan clicked into my head as I smiled back at her and nodded, sharp as a Disruption Blade in its sheath.

Someone had dressed like a Xiaolan assassin. Suvis could do the same. He was already well on his way to Embra from Alaxak to join me. He would arrive within a few days.

Once I felt the razor edges take shape, I relaxed entirely and gave her so genuine a smile she *did* blink. "Why, yes, yes I do."

X

NEV

"AALTOS IS A HEAVILY MILITARIZED PLANETARY SUBSYSTEM." DEVRAK
had requisitioned every infopad on the *Kaitan,* laying them
all on the messroom table. They linked, displaying one image,
and he swept his hands across them, summoning a map in
question. The planet and its moon, both habitable, spun in lazy
orbit before us. "This is where we train our ground troops and
manufacture their equipment."

The Belarius Drive hummed its tune in the background,
activated after coordinates had been programed for Aaltos. As
soon as we had departed from Alaxak, everyone had gone back
to their bunks to try to rest, but only a few hours later, Devrak
had woken me to discuss our next steps and then called a strategy meeting here with the rest of the crew.

His fingers traced out installations on the planet, where

troop counts and arsenal inventories sprang up. Basra questioned the numbers, and I was glad for his curiosity; he seemed to be the least haggard of all of us, and if there was anyone I wanted helping us with strategy, he was the easy choice.

"How familiar are you with the planet, Nev?" Devrak asked.

"Fairly. I trained there for my high-grav exercises. And my father was there regularly for reviews and deployment meetings. I sat in on some of them."

"That's curious." Basra furrowed his brow and sat back in his chair. "There is little reason that a ruler couldn't participate in most meetings and decisions via the QUIN."

Devrak smiled slightly. "Correct. The generals and commanding officers of the Dracorte military are, like much of the family, steeped in tradition. Thelarus, as supreme commander of the armed forces, valued personal interactions and believed it fostered loyalty."

And now those generals all think I killed him.

"Oh, is that why he shook my hand before he took my eye?" Arjan muttered. He leaned back in his chair with his arms folded, shooting me a critical glance.

I knew he blamed me for what had happened to him on Luvos, and while I could see where he might be coming from emotionally, rationally I was having a harder time reconciling the two. I had managed with virtually no sleep since leaving Alaxak, and the exhaustion was amplifying the newfound anger lurking behind my thoughts, waiting to flare up when I wasn't consciously suppressing it. I wanted to grab Arjan, shake him by the shoulders, and ask which one of us had voluntarily chosen to sacrifice more. How much would it take to prove that my intentions were true, or to atone for my mistakes?

Qole ignored him entirely. "So we just cruise in with Nev and he takes over?"

"If only it were so." Devrak sighed. "Officially, the planet is loyal to the new queen, and our mere arrival would cause chaos, infighting, and probably retaliation from Solara before any decision could be made. No, we need the leadership on our side before anyone else on the planet knows we're there, which means we must find a way to meet with them in secret."

Qole leaned forward, frowning, to look at the displays. "I don't see a lot of ships. It might not be too hard to slip through without drawing much attention."

"Correct again," Devrak said. "Aaltos specializes in its infantry. Its navy is small, which is good for gaining entrance, less good for Nev if he manages to convince the generals to follow him. The bulk of the Dracorte navy is under the command of General Illia Faetora of Luvos, who has long chafed under a hierarchy she saw as . . . limiting. Solara has granted her sole command of the fleet in return for her unwavering support."

"So while getting to Aaltos isn't a problem, we have to hope the rest of the generals believe that Nev didn't kill his parents, and that they can defend themselves against the royal Dracorte navy?" I could tell Qole wasn't trying to sound dubious, but the statement wasn't very hopeful.

"Well, that's why we then have to use their strength to blow up a fleet."

"Beg pardon?" Telu said.

"Solara's forces already vastly outnumber ours, but she's expanding her entire navy by thirty percent with a new fleet the Treznor-Nirmanas are building for her on Valtai. Under no circumstances can we let her acquire this fleet."

"And why, pray tell, would we want to blow up this fleet and not attempt to . . . acquire it ourselves?" Basra asked.

"Because only the Treznor-Nirmanas can cede control of the fleet to the rightful owner, namely whoever has paid for it. Besides, attempting to steal it—and that's assuming some slight chance of success, which we wouldn't have—would be an act of war against an even greater power than your sister's. It would look bad for Treznor business, so they would eliminate us with due haste."

"So . . . we blow it up instead. Who came up with this idiotic plan?" Telu asked.

"I did," I said. I nearly wanted to pull a face at her.

"It was rather clever, actually, given what we have to work with," Devrak said, and I felt a warm glow of pride.

"So, we go to Aaltos, talk to some generals, quietly blow up a fleet, and then hope we survive the rest of the Dracorte navy?" Qole amended.

A mirthless smile tugged at my lips. "Not only that, I have to pass the Forging."

"The Forging," Qole echoed, tasting the word like something dirty. "What is . . . wait, don't tell me. Another family tradition. Is it dangerous?"

I was irrationally pleased with her being protective, and that, of all things, put me in a better frame of mind. "Not impossibly so, no, although Devrak's silence on what's involved isn't exactly encouraging."

"The Forging was meant to be a barrier to direct control of the military from the royal family, unless they proved themselves wholly capable," Devrak elaborated. "Solara refused to undergo it, and thus she should have been forced to pass her desires to her generals for them to act upon; she shouldn't be able to provide explicit military directives. To get around this, she has all but dismissed her generals, other than Faetora, and they resent her. Surviving the Forging when Solara refuses to acknowledge the tradition would demonstrate Nev's respect, integrity, and prowess all at once."

"And all regicide on his part forgiven?" Basra wondered out loud.

Devrak only said, "Leave that to me. Now, I must discuss a few things with Nevarian in private."

"Anything you two have to say, you should be able to say around us," Arjan said. "You can't expect us to trust you if you don't return the favor."

"Trusting Eton almost got Nevarian killed," Devrak replied without rancor.

"You know what trusting Nev got us?" Arjan bit back, his single eye burning at me. Basra put a hand on his shoulder, squeezing. Arjan looked up in surprise. He obviously hadn't noticed Basra moving around behind him.

They still hadn't been speaking to each other much, not since Arjan had snapped at Basra's offer to help financially with a replacement for his eye. Basra's wealth wasn't the only problem; Arjan's resentment had been building ever since he'd discovered that Basra had kept his true identity as Hersius Kartolus a secret from him. It wasn't only me who'd angered him.

Basra didn't say anything but left his hand resting there, and Arjan sighed, reaching up to clasp it for a moment.

"You can talk to Nev—Nevarian—alone for anything entirely private," Qole said finally, her sharp eyes noting the exchange. "We won't listen in."

"*Nevarian?* Wait, do I have to call you Your Loftiness now?" Telu asked with a wicked grin, as we all stood from the table.

"Only if I can call you Your Shortness," I said, without missing a beat.

She punched me in the stomach, for which I was oddly grateful.

"So it hinges on the test," Basra said in summation. He crossed his arms, looking at me carefully. I recognized his expression; I saw it on his face after every Shadow run, weighing the optimal cannery to sell to, what third-party deals might be available. He was calculating something, and I was a variable in that calculation. "Are you ready for it?"

"It doesn't matter," Qole said before I could respond.

Devrak frowned. "No?"

She shook her head. "No. Nev has two options. He can fight, or he can give up. Pass or fail, we've all chosen the route we have to fly."

———

"She would have been remarkable if she had gone to the Academy." Devrak swirled the last few dregs of tàs in his cup thoughtfully. We'd ended up staying in the messroom once everyone had filed out.

I'd considered the same thing and had come to a different conclusion. "I believe her not going is one of the reasons we haven't seen the likes of her before."

Devrak inclined his head in deference to my opinion. "Without a doubt. Unfortunately, that is also why you have to distance yourself as soon as possible."

I took a deep breath, steadying my hands on the table. I had been dreading this conversation since I had brought Qole to Luvos, back when I hadn't been willing to acknowledge what I was feeling. But even then, I had known that expressing feelings for someone of low birth would be difficult for even the most open-minded of the nobility. Like Devrak.

"You think she's beneath me."

A pained expression crossed Devrak's face. "I'm afraid that's not it at all. No, it is the simple fact that you have both chosen to pursue goals where success is achievable only through separation."

"I see." My hands tightened into fists, and anger crept into my words. "So somehow being a better ruler than Solara means I have to hurt those near me? Push them away? Focus on myself?"

"I would advise that you not measure yourself against Solara, but against what makes a righteous ruler. You need allies, Nevarian, and you need respect." Devrak leaned forward intently, and I felt the pressure of his presence, decades of listening to him as a mentor. "You will win that with a properly chosen marriage. Your life is not your own now, and attempting to choose relationships for personal gain will not only harm anyone who supports you, but will put this entire crew in danger in the process. Their place is not at court, and I suspect you know this. I suspect *Qole* knows this."

I sat silently, not wanting to meet his eyes, formulating a hundred responses in my head. The man was a master not just of the martial arts but of cornering my thoughts and disarming my arguments before I voiced them. There was a terrible progression to everything that had started unfolding as soon as I had made the choice to fight. *Helping Qole means leaving Qole.*

Devrak watched me, and I wasn't sure whether I was going to rage, laugh, or cry.

Somehow, I managed to merely sink deeper in my seat and give a weary, "Yes, yes." I wanted to add *I've heard it all before,* which I had, my entire childhood. It was just that now it was applicable.

"I'll leave you to think on this. Get some rest, and let's talk after that."

I sighed with relief when he exited, which turned into a groan when Telu entered almost immediately afterward.

"What does it take to be alone?" I closed my eyes.

"Not hanging out in the messroom," Telu said, moving to the galley to pour herself a drink. "What's got you feeling so sorry for yourself?"

"Seriously?" I cracked one eye. "You must have the most epic sympathy standards of all time. Should I start with my parents dying, or something else?"

She sat down at the table with a full mouth, then swallowed. "Happens to everyone eventually. Be happy you didn't feel the need to throw your dad in jail to rot like I did. Anyway, I don't think that's what's gnawing at you right now."

I closed my eyes again and let my hands fall to my sides. "You are the missing piece of the advice puzzle, I'm sure. Tell me what's bothering me."

"You're bummed that Daddy 2.0 just told you to distance yourself from us."

I sat up straight. "Telu, you have to understand . . ."

Telu rolled her eyes. "Scrap that. I get it. You're going to be king on Luvos. Qole is going to run Alaxak. I'm going to, beats me, code a script to cry everyone a river. None of this is going to be all huge catches and good times. *But.*" Telu leaned over the table, and I saw both her eyes glittering through her shock of hair. "You need to make sure you and Qole have the same destination in mind, when it comes to the two of you."

"We hadn't . . . we haven't really talked about any mutual destinations before now. I mean, I've had ideas. . . ." So many ideas. Of building something with her on Alaxak that could belong to both of us. Of being with her, only with her, for the rest of my life. But I'd never voiced any of that to her. "It was too soon," I said aloud. "But now . . . none of that is possible anymore."

At least, not in any form that I'd figured out how to articulate to her, yet.

"That's scat. What is this, some stupid drama vid? You'll just hold off on admitting your feelings for her, because that's *so* obviously a good idea?"

"That's assuming that Qole feels the same as I do. She's never . . ." I felt like squirming in my seat, suddenly as awkward as a child being asked to confess something unpleasant. "She's never said anything, either."

Nothing that spelled out what was in my heart, the words I'd almost spoken to her on the beach in Gamut:

I love you.

It almost seemed cruel for us to do so now. Qole knew what declaring myself king meant. I would be taunting myself, at least, if not her, with could-have-beens. There were still . . . paths . . . but none as perfect as they had once lay for us in my mind. None that might look appealing to Qole.

"Sounds to me like you're afraid of getting your heart broken," Telu said, hammering into my thoughts. "You do what you have to, just don't break *her* heart while you're at it, is all I'm saying."

"The voice of compassion, as always."

"Damn straight."

"And by the way, that was supposed to be a private conversation."

"Please. The old man wouldn't have stayed here if he hadn't intended for me to eavesdrop."

———

"Come in." Qole's voice was distracted after I knocked on the door to her quarters, and I saw why as I entered. She was engrossed in her infopad, and I knew she must have been reading communications from Alaxak on the QUIN. She was lying propped up on her bunk in a gray tank top and short bottoms that clung to her in a way that made something in my throat catch.

She didn't look up right away, raising a finger as she finished what she was reading. There was a time when Qole would have been startled at me being in her private quarters, but over the past month it had become a thing of comfortable regularity, and for a second she had slipped back into that place. I wished I could have.

I cleared my throat. "Do you have a minute?" Not that I knew what I wanted to say to her. Rather, I did—I *wanted* to tell her that I loved her and never wanted to be apart—but that was the opposite of what duty demanded I say. So I was more content to just hear her voice.

She glanced over and gave me a wry grin. "Exactly one minute. Starting now."

I settled onto the floor, leaning my back against the wall. "Oh good. Given that we are traveling through distorted spacetime as we speak, I will choose to interpret that as meaning I have infinite time."

"Even I know the Belarius Drive doesn't distort time, just space." Qole sat up on the bed and crossed her legs. "What distorts time is reading over supply lists and having people ask where I think they ought to be distributed after the attack."

I made a sympathetic noise. "My mother always said that being a leader is a glorious term for being the person everyone delegates to."

Qole snorted. "If things were getting delegated to me,

there would be at least some level of organization. The villages all mostly self-govern, but there are decisions the new governor would have made that no one really wants to make. And I'm the person they are asking. It's ridiculous. Hiat would be much better at this. I just can't risk giving him the power." She slumped, rubbing her forehead. "And I keep hearing . . . Well, I can't blasted focus."

I wasn't used to seeing Qole looking so small, so young. Her assurance was such that it was easy to forget her age. But the vacuum created by the uncertainty of others was filled so naturally by her decisiveness that I wondered if she would just give all of herself up, let herself slip away into nothingness, consumed by responsibility.

I wanted to sit by her, put my arm around her, find a way to give her some of my strength, but I knew I couldn't. I needed to prepare for the inevitable. To distance myself, as Devrak had instructed. Besides, Qole likely no longer wanted to be with the person I was now—not only royal, but the worst of them all, a king—and especially not in the limited capacity in which I was available to her. *If* she had ever wanted me wholly, before.

But then I was sitting next to her, my arm around her. I couldn't even remember deciding to do it. She sighed, her body relaxing against mine.

"I can't believe you need to go through another family ritual where you suffer pointlessly to prove something."

"Sounds like life," I grunted.

"Don't steal my words." I heard the smile in her voice.

"If I stole your words, they would be a lot angrier."

"Do you think I'm angry?"

I paused. "Well, I believe we're all keenly aware that you can get angry. But no, I don't think you're a fundamentally angry person. Angry people are looking for something to tear down. You only ever try to build up. You believe in a better future."

Qole shook her head, the movement of her hair distracting against my cheek. "No," she said quietly, "I just believe in what we have. That it's worth fighting for. I'm not sure things will get any better than that."

"They will." I hadn't intended for my tone to be so adamant. "Humanity wouldn't have survived after the Great Collapse if things couldn't get better. Unifier knows, the systems have been awash in the blood of warfare, but we've had relative peace for a hundred years. Things do get better."

Qole laughed. "How do you do that?"

"Do what?"

"Keep believing in something better despite all evidence." One of her fingers dug into my ribs.

"Well, that's just what you inspire in me." I tried to say it lightly, feeling awkward at how true it was.

She rested her head against my shoulder. "Great. Then we're both delusional."

Amid the worst chaos of my life, I somehow felt more at peace than I ever had. I knew I should get up, leave her side, go out the door that would set us on our separate paths, with our separate burdens.

I didn't move. I could think of no better weight on my shoulder than hers.

———

I only realized I had fallen asleep when I woke up. The gentle haptic touch of the new wrist-comm Devrak had given me informed me of his message. *Time to train.*

I blinked, trying to clear the fog out of my brain. I must

have been in a deep sleep, something I hadn't experienced lately. It should have left me feeling better, but I only felt disoriented.

Qole was curled next to me, my arm around her. I gently extracted myself and drew a blanket over her, which she snuggled into without waking. Her face was relaxed, free of worry, and sinking down beside her to sleep for a week seemed like it would be the ultimate victory, the moment the Unifier had promised.

I turned away. I'd had my stolen moment. It was time to work.

———

Devrak was waiting for me in the hold, dressed only in black pants and a short-sleeved shirt. The hold was always cold, and I wondered how he wasn't freezing.

In one hand, he held a similar set of clothing, which he tossed to me.

"Get dressed," he instructed.

I raised an eyebrow. "Here? Trying to teach me a lesson in immodesty?"

"Preparedness." Devrak crossed his arms. "Who comes dressed in a coat and pants that thick to a training exercise? The time is coming where you will not be able to rely on others to be prepared. You will be alone in every decision you make. A failure to think ahead will simply become failure."

I fought to not roll my eyes as I changed. I had been trained to be a ruler since my earliest memories. I had been given every lesson, every example, for years. What could Devrak teach me in the next few days that would be useful?

His fist connected with my solar plexus as I turned, and I

doubled over, mouth open, trying desperately to wheeze. He stood and waited while I struggled, before I finally straightened.

"Okay, is this just beat-up-on-the-prince hour? I . . ."

His fist blurred for my stomach and I blocked it, then the next strike at my face, then four more so rapidly there was no thought, only movement. I danced backward from the onslaught and Devrak followed steadily.

"This is why you lost to Suvis. You are rooted in the past."

"What?" I desperately dodged a combination, attempted a snap-kick to drive him back, and was only tossed to the floor for my efforts.

"You are not a prince. You are a king. You gave up on your past life when you were exiled, and you never claimed a new one. What is your purpose? What do you fight for? Suvis knew exactly what he was after, and he achieved it."

I scrambled to my feet. "Suvis? Hold on, Devrak, I can't talk and fight. . . ."

"Fight and think, or talk and be beaten." Devrak pressed the attack without remorse.

I blocked, feinting, and moved backward in an attempt to catch my breath. *Breathe.* I calmed myself, and as I did so, it became obvious I could block most everything with relative ease as long as I stayed on the defensive, always moving. "Suvis was a Bladeguard. He's older than me, but I remember him. Was he one of the ones I attacked in the citadel? Was that why he was willing to assassinate me?" Guilt surged in me, which I hated. Suvis was not someone I should feel sympathy for; he was a murderer.

Devrak shook his head, never relenting, his assault steady. "No, those Bladeguards are all dead." I wondered if he intended for me to feel as wretched as I did at that. "Suvis was sent on a black-ops mission that went awry. He disappeared, assumed dead, only to reappear over a year later. He claimed to have been taken by slavers on a privateer vessel before escaping. But he was different, afterward." He stopped, regret creasing his face. "He should never have been given a health clearance. But your sister insisted he be her personal guard."

I remembered the strange way Suvis fought, and saw my opportunity, driving myself forward, knee first.

Devrak blocked it with both hands, sliding backward, happiness lighting his eyes.

"Yes! Defend, distract, find the opening. You're still a quick study."

I wiped my brow, grinning at the praise. It had been a long time since I'd felt successful at anything. "Why, thank you."

"You're welcome." Devrak grinned back, his teeth flashing. "And you still have a lot to learn."

XI

BASRA CAME UP WITH A NEAT PLAN TO GAIN ENTRANCE TO AALTOS.

He made some comms over the QUIN, and then we stopped off at a trading station in the darkest depths of the Dracorte system, far from any smaller planetary subsystems. It hadn't always been so remote, as a once-teeming hub near one of the intergalactic portals that was now only a floating ruin. Four hundred years ago, the portals had connected different systems of our galaxy together using instantaneous transportation, technology that no one fully understood after it catastrophically malfunctioned and vanished in the Great Collapse. Since then, Belarius Drives took us where we needed to go using faster-than-light flight. But they couldn't take us everywhere.

The portals had not only interlinked our galaxy, but they had once connected us to other galaxies, each one as big and complex as ours, with many different systems, planetary sub-systems, and peoples. The Belarius Drive couldn't travel that far, not in human lifetimes. Entire galaxies had been lost to us, and now only the skeleton of such wondrous gateways remained. The ruin stretched longer than the station, even if it was only made up of empty girders as thick as skyscrapers.

The station itself was a multi-tiered conical complex that spun slowly around a central axis, each level meant for a different type of trade. Once largely abandoned after the collapse of the portals, its remoteness now served it well, since smugglers and black-market dealers had moved in. We fueled up in one section of the city-sized station, and then headed to another that, even from the outside, looked decidedly seedier. A steady flow of ramshackle hulks that barely looked fit for flight was swarming in and out like insects from a nest.

We didn't stay long, because, in no time, Basra managed to secure new identification records for the crew and new registration files for the ship—all forgeries, of course—completely covering any digital trail that could link us to Alaxak. The cost must have been astronomical, because the quality was high enough that the documents would stand up to official scrutiny. To complete the picture in a more tangible way, he also bought an entire load of black-market cargo, with which we filled the hold.

There was something fittingly ironic about smuggling in the rightful Dracorte king onto Aaltos with a load of illegally trafficked goods. If we drew suspicion, crime would be our cover story for a legitimate mission, rather than the other way around. Only Basra could have come up with something so twistedly brilliant and bewildering.

Despite the absurdity of our situation, the danger of getting caught was still real as we approached Aaltos. There might have been plenty of civilian traffic to hide us, but it was still a planet dominated by the military and all the protocol that involved. The ship comms were quiet, everyone seemingly taking turns holding their breath. Aaltos grew in the viewport, coming into focus like the features of a fast-approaching stranger whose intentions were yet unclear—friend, foe, or entirely disinterested?

If planetary security found out who we really were, they would be much too interested.

The planet's face was gray and lined—rocky canyons, Nev had told me, carving deeper than any I had ever seen between winding chains of mountains. The elevation varied so much in places that it was easily discernible from space. It seemed a harsh planet on which to live, especially with the higher gravity. Which was part of the reason it made an excellent military training ground.

I was shocked when we were approved to enter the atmosphere without incident or delay, though perhaps I shouldn't have been. Not even Devrak had been able to find anything to fault in our new, forged identities. I brought the *Kaitan* down at a quieter shipping spaceport just outside the capital, AS-01, a name that told of the planet's functional history, the letters standing for "Aaltos Settlement."

"Can we . . . *not* sell this?" Nev murmured, grunting as he set down a crate. "I probably banned some of this stuff myself."

"You expect the captain and me to miss out on a profit because of your qualms?" Basra asked, without bothering to look up from his infopad. "You chose your own mode of transport, *Your Majesty.*"

Arjan was grinning, probably over the fact that Basra, at least, could still put Nev in his place. Basra and my brother were exchanging smiles and covert glances more and more, a sight that filled me with happiness. I managed to keep a straight face.

Soon, a woman, one of Basra's hundreds, if not thousands, of contacts through his role as Hersius Kartolus, who looked surprisingly prim and proper rather than shady, met us to begin arranging the selling of our goods. She moved easily in the heavy air, unlike the rest of us. Once Basra gave her some instructions, we left the cargo in her hands. I chose Telu to stay with the ship, where she would be able to send or receive messages through encrypted channels, in case of an emergency.

"I had to stay on the ship last time you guys got to explore a new planet," Telu groused.

"Yeah, and I lost an eye when we did, so don't feel too bad," Arjan snapped back.

Maybe I should have ordered Arjan to remain on the *Kaitan,* but I didn't think he would stay put.

A hired shuttle took the rest of us into the city, more specifically to the Dracorte Military Headquarters, which included both a base and an enormous academy. The city rose gray and striking all around us, reflective steel buildings towering to mirror the stormy sky. If the capital of Nev's homeworld, Dracorva, had looked as intricate and beautiful as frost on a windowpane, AS-01 was as sleek and practical as the tempered glass beneath it.

Nev took my hand in the shuttle, causing me to start. I realized I'd been making a fist as I stared out the viewport, my breath getting shallower. Across from me, Arjan's jaw was tight as he peered outside too. As he'd reminded Telu, things hadn't gone so well for us last time we were in a major Dracorte city. Not only had Arjan lost pieces of himself, we'd all nearly lost our lives and had to end many, many more. But maybe, with fewer frilly trappings than Dracorva, AS-01 wouldn't be hiding as many horrible surprises.

Even if that were the case, this situation was about to entirely depart from the realm of my control. I would no longer be able to protect the crew on my own. We'd placed all our trust in Devrak, I realized. At the slightest word from him, all of us would be arrested and quite possibly executed for treason. Even Nev.

I tried to assure myself that Devrak could have done that multiple times already. There would be no reason for him to wait until now if that had been his intention, aside from dramatic flair, and he didn't strike me as the dramatic type.

He directed our shuttle to a private back entrance to the main base headquarters, where we were stopped at a gate. I definitely held my breath, because if we didn't make it to the highest levels of authority before being discovered, then those lower down might report us to the wrong people. At least Nev was wearing a small device clipped inside his jacket that masked his true biometric signal by transmitting a false one, so he shouldn't set off any alarms. Devrak handed over all our ID chips—his real, ours fake.

The guard on duty barely glanced at ours, but he sure stared at Devrak's, then blinked at the man himself. "Right this way, sir. Proceed to sector A, and I'll inform—"

"General Talia," Devrak finished for him—an order, rather than a suggestion. He was leaving nothing to chance. "I would like to meet with her and General Gavros in private."

———

My unease wasn't alleviated when we were led on foot through several pairs of high-security checkpoints and down long, smooth hallways, into a room with a thick door. Anything this sterile gave me flashbacks to both the Treznor and Dracorte laboratories where royals had tried to dissect me and *had* cut into Arjan. Windows lined the room, the reflective kind that didn't let you see out, only let observers see in. The only furnishings were a steel table and chairs, all seamlessly attached to the floor, perhaps to prevent someone from trying to break the windows with them . . . as if people were often kept here against their will.

Devrak announcing his departure at the door *really* didn't help.

"I'll be back as soon as possible, but likely only for you, at first," he said to Nev. He had been careful not to use Nev's name or title yet, or to give any other indication of who he might be.

Nev didn't seem alarmed by our accommodations. He only nodded before Devrak left and the door sealed behind him. This must have been routine procedure or something. But Basra leaned against the table, arms folded, not looking happy about being locked in here, and neither Arjan nor I could keep still.

It took less than an hour before Devrak came back, but in that time, both Nev and Basra had tried to stop me and Arjan from pacing by catching our respective hands. And yet, when the door slid open, it wasn't *only* my brother and me who betrayed our nervousness. All four of us spun or leapt up.

Devrak wasn't alone. A dark, cynical part of me expected guards with photon rifles, or maybe even Bladeguards, to be accompanying him. But when he stepped aside, he revealed the last person I could have imagined.

Marsius Dracorte III was short enough to hide behind Devrak's back because he was only eleven years old—and barely eleven, at that. Nev had only recently remarked, bitter-sweet, on the passing of his little brother's birthday. Marsius peered into the room around Devrak, hesitant. His eyes widened when they caught sight of Nev, and even with Nev's disguise, Marsius's eyes immediately began to fill with tears.

"Marsius," Nev said, choked. When the boy didn't move, he added, "It's me. Devrak, can I get rid of this?" He waved at his face. Devrak had barely nodded before Nev was already fishing out his contacts and popping his features back into perfect shape. His beautiful face blanched when Marsius only glanced back and forth between it and Devrak. "I didn't . . . I promise it wasn't me. . . ."

"He has already heard as much," Devrak said quickly, when Marsius still didn't seem able to speak. "I just explained everything to an assembled panel of generals, and Marsius was in attendance. They now want to hear it from your lips, but first, I thought . . ." He looked down at Marsius, his forehead creasing in concern.

I was looking at Nev the same way. One harsh word from Marsius could break him; I knew it. I desperately wanted to take *his* hand now to comfort *him,* but I waited. We all did. The silence stretched another painful moment.

"You"—Nev swallowed—"you don't believe I killed them, right, Marsius?"

The boy's lips trembled, and then he was hurtling around Devrak and through the door. Nev opened his arms as his little brother flew into him, and it wasn't long before Marsius's strangled sobs echoed through the room, muffled in Nev's neck.

"Shh, I've got you," Nev murmured, eyes closed. He stroked Marsius's hair, rocking him slightly back and forth.

Marsius tried to talk, but all I heard was a jumble of "Sol

said it was you, but—Mother and Father—and then you were gone too—" between the gasps and sobs.

I swallowed the lump in my throat and looked away, blinking. The boy had lost his parents, and had lived until now thinking his own brother, his hero, had been responsible ... when it had really been his sister. My fists clenched. I didn't think it was possible for me to hate Solara any more than I already did, but I was wrong.

I heard a voice: "No."

It was Nev's. I turned back to him, but his eyes were still closed and he was murmuring to Marsius, "I'm here for you now. I'm here."

I did a quick check for any visual hallucinations. For a split second, I thought I saw a dark outline of a person standing in the window's reflection, near where Nev would be, but then I blinked, and it was gone.

Luckily everyone was too focused on Marsius to notice any strangeness in my behavior. When my gaze returned to them, Nev was standing, surreptitiously wiping his own eyes with one hand, the other holding his brother to his side. Marsius's face was red and splotchy, and he dragged the sleeve of his deep-blue uniform, military cut, across his nose. They were an endearing likeness of each other, separated only by years and responsibility.

"I believe you know at least Qole and Arjan," Nev said, squeezing his shoulder. "This is Basra, Marsius, a good friend of ours."

Marsius blinked his shiny silver-gray eyes and looked at our little group with uncertainty. The three of us probably weren't the most comforting sight.

"Hello," Basra said in return, his tone oddly tentative, for him. His expression was even more unusual—mildly perplexed

215

and maybe even reluctant, as if Marsius were a potential buyer to whom he had no idea how to make a pitch.

I could guess why. Marsius had heard *Nev* wasn't responsible for any of his heartbreak, but the last time we'd seen him in Dracorva, we'd left parts of his home in smoking ruins. Basra had also single-handedly threatened to financially ruin his family. I couldn't imagine what Solara had told the boy about us. Like Basra, I waited for Marsius to make the first move, so I could follow his lead. And Arjan, I imagined, had no desire to indulge a member of the royal family who'd hurt him, no matter how young or innocent the kid was.

Or maybe I was wrong.

Arjan rolled his eyes, muttering, "Ancestors' sake, you two," and extended his hand to Marsius. He hadn't spoken to me in that warm, chiding tone in ages, and I'd never heard him use it with Basra. A lot louder, he said, "Hey, kid, I missed you."

Nev's brother went right for him. Instead of simply taking Marsius's hand, Arjan seized him in a one-armed hug, clapping him heartily on the back, and even lightly slugged him on the shoulder afterward. Devrak tensed, but it drew a startled laugh from the boy who'd just been crying his eyes out.

Basra and I exchanged a glance, probably looking similarly sheepish and relieved. Maybe it was just that neither of us knew how to act around children. Nev caught the look between us and swallowed a laugh behind his hand.

"You're taller already!" Arjan exclaimed to Marsius. "You'll be old enough to come Shadow fish with us in no time."

"*Could* I?" Marsius said.

"Of course," Arjan replied, without even pretending to defer the question to Nev or Devrak.

Ancestors, he was good. Perhaps I shouldn't have been surprised. Arjan was an older brother, like Nev, and had grown up with me to care for. As the youngest in my family, I'd never been around many kids. Perhaps Basra hadn't, either—a thought that made me wonder for the hundredth time what his childhood had been like, and how he'd ended up here in this room on Aaltos with me and my brother.

"Did you practice those knife tricks I taught you?" Arjan continued, as if it were the most natural thing in the world to converse with eleven-year-olds. About knives, no less.

"Yes! But, hey, what happened to your eye?"

Arjan glanced at Nev. "It was an accident, but I'm fine now. Honestly, I think the eye patch is pretty swift." He even used the slang that younger kids were using on Alaxak. "What do you think?"

"Swift, yeah," said Marsius, trying out the word.

The kid, at least for now, didn't need to know his dead father had been something of a monster. Nev didn't hide the appreciation in his eyes when he nodded at Arjan behind Marsius's back.

This relatively private visit from his little brother had probably been a gift from Devrak. But it was because of Arjan that Nev could see him *happy* again this soon. Nev's expression was so soft, I could see that too was a gift without measure. I knew Arjan had done it for Marsius, not Nev, but still, there might be hope for this crew yet.

Except, of course, Nev wasn't my crew anymore. He was a king, and he was about to go declare himself so to a pack of generals.

As if remembering himself, Devrak cleared his throat. "I'm sorry for how brief this reunion must be, Your Majesty, but we must depart. Marsius, you can at least accompany us to watch the trial."

"I don't want to just watch. I can testify, I can—"

"Trial?" I said, interrupting Marsius without meaning to. "You mean Nev still has to prove his innocence, even *before* the Forging thing he has to do afterward to make everyone happy?"

"Your concern is touching, Miss Uvgamut," Devrak responded sincerely, "but it's a matter of protocol . . . something His Majesty must undergo."

"And what about us?" Arjan asked, keeping his tone in check—again, probably only for Marsius's sake. "We can't come?"

I imagined it was more out of discomfort at being locked in this room or maybe mistrust for what Nev might say about us, rather than a show of support.

"Yes, Devrak, why wouldn't they be able to come too?" Marsius asked, clearing his throat to make his voice deeper and more even. The change in him already was astonishing.

"Perhaps they can meet us at the trial in a short while, Your Highness," Devrak said to the boy. His tone grew gentle in a way I hadn't yet heard. "But Nevarian needs to speak for himself first. The others can join us after that."

Nev frowned, mirroring my own expression. "But they surely needn't stay in *here* in the meantime."

Devrak blinked. "Of course not. Not anymore. I'll have someone show the three of them to our guest quarters."

"I could have shown you if I weren't going to the trial," Marsius said confidently, and then added, apologetic, "Not that the rooms are very nice, but they're better than this." He obviously had no clue where we'd just come from.

Basra's voice was quiet, but it carried. "Since we're all acknowledging whom Nev is now, I don't think I need to remind *anyone* that Qole is his critical ally as the leader of Alaxak, not a common guest."

The words were careful, but they were nonetheless a warning meant for Devrak's ears. I didn't want any special attention, but still, I was absurdly grateful to have someone looking out for me.

While Marsius might have been young, he wasn't stupid by any stretch, and his eyebrows scrunched at the sudden shift in atmosphere.

Devrak looked both embarrassed and slightly beleaguered. "A reminder isn't necessary, no, but this is a military base, and all quarters are appointed in a similar . . . utilitarian . . . style. I'll be sure to give word that you're all to be treated with the best we have to offer."

Basra shrugged. "That's all I wanted." *The best,* he meant. He waved a hand at the door, as if he were in charge here. "Carry on."

Arjan and I met each other's eyes. Maybe it was the stress, or the endless absurdity of our situation, but I could tell we were both ready to burst out laughing.

And then, for a moment, I loved them all so much it hurt: Arjan, Basra, Telu—I couldn't think about Eton, because it hurt too much in a different way—and Nev, most definitely Nev. They were all my family, if not my crew. And, hell, if my crew could include my impossible brother and one of the richest people in the galaxy, why not a king?

Whatever Arjan and I were feeling, it was good we held it in, because it wouldn't have lent Basra's assertions much credit. I was supposed to look the part of a world leader, facing the king of *many* worlds. I managed to meet Nev's eyes with the right amount of soberness, if only when I remembered where he was going.

Nev, for his part, took me in with his gaze, as if this were the last time he might see me. I hoped with all my heart that

that wouldn't be the case. Even so, I had to resist the urge to hold on to him, no matter who was watching, just like I'd had to resist laughing a moment ago.

Even Shadow didn't make me feel as unstable as Nev did.

But before I knew what was happening, Nev took three powerful strides across the room, seized my face with both hands, and drew my lips to his. I forgot everyone then, and even my own craziness. The world shrank to his mouth on mine, until he pulled away. When he did, I had to steady myself on his arms, blink to regain my focus. Basra characteristically appeared unmoved, Arjan was staring at his toes in embarrassment, Marsius was grinning enthusiastically, and Devrak . . .

Devrak didn't look happy. But I didn't care.

"Make it work," I said to Nev, a little breathless.

A wince flickered across his face, and I wondered if he'd read something else into my words. But when he responded, his voice was steady. "I'll try my hardest." He backed away, his hand trailing mine for a lingering moment, and then he was out the door with Devrak, Marsius on his heels.

———

As Devrak had promised, guards—*without* their photon rifles at the ready—directed us to spacious, if simple, rooms shortly after that. They were merely doing their duty and filling in where there would have been servants in a place like the Dracorte citadel. So I was relieved when, unlike servants, they left me by myself in front of one room and both Arjan and Basra by another, at the latter's insistence. He obviously wasn't bothered by anyone knowing he and my brother were together, and Arjan was happy to join him. I might not have wanted guards or servants around, but I felt a pang to face my own door alone, after seeing them vanish inside together.

If I'd hoped for strangers to let me be for long, though, I was disappointed. A firm knock sounded throughout my apartment after I'd barely had time to take a quick shower. I'd been pleased to discover there were showers instead of ridiculously oceanic bathtubs like there had been on Luvos.

I opened the door with wet hair and only a towel wrapped around me. A woman stood outside, slightly taken aback.

I blinked right back at her. I had no idea who she was, but she was wearing a well-decorated blue military uniform and was carrying a garment bag folded over one arm, her hair pulled up into a tight golden bun.

She regained her composure and held out her hand. "Miss Uvgamut, I'm General Talia. His Majesty is finishing up with the others, but Devrak took me aside to mention that you may have arrived without proper attire."

It took me a few seconds to realize what she'd said, because I was too busy noticing she'd called Nev *His Majesty*—which meant they believed him.

But then my mind caught up. "*What?* You brought me something to wear?"

"Oh good," she said, letting herself in. "You *are* about my size."

"Thanks, but . . ."

She took in my offended tone, my wet hair, and my clothes discarded in a pile next to the washroom door. "Let me be blunt, Miss Uvgamut. Clothes are like armor to a Dracorte, and your measure taken from them. Forgive me if Devrak thought you might wish to feel more at ease in this regard, or if I cared enough to come in person to guarantee it. After all, I

221

should be listening to His Majesty speak on both his behalf and yours at this very moment."

"Then why *did* you come?" I asked, gathering my towel self-consciously around me. "Why *do* you care?"

"Because I already believe His Majesty and what he has to say about you. And I know what it feels like to be a woman in a room mostly full of men, with every single one of them taking your measure with their eyes." She held out the garment bag.

"Oh," I said, forgetting everything I had been about to say. "Well. Thank you."

I took the bag from her. She didn't seem to be going anywhere, so I unzipped it right there.

I was expecting some showy gown, like the one Solara had stuffed me in on Luvos, but instead there was a sharply cut black jacket over a narrow knee-length dress. It was almost like a military uniform in its simplicity, but elegant enough for a diplomatic envoy. She lifted the black leather boots she'd been holding under the garment bag. They were sleek and shiny, similar to my old pair in name only, and an exact fit for the dress.

"Huh," I said. "This is kind of perfect."

"I thought it would be."

It suddenly occurred to me that she and Jerra might like each other. I had to swallow yet another laugh at the absurd thought. Talk about worlds colliding.

"I can also put your hair in a twist," she offered casually, as if she did this every day as a general. "Neat, nothing flashy."

Great Collapse, what all had Devrak told her? That not only were my clothes hopeless, but my hair was too?

"No, thank you." My usual braid would be just fine.

At least I knew she wouldn't try to put any makeup on me, because she didn't wear any herself. I hadn't minded it, exactly, when I'd worn it once in the Dracorte citadel, but it had made me look like someone I wasn't. Talia didn't seem to want that. She wanted me to look like myself, just in different clothes. And I was surprisingly grateful.

———

After I was dressed, and my long black hair was back in its braid, I followed General Talia down the stretching, plain halls into something resembling a courtroom. The boots were too tight, so I was a mixture of relieved and nervous to finally make my way inside the high double doors. The room was huge, carpeted in deep blue and lined with flowing silver benches, but it was only dimly lit along the floating shelf-edge of the ceiling, casting an almost sinister glow over the faces arranged in a line at the end.

Nev and Devrak stood before the long table of uniformed men, with a scattering of witnesses filling the benches behind them. Both had washed and changed as well, Devrak into a blue suit like so many others here, and Nev into something similar, but with a silver sash overlaying the top, a black cape draped over one shoulder, and a thin circlet on his brow. It was probably the best they could do for kingly attire. He didn't turn; he hadn't heard me enter.

General Talia left me in the aisle between benches to go take her place up front. Not every seat was filled at the table, so her absence hadn't been glaringly obvious. I wondered who was missing from the group, and why.

Solara was probably the why.

I was relieved to spot Arjan and Basra on the benches toward the back, so I didn't have to venture any farther into the room. Arjan had worn his same clothes, likely in a stubborn statement, but Basra . . . Basra was in a sleek dress, with eyes and lips lined in a lush reddish purple, brown crest of hair in a sleek wave along one side of her face. *She* was definitely female at the moment.

I sat next to her and leaned over self-consciously, keeping my voice quiet. "You got to dress up too?" Not that I was surprised; she seemed reluctant to pass up the opportunity during a formal occasion. "Who loaned you *that?*"

Her dress was significantly fancier than mine, a sleeveless silky green sheath that showed off her coppery shoulders, now strong and squared instead of in their usual indifferent slouch.

"Excuse me," Basra whispered in mock offense, "this is *mine.*"

She must have had it in her bag or sent for it from the *Kaitan.* Of course she would have a gown, or maybe fifty, on board. I'd seen Basra in a dress more often than the crew saw me in one. Arjan stifled a smile, unselfconsciously seated with his thigh along hers, her hand clasped possessively in his lap.

Again, I was happy for the improvement between them, but I had to swallow a twinge of jealousy as I looked up to watch the proceedings.

It seemed they were just wrapping up. A man with silver-streaked dark hair leaned over an infopad, and his voice rang in the room, artificially amplified.

"So we have an agreement, then, Your Majesty. We will fully back your claim against your younger sister, Solara Dracorte, based on the strong evidence provided that you did not commit regicide against the late King Thelarus and Queen Ysandrei, and that she in fact did, thus nullifying her own claim

224

to the throne according to statute 311Z. We will also support granting Alaxak's sovereignty, with the understanding that we will maintain strong political and economic ties."

He cleared his throat, and Nev bowed his head, looking anything but triumphant for some reason. My nervousness grew as the man continued:

"And in return, Your Majesty will immediately complete the Dracorte Forging in a manner satisfactory to this panel. You will then swear to do everything in your power to end your sister's unjust reign as soon as possible. And finally"—the words fell like a sword—"you will, with the utmost urgency and under our advisement, find the most advantageous match for a queen, preferably one that binds the Dracorte name to another royal family's. With civil war upon us, now is not the time to be concerned about weakening bloodlines. It's about strengthening our chances of survival."

It took me a second to process what he'd said under all the official language. Devrak put a hand on Nev's back, as if pushing him forward.

Nev nodded slowly, oblivious to the fact that my heart was shattering in the silence behind him.

Both Basra and Arjan were casting sideways glances at me, but I didn't look back at them, refusing to let my face show what I felt.

I knew this was politics, but that didn't ease the piercing sting in my chest, the ache like I couldn't breathe. It didn't calm the rising fury, at Nev, at myself. He should have spoken to me first in private, but I also shouldn't have left myself vulnerable.

We were a lost cause. This was the inevitable conclusion, and I should have seen it coming.

But the man seemed to believe there was reason to doubt.

"Do you agree that such a match *should* solidify and

increase your standing in the systems against the usurper, So-lara," he pressed, "that we *need* the support of the other families to succeed, and that you *will* take our recommendations for a queen under strong consideration—Princess Xiaolan Daiyen being top among them? Do we have your binding word as King Nevarian Thelarus Axandar Rubion Dracorte?"

Nev let out a deep breath that he seemed to have been holding. "You do. I swear it, by my blood and my throne, in my name and the Great Unifier's."

Even though he was facing his generals and not me, he might as well have been speaking the truth that he'd been try-ing to communicate to me earlier, with his desperate kiss, his longing eyes, and his sliding grip. The word that was the last thing I'd wanted to hear, and so I'd been foolishly pretending that he hadn't been saying it, like another hallucination:

Good-bye.

I slipped away from Arjan and Basra, leaving the room be-fore Nev could turn around and see that I had been there at all.

XII

NEV

I SAT UP IN BED, SWEATING. AFTER ALL THESE WEEKS, IT WAS THE SAME thing that replayed in my dreams. Eton and the young guard grappling during our escape from the Dracorte citadel, just before Eton had taken off most of his skull with a single shot.

I pinched just below my eyebrows, trying to wake up. I hadn't even been the one to kill him, but my mind couldn't let it go. He had been doing his job as best he could, thinking he was serving a good cause. Now he was gone. Witnessing his death had been the first time I'd grasped the true weight of the price that others would be paying for my choices. I'd been told such a thing my entire life, but all my intellectual understanding had evaporated when exposed to experience.

I climbed out of my bed, which, after the *Kaitan,* was so comfortable I found myself having trouble sleeping in it, and padded across the thick carpet to the window that overlooked the Aaltos military complex. In the dark, the pulsing veins of flight paths streamed between towers garrisoning thousands of troops, and in the distance, I could see the gouges in the earth that belonged to Irgath, the deepest canyon on Aaltos. In the night, they looked like black cracks. But they were many miles wide, and thousands of feet below the surface lay the valleys where agriculture was still the primary way of life, cradling a culture that had started after the Great Collapse had wiped out contact with civilization. The heavier gravity here made for sturdier stock, with regard to both crops and human populations, and so the people were prime targets for military recruiters.

For the first time in my life, I wondered if they would be happier had they been left alone. Now, if we went to war, those families would send their children, children who would be just as eager to do their duty as the young guard in my dreams.

Ever since leaving Luvos, I had lost all desire to be a ruler. What I was doing now felt like necessity, and returning here didn't feel like coming home, but revisiting a graveyard of hopes and dreams that had belonged to a different person, a different life. The last time I had stood, viewing the traditional domains of my family, my father had stood behind me, encouraging me to give up Qole. Now I was facing a test. If I succeeded, I still had to give up Qole and take my people into a civil war.

I glanced back at the bed with an irrational hope that I would see her there, her black hair sprawled across a pillow. A hope for a reality that I was supposed to abandon but couldn't stop imagining.

Instead, my black-and-gray combat suit had been laid out

beside the bed. Dawn was touching the darkness, and it was time to get ready for my Forging.

———

Something about the woman inspecting me was unsettling, but I couldn't place it.

The top of her head just reached my shoulder, but she was built in the sturdy manner that indicated she was a native of Aaltos. All that was really visible as she examined my wrists and waistband for any hidden items was a shock of white hair. Dressed in the plain khaki jumpsuit of the countless orderlies that inhabited military installations, she was missing any indication of rank on her shoulders.

I had taken a mag-rail from headquarters that had dropped me steadily under the surface of the planet. Now we were in a cavernous stone space. An ancient light fixture in the ceiling illuminated a set of doors at the opposite end. Heavy, tall, and bound with iron, they were relics of another age. After the Great Collapse, before the Belarius Drive connected planets, the humans on Aaltos had built a latticework of trails and tunnels to reach up from the deep canyons, especially Irgath, to facilitate trade and the transport of food. This would have been one of the largest of those.

"What's your name?" I asked her, wondering why she had no identifiers.

"Not important," she said dismissively, patting down my torso.

She was checking me for illicit items that might give me an edge in the challenges ahead, which I found vaguely amusing. "I'm not sure what you think you'll find. Hard to prepare when I don't know what I'll face."

"Like life, you mean?" She grinned and stepped back, wiping her hands in a show of being finished. She didn't seem nearly as old as her hair would suggest, her open face lined more by weather than age. "Just doing my job."

I nodded. "Far be it from me to stop anyone from doing that."

"No? Weren't the guards you killed doing theirs?"

The question took me off balance. I had faced variants of it multiple times, but now that the trial was complete, I had assumed subordinates would return to treating me with the kind of respect and deference afforded to royalty.

Apparently not.

"I gave the guards a choice to abandon their duty in favor of what they knew to be right."

"Are you fighting Solara out of a sense of duty or rightness now?"

I almost ignored the question and told her to be about her business, but exhaustion gnawed at my bones ... and fear. I hated admitting I was afraid in halls that should belong to me, but so much depended on me that my fear, at least, was impossible to ignore.

Admitting it helped me bite back the words. If I was afraid, in a position of privilege even now, then how would someone feel who had to follow a potentially unstable leader?

"Both. It's my duty, and citizens' rights are being trampled, so it's right to defend them," I explained. "Given the context, my actions are both morally and lawfully grounded."

"True." The orderly tilted her head, bright amber eyes on mine. "But citizens' rights are trampled every day and no one bothers to do anything. Tell me the real reason you fought for Arjan then, and Alaxak now."

Everyone kept questioning my motives, as though I had secrets within secrets. A flash of irritation shot through me. *Pretty sure I have fewer secrets than anyone I know.* She wanted plain talk? Fine.

"It's simple. I wouldn't have been able to live with myself if I hadn't taken action."

"I see." She rubbed her thumb and forefinger together, examining a nonexistent mote between them. "I wouldn't have taken you for a moral narcissist."

"Excuse me?" I narrowed my eyes. "What do you mean?"

"I mean, do you think of morality in terms of how it makes you feel, or how the consequences of your actions affect others?"

Not only had my own father put that question to me back in Dracorva, I had asked myself the same many times, going over it in my head so often it felt like I was a planet locked in an eternal orbit, the end to which would only be eventual destruction. Father had often mentioned the *greater good,* but what was the greater good? Stability of the system? Saving as many lives as possible? Or was it sacrificing either stability or lives—or both?—in a way that would benefit others later? Qole, the only person to whom I might have spoken about it, had no doubt in her mind that breaking Arjan out of the citadel had been the right thing to do, and that challenging Solara now was, too. At least, I assumed so. It wasn't that I doubted our actions myself, but for some reason, that surety gave me little peace lately.

In the end, it all made me very weary. I could debate morality with the best of them, but I couldn't summon the enthusiasm now. So I shook my head.

"I do what I can, when I can. But if I see an injustice that my family caused, then I should be the one who rights it. How do you think I should have acted?" I paused. Maybe someone as outspoken as she was would have something new to say. "What would you have done?"

"Doesn't matter, I wasn't there. And we make our choices alone." She shrugged and gave me the circular benediction of a priest of the Unifier. "I pronounce you clean and ready for the Forging. I'll open the door."

The motion pulled back the sleeve on her jacket, and the gold bracelet with the three interlocking circles symbolizing the Unifier flashed on her arm.

My eyes widened. "You're a priestess?" As far as I knew, there weren't any priestesses in the branch of the Unifier's Faith practiced in the Dracorte system; female clergy members weren't forbidden, exactly, but it wasn't accepted. Other families and systems had other practices, which was cause for endless debate and rancor.

She walked to the control panel embedded by the door and held her hand up to it for a moment, and something large inside the stone walls shifted. "I am. My position has existed for as long as people have been on Aaltos. I am here to provide a different point of view on the Forging."

The Forging had already begun, apparently. This little exercise was part of it.

"And what does the Church think of my actions?" I had wanted to ask the question since leaving Luvos.

"I don't speak for the Church, Prince, any more than you speak for your people," the priestess said, not unkindly, as though disabusing a child of a favorite notion. "I do know we are unified in self-sacrifice, not sacrificing one another. And as for politics"—she snorted—"pah, what business is that of the Church?"

"The morality of government is of paramount importance," I countered, somewhat shocked by her words.

She laughed outright. "Government is the sum of individuals, and you can't legislate yourself into being a good person, I'm afraid."

I had hoped for something that would fortify me for whatever lay ahead, or let me cast away any doubts in setting aside the old in favor of the new. Her answer left me feeling as muddled as before.

I stepped for the door. As I advanced, it rose, until I stood at the entrance, trying to discern the way ahead. Beyond it, there was no light, no visible path.

I looked at the priestess and raised my eyebrow. "Any tips?"

"Don't do anything stupid."

"Worth a shot." I shrugged and stepped into the darkness beyond. The door behind me closed, and the floor began to drop.

———

In the dark, the descent felt eternal, so long that apprehension turned to boredom. If I hadn't been used to working on the *Kaitan,* I would have stumbled from surprise when the motion finally stopped and a door groaned open in front of me.

I stepped out onto a bed of scree. It dipped into a rolling valley, the shadows startling with cold, the distant sunlight both inviting and blinding. A valley stretched away for several klicks before rising again, the trees giving way to grass, then back to trees that did their best to scale cliffs stretching higher than imagination permitted. There was a patchwork of farmland in the center of the valley, split by a shining ribbon of a river that encircled a tiny walled village. This was clearly Irgath, home to a way of life far removed from the concerns of royals. The only noise was the distant roar of wind in the cliffs above.

Arranged in a semicircle directly in front of me were five people in black suits identical to mine. I stopped, regarding them warily. It seemed unlikely that I would be sent here to make friends.

They ignored me, hunched around an infopad, arguing. I approached cautiously, still roundly ignored.

"If we can get to a communications array, we can call in a fleet." A woman with a face like a collection of knives was speaking.

A much-too-handsome man shook his head. "There's no time. There's a shuttle in the village. I say we take that, use it to infiltrate the docks."

I cleared my throat. "Ahem. What, exactly, seems to be going on?"

I received a series of impatient looks. "You're late," Tall, Dark, and Handsome said testily.

"Am I?" Several things had become immediately clear: we were expected to fulfill a mission, there was no designated leader, and he clearly was hoping to receive that designation. I left the posturing to him. "Apologies, I took a few moments to discuss philosophy."

As he processed this, I glanced at the infopad. Its contents made me blink. It showed a readout of Aaltos construction docks. But there *were* no construction docks in orbit above Aaltos, and the ones in the readout looked exactly like those on Valtai. Solara's new fleet.

"I take it we're supposed to find a way to sabotage that operation," I said, as nonchalantly as I could muster. I was unsettled to see so close an approximation of our actual battle plans.

"We have a small window of time to neutralize it." The

woman sketched out a few lines, showing where we were. "How is up to us."

Ground-to-vacuum operations weren't unusual but were typically undertaken with a great deal more equipment than we had. Handsome's plan sounded like the most expeditious.

"So, shuttle, orbit, success," I said, unable to keep the sarcasm at bay. "No possible complications."

The woman's lips twitched in approximation of either a frown or a smile. "We need to plan for complications, though. Starting with the fact that we need to gain access to the village, which was built at the height of post-Collapse turmoil. It has stone walls several times our height, and the entrance is monitored. If we're caught, they won't be giving the shuttle to us."

I frowned. "Wait, are these unsuspecting civilians down there? An actual village?"

The sharp-faced woman nodded. "These villages have been used in training exercises for centuries. It's an honor, and the reward is substantial."

"So . . . we need to avoid civilian casualties, then."

The woman shrugged. "I didn't say that. They will treat us the same as anyone, regardless. It's part of it."

"If they catch us, they'll regret it." One of the soldiers smiled.

"Dispensing regrets isn't the goal," I said, determined not to see how far these soldiers would go. "The goal is to get over the walls unseen, commandeer the shuttle, and be gone."

"Unseen? Floated over many walls, have you?"

My fingers flexed in muscle memory. "No, but I know my history. Fine as they were, the stonemasons of old Irgath did not build perfectly smooth walls."

A few uncertain glances were traded, but the woman nodded. "Worth a shot."

We didn't deliberate. Action decided, we moved quickly, each position determined, scouting and signaling to one another in silence until we found the section of wall we thought would be best. I had to admit, it felt good to be part of a team again. To know my role, and how to fulfill it. I hadn't felt such confidence since I'd boarded the *Kaitan.*

In a way, the moment I had met Qole had changed my understanding of the world and myself, made it less comprehensible. Nothing like a crisis of morals to shake your confidence. Perhaps the realization should have discomfited me, but instead, now I had a moment of surety: lessons learned had compensated for confidence lost.

We were professionals, trained at the highest level, myself even more so than my companions. So I wasn't surprised when, even in broad daylight, our presence went undetected. We didn't even slow when we approached the wall, looming above us, a dark shadow against the bright sunlight, its presence as intimidating as the increasing roar of the wind. The sharp-faced woman, who I learned was called Aris, crouched at the base of the wall, cupped her hands, and from a full run, I launched myself at her makeshift step. She lifted as I jumped, and my fingers latched onto the rough rock above.

My toes scrabbled, caught, and held on to crevices beneath me, even as I reached down, hand outstretched for the others.

There was no need to look. A strong hand grasped my wrist, and the moment I felt the pressure, I heaved. Then they were above me, grunting as they pulled themselves up to the upper ledge. I became a human link, channeling soldiers below into the peaceful world above. The last one reached down, grasped my aching arm, and hoisted me up onto the wall.

I crouched, wary of our exposed position, but there was nothing to fear—no one was there.

No one was on the wall. Nobody on the narrow paths between the tidy stone houses that barely reached the height of the walls. The realization began to sink into me, as I surveyed the village below, that it was deserted. The roar of the wind was stronger here, an eerie contrast to the emptiness of the streets below.

Cold pooled in my stomach; something wasn't right. I glanced at the others to see if they realized that our good fortune stretched credulity, but if they did, they gave no sign. They moved on, jumping to the nearest house and melting down the side of walls into the narrowest of alleyways when the distance became too great.

As I followed, I remembered my rooftop escape from Nirmana with Basra, a brush with another way of life, one so foreign from my own. I couldn't help but wonder about the lives of the people in the houses we passed.

As it turned out, the entire population of the village was crowded around the landing platform—the shuttle, in particular. But after a moment's reflection, I realized that it was a sizable gathering, yes, but it was almost entirely composed of either the very young or the very old. It was the village, but only a part. I drew up short, trying to understand. The cold in my stomach began to solidify into fear.

"Stand aside!" The handsome man of our group, Bentus, did not hesitate. He strode forward, power radiating as the crowd parted before him. "We're taking this shuttle."

"What?" A young boy remained in his path, uncertain in his defiance. "What do you mean . . . Ow!" he cried as Bentus's hand on his shoulder tossed him out of the way.

I still didn't say anything. It was clear that in just a few steps, we could be in the shuttle, in orbit, and perhaps on our way to a successful conclusion to these games. But this was a test, I was sure of it, a test that was using innocent people to see how I would react as a ruler.

The problem was, I had no idea.

"That's *enough.*" The voice was clarity, conviction embodied. For one elated moment, I thought Qole was here with us, and I looked up.

It wasn't Qole, but everything about her reminded me of Qole. The woman's youth was inconsequential next to the intensity of her eyes, her utter lack of fear in blocking our group. Purpose, not bravado, brought us to a halt.

"Whatever reason you're here," she said calmly, "it has to change. Everyone is in danger. If we don't all board the shuttle, we're going to die."

"What do you mean?" A strange surreality crept under my skin. Like the dreams that visited me at night, I was being forced to revisit what I couldn't change. "What's going to happen?"

"The dam"—the young woman enunciated each word like a chisel—"has burst."

My mouth went dry. "That's not wind," I said, almost a whisper. "Is it?"

There were many dams in these canyons, I knew, holding back enough water to make an inland sea.

She shook her head. "It's the Irgath River. It's far away, still, but it's coming. And when it does, nothing will be left."

"Then we need to go *now.*" One of the members of our group couldn't keep panic from fraying the edges of his voice. I couldn't blame him; the roar was ever present now, and I wondered if I would see a solid wall of water if I peered up the canyon.

"We can't! Not everyone is here!" the young woman shouted. "We're farmers, not soldiers on a training mission.

Most of us are out in the fields. I've sent people to warn them, and organized the rest to be ready when they get back. They won't be long, I promise."

"Then we'll send your pilot back to pick them up," snapped Bentus. "We're a little short on time to hold out for a pack of dirt-diggers."

"No." A thousand speeches were in the strength of her refusal. She slowly drew an ancient ion pistol from her belt, the chamber whining to life as she did so.

She was better than him in every way but one: force. With savage satisfaction, he kicked the weapon out of her hand, and his fist flew to her face.

And then my hand was on his wrist, my fingers white from pressure, stopping him. I couldn't remember deciding to, but there I was, staring into his outraged eyes.

I threw his arm aside, sending him staggering back several steps. "This is a *game* to us," I bit out, my voice uneven. "It's not to them. We wait."

His face purpled, but it was Aris who spoke. "It might be a game to you, Prince, but for us, it's our future. We need to succeed. We have people depending on us."

"I believe you." I stared her down. "But wanting to advance is not the same as wanting to survive."

There was a moment of silence as the two of them gathered to face me, arms in a fighting stance. The distant roar of unimaginable tons of water was the only backdrop, taunting me with the stupid insignificance of our standoff in the face of it. With my inability to change the future.

I barely had time to swear before they were on top of me. I brought my forearms up, blocking punches, my legs working frantically to give me ground and counter the kicks they sent my way. I tried to sink myself into the calm, invincible peace I had felt when I'd fought my own guards in my family's citadel. I reached for the surety that had guided my hands.

But I couldn't find it. I was in the same place, in a sense, in a position re-created by the very people who were supposed to serve me. And then I suddenly understood the test. Whoever was conducting the Forging wanted me to make different choices, to show how ruthless I could be, but not against my own soldiers. They wanted me to dismiss the villagers' peril and take the shuttle. Winning this tussle would mean I'd failed a clear test of my ability both to lead troops and to accomplish the necessary goal, whatever the cost. It would mean I'd fail the Forging. And failing the Forging meant losing everything. My ability to help Qole.

In a sick twist, I had to refuse to defend these people to continue defending her. But the only way to do so required killing the very thing that made me want to help her in the first place.

I found I wasn't capable. I wasn't filled with certainty or peace, but I knew that much.

They rushed me, and I twisted, watching a kick fly past. I felt a detached sort of pride in dodging the next serious attempts to bring me down, as routines born of endless drills came to life. I danced back, avoiding each strike. To the untrained eye, it would have been beyond impressive that not a single blow landed from five opponents. But I knew I had committed a grave tactical error: despite wanting to protect the villagers, I didn't want to fight these people, my own comrades, again, and with that mind-set, I had failed to map a strategy to win.

The realization came just a few seconds too late, even as one of the soldiers tried to tackle me. I met his attack by unimaginatively throwing my weight into him. He was a husky youth, wild-eyed, and my feet scraped across the stone as he pushed me backward. We grappled for a few seconds before something hard connected with my jaw, rattling my vision. I dipped my head, tried to use him as a shield, felt someone kick my legs out from under me, tried to roll, and was lifted into the air. The stone flashed into my field of vision.

The crack echoed through my skull and pain seared colors too bright to bear across my vision. Then it was black.

There we go, all done, I told myself. *Forged right out of existence.* I couldn't pry my eyes open, but I heard the sounds of combat around me, the dull thud of fists on flesh, the grunts and pained yells. It was all just so stupid, I thought deliriously, as I felt blood pool underneath my face, mixing with the shooting pain spreading from my temple. If this was what was involved in ruling, I wanted no part of it.

My eyes flickered open to see the feet of others shuffling past me. My vision swam, blurred, and I closed my eyes again, ready to let the blackness wash the pain away. It was after they were shut that my brain informed me of what I had seen.

Qole, doubled over and gasping, trying to fight in a battle that could only end one way.

My eyes opened again. The pain roared back, louder than the water, but I welcomed it, let it fuel me. I knew my mind had played tricks on me. I knew it wasn't Qole, but I knew something else: my father had felt the same way as the conductor of this test. He'd thought the only way to defend my family, to rule, was to betray his own values.

I wasn't him. Qole had taught me that.

And, bigger picture be damned, it wasn't in me to let these people be sacrificed.

I stood up.

When I had fought the Bladeguards, I'd felt peace. It wasn't peace that flowed through my veins now, but rage. Rage at the injustice that seemed to follow my family everywhere. Rage that everything that mattered to me was in danger. Rage that, despite the skills and abilities beyond the reach of many I had been given, I could effect little change for the better with them.

Well.

Adrenaline flooded my body, and my vision narrowed on the nearest soldier. He was in the act of planting a foot against the chest of an elderly gentleman who had dared to intervene.

The kick never landed. Almost casually, I snatched his hair and yanked his head back as I snapped a kick to the shin of another soldier. As that target crumpled, gasping, I pulled harder, bringing the hair, and its associated skull, to meet my knee.

They rallied, retaliated. They had only just brought me low, and could do so again; I could see the thought on their faces. But that had been Nev, uncertain and alone. This was Nevarian Thelarus Axandar Rubion Dracorte, and I had righteous fury on my side.

Bones cracked, joints popped, and limbs bent as I held nothing back. I dismantled them. They reeled back from me, clutching at battered parts of their bodies, attempting to regroup. Aris scooped up a rock, and without a second thought, I kicked up the photon pistol that had been dropped on the ground, snatched it in midair, and pressed it to her temple.

Everyone froze, as we locked wild eyes. My breath heaved, and my hands throbbed with what were sure to be shattered bones.

Out of the corner of my eye, I saw the kneeling form of the defiant young woman, so much like Qole, and my finger tightened on the trigger at the thought.

So much like Qole.

My hand started to shake. Everything here had been en-
gineered. There was no organic element in any of it, outside
the pain. I was an insect under glass, put under the precise
pressure that would squash it. A web of choice spread out before me, each rippling consequence as horrible as the last: Win
the Forging, destroy the village. Save Arjan, destroy my family.
Help Qole, lose her forever.

People with centuries of resources, of experience at deceit,
ruled these systems, and as much as I might imagine otherwise,
I was, one way or the other, a pawn in their games.

The water was now an overwhelming roar, ever closer than
before. Whatever else was fake, that danger was real.

My finger tightened on the trigger. I turned, walked into
the shuttle, and shot the control panel to slag. *If I can't win*, I
thought, *it might be time to play a different game.* Ruthless as the
generals might be, I didn't think I was a resource they were
willing to let go just yet. It was a bluff I was willing to call.

I stepped back outside, to the stunned gaze of the crowd.
"There," I said, calm for the first time in days. "If they want
anything useful out of me, they're going to have to save the lot
of us."

They hadn't bothered keeping us in suspense. With a nausea-
inducing lurch, gravity had reversed, and we were lifted up the
cliffs. Below us, a gargantuan wave careened along the canyon
walls, scattering the village as though it were a toy model. I
was launched at a different angle and trajectory than the others
and, just before I slipped out of consciousness, had time to
think on how impressive and rare the tech was that allowed
tractor beams to be used on humans directly.

I came to when I was dropped unceremoniously on the rough-hewn stone ledge. On one side, the shelf ended in a cliff that plunged farther into the canyon. On the other, sitting upon a stone platform, was everyone else: Gavros and Talia and the other military leaders. Devrak was there too, as was Qole and the priestess, all of them seated behind a table. The priestess was still dressed in her simple khaki jumpsuit; her presence was utterly incongruous next to the uniforms on either side of her. Even Qole fit in better. Or at least appeared to. I shivered.

The generals looked concerned, worried almost. Gavros stood, an infopad in front of him, where I could only assume notes on my performance had been accumulated. Talia tried to speak to him, but he launched into the verdict.

"Your tactical ability is demonstrably sound. Your strategies, if rash, are effective. We will consider that a moderate success. As for the rest ..." He set the pad down. "It saddens me to say that in the history of this trial no one has failed quite so profoundly."

"What?" I was incredulous. "Because I can read the end game and see how pointless it is?" I knew it was wiser to bite my tongue, but exhaustion wore away diplomacy. "There was one end to that, General—either I stripped away my humanity, or I lost. I wouldn't be fit to rule if I made that choice."

"That you think in such narrow terms is a failure itself," Gavros said angrily. "The test is different for everyone. Your grandfather Axandar's was a test against aggression, and he won without striking a single blow."

I squinted. "Er. How?"

Gavros waved an impatient arm. "Someone tell him."

Devrak stepped up beside me. "Your grandfather threatened to outright kill anyone who fought him, but to reward anyone who joined him," he said quietly. "Everyone opted to join, particularly given his reputation."

Distantly, I wondered if my father had accomplished the same, completing his Forging without violence. But I knew the answer without asking. My father and I were a lot alike in some ways.

I tried to grasp for an excuse even as shame nipped at me. "That . . . sounds like cheating. It's no different than what I did."

"Cheating?" Gavros was incredulous. "How many rules did you hear us announce?" He sat down with a huge sigh. "The problem isn't that you chose to break the rules, because there aren't any. What you just did was impressive. It was more than impressive. But instead of convincing others to follow you, you threw a tantrum."

"I wouldn't call that a tantrum, Gavros." Talia spoke from her seat. "I would say that he became a leader."

"He can't just opt out of difficult decisions in real life, Talia."

"No," she agreed, the faintest trace of acid entering her words, "but eventually every leader realizes they have to act without the approval of others."

"There is also the matter of Ms. Uvgamut," added Gavros.

Qole's eyebrows shot up, and Talia's voice grew colder. "Oh?"

"Indeed," I said. "What about her?"

"As we feared, being reminded of her is what galvanized you to continue fighting. You fight for her sake. You lose motivation when you fight for duty's sake. This behavior in a military commander isn't fitting—"

"He may be the first fit candidate I've seen."

That voice drew everyone's eyes, stopped the words in our mouths. It was the priestess who'd interrupted us. Surprise rippled through the others.

"Why?" Gavros demanded. "A priestess hasn't approved of someone in living memory."

"It's happened only once before," she agreed. "What we look for we seldom see in anyone: humility."

"He isn't displaying a great deal of humility, priestess," one of the other generals grunted. "Seems proud something fierce to me."

"I never said he was perfect," she said, her voice suddenly sharp. "But he didn't shy away from my questions when he had no idea who I was. He refused to impose his own will on the test before being pushed to a breaking point, a breaking point born not of a desire to win, or a fear of losing, but caring for someone else. Whatever is driving him, it isn't pride."

Gavros considered her carefully. "He's willing to bloody faceless subjects but cannot bear to see someone he cares about hurt? That is more selfish than it is moral."

The priestess nodded. "It won't be if he grows past that, and instead uses what he cares about as inspiration to do what is right at all times. I believe he will." She paused, a curious expression on her face. "It would change everything."

My father had advocated what amounted to ruthlessness to achieve the greater good. I had chosen to respect the individual. I didn't see how, but the priestess seemed to believe that the two could intersect.

If that was true, I might have a way forward.

Qole caught my gaze and jumped off the stone platform to stand at my side. "I think you are all forgetting something else." Her voice was loud against the canyon walls, without a trace of uncertainty.

"Ms. Uvgamut," Gavros said with strained patience. "You were invited here as a courtesy to the Alaxan ... government. And because"—he paused, looking at Talia—"people insisted. But that doesn't give you permission to speak."

"I didn't ask for permission," Qole said flatly. "But I mean no disrespect all the same. I'm just reminding you that you're bickering over details." She raised her hand to me like a blade. "The question is: can he lead an army? You aren't voting for who rules you in peacetime. You're voting for someone who can keep Solara from crushing us. You're voting for someone Alaxak will ally with, trade with." She shook her head. "This isn't about who got the highest score on a test. You're voting for a chance. For someone who can beat the odds."

There it was again—the gravity that drew everything that was real, centered it and anchored it. I could feel it working on me, on everyone around us. Qole looked at me. "Speaking from experience, I don't know anyone who is better at beating the odds."

She believed it, believed in me. In that moment, so did I.

Devrak chuckled, and Gavros looked to either side, as if seeking help.

I walked forward and put both my hands on the table, looking each of the generals in the eye, one by one. "By right and by birth, I am the king," I said quietly. "That is not in dispute. Whether by force or law, I claim the throne. As for the results of the Forging, I will respect the laws of our people and let you decide."

I turned and staggered closer to Devrak and Qole. My vision swam. "Huh, I think I might need a medic," I slurred.

The last thing I saw was Qole and Devrak, catching me.

——

I was unconscious in the med bay when they decided that I had passed. The decision was unanimous in the end. Whatever reservations Gavros had possessed, he'd apparently changed his mind.

Shortly thereafter, I was up and walking through the hallways—no longer an exile interloper, but a young man in his own domain. After a full scan, medics had replaced ligaments, regrown tissue, drained fluid, and siphoned away pain, so that I now felt as if I had experienced only moderate exercise. I'd felt worse after a day of regular work on the *Kaitan*.

I rubbed my temple absently. I was going to be king. I had grown up knowing this day would come, and I had known it would be a grave one, depending as it did on the death of my parents. But as events unrolled around me, it all seemed much too fast and large to properly grasp—a meteor wiping out everything that had come before, heralding a new age.

Whether I fully understood them or not, I had to trust my instincts, and that meant I had to talk to Qole. I consulted my wrist-comm to locate her room. I had a small window before advisors and assistants descended upon me, planning my unveiling and our next moves. I had to talk to her alone, first, to explain our new situation as best I could. The problem was, I had no idea how. If I couldn't explain it to myself in a way that didn't upset me, how could I to her?

I still had to try. There was a part of me that hoped she wouldn't care. The other part of me knew I'd be hurt more than relieved if that was true.

I found her room easily and held my breath as I knocked on the door. I didn't know if she would be there, but I knew that when Qole needed to think, she would be by herself. The door cracked open, and Qole peered out warily, reminding me how unlikely it was for her to feel safe here.

I tried to smile. "Hi. May I have a moment?"

To my relief, she nodded and stood back. "Of course. How are you feeling?"

"Much better, thanks." I stood in the middle of the room. "Your suit is very flattering." It hadn't been what I wanted to say, but in the absence of useful data, my brain had decided to go with what was first on my mind. The outfit was more than flattering; the military cut was striking, composed of precise strokes that broadcasted the powerful mind and body within.

"Thanks," Qole said hesitantly. "I've heard that a lot. I guess everyone thought I would be dressed in dirt and dripping blood."

"Cloaked in Shadow." I spoke without thinking.

Qole smiled despite herself, then sighed. "I wish it were just a cloak. Then I could take it off." She sat on the windowsill of her room. Beyond, the spires of the military barracks shot into the air, creating a staggered blue pattern of visible sky.

"Anyway," she continued. "I heard the good news. You're going to be the next king. What's next?"

"I'll announce my resurrection and gather supporters. Find allies." She winced, and I knew then that she'd heard *how* I was supposed to go about finding allies. "Look, Qole, I'm sorry."

Qole crossed her arms. "For what?" But her tone said she knew exactly what. I grimaced, and yet felt a guilty thrill. She *did* care. She *had* been imagining a future with me, like I had with her.

And now . . . I didn't know what now.

"I assumed you knew about . . . about my need to marry. I shouldn't have, but you've already been exposed to how royal politics work."

Qole narrowed her eyes. "Is this how it's going to be? *Assume* your allies are fine with however you want to use them?"

I blinked. *Allies? Use?* I had expected a more personal approach. "I, no. You must know this isn't *my* choice."

"It *is* your choice. You're the king," Qole snapped, the color in her cheeks rising. "How you treat people is how you will rule, Nev." She swallowed and turned to the window, putting a hand on it as if she could escape. I couldn't respond, because what she said felt right.

Her voice was quieter when she spoke again, sounding as vulnerable as she suddenly looked. And there she was—Qole, *my* Qole, not the captain or the planetary leader. "You led me to believe we had something. That there was hope."

"We *do* have something," I said desperately. *I will fight for it,* I wanted to add, *I haven't given up.*

"I'm not ignorant." Qole turned on me, her hands turning to fists. "I knew things would change. I knew they would be harder, or maybe impossible. But I was trusting that we'd tell each other when things became impossible, like you tried to do in Chorda. I trusted *you.*"

I gestured uselessly. I knew I shouldn't be frustrated, or angry. I knew how hard it was for someone like her to trust anyone like me. How hard it was for her to trust, period. But I was tired of being the person in question all the time, whose position or past made everything about him suspect. "Very well, then. I am telling you. If I am to be king, if I am to protect Alaxak, then I will be forced into a diplomatic marriage. We can't . . . we can't have everything we *both* want. But that doesn't mean we have nothing."

Hurt registered on Qole's face, and anger. She hesitated, then walked to the door, opened it, and gestured toward the opening. "Great. Thanks. Devrak has set up a strategy meeting later today. I'll see you there."

Now there was no thrill. Only a feeling like I was falling. "It doesn't have to be like this."

She waved a hand in the air. "Oh, this conversation again? How could it not be, Nev? Tell me." Her words were derisive. "I wait for you to sneak away from your royal queen once a year to visit your common mistress on her far-flung frozen planet? Well, how about I tell you something?" She squared her shoulders. "I can't. I can't do that to myself, even if you could. I have more pride than that."

"That's not what I want."

"Then what *do* you want?"

I wanted her, but I couldn't have her. I stood, searching for words that could salvage the situation. But there was nothing. Maybe she wasn't *my* Qole anymore. She might have been, once, without my fully realizing or appreciating it, but not anymore.

"I . . . ," she started. "I can't keep doing this, Nev. I can't keep pretending." She pressed her palms into her eyes. "It's going to tear me apart."

"I know. I understand." But what I knew or understood wasn't in line with what I felt. What I felt was that this road we were walking down now, away from each other—*that* would tear me apart.

And there was no reasoning with that as I walked away from her.

Recessional

THE GREAT BELLS OF TENÉRUS'S GOLDEN TOWERS RANG OUT AT THE tragic news. It was, to hear the whispers that were both subdued and perversely titillated in the Belarius palace halls, the most daring assassination ever carried out, against a person no one thought could be touched, by an assassin who *might* have been sent by the last royal family anyone expected. I felt quite proud of it all, but the tolling went on so long that it began to give me a headache.

There was no escaping the sound, especially not where I was headed. The palace lifts took me most of the way, but there was still a long, austere hall to traverse before reaching my destination.

There, coming the opposite way, I bumped into Daiyen Xiaolan.

Her long black hair fell around her shoulders and over a

more conservative, long-sleeved traveling gown of midnight blue. Her loose, unadorned tresses made her look more like a little girl, more innocent—a look as calculated as mine. But a hairstyle wasn't nearly enough to combat the rumors, in her case.

She stopped a few paces from me, meeting my eyes levelly. "Mother and I are leaving Embra in an hour, but his guards won't even let me offer him my condolences." There was no sadness in her tone, but had there been, I would have taken it as fake. Her smooth mask was the more convincing indication that she might be feeling out of sorts.

"That's such a pity," I said with a concerned scrunch of my brows. "But you must understand their concerns."

"That was *no* Xiaolan assassin." Her fury, all too real, was now barely contained. "And you know it."

Of course I did. It had been Suvis, dressed as one. The Xiaolans didn't even have a strong motive to make such a move, but most everyone was so laughably gullible, believing only what they saw on the face of things.

"I'm afraid I only know what I've heard in the palace." *Everyone is gossiping about it,* I didn't add. *About* you. "But I have no doubt your own intentions are pure."

A wonderful nonstatement, that. Pure *what?* Pure malice? Pure greed? Pure jealousy? One could read anything into it.

Her sharp eyes narrowed. Even amid what might be a truly disappointing and grievous situation for her, they were as perfectly black-lined as ever. I grudgingly respected that.

"In fact," she murmured speculatively, "I wonder why the assassin didn't come for me."

Because then it would have been far too obvious who had sent him. "That would have been equally tragic. Heathran would only be mourning you instead of his father." Besides, I'd be happy to have her killed *eventually.*

253

"There will be no mourning my absence now, hm?" She cast her gaze down to the gold-streaked marble, her tone falsely pensive.

"I'm *sure* he doesn't think you responsible."

She didn't bother to dignify that with a reply. Even if no direct ties linked the assassin to her, she was suspect, to be forever associated with the Elder's death—an assassination so astounding it surpassed even my parents'. Heathran would have a hard time ever looking at her again without thinking of it. Any relationship between them, or their families, had been effectively poisoned.

"I hear Nevarian is alive and has declared himself king," Daiyen said, as if in passing, not like it was explosive news.

Nev, the stubbornly persistent bastard, had revealed that I'd been the one to assassinate my parents and then frame him for it. At least, so far, no one seemed to be taking the accusation seriously, other than the generals on Aaltos. In this case, my past reputation was serving me well. Solara Dracorte, the bubbly social butterfly, the conniving mastermind behind the *second*-greatest assassination in recent memory? It was ridiculous.

And it had occurred to almost no one that I could be behind the greatest.

But perhaps one person knew better. Daiyen had raised her eyes to hold mine again, this time with sharp, seething hatred. But then her gaze drifted over my shoulder.

I turned and cursed inwardly. Shadia Belarius was headed toward us—worse, toward her brother's quarters. Now that I'd seen her, it would only be proper for me to cede Heathran's time to a grieving member of the family. But this was my precious window, and I couldn't let her occupy it.

But Daiyen swept by me without another word. When she

reached the girl, she took her into her arms. Over her shoulder, Shadia's face crumpled, and she wept.

Shadia, at least, didn't believe her at fault. For the moment, I didn't mind. In fact, I almost could have thanked my erstwhile rival. In trying to prove the genuineness of her sympathy, Daiyen was helping me still.

Taking advantage of Shadia's delay, I continued down the hall to reach Heathran before his sister could. Now that she was in the middle of what could be deemed a social engagement, I wasn't breaking decorum, and she *would* be if she intruded upon my private moment with her brother.

Guards flanked the gilded double doors, which were towering, unadorned, and imposing, like the rest of the palace's features. Even the guards themselves were the same.

I clasped my hands demurely in front of me. "Please let His Highness—excuse me, His *Majesty,* the Elder—know that Queen Solara Dracorte is here to see him, if he will have me."

One of the guards touched his ear and murmured into a comm. The gesture acted as a reminder, and I discreetly reached up, as if toying with my hair, to shut off my own. I didn't want anything interrupting.

The guard's eyebrow twitched in surprise at whatever he heard on the other end of his comm. *Good.* I'd done well enough before, but now would be the tricky part. After another "Yes, Your Majesty," he turned back to me. "He will see you." He bowed his head as he opened a door.

The interior was dimly lit, golden lamps glinting off the gilded furniture and trim. The white marble floor was pooled in light as I stepped over it, to where Heathran was seated, head bowed, on a simple purple-upholstered divan with golden legs.

I needed him to look up at me in this perfect lighting.

I paused in front of him, hugging my arms in a vulnerable stance. A sob hitched in my throat, the sound delicate but audible in the silent sitting room.

He looked up in surprise, since it was certainly no noise Solara Dracorte had ever made in public. His red-rimmed eyes widened farther. My plain white gown of mourning glowed in the lamplight, modestly covering me from wrists to toes with a high neck and long, wide sleeves. My only concession to his taste was a thick gold collar that clasped my neck. Otherwise, I was what he would least anticipate.

Heathran wasn't stupid. His father had just died. He would expect people—especially someone like me—to appeal to him in any way possible to get what they needed. To take advantage.

In our distrust, at least, we were alike.

"Heathran," I choked. "I'm so, so sorry. Words cannot describe . . ."

He had to blink several times and clear his throat before he could speak himself. "Thank you, Solara. Please, sit." He nodded to the spot next to him on the divan.

I slid shakily next to him, not so close as to be indecent, but not too far.

"I know only too well how you are feeling." I wrung my hands, without overdoing it. "The pain is so great, and for an heir, the burden so overwhelming."

"You, of anyone, would know how I feel," he murmured, looking down at his own clasped hands, not at me.

Still, this was a response he expected. That wouldn't suffice.

"I do. I wasn't sure if my father loved me, either."

His eyes shot to me. It was a gamble, telling such a raw truth and expecting him to admit his own, but at least I had his attention.

"The problem is," I continued, "that didn't make me love

him any less, or ease the burden of his passing. It almost makes it worse. To be left with so much responsibility, without knowing if one is worthy . . ."

"Solara," Heathran said, his voice barely a whisper. "I'm sure you'll make an excellent queen."

He was genuine. The gamble had paid off.

I held his eyes. "And you an excellent king. I feel like I understand you like no one else." Finally, I let myself lean closer and put a hand on his arm. "If there is anything, *anything* within my power to do to ease your sorrow, just give me word."

"Your . . . being here . . . is a comfort all its own." His soft, higher-pitched voice was beginning to sound huskier for a reason *other* than grief.

My face crumpled, and my body caved toward his, as if I couldn't help it. Now that I'd gained his trust, he would believe it. I collapsed onto his shoulder and let loose a muffled sob. His arm immediately came around me, strong and warm—not at all like the formal, stiff responses I'd gotten from him before.

"At least your system is whole," I gasped. "I *wish* that my parents' assassin were a nameless Xiaolan hireling—if indeed that is who it was," I amended in a gracious murmur into his shoulder. "It was my own flesh and blood who took my parents from me, and who is now trying to betray me more than he already has. Can you imagine? The distance between my father and me was one thing, but I once thought Nev and I were close. It would be as if Shadia . . ."

"I can't even think it." It was another risk mentioning his sister, in case I triggered a defensive reaction, but fortunately his voice was only brimming with sympathy. And if I planted even the slightest wariness of Shadia within him, so much the better. She was obviously too close to Daiyen, despite the rumors, and so she might also object to *my* new closeness with Heathran.

"Yes, you have your sister," I said in an approximation of numb grief. "Be grateful, despite all you have lost. You still have *someone* who loves you. I fear that the evil lies of my once-brother have even turned young Marsius against me, never mind several of my generals. Marsius was stationed on Aaltos, studying to become my supreme commander. But now . . ." My voice hitched. "I am utterly alone in the galaxy. I have no one."

His hand squeezed my shoulder. "That is not true, Solara."

I pulled back. If I looked at him with innocent confusion, it would give the lie. So instead I scoffed and glanced away, as if I didn't trust *him*. "What do you mean?"

He turned my face back to his, his dark eyes burning as warm as the golden lamps around us. "You have me. I will not allow you to suffer alone. Just as you promised on my behalf, you can always turn to me if you need anything, anything at all. I'm here for you."

With that, the solution to my final problem fell into place. Money to combat Nev, the drones, and the other royal families' ire would be of no concern. There was no more Daiyen or Belarius the Elder to stand in my way. And all without weakening my family name with marriage, or giving Heathran much of anything in return. It was just as I'd guessed: Heathran, feeling out of control in his grief, needed someone to care for amid theirs. It was a way for him to feel more *in* control, as if doing something for another would fix what had happened to him.

My lip quivered in what Heathran assumed was an emotion of another sort, drawing his attention. "Oh, Heathran . . . ,"

I breathed. My eyes widened, swallowing his with the full force of my most defenseless, longing gaze.

He leaned forward.

It may have been another test. Even if it wasn't, there was no way I would capitulate so soon, not after the chase he'd led me on. Where was the fun in that? I pulled back at the last second. "My apologies ... I ..."

Heathran immediately removed himself to a respectable distance. "*My* apologies. It's too soon."

"No, Heathran, of course not. I wish to see you again, but my emergency comm is buzzing."

He waved me away, definitely understanding such things. I even got a rueful smile from him, and I felt like I'd won the night.

Unfortunately, as I left Heathran's quarters and reactivated my earpiece, I realized that I'd been honest about more than I'd intended. My emergency comm *was* buzzing, and a series of messages were waiting from Suvis and those generals still loyal to me. It didn't take me long to gather the gist of them all:

Aaltos is mobilizing.

I wished I'd received the warning sooner, but the delay had been worth it. Besides, Nev was likely headed to Alaxak to defend it from further attack—a fool's errand. Even if a rag-tag fleet of fishermen had somehow managed to take down a battle carrier and its accompanying starfighters, there was no way, even backed by Aaltos, that they could fight off the fleet currently mobilizing around Luvos—a fleet that wouldn't be there for long.

I suddenly froze, pausing in the middle of the hall, un-caring about the curious looks I received.

Nev might already be well aware of that. He'd proven

himself far craftier than I'd given him credit for. I wasn't entirely positive, but beneath his arrogant swagger, his overused muscles, and his unceasing bluster about right and wrong, he might actually be able to think like a king.

So *where, then,* I wondered, *might he be headed?*

XIII

QOLE

"That," Telu said, *"doesn't look anything like Aaltos."*

She was right. As militarily adept as the Dracorte world had been, it was spare on orbital security. Now, through the *Kaitan's* viewport, the planet Valtai, the seat of the Treznor-Nirmana family council, made Aaltos look more like Alaxak in comparison.

I'd never seen so many cargo stations, docking bays, construction docks, or weapons platforms, hovering above the atmosphere like planetary rings. Not to mention the destroyers. Many were docked, either under construction or shiny new and ready to launch a hundred plasma missiles on command. But a few were much more active, patrolling the planet's perimeter.

"This might be a problem," I muttered. Nev glanced at me

from the copilot's station, probably because it was one of the few things I'd said within his hearing all day.

There was nothing to say to him. I didn't even want to *think* about our situation—whatever that situation was, whatever I had imagined it to be. At some point, *somehow* I'd finally let myself imagine that we, Qole and Nev, together, could work without the universe cracking apart. Indeed, it turned out that the universe was pretty solid, and it had *solidly* inserted itself back between us. Or maybe it had been there all along and I'd been living in a strange warp in space-time this past month.

Like now. It might have looked like we were only an arm's length from each other on the *Kaitan's* bridge, so close, like our fingers could touch if we reached out . . . but we couldn't, not ever again.

He was meant for someone else. He always had been.

I wouldn't have even thought a king—one destined to marry a princess or queen from some other royal family— would be permitted to stoop so low as to ride with us on the *Kaitan* again, but that was part of the plan. We were back in disguise.

Our approach to Valtai was much the same as Aaltos: slip in and hope nobody noticed us. The problem was, somebody in the extensive Treznor-Nirmana security system was bound to get suspicious.

"Bribery, if worse comes to worst?" Basra said from his station beneath us.

"Someone will turn us in," Devrak said, seated next to Nev. "They have spies everywhere."

"Hack their radar systems to mask us?" Nev suggested next, with a glance down at Telu.

She snorted. "They still have viewports, genius. We'll look even more suspicious if we appear there but not elsewhere.

Besides, if they detect anyone hacking their system, they'll be on even higher alert. Planetary security on a capital world like this is mega different from an unsuspecting battle carrier."

I almost expected Eton to chime in with something like, "Blast straight through them, then," until I remembered he wasn't up in the weapons turret. Something pinched in my chest. Maybe one of the many pieces of my heart, grinding against the others.

Arjan wasn't around, either. He wasn't off the ship, but he was in his quarters for some reason. Whatever the cause, it irritated me. Here we were, trying to subtly infiltrate an enemy planet and not-so-subtly blow up a fleet, and Arjan didn't feel the need to watch? Sure, Nev had taken the spot Arjan usually occupied when he wasn't in the fishing skiff, but only because my brother wasn't there to begin with.

The plan was to sabotage the fleet the Treznors were building for Solara before it could be used to bolster her ship numbers—a plan that Nev had come up with that everyone from Devrak to Talia to Basra had decided was the way to go. Maybe because none of *them* would flinch over what those battle carriers and destroyers might have cost. I thought it was a waste, but there was no way to steal the ships without access codes that only a member of the Treznor-Nirmana family possessed. This was the best we could do, I was forced to admit.

Without a large fleet of our own, our strategy was to use ground troops, slowly and quietly ferried to construction docks hovering in Valtai's orbit, overwhelm security, do the job with high-energy explosive charges, and then leave before either the Treznor-Nirmanas or Solara could rally.

Just out of range of detection, we had twenty of our own destroyers—all we had—commanded by Talia and Gavros and accompanied by a small fleet of innocuous shuttles loaded with troops—two of which had already landed at the construction docks under various excuses, while carrying elite covert-ops teams trained on Aaltos for precisely such missions. Now we just had to join them. We'd come separately to make sure the coast was clear for Nev and Devrak, and because I was the best pilot for a quick getaway. If all went as planned, the destroyers wouldn't even have to get involved. The last thing we wanted was a standoff with Nev as hostage, giving Solara all the time in the systems to show up with an armada.

"We'll be fine," Nev said. "The other two shuttles made it, and we will too."

I wasn't sure how he could be so calm, especially since he had the most to lose if we were caught.

Telu voiced my thoughts exactly: "Yeah, and those shuttles didn't look quite as strange as we do. Even with our new registration numbers, we look like mercenaries or smugglers at the very least."

"This would be a fine time to remind everyone that the king should probably not be on a strike mission," Basra murmured.

It had made the most sense for Nev to stay back with Talia and Gavros, but he'd refused. He'd officially declared Solara a traitor and himself the Dracorte king over the QUIN, calling for his family and all their subjects to follow him.

"The last thing I want to do now," Nev said, repeating a familiar refrain, "is hang back from danger. I must set myself apart from Solara, charge into battle like my father would have done. That's what will earn me respect."

Apparently, the Forging *still* wasn't quite good enough.

And yet, as much as I didn't want to relate to Thelarus Dracorte, or for Nev to emulate the man, I understood. I couldn't imagine forcing others to do what I myself wouldn't.

And at least it gave me an excuse to be a part of . . . this . . . for a little longer. Nev's presence on the *Kaitan* was the only reason I hadn't set a course back to Alaxak and left this civil war to people who knew what they were doing. A small voice—not a hallucination, thank the ancestors—wondered if, behind his logic, Nev had the same desire to stay closer to me.

But that was stupid, and might as well be a delusion. Because we weren't—couldn't be—close.

"Where's Arjan?" I demanded in an exhale of frustration that really had nothing to do with my brother.

"Dunno," Telu said from below.

"Well, someone go find him."

To my surprise, Nev jumped up. It wasn't just that he was a king, as I was constantly reminding myself; it was that he and Arjan didn't get along very well. Or, at least they hadn't. Ever since Arjan had comforted Marsius, Nev had been polite and considerate around him. He probably wanted to prove that he didn't mind fetching him, both to me *and* Arjan.

But Nev didn't look polite, or considerate, when he came storming back onto the bridge a few minutes later. He looked absolutely furious. "We need to turn around, go back."

"What?"

Rather than respond, he pointed directly behind him.

"Oh, Great Collapse," Telu said, seeing whatever it was before I could.

Marsius came slinking up the bridge stairs. Devrak put his face in his hands, only bringing them away to rub his temples in what looked like restraint. Maybe to keep from yelling.

I had no such restraint. When I could find my voice, I shouted, "What in blasted hell is he doing on board?"

Nev kept pointing, until Arjan came up after the boy.

"He did this," Nev ground out, any attempt at friendliness

gone from his voice. "There was no way Marsius could have stowed away on his own. There were too many people watching him, too many ways for him to get caught. He didn't even know this ship, and yet he was in Arjan's quarters, playing cards with him like this is all some sort of a game."

"I know it's not a game," Marsius insisted. "And it's not Arjan's fault."

Basra's voice drifted up from below. "That's why Arjan has been so happy to sleep in my room, instead of having me over. I thought it was because he'd finally realized my decorating was superior."

Basra's quarters on the ship had little to no decorations, despite the metal wardrobe locker that was packed with sparkly dresses. That explained his dry tone, and the hint of rebuke. And maybe even sheepishness that said *I should have known.*

Arjan didn't look sheepish, not in the slightest. He folded his arms and stared defiantly at us all over Marsius's head. I wanted to punch him.

"I wished to help," Marsius said. His voice was quieter, but steady.

"Why?" Nev demanded of Arjan, ignoring Marsius entirely. "Is this some attempt at revenge? My family hurt you, so you want to hurt them?"

Marsius looked at them both questioningly. "Wait, how did we hurt—"

Arjan spoke right over him without answering. "You think I would do something so disgusting? Only a Dracorte could think of something like that."

"And I *can* help," Marsius interjected before Nev could. "If Solara catches you, I could try to convince her to let you go."

"One," Nev said, ticking up a finger, finally addressing Marsius, his restraint audible, "she wouldn't listen to you.

Two"—a second finger followed—"what happens if the Treznors catch us instead? What then? What were you *thinking*?" Once again, he directed his anger at Arjan.

"I did it because this was what was best for him," Arjan growled. "He didn't want to be left behind. He hates Aaltos, and he misses his family, which you would have noticed if you weren't too busy being king."

"So you think bringing him *here* is better?"

"It's better than where he was."

"Are you mad? This isn't about his personal happiness; this is about his safety!"

Arjan blinked, and I realized he truly hadn't considered the danger. He was a Shadow fisherman, dodging death in the skiff every day, so his perspective on what counted as dangerous was skewed, as mine often was. But even more, lately, Arjan seemed to be living in the moment, rather than looking too far ahead. "One isn't more important than the other," he said.

Nev shook his head. "How dare you risk my brother's life—"

Arjan barked a laugh sharper than one of his throwing knives and nodded at me. "And what is it you think you're doing with *my* sister? Wait, is it because she isn't royal, so her life matters less? Is it because she's easy for you to use, because she loves you?"

"Arjan!" I yelled, barely holding the *Kaitan* straight. *I* hadn't even admitted that to Nev yet . . . and I wasn't ever planning on it. "That's none of your damned business. Besides, I'm old enough to make my own decisions, unlike Marsius. I'm your *captain,* no less, and you had no right to bring him on board without my permission. Which I *wouldn't* have granted." I was furious, but more than that, I wanted to bury what Arjan had said in an avalanche of words.

He tossed his head, scoffing even though Nev had fallen silent with a stunned look on his face. "Yeah, well, at least I didn't bring him here because I want to use him in any royal ploy or plot or scheme. I let him on board because he needs family. He needs to feel needed. Better yet, he needs people like *us.*"

That hardened Nev's expression a bit, but he still didn't argue. He only turned to Devrak, locking eyes with the older man for a minute.

"We can't go back," Devrak murmured eventually. "We'll most definitely give away that something is amiss and jeopardize the others if we turn around right now."

It was Nev's turn to scrub his hands over his face. "Devrak, how can we take the risks we must with him on board? And risk losing two of the last three members of the Dracorte family?"

Neither of them looked my way, carefully, but we were all thinking it, especially Arjan—who *did* look at me pointedly: Nev was, of course, willing to take risks with the rest of us. But unlike what Arjan thought about that, I saw it as a sign of respect.

I knew it was. So why was doubt now crawling into my brain?

I'd felt it from the beginning between us, that gravity tugging us together. But while I'd been drawn to Nev for some unfathomable reason I couldn't describe, some undiscovered law of physics that seemed to defy reality, he'd always needed something from me. Even when he was exiled, without a home or purpose, he'd needed somewhere to stay, something to do.

Was Arjan right? Could Nev not help using me because he was a royal, a prince, and now a king like his father, just like I couldn't help letting him, because I was stupidly, hopelessly in love? Had this love made me weak?

"No," a familiar voice said.

I looked up, thinking Nev had somehow responded to my thoughts, but he and Devrak were still bickering quietly. I'd heard his voice, though.

Only in my head, even though it had seemed spoken in my ear. Maybe I wasn't weak, just crazy.

"We should be fine," Devrak said with a decisive air, "as long as we don't get caught."

That was when I saw the approaching ships out the viewport, and the alerts on my feeds. A pair of starfighters on patrol. Except they weren't flying in standard patrol formation; they were headed straight for us.

"Um," I said.

"Hm, yes," Basra said. "You know that worst-case scenario I was trying to plan for, and that our man Devrak was simply hoping to avoid? That might have just arrived."

"Maybe they only want to say hi?" Telu suggested halfheartedly.

Our comms beeped. "Transmit your registration and your itinerary," a hard voice said.

"It should pass inspection," I muttered. "Send it, Telu."

And then we waited. I had to resist tapping my fingers nervously on the dash. Next to me, Nev's jaw was tight.

"Please proceed to containment bay twenty-one," the voice rejoined. "We're going to conduct a routine search of your cargo."

I cursed. Our cargo, this time, was not stolen goods, but a load of Shadow for use in emergencies. That, combined with our stowed fishing net and our general appearances, might be enough to tell them where we were from, and whom we were carrying. Especially with Marsius on board.

"Unifier's sake," Nev said. "I can disguise myself, but I don't know what the drugs will do to someone Marsius's size— they're calibrated for me." He glared at Arjan.

"If they search us thoroughly," Basra said, "they'll probably take a biometric reading anyway."

Much like masking a ship's signal, biometric scramblers worked only when one wasn't staring right at the person in question and wondering why they couldn't get a clear reading.

"Both of you need to hide," Devrak said. Meaning, of course, the two royals.

Nev threw down his hands. "I didn't come here to hide! Best-case scenario, this holds us up and aborts the mission."

"It's still better than it could be."

Another comm beeped. "Uh," Telu said, "this one is scrambled."

Maybe it was from one of the generals, and *they* had a plan. "Open it," I said.

A rich, agreeable voice filtered into the *Kaitan*. "Why, hello. At least one of you might recognize me. A pleasure to speak with you again, Nevarian."

Nev let loose a fluid stream of curses that even made Telu raise an eyebrow.

"Who is this scat-bag?" she demanded.

"That *scat-bag*," Devrak said flatly, "is King Makar Treznor-Nirmana."

For a few seconds, we all stared at Devrak. Then Arjan burst out laughing. I stared at him not doubting just my own sanity, for once.

"Arjan?"

He could hardly get out a word and waved a hand in my

direction. "It's just . . . too perfect," he gasped. "How do things like this always happen to us?" He struggled to swallow his laughter. "Well, I know how," he added, wiping a tear from his eye. Then he gave an acknowledging nod at Nev.

"Speak for yourself," Nev snapped.

"It could be a bluff," Telu said, ignoring them both. Basra shook his head, but she went on. "How could he know for sure that Nev is on board, and isn't the guy, what, totally powerless right now and under house arrest, or something?"

Nev and Devrak shook their heads. "If Makar is moving this boldly, he knows Nev is on board, and he is a far cry from powerless," Devrak said.

They both looked worriedly at Marsius, who flushed and looked down at his toes. "I just wanted to help," he whispered.

Nev closed his eyes, took a deep breath, then stepped up to the comm. "Hello, Makar. A pleasure, I'm sure."

"Yes, so *good* to hear your voice," Makar responded warmly. "If only everyone knew you were here, we could give you the proper welcome you deserve."

Nev's response was tight. "I'm fine with minimal fanfare."

"I thought you might be, which is why I'll give you a choice. Either transmit this clearance code to those starfighters and then land at these coordinates to my country villa"—the information appeared over an encrypted feed—"or else I'll let them know to have a nice hot cup of tàs waiting for the new Dracorte king upon his arrival . . . oh, and to properly welcome the other guests in those two shuttles that are waiting at the construction docks." There was a pause. "It will be *so* lovely to meet as equals."

Like Makar, none of us imagined we had much of a choice.

Makar's "country villa" was in fact a sprawling compound of glass, steel, stone, and dark woods, many-winged and tiered, some levels looking almost like they hovered in midair through a trick of the architecture. I set the *Kaitan* down on the inside of a towering black wall that surrounded the place, holding back a leafy jungle.

The planet, where it wasn't built up with towering, glossy cities, was in fact covered with green, we'd realized, once we made it beyond all the orbital interference and into the atmosphere, where we could see the surface unobstructed. I'd pictured Valtai more like Aaltos for some reason, craggy and severe, but vines stubbornly clung anywhere they could manage, even to steel and glass.

The humid air hit me like a wet towel when I stepped out. Not far behind it, the heat was another slap in the face. I started sweating almost immediately under my coat.

"Ancestors," Arjan wheezed, tugging at his own jacket to let in a nonexistent breeze. "How does anyone live here? You can't breathe."

"It's like a sweaty little fat man is sitting on my chest," Telu added, a hand over her heart. Both Devrak and Nev cast her looks, seeming mostly unbothered by the heat themselves, but she only shrugged. "Hey, that's what it feels like."

"Is it an experience you're familiar with?" Arjan snarked.

Basra, having been born in the heat of Nirmana, the royal desert planet, was totally unaffected. In fact, he strode down the ramp without waiting. "Let's meet yet another king, shall we? You'd think it would get old by now." He said it like it was very much getting old.

A servant came out to greet us and take our jackets. Basra only tossed his in the servant's general direction and strode right into one of the villa's several sets of glass double doors.

A man stood in the shining, sleek foyer, his dark hair thick and wavy, his suit white against warm brown skin. He looked to be in his forties, but he was probably older, knowing royals. Whatever his age, he was strikingly handsome. Sensual lips curved into a smile, but before he could open his mouth, Basra spoke.

"I'm Hersius Kartolus the Thirteenth." He pulled up a loose sleeve and his glowing holographic tattoo sprang into the air above his extended forearm, showing a blue-and-black closed-end double helix with exactly thirteen spirals—his unique form of identification. It marked him as one of the richest individuals in the systems. "I'm not in the mood for pleasantries, so let's get right to it."

"Ah, so you're the latest Hersius," Makar said, unruffled.

Telu folded her arms and eyed Makar. "And you're the scat-bag."

Devrak coughed into his fist.

Makar's perfectly manicured black brows shot up. "Well, I think I like *you*."

Telu looked taken aback by that, but the king had already turned to the rest of our group. "These must be the other Alaxans," he said, his eyes sweeping over Arjan and me to rest on Nev. "Along with *King* Nevarian Dracorte, Devrak Hansen, and . . . oh my, is that Prince Marsius? How you've grown!"

Marsius stepped out from behind Nev, trying not to look like he was hiding and only halfway succeeding. He bowed properly. "Hello, King Makar, I'm pleased to see you again."

"I'm sure." Makar clapped his hands. "Refreshments? A moment to primp?"

"We didn't come here to have our nails done," Basra said. His words had the desired effect. Makar glanced at his hands, and, indeed, Basra's nails were a nice shade of metallic purple.

Makar weathered it without comment, or even another raised eyebrow.

"Right this way, then." He gestured to another pair of doors.

We made our way into a sitting room filled with black chairs that didn't look like chairs, or anything that could be sat upon at all, so half of us remained standing. Makar took a seat, as did Basra, Nev, and Marsius. Maybe they were used to such furniture. Devrak looked too wary to sit, rather than unsure of how to go about it.

"Let's get right down to it, at your request," Makar began without preamble, "since I know someone else who just can't wait, either."

"What do you mean?" Nev asked.

"Let me start over. I know why you're here. You want to sabotage Solara's fleet that my family has been so industriously building for her. I was for your plan, since it would weaken your sister, put her more in our debt at the same time, and, quite simply, vex her, which would please me above all."

"So why all of this?" Nev gestured around.

"Because Solara is here."

"*What?*" Half of those sitting were standing again—Nev and Marsius behind him. Only Makar and Basra remained seated, the latter regarding the other levelly over folded hands.

"I don't mean *here,* in this house." Makar raised an infopad, and what it showed on a vid feed nearly made my heart stop.

It was a fleet, in space. A massive fleet. An armada. At least ten battle carriers, too many destroyers to count, and no doubt hundreds of invisible starfighters. And it was looming, in real time, just outside the range of Valtai's planetary defenses.

"The First Dracorte Fleet," Nev murmured, stunned.

"She has come to collect her *new* fleet ahead of schedule,"

Makar said, his tone casual, as if she'd arrived early for dinner. "And it appears she brought reinforcements. A number just shy of what my family would perceive as an open declaration of war."

"How . . . ," Nev began, then swallowed. "How did she know we were here?"

"She doesn't, not for sure, but she suspects. Smart girl that she is, she wouldn't wait around on a hunch like that."

"Wait, how did *you* even know we were here?"

"Half of the Treznor-Nirmana spy network is still mine." He smiled. "The better half. Besides, ever since one of my destroyers encountered the good ship *Kaitan Heritage* back when you were only a prince, I've been on the lookout for it. It's quite the unique ship, you know. Also, I recorded *her* biometric signal during that little encounter." He pointed at me. "Do you think the rest of us simply forgot about her after the implosion within the Dracorte family?"

I opened my mouth, then closed it. The ground felt unsteady beneath my feet. I wasn't quite sure what was going on here, so I figured it was better that I stay quiet.

"What do you want?" Nev said, his voice low after glancing at me.

"I still want to help you. The only possible course of action for you now, since you can't very well blow up the fleet anymore without igniting open war between your family and mine, is to take the fleet and this fight elsewhere, with us as your new business partners."

Devrak spoke slowly. "Treznor-Nirmana would ally with Nevarian?"

"Well, *I* would ally with you, and the rest of my family would be forced to stand behind me with a fleet like that at your disposal, and thus reinstate me to full power. It would be too messy and embarrassing, otherwise." He hesitated. "We won't go to war for you, but our financial and political backing should be enough to give Solara pause and to stop this silly tussle between the two of you."

"Helping you reinstate yourself *should* be enough to recompense you for your help," Basra said behind his hands. "But it's not."

Makar nodded. "Too right. Giving a fleet to you, without payment—ships that could later fire upon erstwhile allies, if they felt like it—would be foolish. I would need something stronger to bind you to me, first."

"You want a trade agreement, no doubt," Basra said. "You want access to Shadow, through Nev's alliance with Alaxak."

I gritted my teeth as Makar nodded again.

"But . . . even a trade agreement isn't quite enough," Basra continued, reading something in his face.

"You could go back on your agreement with a stronger fleet," Makar said, shrugging in a show of justified concern. "Allowing you to thwart Solara is one thing, since she has irritated me so. Allowing you to beat her, take the throne from her, and reunite your divided family, is quite another."

Of course, the Dracortes had been in competition with Treznor-Nirmana for a very long time. It didn't matter that Nev was fighting against Solara, Makar's personal enemy. Nev was still a Dracorte.

"What do you have in mind?" Nev ground out.

"The girl stays with me." He nodded in my direction, making me blink. "I know she's valuable to you, and all the systems, with the power she can wield." Of course he knew. His scientists had nearly cut me open on a table. "Once I've regained power, we've established a robust Shadow trade, and I've learned what I can from her, I'll let her go."

276

Nev's voice was dead. "Absolutely not."

Makar held up his hands. "Nothing untoward will be done to her, of course. All research will be painless."

"No. And besides, she isn't mine to give or take. I've granted Alaxak sovereignty, and she's their interim leader." Nev smiled without a hint of mirth. "That wouldn't be a terribly diplomatic action on my part."

Makar drummed his fingers on his knee and pursed his lips, which I suddenly didn't find sensual at all, but repulsive. "That is a conundrum." He didn't sound bothered, and I realized why a second later. "I didn't think you would agree anyway, so how about something else? If you won't give me the girl, why not give me . . . yourself?"

Nev took a step back, nearly knocking into his chair. "What in the systems are you talking about?"

"Renounce the Dracorte name entirely, marry into my family, *become* a Treznor-Nirmana, and you will go debt-free and have all the ships to combat your sister that you want. Your generals and forces can go with Solara or stay with us; their choice."

I'd barely heard anything after *marry into my family.* The words bounced around in my skull like a ricocheting photon blast, leaving me stunned. I'd known this was coming, but not *this* soon. And not in this way.

Nev regarded him for a long moment. Or maybe it only felt long because I was holding my breath. Everyone was. "The planetary subsystems I hold now will of course join the paired Treznor-Nirmana systems," he guessed finally. Makar nodded. With that much offered to his family, even without the ships or troops they didn't really need, the Treznor-Nirmana council would definitely be forced to return power to him. "Not all of them will follow me," Nev insisted. "Some would resist."

"And they'll be caught between Solara's army and ours. Of the three, I know who would win. Besides, they're not my biggest priority."

Nev exhaled. "Ah. You also want our Shadow refineries and research stations, and our exclusive trade rights with Alaxak."

This was beyond a trade agreement. This was full access to Shadow. Makar gave another nod.

I couldn't keep quiet any longer. "We're not trading with *him*," I spat. "You can give away what's yours, whether that's the Shadow we trade with you or your own planets, if you want. But you can't give away what's *ours* by right to grant."

Nev threw a hand at me. "Qole, I don't want to do this."

Makar arched an eyebrow at me, waiting for my response—as if this were his evening's entertainment.

I tried to ignore him, to keep my voice steady. "But you're thinking about it." I couldn't help the next words to escape my lips. "How could you?"

I knew why: Solara's ships in the sky. Our imminent capture and likely execution, or a suicidal last stand. The lives of his generals and subjects, hanging in the balance. Even if we somehow managed to escape and slip back to Aaltos with our forces, there was likely no way for Nev to win the civil war with Solara gaining possession of her new fleet. Fighting wasn't always the answer, and Nev had proven he understood that, as a king. But that didn't make it any easier to bear.

Makar sighed loudly. "Ah, lovers' quarrel, hm? I guessed as much." I rounded on him, but before I could get out a word, he said to me, "It's not as if such relationships are rare, and of course you wouldn't have to worry about any competition in that sense from my daughter. After all, she's only twelve and not to come of age for quite a few years yet. By then"—Makar shrugged—"who knows. Perhaps you'll have tired of him." He tossed his head at Nev.

"She's *twelve*?" I said, just as Nev said, "Your *daughter*?"

We both found different things about the proposal surprising. But then, it was fairly common in Nev's world to be promised to someone at such a young age. Most royal marriages were arranged—his own, with his cousin Ketrana, had been arranged by his parents when they were around that age. Then again, they'd *both* been that old, not one of them nineteen.

Nev was far more concerned about *who* she was. "You have a daughter? How does no one in all the systems know this?"

"I'm *eccentric*, remember? I like to keep secrets. I also like for my heir to not be assassinated before she can speak." His expression wasn't amused, even if his tone was. "We live in dangerous times, as you well know: your parents, now Belarius the Elder, and the attempts on your own life . . ."

"She's your heir, too?" Nev's voice had grown fainter.

"Declared and sealed before Unifier priests that were sworn to secrecy under pain of excruciating death, and such. I can show you the documents if you wish."

Nev shook his head, covering his eyes with one hand. "Let me get this straight. You wish me to marry your daughter, knowing someday I might sit on your throne?"

"*Her* throne, mind you, and you will only sit next to her under our name, not your own." He grinned fiercely. "Keep in mind, only the Nirmanas are patriarchal, not the Treznors. It's her rule."

"Still, that's a new way to treat rivals."

"By assimilating them? I assure you, it's quite an established technique. The Nirmanas are a case in point. Besides, there's the added benefit of the snub to my family, in repayment for how they've treated me. Not only will none of them be chosen as heir, none will even marry my heir."

Nev dropped his hand. "As far as I know, you don't even like *me*."

"I wasn't too enthusiastic about my wife, either, but I married her to bind our families together. And I like your sister far, *far* less than either of you. Can you just imagine how this would irk Solara? I think she'd prefer civil war." He smiled at the thought, a genuine smile.

Eccentric, indeed. More like mildly psychopathic.

"Your wife's name survived," Nev pointed out.

"Well, yes, because Treznor wanted their entire family. I'm happy to let your sister sink with the Dracorte name—into debt, disgrace, oblivion, or all three. I just hope *you're* smart enough to know when to abandon ship." He brushed at his jacket. "Reciprocal feelings of affection aren't a requirement between myself and a son-in-law, but I can't abide stupidity."

Nev flinched at *son-in-law.* Or maybe it was the prospect of the Dracorte name brought down.

I didn't mind that so much as the thought of losing Nev. Of his trading himself for our survival—his, mine. I didn't particularly care about the Dracortes, but I cared about him. Without his pride, his self-respect, his duty, he would be a shell of himself.

Not to mention what might happen to me, or Alaxak's sovereignty, *before* Nev was able to sit on the Treznor-Nirmana throne. I didn't trust Makar farther than I could drop-kick him, which was all I really wanted to do.

Basra's lips were pinched, almost like he figured it was the best course of action, but he didn't like it. "*This* is why you don't bring royals on covert ops," he muttered.

Everyone else was thinking. Marsius looked stunned. Devrak looked sick. Both Arjan and Telu looked as worried as I felt.

Maybe not quite as worried. "Nev . . . ," I began, desperation in my voice that I couldn't hold in. "There has to be another way."

"It's either my plan or you try to fight your sister's navy with only twenty destroyers," Makar stated bluntly. "Not only will Alaxak's attempt at independence become a quaint footnote in history, but you'll lose it all: your throne, your ships, your loyal subjects' lives, and maybe even your own life. Definitely the lives of those you care about most." His eyes wandered over me and Devrak. He paused. "Or perhaps I can just call my family right now and turn you all over to them, so they can turn you over to Solara, minus all the pointless bloodshed. That's what will happen if you try to sneak away—fair warning."

"And no financial incentive will sway you to be more reasonable with your demands." It wasn't a question from Basra.

"I don't need money. I want power returned to me, I want more of it, and I want our competitor's name ground into dust. Is that so unreasonable?" Makar didn't wait for an answer. "Don't you even want to get a look at your potential bride first, Nevarian?"

I could think of worse imminent horrors, like Solara's fleet, but Nev's jaw hardened, as if what Makar said were unspeakable. "Don't tell me she's here."

Makar touched a comm at his wrist. "Rava, do come into the sitting room, won't you, dear?"

Nev winced. "I've no trouble imagining that you could subject Qole and me to such an awkward situation, but you would call your daughter in here to embarrass her? Are you truly a monster?"

281

Makar's eyes grew flat, looking almost black. "Be careful, young king, in your assumptions. And if you offend my daughter, or shame her, you will live only long enough to regret it."

He might as well have tied a ribbon on it, so neat was his trap. I almost wondered if he'd anonymously tipped off Solara to our presence in order to arrange it all. But no, she'd have had to embark on the journey days ago, well before Makar knew we were here. He was probably right, and she was simply too smart.

I wanted to close my eyes when the soft whisper of slippers over the glossy floor announced a new arrival. But I couldn't help looking.

Rava Treznor-Nirmana was beautiful even at twelve, a perfect flower bud before blossoming fully. She had cascading curly brown hair and coppery brown skin that was somewhere between Basra's and her father's—Nirmana and Valtai. Huge golden-brown eyes stared around the room at us all, and she smiled timidly as she curtsied.

"You sent for me, Father?" Her voice was like a small chime. "Oh, we have guests! How exciting!"

Makar held out his hand, and she immediately went to him and took it. He opened his mouth, but Rava spoke before he could. "We rarely have guests, and never any my age." She beamed at Marsius. "Are you here to visit me?"

"I—" Marsius began, flustered.

"No, my dear," Makar interrupted. He wasn't about to let a second child talk over him, though he looked more amused than irked at his daughter's flood of words. "But *he* is." He held Rava's wrist up to Nev.

My guts twisted like a rag being wrung out. The girl was so sweet, so innocent-seeming, being used in a power play just like the rest of us, and yet I hated her so much I could hardly stand it.

Nev took her hand. Of course, it was the only polite thing to do. He bent over it and kissed her knuckles. "Princess Rava, I am King Nevarian Dracorte."

"*Oh,*" she gasped. She wasn't nearly as polished and poised as other royals, who were used to a life at court. In fact, I'd probably met more royals than she had. "I've heard of you! You . . . you're exactly as I've heard you described." Meaning, *as handsome.* A warm blush pinked her cheeks.

I bit my lip so hard I briefly worried it would bleed. What if Nev was able to like a princess more genuine and kind, less cynical and calculated?

"And you're just as lovely as your father promised," Nev said. The words were smooth, elegant, but there was nothing underneath them. His silver-gray eyes were dull.

At least there was that. Or maybe I was a selfish, jealous idiot and I should have wished Nev all the happiness in the systems, especially if it saved our lives.

If it saved our lives.

Rava's own eyes went back to Marsius. "Then *you* must be Marsius Dracorte, all the way from Luvos. I can give you a tour of the house while you tell me what it's like there. Do you have other princes and princesses your age, or—"

"Rava, dear, now's not the time for chitchat." Makar didn't look entirely pleased with Nev's response, but he wasn't displeased, either. He leaned back in his chair. "Now, Nevarian, what is your decision?"

XIV

I WAS PAINFULLY AWARE OF THE SILENCE THAT SETTLED AROUND US.
Everyone was waiting for me to speak.

But I didn't know what to say. To say yes meant not being
king. It meant truly giving up any hope of a future with Qole.
To say no seemed to doom everyone here, and the systems, to
Solara's rule. I couldn't remember ever seeing my parents at a
loss for words.

Maybe it didn't help that I didn't want to be king. People
spent lifetimes scheming and killing to gain power, people like
my sister. But to me, such a position was only about duty. I
wanted to be with Qole, only Qole, who was standing there
and looking at me with an expression that made my chest hurt.

"You may want to decide soon." Makar poured himself a
glass of something golden out of a minimalist decanter. "I'm

in no hurry, really, but your sister"—he tapped at the infopad with raised eyebrows—"seems very anxious. I have to give her credit; she's decisive."

What I wanted was for everyone I loved to be safe. And in the end, of my miserable choices, none of them left me with Qole anyway. Outside of my pride or any hope for personal happiness, this might not be the worst outcome.

I opened my mouth. The words clawed in my throat, not wanting to come forth.

"Perhaps I could help." Everyone swiveled to stare at Marsius.

"Excuse me?" Makar looked more curious than confused, like a predator that had spotted interesting movement on the horizon.

I'd hardly been paying attention to Marsius until now, other than to make sure he wasn't in any immediate danger.

Marsius cleared his throat and spoke up a little louder, bolder. "King Makar, perhaps you would consider me?"

"What?" I said.

Marsius hardly glanced at me. He walked right up to Rava and bowed deeply. "Princess, forgive my boldness, as I know we have only just met, but I find you . . ." His composure failed him for a moment but he rallied. "Quite charming."

While I'd been lamenting my fate, he'd apparently been staring at Rava, his face aglow with genuine interest, but also understanding. He knew *I* wasn't interested, especially since he'd seen me kiss Qole, and he also knew what was at stake here.

Makar scowled. "Oh no, no. Wait." For once, I completely agreed.

Marsius carried on, taking Rava's hand. "Would you . . .

I mean, I would be honored if you considered me instead of Nev. As you say, we are more of an age, and I've been lonely. You might be too, living here by yourself? And"—he glanced at Makar—"it seems it may be good for both our families."

Marsius had said so many times that he wanted to help. I'd written it off as childish earnestness, but I had to remind myself that even at age eleven, he was already well versed in diplomacy.

Rava's blush looked like it might combust her, and yet she could barely contain her sweet smile. "Prince Marsius, you honor me. I *have* been lonely, and I would adore a friend! But of course, Father must approve." She rounded on her father, eyes agleam. "Oh please, Papa. Please!"

Makar rubbed his brow and made a vague hand gesture. "I see. Dearest . . ."

I could sympathize. In a way, it was a definite compromise. Makar would have an alliance by marriage, and if Marsius stayed on Valtai, he and I both knew that would be the equivalent of a hostage to ensure my general cooperation. At the same time, it was impossible for him to gain any of my subsystems through Marsius, or, more importantly, to subsume the Dracorte name. We would both benefit, and we would both have one another to consider.

And it made me sick to my stomach.

"Marsius—" I started, but Makar cut me off.

"Really, Rava, this little fellow instead of . . . *King* Nevarian, perhaps?" It astounded me that he even considered her preference in the matter, since he was happy to betroth her to a man seven years her senior, but perhaps he would never have followed through without her consent. He seemed to care deeply about her, in his own way. The man was a puzzle.

She nodded shyly, without even looking at me. "I think Marsius and I could be fine companions."

Marsius beamed.

I glanced at the others. Devrak didn't bother hiding his consternation, but he also didn't look as outright opposed as I felt. Knowing his calculating mind, he was probably thinking: *It might be an out.*

It might be a way, if Makar found it useful. But this was Marsius. I remembered the day he was born, my excitement at seeing his face for the first time. Marsius, an innocent, whom everyone loved, who was the best of what we Dracortes had to offer.

And yet, perhaps, while I'd been too busy with other things, as Arjan had accused, Marsius had been growing up. Perhaps, raised as a Dracorte, he had never been overly innocent in the first place. And ever since his parents had died, his brother had vanished, and his sister had sent him away, maybe he hadn't been happy, either.

"Marsius," I started again, stopping. I didn't know what to do. I could not consign him to a decision he might be too young to understand, but if I didn't, we all might simply die. Even now, precious minutes were slipping away.

Arjan walked over to Marsius and put a hand on his shoulder. Makar tensed briefly at his proximity to Rava but didn't stop him.

"Marsius. I trust you, I do, but for ancestors' sake, the thought of marriage scares *me*. I just want to make sure you know what you're getting into." Arjan spoke directly to him, and I could have cried in gratitude for his caring about him as a person, not as a pawn.

Marsius nodded, looking at him and then at me. "I do, and

I think it's for the best. No one is making me do this, especially not you, Nev. I *want* to. Rava and I could keep each other company, and if it helps our friends and family, then . . ."

"Then it's the thing to do," Rava agreed, looking almost surprised at her own boldness.

Makar sat back and rolled the liquid in his glass. "Well. No offense, but the little one isn't quite the same catch."

"I don't think . . . ," I started to say, with no idea how to finish the sentence. I had to agree, I knew that, but couldn't bring myself to do it.

The power in the room died, saving me from having to respond. A warning klaxon began to sound in such a pure tone that it might have been confused for melodic, if red indicator lights hadn't glowed to life along the ceiling.

"We're under attack." Devrak appeared at my side, placing himself between us and the transparent door to the outdoors. "We should move."

"Correction. *I* am under attack." Makar stood up, setting aside his infopad to call out, "Security monitor, status, please."

"Your premises are under assault, Your Highness," a sultry female voice responded. "Snipers eliminated external security, and a squad has infiltrated the grounds. Your personal detail has been diminished to twenty-four. Now eighteen."

"Unbelievable." Makar shook his head. He seemed unconcerned, if annoyed in principle. "Either the council or your sister has taken it upon themselves to bring me out of my convalescence."

"Given the timing, I would guess the latter." Basra had also positioned himself between Arjan and the door. I would have found it amusing at any other time, since Arjan was twice his size . . . if I hadn't seen what Basra could do with a photon rifle. "And I agree with Devrak's suggestion. We should move."

Makar smiled slightly, almost a smirk. "You don't suppose I trust my security to AI systems and guards, do you? This part of the house is sealed and all but impregnable." He walked to the door, one hand in his pocket and the other holding his drink. "No, no. It was only a matter of time before someone tried something like this here, so I've been waiting. It's just a question of whom, so I can visit their loved ones later. Oh, look, there's one."

A figure in heavy battle armor was striding up the steps. Helmeted, capable of operations in a vacuum or atmospheric conditions, the armor rippled with multiple shield types. It would shrug off most handheld energy weapons and was the very picture of why Disruption Blades had come into use. A white stinger had been etched across the breastplate and on the heavy plasma gun that was pointed at us. Two others dropped from the sky behind the first figure, dust rolling out from the impact of their landing. Jagged fins, edges still glowing where thrusters had burned, folded, and disappeared behind their backs. Their visors were up, the faces in the suits older and so scarred that it took a moment to differentiate between the man and woman.

"The Swarm," Basra said tersely.

Recognition made my spine tingle. Mercenary forces were common, used by both major and minor families to do their business for them. But the Swarm was different from regular fleets. It wasn't made up of desperate people with no other options; it was an army of the best, the cream of the crop, soldiers who had survived a career of combat or been too dangerous to be accepted anywhere else. If you hired the Swarm, you'd be broke, but victorious.

Makar scowled. "Solara thinks mercenaries will hide her tracks?" He turned and walked toward Rava, making a shooing motion with his hand. "Rava, dear, these people are not the nicest. How about you go to your room while I deal with them, yes?"

The first figure stopped at the door, the glistening dome of his helmet melding with the faceplate in a reflective mask. He raised a hand, made a curious gesture, and Basra, closest to him, palmed the door open.

I had one terrible moment to wonder if I had been wrong about Basra all this time, before everyone exploded into motion.

Devrak and Arjan almost tripped over one another trying to head off our attacker and shield Marsius at the same time. Makar dove for Rava and snatched up her arm, likely intending to flee with her in the chaos … and if he left, any hope we had of gaining the fleet left with him. Qole must have seen the same thing, because she strode to Makar in two great steps and, with eyes black as pits, punched him in the chest so hard he went tumbling across the room. I pounced on him and put him in a headlock. I wondered if Qole had killed him with the force of her punch, but Makar stirred in my grip and grasped the arm I had around his neck.

Motors in the suit joints whirring, the armored mercenary stepped into the room, past an unconcerned Basra, and leveled the plasma rifle at Makar.

"Don't move." The voice coming from the speaker was familiar, and I narrowed my eyes. The half of the domed helmet slid back as Eton finished his sentence. "I don't want to shoot you while you're useful," he said to Makar, then nodded at Basra. "Thanks."

I was less surprised by his presence than I was relieved. I might not have been Eton's greatest fan, but in our increasingly hostile situation, I at least knew he was friendly to the crew of the *Kaitan,* if not me.

"Eton?" Qole, resting one hand on the floor and the other on her knee, looked at him uncertainly. "No, that's not right. You can't be here."

My stomach dropped. Her tone was wrong, as though she was questioning what her eyes were seeing. She'd been acting strange off and on, but this was the first time I realized it might be something other than stress. Using Shadow took its toll, but the toll might be higher than she was letting on. How much more would it take to permanently damage her, or drive her insane, like her parents?

Eton misunderstood. "It's me, for better or worse. There's not much time to explain. If you want to destroy the new fleet, we need to move. Solara must have guessed what your plan is, since she's sending shuttles filled with ground troops to claim the ships. Once they get here, we won't be able to fight them all off."

"What? How could *you* know what we intend as well?" I shook my head. "Did we just post this on a media site somewhere? Are there cameras?"

Basra cleared his throat. "The captain fired him. She didn't put a gag order on me, or forbid me from hiring a mercenary force. Although"—he raised an eyebrow at Eton—"it sounds as though with Makar here, we might be able to take the fleet ourselves, instead of blowing it to dust."

Eton grinned involuntarily. "Now we're talking." He tipped his head, and an indicator light in his helmet came to life. "Grounds are secure for the next few minutes. If this is going to work, we need to get you to the dock command center. Let's get going." Other figures moved outside, the active camouflage on their suits making them blurry distortions.

Makar didn't stir outside of raising a finger. "Maybe first explain how threatening me will get you a fleet."

"You don't need your limbs to be useful," Eton replied, pointing with his rifle.

"That is very true," the king acknowledged. "However, it's fortunate that your companions and I just reached an equitable agreement. No need for force."

He was lying, but I was happy to let him have it. Releasing my hold, I offered a hand to help him up. "Indeed, we were just agreeing on everything," I said, putting an edge into my voice. "Such as, Marsius will be engaged to Rava, creating an alliance between our families. As a token of your friendship, you will help us take command of the fleet that you built for the Dracortes. And since we will only negotiate with you, not the rest of your family, I'm sure you'll be back in power in no time."

"And we give you the gift of limbs, also," Telu added, from where she sat, tapping away at Makar's infopad. Somehow, in the confusion, she had managed to calmly sit down and begin working.

Makar took my hand and stood up, wincing, one hand to his chest. He spoke to me, but his eyes were on Qole. "A gift, yes. Thank you." Then he snatched the infopad from Telu's hand and turned to his daughter, who was huddling with Marsius. "Rava, are you all right?"

She nodded, her eyes frightened. "Yes. Are these men going to hurt you?"

"No, they won't," Marsius tried to reassure her, taking her hand. "I think this is just how negotiations are done. I've never seen one like this, but I know they can get tense."

Makar's face twitched. "Precisely."

"Then can we get a move on, already?" Arjan demanded from where he stood by the door, peering out, already armed with a spare weapon of Eton's, a snub-nosed photon pistol. "We're wasting time we don't have."

"Not before he signs an agreement," Qole and I said simultaneously. Without thinking, we both smiled at one another, and a pang of longing hit me. For her, for the way things had been, and might never be again. I moved past it quickly by adding, "And as long as you, Marsius and Rava, are certain."

Marsius gave me a grave, adult nod. *I am acting as a man,* he was trying to say. I didn't see how he could be so sure, but he was willing to make a decision I knew could not be easy, regardless of what he indicated. Marsius might have just saved our lives, and I had never felt as proud of my family as I did then. I nodded back at him. Then he looked at Rava, who returned his smile and then turned to her father. "I'm certain, Papa."

Basra stepped forward, motioning to Makar. "I imagine you have recording capabilities, as does Eton's suit. And, as it so happens, I am a registered witness in the Treznor-Nirmana system. Let us state the agreement."

"I appreciate an impartial witness." Makar's lips formed a mocking smile. He keyed open his infopad after shooting a dark look at Telu. "Though truly, I appreciate you not threatening or coercing my daughter in all of this."

"I don't involve children in my business," Eton spat. "Unlike some."

"Really? Devrak begs to differ." Makar looked between us, noting our blank stares. "Eton . . . or should I say *Teveton* . . . didn't tell you?"

"Makar." The warning came from Devrak, not Eton, who had gone pale.

"Everyone here just seemed like such lovely companions. I thought they would have known."

"I know," Basra said, drawing a surprised look from both Devrak and Eton, "and it's inconsequential. Stop stalling."

The king sighed, activating the recording feature on the infopad and setting it down. "Secrets, secrets. Teveton Gregorus, the bodyguard to Devrak's family, killed his wife and daughter while he was ostensibly protecting them, and then disappeared—to join the Swarm, apparently. Really, I'm shocked to see you both so friendly. I would love to hear all the details someday."

I gaped, trying to process. Maybe Basra knew, but all I had known was that Devrak had lost a wife and daughter ages ago. I'd certainly never connected it to Eton's abrupt departure from Dracorva. Besides, Devrak had always said they'd been killed in a shuttle accident.

Eton's voice, hollow with grief in the *Kaitan*'s hold, came back to me: *They killed her, Devrak.*

As bad as you feel, you can well imagine that I feel worse, Devrak had replied.

My thoughts raced back through the years. Devrak's daughter had been about my age when she was killed ten years ago, which would have made her about thirty now. Still younger than Eton, but not by much. She'd been a passionate and vibrant young woman. Zenaria had been her name. Devrak had told me she loved to cook.

"The details," Devrak said tightly, "are that Eton was framed for an assassination that he had nothing to do with. I knew it at the time, and I could never find him to let him know I didn't hold him responsible."

I couldn't imagine who would have dared mount an attack on Devrak's family, much less succeeded—except for a royal. I wondered if that was why Eton had hated me from the minute he'd known who I was.

"It doesn't matter what anyone believes." Eton's basso voice rose. "I didn't want to go back to that society of venomous creatures like *yourself.*" He pointed his weapon at Makar, and for a horrible moment I thought everything was going to fall apart.

Qole was staring at Eton with a mixture of sympathy and wonder. Part of me thought I should feel the same, but given my history with both men, I felt much worse for Devrak. In any case, there wasn't any more time to consider his or Eton's terrible past, because it would be at the expense of our imminently terrible future. Right now, we had to move.

"Makar," I said flatly, breaking the silence. "What are you playing at?"

"Playing? We're allies now. Friends, practically. No secrets, right?" He patted Eton on the shoulder brightly. "Now, I've called royal security away from the construction docks, so we have time there, but it looks like Solara has smelled that something is off and is well on her way. Let's get this agreement witnessed and recorded, the children to a safe house, and ourselves out the door, what do you say?"

———

In the hurtling frame of the *Kaitan,* we armed ourselves for war. For the first time in weeks, I inspected my Disruption Blades. I hadn't wielded them or even wanted to look at them since Suvis had misused them to kill my parents. But something had changed. They felt like mine again. I had watched their crafting under the hands of the most skilled weapon-smiths the systems had to offer, and I knew every scratch, every detail of the hilts, every worn spot on the grips to a degree that gave me calm now.

I had never been in war, but I had been in battles, and my Disruption Blades were an extension of myself. I activated them, the bright blue light pouring down their center inexplicably reminding me of Qole upstairs.

She wasn't well, I was convinced. As badly as I wanted to ask her what was happening, beg her to take care of herself, I knew there wasn't time, and given what we were headed toward, the words would be foolish. We were all in danger, and I could best protect her by doing my duty.

"Nevarian." Devrak poked his head into my quarters. "We're almost there."

I looked up at my mentor's face, wondering how he could show no trace of fear or worry. Everyone else was either tense, angry, worried, or all three. Guilt stabbed at me for never having known the truth about his family, never expressing my sympathy, while I shed tears for my own. He probably hadn't wanted it.

I still would have wanted to give it.

"Devrak, I'm sorry about your wife and daughter. If I had known . . ."

"You were a child when it happened, Nevarian. It was my burden. And Eton's." He smiled sadly and stepped into the tiny room, boots striking on the polished wooden floors. "I brought you a different sort of burden to bear." It was a large rectangular box of blue so dark it was almost black. He pushed it toward me. "I transferred ownership to you, so only you can open it."

It was unexpectedly light when I pulled it closer. Guessing, I placed my palm on the surface. A pulse of brighter blue radiated from my hand, and the top turned into a hundred tiny squares, folding away into nothingness. I recognized the tech; it was the same as the one that Devrak's armor on Alaxak had displayed.

In the case were folded layers of synthetics, light armor plating, and miniaturized equipment. I lifted something that looked like an armguard. It weighed next to nothing.

"Devrak, this is your new armor. I saw you wear it on Alaxak." Something crawled down my spine, some recognition that had not been there before.

Devrak walked to my side, mouth curved in a small smile. "Not new. I have had this suit for a while now. It's worth several fortunes." He took the armguard I was holding and placed it against my forearm. With a barely audible hiss, it attached to my body, a thousand pinpricks rippling across my skin. "I've been running covert operations for your family for quite some time. I was sent when your father couldn't risk anything being traced to the family. This is the armor I've been using. You would normally inherit your father's, but his was much heavier, and I believe you might prefer a lighter touch."

And it was turned to ashes with the Luvos Sunrise, I mentally added. I shook my head. "Devrak, you should have this. It belongs in your family."

Devrak opened his mouth to say something, then reconsidered. Instead, he picked out another piece of the suit and attached it to my bicep. With a click and sting, it formed a connection to the armguard. "Well, you're the one going into combat right now," he finally said, his voice quiet. He looked up, and put a hand on my forearm. "I'm afraid Solara has called me in."

I was silent. I had been dreading this moment. Ever since

he had found me on Alaxak, Devrak had been running an elaborate game of deception with Solara, sending her reports on his activities and falsifying third-party corroboration, but we had agreed that his potential value as intelligence within her regime was invaluable. Now that the time had come, I couldn't imagine him leaving to join her.

"How can you go to her now? What reason can you give her to have been here? She'll know right away." I was grasping at straws. Inside, I knew there was no scenario Devrak hadn't already considered.

"She actually called me in for additional orders several days ago. She thinks I've been on Aaltos trying to spy on you." Devrak smiled. "So this couldn't be neater. She was likely trying to order me here anyway, and if not, I can claim to have been following you. I have any number of reasons to disappear for stretches at a time; it's always been part of my job. I'm going to take a skiff at the docks, and she'll be none the wiser."

I nodded dumbly, looking at my hands. I hadn't realized until now that, with this growing distance between me and Qole, Devrak had been helping me face, well, everything.

The comm in my room chirped and Qole's voice, her tone carefully businesslike, filtered into the room. "Report to the bridge, please."

———

When we came up to the bridge, Eton was speaking. "I rejoined the Swarm when I left you, watched the job boards, hoping I could still be of use. And then I got the call from Basra that you might need some muscle on the ground to deal with this worm."

Dressed in his own armor, a smooth gray affair, Makar feigned indignation at being called a worm.

"Ancestors, that's great," Arjan said from the copilot's station. "It's good to have you back."

I struggled to keep my face neutral. I wasn't sure what made me consistently less than human in Arjan's eyes, but he was acting as though my latest near death thanks to Eton had never happened. Perhaps it was because Eton was useful now, but that didn't mean I had to like him, or that the past was forgotten.

"No one is back," Qole said flatly, from the captain's chair. "Focus on the job. Eton, brief them."

I expected Eton to at least look chagrined, but to my disappointment he took it in stride. His tone was businesslike, that of a sergeant briefing his squadron. "Right. Solara's fleet is still in a holding pattern, the official distance away from the planet, just like your twenty destroyers, so as not to violate any treaties. Unfortunately, she has sent troops to secure the construction docks in orbit." He raised his wrist, and it projected a small holo of Valtai's orbital airspace. The new fleet was shown safely locked away in its docks, hovering well over the planet's surface, and our additional shuttles from Talia and Gavros were blue dots that had almost reached it. But at the outskirts of the holo were twice as many red dots making their way toward the same destination. Eton pointed a finger at a small station attached to the construction docks. "That's the command center. The fleet can only be claimed there, and Solara has sent a security detail to hold it, since she guessed something was up. If we act quickly, Nev can redirect some of the troops he sent for the ships to secure the command center before her, so Makar can pass control of the fleet to him." He nodded to Makar, who handed me his infopad.

"For a purchase of this magnitude, several safeguards are put into place," Makar explained. "Only someone with the appropriate rank can authorize the release of the vessels, and only with the presence of the purchaser. Or their direct beneficiary after death, of course." Makar shrugged at me with indifference. I wanted to punch him.

"In lesser circumstances, it could be done remotely," Eton continued, "but for something like this, both parties need to be present at the control center on the docks. Right now, Solara's being careful with troop numbers, but as soon as she catches a whiff of the Swarm and our possible victory, she's going to respond with more force than we can handle—in minutes, not hours. We have a small window."

"What about planetary security?" I asked.

Makar smiled. "They have conflicting orders: to support Solara, from my family council, and to stand down, from me. They're listening to me. We typically stay out of purchaser squabbles. Whoever lives can pay."

Whoever lives can pay. Of that I had no doubt, but I wondered who would end up paying the ultimate price. Some part of me knew that trying to capture an entire fleet with Solara waiting to attack was unlikely to end in success.

I didn't have a chance to respond when the *Kaitan* bucked and Qole put us in a swooping dive, almost dropping me to the floor.

"We're taking fire. Small arms," Basra reported from his station below.

"Strap in." Qole's mouth was a grim line. "It's about to get rough."

———

The construction docks were in orbit, barely. It looked a lot like the water docks on Alaxak: a series of long, flat open-air pathways branching off several central hubs, with arms at ninety-degree angles, and ships parked in rows. Only, being above the atmosphere, there were many layers of docks, cranes, and scaffolding between them so each project could be accessed from any point in space. At the center of it all was our goal: the dock command center. Suspended in midair, surrounded by the shimmer of mag-field supports, the command center was a simple transparent globe several hundred feet in diameter. From far away, the whole thing reminded me of the lace of Dracorvan architecture. Up close, it was as rough and utilitarian as an electrical circuit. In the distance below, visible through a patchwork of girders and clouds, was the humbly named Makar Ocean, the blue curve of the planet disconcertingly close.

Around the docks was an expensive containment field for breathable air, so techs and engineers could work in atmosphere rather than vacuum. Now, it rippled with color from the erupting firefight. Gray-clad troops appeared and disappeared like insects among the storage containers and equipment inside, and stray bolts of energy escaped from the containment field like a deranged rainstorm. It made it hard to appreciate the view.

Qole ignored the stray fire, trusting the sturdy hull of the *Kaitan* to shrug it off. She looked up at me. "Where?"

Activating the lenses in my eyes, I scanned the structure for a safe space to put down. We couldn't have known where until now. Red silhouettes—our enemies—flickered out around the figures nearest the tall command center tower in the middle of the platform. Blue overlays dotted the locations of other, closer troops. Our forces.

"There." I pointed to a space intended for a future construction project, right near the command center, but free of Solara's troops.

Qole nodded imperceptibly, her fingers flexed, and the *Kaitan,* air rippling from the heat of its backwash, rocketed sideways like an angry insect and settled into the space with comfortable precision.

"We're here." Qole's hands flew over the controls as she began shutting the *Kaitan* down.

I was suddenly scared, rooted to the spot. Outside would be the scream and roar of weaponry and smell of death. Again. And as much as I had thought I was past it, every horrible moment of the last month came rushing back to me. So many people dead, so many as a result of things I'd done or been involved in. My hands started to shake, and I looked down at them. Every death felt like a personal failure. And stepping outside meant confronting that.

I met Qole's gaze. There was concern on her face, but her eyes were steady. She knew what she had to do, and she was going forward.

I felt myself come back together as neatly as Qole had landed the *Kaitan.* People would die; I knew that, and I knew I couldn't change it. But *we* wouldn't. And hopefully, we'd save more lives than we lost today. But then, as Qole reached for the last switch, I saw that her hands were shaking too.

"We're going to make it," I told her. She opened her mouth to reply, but I raised a finger. "And don't tell me I can't know that. The only thing we've consistently done is survive, so I'm going off evidence here."

The corners of her mouth curved up in the smallest of smiles. "You've got me there."

For a single precious second, that smile was the only thing

that existed. I couldn't imagine a better world than one where she would find something to smile over, and I wanted to create it for her.

It flickered and disappeared, and the captain was back. "Now let's get to work."

Our group wound through the abandoned construction toward the command center, alternately crouching and covering one another as we went. We made for my troops, which I could see in my lenses.

My troops. It was strange to think of those men and women as fighting and dying, trusting in my command, my ability to make decisions.

We broke into the open of the platform, and the firefight was spread out before us. Streaks of energy flickered between two positions, ours and Solara's, debris scattering from blaster fire. Shields flashed and hummed, their incandescence lighting the spiraling smoke that drifted over the battleground. My troops had formed a defensive perimeter at the entrance to the command center.

As advanced and ostentatious as anything of Treznor make was likely to be, the transparent sphere of it was connected by a thin, almost invisible clear elevator shaft to the platform below. It was the only way in.

A woman ducked near me, half her helmet covered in dried blood, her armor striped with scorch marks. "Your Majesty." She saluted crisply. "Commander Aris." Without her name, I would have recognized her voice, even drowned out by weaponry, sounding through the comm in my ear. She was the sharp-faced woman from my Forging. "We mobilized a few minutes too late to take the command center. We're pinned. Our equipment was intended for an infiltration mission, not heavy combat. Without heavy losses, I doubt we can go on the offensive."

"Copy." I knew what she was asking: Did I want them to engage in a suicide charge? I was amazed by her loyalty but grateful I didn't have to contemplate such a thing. I brought up an overlay of the battlefield on my lenses.

"Even if we manage to win here, Solara will have already sent a small party up to the control center." Basra's voice filtered into my ear, his meaning clear. If Solara secured the control center for her own arrival and arranged for another royal family member to sign the fleet over to her, we would be done. *We're almost out of time.*

I traded glances with Eton. "Commander," I said to Aris, "lay down any visual cover you have left. All of it. Then hold your fire and, on my mark, charge the enemy position."

It still *sounded* like a suicide charge to her; she just didn't know it.

She didn't even blink. "Copy." If I'd doubted her bravery in the Forging, I didn't now. Then she winked through her visor. "But if I survive, I want a rematch." She turned, adjusted her comm frequency, and began to bark orders. Dozens of canisters arched through the air, trailing plumes. They landed with a spin, smoke pouring heavily from them. In addition to the smoke, infrared and electromagnetic signals were pulsing as well, there to scramble every sensor the enemy had, visual or otherwise.

I waited, counting down from ten to myself. *Ten, nine, eight.*

All fire ceased from my troops as smoke filled the air. Enemy fire still lanced through, the colors almost beautiful if it weren't for their deadly intent. *Seven, six, five.*

The smoke rose high into the air, the circulation vents wafting it over us in a fog. *Four, three.*

As the fog started to peel away, suddenly I could see the ghostly figures of the Swarm hurtle through it. My troops hadn't come prepared for heavy combat, but the Swarm was famed for nothing but. Their powered combat suits let them leap with murderous velocity directly into enemy positions. Their mass shattered shields and soldiers alike, sending shock waves through the duracrete beneath us. Once in enemy positions, they methodically opened fire with heavy plasma rifles that scorched holes and rendered commandos to ash.

Two. One. "Mark." I spoke into the comm, and our troops rushed the enemy. I whipped both Disruption Blades into my hands, and after a few running steps, I jumped.

Devrak's suit, which I was now wearing in full, wasn't powered in the same way, but its tiny servos would, on command, provide extra force. I couldn't use it indiscriminately, but I chose to activate them as I pushed off, feeling the rush of power as I leapt farther than human muscles could propel me. I landed in the enemy position and went to work. My Disruption Blades glowed in the smoke, leaving trails and patterns as I used speed to my advantage. Each strike deactivated shield stations and damaged weaponry, making an open path for soldiers behind. The smoke cleared in front of me, and I saw two of Solara's Bladeguards doing the same to a member of the Swarm: deactivating his suit with their swords, then following through with blaster shots and blade stabs to the faceplates. I caught one of them by surprise, slashing through his defenses and armor, while several precise shots from behind me dropped the other to the ground.

Basra's voice sounded in my ear. "You're welcome."

"Show-off," I muttered, turning.

Through the smoke, Qole filtered into view, wearing the combat suit Talia had given her. Dark interlocking rings covered her limbs and lower torso, while thin armor plates covered her chest and shoulders. Brown synthetics scooped from her neck down to the armor, allowing for flexibility. An insignia was burned onto her right shoulder plate: three stars over three waves that represented the fledgling Alaxak government. With this, she still wore her original leather boots and gloves. A plasma pistol was strapped to one thigh, and she cradled a rifle as though she had been born to it. Arjan and Basra were close behind in matching suits of their own, Arjan with his knives strapped across his chest.

They ran with grim determination into the breach I had made, laying suppressive fire as Eton had taught them. If Qole was afraid, she didn't show it, naming targets to Arjan and Basra as Telu relayed enemy positions from the *Kaitan* while parsing endless feeds—video, radar, heat-sensing, and anything else she could get her hands on.

I couldn't watch for long; we only had precious minutes remaining in our window for success. I left them, darting through the combat field, relying on my suit to keep me safe as I headed for the elevator that led to the command center hovering in the air above us.

"Eton," I ordered, "now."

Eton landed before me, his arm wrapped around Makar's waist, and cracks spread in the duracrete below his feet at the force of his impact. He set Makar down, and the Treznor-Nirmana king dusted himself off with dignity. With a twist of his hand, he opened the elevator doors, and the three of us disappeared inside. We were gone before our attackers even realized what had happened.

"Telu," I said. "We're in."

"Good job," she responded. "Qole is going to help Aris secure the entrance."

My heart hammered. I wanted to be there with Qole, fighting. But the only real thing I could do to help her was leave her. It was becoming a familiar pattern. One I hated.

At another gesture from Makar, the platform beneath us lurched. Gravitational dampeners kicked in, and we stood comfortably, watching the battle recede behind us as we shot upward.

"Telu says sensors confirm a small group is already in the command center," Eton reported. "I should be able to over-whelm them pretty easily."

Makar smiled. "My, aren't you confident. How easily, do you think?"

———

"Quite easily, I see" was Makar's only comment minutes later, as we stepped past the scorched bodies of the soldiers that had been waiting to ambush us. That was all they could have done, since they couldn't get inside the inner control room without Makar.

Outside the crystal-clear sphere of the command center, the construction docks floated in the vacuum of space, a maze of equipment and ships—almost every one part of Solara's commissioned fleet that we were about to steal. It was an impressive view, with the inside of the control center even more ostentatious. From an outer circular walkway, another narrower catwalk ran to the middle, where the control room was suspended. It had a dais with a command terminal and was surrounded in a transparent bubble itself, scenes of ancient victories engraved by lasers on the surface. It was a place designed to impress, to entertain visiting royals as they claimed their new purchases in pomp and circumstance. As a result, there were also shuttle launches attached to the outside ring of catwalk: escape pods.

Telu's voice sounded in my ear. "Nev, gotten anywhere yet? Solara is dropping something like a hundred shuttles. Give them twenty, and they will be all over you."

We ran across the catwalk, Makar shouting as he led the way. "After I enter the access codes, the system will take readings of both of us. Don't leave or it will restart!"

"How long will this take?" I couldn't keep the tension from my voice as he waved open the door to the interior control center. "Solara is sending reinforcements."

"It takes longer than it has any right to," Makar replied. "If you want whoever is going to man your new fleet to get here before Solara, I would suggest you issue the command to them now."

I had been holding off for a reason. On the way from Makar's to here, I'd already used the QUIN to message Talia and Gavros to let them know that the plan had changed, that now we were seizing the fleet, not destroying it, and that we needed hundreds of reinforcements ready to crew our new ships. They'd had the numbers waiting on board dozens of shuttles as a contingency, in case I had been captured with our small strike force during the sabotage mission. In such an event, they would have thrown all caution to the winds and openly defied the Treznor-Nirmanas to get me back and to try to steal the new ships. It would have been a desperate, last move, since it would have meant war with both Solara *and* Treznor-Nirmana.

But that was before Makar had taken our side.

Now those shuttles were near, but I'd ordered them to wait just out of range of the docks. Because if we didn't seize the new ships in time, everyone I sent here would be sitting targets for Solara's fleet. They would be putting their faith in us. In me. I shook my head. *It's official. I hate my job.*

I stood in the doorway to the interior control sphere, watching Makar awaken the ownership programming, and gave the order for the shuttles to land.

"Affirmative, Your Majesty. Have you taken control?"

I grimaced. If this didn't work with Makar, this order would sentence all of them to death. "No, but I will have by the time you get here."

A thick palm punched into my back, and I flew face-first onto the catwalk of the control sphere, blood in my mouth as the shriek of a plasma rifle sounded behind us. The rifle shrieked twice more, and I rolled over to see Suvis in midair outside the elevator, just as he buried his Disruption Blade into the faceplate of Eton's power suit. Energy discharged from the sword in a corona, and Eton dropped to his knees, wobbling there for a terrible moment in the heavy suit, his plasma rifle crashing to the floor, before he fell onto his back with an enormous clang.

Face invisible in his skintight black mask, Suvis stalked toward me, Disruption Blade in one hand, photon pistol in the other. Two scorch marks marred Suvis's suit, the blistered skin oozing, but they seemed to have no effect on him. I glanced around for my gun and saw it on the bottom of the command-center sphere, fallen off the catwalk when Eton had pushed me out of the way. The pistol was as good as gone, and my blades wouldn't help me at this distance. Suvis took aim.

Before he could fire, the transparent door to the control room slid shut between Suvis and me, sealing itself with a pop. A moment later Suvis's shot scoured the surface before my eyes in an ugly streak.

I sprang to my feet, Disruption Blades humming to life. "Open the door," I snarled at Makar. "I'll end him."

"There is no time." Makar stepped up to the command terminal on the center dais.

I didn't move. "He'll kill Eton."

"He looks quite dead to me already." For once, Makar's response was completely serious. "If you want any chance to beat your sister to this fleet, we must do this now." His fingers danced across the display panel's interface.

"Welcome, Your Majesty," a synthesized, sexless voice intoned. "Initiating ownership transfer protocols."

Every fiber of my being wanted to slaughter the wretched man inches from me. There was a twisted justice to Eton being felled by the very person he had abandoned me to, but I could find no pleasure in it.

I tore myself away and stalked toward Makar. He was right. *This isn't about stopping the weapon; this is about stopping that hand that wields it.* I repeated the thought over and over, using it as a mantra to keep my reason.

As soon as I reached Makar's side, another light glowed to life on the terminal display. "Codes authorized. Gathering biometric data," the voice announced, the last words muffled by the crack that came from behind us.

Suvis had driven the point of his Disruption Blade into the door. He did it again. And again. He paused to fire at the same point with his blaster, then began chipping away with the sword again.

"Um . . . that looks like it might work," I said.

Makar glanced at his progress. "It might. If he breaks in before the process is complete, one of us will have to deal with him."

I stared, fascinated, as Suvis continued. His pace was machinelike, unwavering. The cracks spreading in the dura-plast paid testimony to his determination.

My eyes traveled to where Eton lay, perhaps dead or dying. I wondered how I would explain to Qole and the rest of the crew what had happened, especially if his sacrifice had been in vain.

That was when the breastplate of Eton's suit exploded forward and a single fist shot into the air.

Rising from the husk of his suit, face bloody from a long gash down his cheek, Eton emerged. He snatched the heavy breastplate with both hands and heaved. Somehow, Suvis brought his arms up in defense as it struck him, driving him against the door. His pistol fell out his hand and bounced off the catwalk into the air. Straightening, Suvis maintained his grip on his blade and hefted the breastplate as if it weighed nothing, perhaps to hurl it back at Eton.

Before he could, Eton pile-drived against his own armor plating, pinning the assassin and latching onto the hand that held the Disruption Blade. Suvis dropped it, then, in a movement so fast I couldn't follow it, snatched it out of the air with his other hand. But Eton was already moving back, taking the breastplate with him. Suvis stabbed at his torso, but Eton raised the breastplate and smashed it violently aside. The blade merely clattered to the catwalk.

"Biometrics collected," the voice informed us, calm and oblivious to the chaos outside. "Verifying."

Suvis pounced, placing his foot on top of the breast-plate and using it as a launchpad to leap even higher. Then

311

he dropped, bringing his knee down on Eton's head. Eton toppled backward like a felled tree, the breastplate clattering out of nerveless fingers.

"Pity he didn't last longer. We need a bit more time," Makar said with a sigh. I couldn't respond.

Suvis drove his knee down yet again. I would have broken away, run for the door, but Makar had hold of me with a steel grip.

He's going to kill Eton, and I'm just going to stand here and watch.

Eton caught Suvis's knee. He should have had a fractured skull. Instead, the muscles in his arms bunched like coiled cables, and with a heave, he threw Suvis back.

Suvis landed in a roll, and Eton stood. He moved slower, carefully, with determination. With perfect form, he settled into the defensive position that Devrak loved. Instead of the typical fury, his face was calm, and he smiled a bloody smile, beckoning with one hand.

"Biometrics confirmed. Welcome, Nevarian Dracorte. Please acknowledge your desire to complete this transaction."

"Yes, yes!" I shouted. "I confirm."

Suvis and Eton met, arms a blur, feet dancing. Eton would deflect, trap a limb, and attempt to engage, only to have Suvis pummel him from another direction. But unlike Suvis's fight with me, Eton didn't seem to get worn down. Instead, he absorbed each hit, and his smile only grew. For once, he was exactly where he wanted to be, where he needed to be. Every strike, every punishing blow, fed him. He was the shield, the last line. And he was willing, happy, to pay the price.

"Your Royal Majesty King Makar Treznor-Nirmana, please confirm to complete this transaction."

"Confirmed," Makar said, then looked at me. "There. All done." He keyed open the door.

I hurtled through even as Suvis somersaulted backward, retrieving his sword. He twisted to meet both my blades with his one, their lights intermingling and flickering between us.

"I will kill you," I snarled, my face almost touching his.

He headbutted me and whirled to meet Eton.

And for the next few seconds, Suvis held both of us off. I had expected him to crumple under our attack, not become even faster than before. His sword flickered between us so quickly that it felt impossible that he was responding to our moves, seemingly anticipating them instead. My blades sparked against his, Eton ducked and danced, and neither of us could connect.

Until I trapped his blade with both of mine, and Eton snap-kicked him in the chest.

Suvis twisted uncannily in midair as he fell, his hands grasping the edge of the catwalk by his fingertips. He swung underneath it, caught the other side, and heaved himself back up to our level.

Eton and I both stared. "All right," I said. "That's simply ridiculous."

Suvis didn't stay to argue. He turned and ran, legs and arms pumping, straight for a shuttle launch bay. Eton and I gave chase, only to have the launch door close in our faces.

As we watched the shuttle depart, engines flaring in the darkness of space, I remembered Makar and turned, only to see him at another shuttle bay. He waved cheerfully. "The fleet is yours, my future nephew-in-law. I will be watching with total attention. Best of luck." And then he, too, was gone.

"Well, wonderful," I said, for a moment overwhelmed with

simple irritation. I looked to Eton, to see he had silently slid to the ground, clutching his ribs, eyes shut. Of course. He had seemed incapable of pain, but the amount of damage he'd just absorbed would have leveled most men several times over. Instinct took over and I kneeled by his side, fumbling for the medi-kit pouch on my suit.

Telu sounded in my ear, her voice almost panicked. "Nev, for the love of the ancestors, respond." I'd been hearing her before now only vaguely, the volume down so I could concentrate. "Eton has gone offline. Are you all right?"

I wiped the sweat from my brow with a shaky hand, prepping a stim for Eton. "Affirmative, Telu. The fleet is in our possession. Eton is okay. We had some, uh, excitement."

"I've about had my fill of excitement, so keep it down a notch," she snapped. "Solara is pulling back her shuttles. She knows you have the fleet. Makar's confirmation sent out a detectable signal."

At least that was something. Without her here on the docks, we'd have more time to mobilize. It was going to take a little while to get pilots into the ships, boot them up, and warm up the engines. "Right. Keep me informed. Give me two, I need to take care of something."

I pushed the stim against Eton's thigh, and it injected with a hiss. He gasped with relief. I moved to his face next, placing a plastiskin patch on his gashed cheek.

He cracked an eyelid and looked at me. "Thanks."

He was bruised, bloody, but alive. And I was alive thanks to him. "The least I could do," I said shortly.

He chuckled. "We make a pretty good team, I guess." Then he opened both eyes, his expression serious, and dragged himself into a seated position. "I'm sorry I didn't realize it sooner."

He held out a hand. "I have a lot to make up for, if you'll let me."

I stared. Eton had tried to kill me not once, but twice. Maybe three times, depending on how one counted. From the day I had met him, he'd been hostile and rude. He had betrayed me at one of my lowest points, while pretending to be, if not a friend, then at least a partner-in-crime.

"You never give up," I said slowly, not taking his hand. "At every turn, you keep trying again."

Eton kept it extended. "Like I said, I have a lot to make up for. I just do what I can."

I'd said the same words to the Priestess of Truth. Eton had been struggling for the same thing as I. To somehow, in some small way, make things better. To keep those he loved safe. And in the process, he had hurt me very badly.

If I couldn't forgive him for that, if I couldn't see his struggle to redeem himself, how could I expect anyone to tolerate my mistakes? How could I hope for someone like Arjan to ever forgive me, no matter how hard I tried?

If any of us were to stand a chance in what came next, we *all* needed to act as a team.

I took his hand. "New start," I said firmly.

Eton blinked, surprise on his craggy face. Then he smiled, a genuine, happy smile. "Deal."

"Nev! Eton!" Qole called out from behind us, and I turned to see her exiting the elevator. Relief washed over me to see her unharmed. Basra and Arjan were with her as well, Arjan missing several of the knives he had been carrying before. They looked between Eton and me, their faces questioning.

"No, I didn't do this to him," I said with a sigh, standing from my kneeling position.

"As if," Eton rumbled. "When you get as good as that guy, I'll ask you for lessons."

"Hey," I protested, but then held out my hand, this time to help him up. He clasped it, and I pulled him to his feet with a grunt.

I was unable to contain a grin at the mystified expressions on the others' faces. I looked at them, these extraordinary people arrayed to either side of me, and for the first time, I felt a glimmer of hope. I'd thought I had to push everyone away in order to do what my position demanded of me. But perhaps we could do this. Together.

Telu's voice sounded on the comm again. "Nev, Devrak needs to talk to you. I can transfer him to you when you're ready."

I went still. Even though we had set up a way for him to contact the *Kaitan,* I knew he wouldn't be contacting me so soon if something weren't wrong. "Put him through."

Devrak's voice was quiet. "Nev, there isn't much time. Listen carefully. I've been accepted on the ship, with no security restrictions."

I glanced at Qole, frowning. "That's good, right?"

Devrak ignored my comment. "Solara gave the order to an advance team of destroyers to enter Valtai's orbital airspace. She's going to destroy the ships in their docks, Nevarian."

I broke out in a sweat. "She can't. Treznor-Nirmana will consider that an act of war; they'll attack her fleet."

"That's what I told her. She said now that you own it, they will treat it as a civil war and stay neutral. It helps that she's only sending a few ships. She's right, Nevarian—no one is going to stop her."

There was no time to power up the ships before she made her move, especially not the Belarius Drives. Defense was impossible. *Escape* was impossible. Even if we boarded the shuttles our forces had come in on, she'd blow us out of the sky before we could get far enough away. The realization settled over all of us in the command center with the same quiet, heavy chill of a mausoleum.

"What about Talia and Gavros?" I asked desperately. "Their twenty destroyers could make the difference in our fleet getting operational here." They'd been holding back for diplomacy with the Treznor-Nirmanas, but now, apparently, that wasn't an issue.

"If they can get there in time. The chances are slim." Devrak's voice cut into the silence. "Unless I ensure things on this end."

I couldn't respond. I knew what he wanted.

He was asking for approval to assassinate Solara.

"Nev, she will kill you all without a second thought." The voice in my ear was gentle, despite the words. I couldn't remember him calling me by my nickname ever before. "She's a monster."

She was. I knew it was true. But she was also my sister, my own blood, and a person who could have been my close friend. Now I was going to order her assassination because we were both struggling for the same thing. Grasping for power, for the crown.

Besides . . .

"Devrak, killing Solara is a suicide mission," I said. Qole's eyed widened, and I held them, something steady.

"Not necessarily. I have options, and Suvis isn't here. But . . . Nevarian, I'm a soldier. We can all die at any time. And we have little time to act."

I bit my lip, looking down. In the end, this wasn't about power. It was about survival—Solara or thousands of people.

I couldn't think of it as Qole or Devrak.

Unable to look at the others, I walked to the edge of the walkway and gazed through the glass beyond. I could see our boarding shuttles at the construction docks nearest to us, the power flickering on in the battle carriers and destroyers. Each light felt like life—*lives*—behind which a team of people worked frantically, who believed in my leadership, who believed that Solara's rule was wrong.

Something cold and hard settled around my heart. "Please make it quick."

"Yes, Your Majesty. You're doing the right thing." Not giving me a chance to argue, he added, "It will be best if you comm your sister when I give a signal, keep her focus on you. I'll click open an encrypted line to Telu when I'm ready."

"Devrak . . ." I worked hard to keep my voice steady, as calm as his. "I need to you to know that you're my friend."

"I dislike good-byes." I couldn't see his face, but the smile in his voice brought it to mind vividly—that brilliant, rare grin, the laugh lines in his brown skin, and the eyes that seemed too gentle for what the hands were capable of. "But, my king . . . my friend . . . we will speak when this is over, I promise you."

I nodded, feeling foolish, knowing he couldn't see me. "I believe you."

There was the faint tone of his disconnect, and that was it.

XV

THE CONTROL CENTER WAS QUIET AS NEV WAITED FOR THE SIGNAL FROM Devrak. Telu was nearby, infopads in hand, keeping Devrak's comm channel secure. She also helped Eton bind a few final bandages with a tenderness I hadn't noticed in her before, nearly like how Arjan and Basra were fussing over each other. Telu must have missed him. I had too, but the moment my feet tried to lift in his direction, my body froze, like I was about to step over an edge.

I stood, effectively alone, trying not to feel the empty space around me like a chill. They all had someone to comfort them, except for me. And Nev. We both stared at the still-black vid feed, ready and waiting to come alive with Solara's image.

I jumped when I felt an arm around my waist. Telu stood at my side and gave me a squeeze, along with a tentative smile. "How you holding up?"

"Fine," I lied, my voice tight. I didn't want her to know how much I appreciated her presence. If I didn't need self-pity, I didn't need *her* pity, either.

Another arm came across my shoulders from the other side . . . Arjan. "If anyone can do this, Devrak can," he muttered. "We'll make it."

Together, my brother and Telu made a sandwich with me between them. My family, surrounding me. Hadn't it been just us in the beginning? I'd felt so stable and self-sufficient before, but now, being responsible for them sometimes made my loneliness feel like it was enough to crush me.

"I am here," Nev's voice said.

I glanced at him, trying to stifle my urge to gasp. It had sounded like him, but I knew it was impossible.

I closed my eyes and clenched my teeth, willing myself to calm down, my heartbeat to slow. That was another reason I couldn't get close to anyone. When insanity finally enveloped me in its long-promised embrace, it would be better if no one else was nearby.

And it was already happening.

Maybe Shadow, in my blood and bones from the very beginning, had been my closest companion.

"Yes. You are learning. We are learning." Nev's disembodied voice, speaking those words, made me shiver.

"You sure you're all right?" Telu murmured softly.

"I said I was fine." I slipped away from both her and Arjan in case I shuddered again and they felt it. They both glanced at each other. Telu looked hurt—but not for long. Her fingers went to the comm at her ear.

"Devrak clicked his channel open!" she said, hurrying to her array of infopads, laid out over the top of a control panel.

"Two clicks, which means Solara's in her office on the *Volassa*. I'm requesting an open line now."

It took only thirty seconds. We all stared, barely breathing, at the vid feed until it blinked into life.

Solara stood on the other end. She shone like a star, as usual, and wore a small smile on her face. Every muscle in my body flexed. Nev faced her, seemingly calm, his eyes tired, his hair mussed, but his shoulders squared in his armor, the control center transparent behind him. The rest of us were even more haggard. Solara was no doubt taking us all in with pleasure. If I could have leapt through the feed to strangle her, I would have.

A private office looked to be in the background of Solara's feed, paneled in dark wood. Only the edge of a holodesk was visible in front of her. There was no sign of Devrak yet.

"I must say, I'm surprised," she said, her voice smooth and almost pleasant, if not for the brittleness, like ice ready to crack. "I didn't think you were one for begging."

"I don't want to beg," Nev said, his expression still, his voice as level and taut as a tightrope.

"You wish to hurl more false accusations at me before you face justice?" she added, probably for the benefit of anyone else who might be listening, in case we were trying to set her up. "Now, that *would* be more like you."

"I just want to talk, Solara."

"Do you wish to discuss the weather? The latest fashion in Dracorva? I'm all ears, at least for the amount of time it takes my destroyers to reach you."

"I want you to rethink what you're doing. It doesn't have to be this way."

I remembered him saying the same thing to me on Aaltos— the same hopeful, futile words. They were futile in Solara's case even more than mine, because more impossible than a future with Nev and me together was a compromise from a power-hungry sociopath.

"Oh?" she asked breezily. "What can it be? I'm sure you'll tell me anyway."

"We're *Dracortes*, Solara. This is beneath us. The systems are watching, and—"

She scoffed and folded her arms. "Do not preach to me about family honor, *brother*, when you were willing to throw it all away for an infatuation. And please spare me a further lesson about the supposed morality of what you did. We're both just fighting for what we want."

Nev pressed on. "Well then, hear me as your brother if you won't as a Dracorte. We are blood, Solara. We grew up together. We've dined and laughed and danced together more times than I can count. Can you really do this to me, destroy me, while looking me in the face?"

He looked so sincere, even to me. I hoped this was part of the distraction and he wasn't *actually* trying to convince her. His naïveté had hurt him too many times.

Solara stared at Nev. I could see nothing in her steely, silver-gray eyes. No hint of remorse or glimmer of feeling.

A knock sounded through the feed, rapping on the door to Solara's office. Her face lit up, then. "Ah, yes. I wanted you to see him. To realize where he truly stands, which is *not* with you." She tipped her head. "Come in, Devrak."

Devrak appeared in the background, looking entirely at ease.

Her voice went plaintive. "Devrak, Nev is on the feed, trying to talk me into pulling back. Do you think I should listen?"

Devrak arched an eyebrow. "Strategically unwise, unless he plans to admit his guilt in your parents' murder and abdicate his false claim to the throne, so we can put him through proper channels for justice."

He was obviously acting, but he was putting on a good show. Almost too good. He had to be, for Solara.

Her smile was predatory. "See, Nev? No one believes your lies. Not your sister, not your old mentor. You're a traitor to your name, your blood, and your subjects, and *this* is justice." She nodded in Devrak's direction without taking her eyes from the feed. "It must hurt your sanctimonious sense of moral superiority to know that someone like Devrak is loyal to me."

Nev didn't have to pretend to glower.

This was the time for Devrak to strike. But he didn't move. I started to feel nervous.

"You need more convincing, I think, brother dear," Solara said, her eyes narrowed at Nev. "Devrak?"

"Yes, Your Majesty?" he said levelly, clasping his hands behind his back.

"Are Talia and Gavros coming to Nev's aid?"

Devrak's brow furrowed. "Your Majesty . . ."

"It's okay, Devrak. We can tell him now. It's too late for him to do anything about it. Did you or did you not bring Talia and Gavros my terms and convince them to stay out of this fight?"

Devrak's face smoothed—resigned. That was when I knew we were in trouble. "Yes."

"No," Nev said immediately after.

Solara grinned like a girl with the winning hand at a card game. "Check your feeds. Are the twenty Aaltos destroyers rushing to your aid?"

No, I thought, echoing Nev. Not only Devrak, but *Talia* would never . . .

Telu cursed. "Great Collapse, she's right. They said they were coming, but . . ."

"But never trust a royal," Arjan ground out.

"But they're not headed for the docks," Telu finished, sounding on the verge of tears. "They're close, but moving around the other side of the planet, out of the potential battle zone. There's no way they can get to us in time before Solara's destroyers do. They're not even *trying* to."

Solara sighed. "They knew it was a lost cause."

Eton was frozen, staring as though he couldn't believe what he was seeing. Basra was too, but like he *could* believe it.

Nev looked gutted. "Devrak . . ."

"I'm sorry, Nevarian," he murmured. At least he met Nev's eyes straight on when he said it. "I had to."

"My loyal servant," Solara said, but she was only looking at Nev, gauging his reaction. The world felt like it was collapsing under my feet. It was all over.

That was when, on the feed, Devrak stepped silently up behind her. Maybe, even after setting us up as sitting targets, he still planned to kill Solara. It was the least he could do.

But before he could make a move, Solara turned and held out her hand, as if for Devrak to kiss her ring, pay homage to her.

Devrak took her hand with his right and bent over it. His left hand tucked behind his back. This was it. He could still strike her down when she least expected it. When he looked up at her, I recognized the gleam of victory in his eyes, and the sudden flash of fear in Solara's.

But then Devrak suddenly went rigid, straightening with a gasp. His eyes bulged. A dagger, sharp and gleaming, clattered from his left sleeve.

Solara pursed her lips. "A dagger? How messy."

Devrak wasn't moving, only standing frozen, his expression alarmed.

Nev lurched forward, but he caught himself, bracing his arms on a control panel. "What's happening?"

"My hands are coated in a neurotransmitting paralyzing agent. It's instantaneous, and lasts for about forty-five seconds." She bent to retrieve the dagger. "I knew betraying you would be so hard on him that he'd try something drastic. He did have such a soft spot for you."

Nev sounded afraid. "What are you doing?"

Solara came around to Devrak's shoulder. She tapped his arm with the blade. "I told you he stands with me—if only when forced." She sighed and gestured dramatically, as if this were all a game. "But see, look how loyal he is now! At my command, he stays his hand and holds still."

"Solara . . . ," Nev said, choked. I didn't know what he planned to say, and apparently he didn't either.

She held his eyes again. "You thought to distract me with this little ploy, to pluck at my heartstrings and wring a sad song from me, while Devrak put a knife in my back? What is it you said? *Can you really destroy me, while looking me in the face?*" With a wicked smile, she added, "Now, now, you *have* changed."

"Solara . . . Sol . . . if this is just between you and me, then—"

"Yes, how about I distract you instead? Why don't *you* sing for *me?*"

In one quick motion, she drew the blade across Devrak's throat. A spray of red droplets hit the feed.

It felt like the air was sucked from the control room at once, leaving all our mouths open, our lungs struggling to work in a vacuum. The blood began to pulse down, at first in a few trickles, then a flood. Like Devrak, none of us could breathe, or make a sound.

Solara didn't have any such trouble. She tapped the bloody knife against her bottom lip and said, "After all, Devrak won't be able to."

My hand was over my mouth. A strangled noise escaped Eton. Nev's fingers dragged down his cheeks, as if he wanted to cover his eyes but couldn't look away. Devrak's life poured down the front of his jacket in a red waterfall. He was gurgling, choking, spasming, but he still couldn't move. His muscles locked him in place for us all to keep watching.

Solara tossed the dagger on her desk. "Really, I'd have preferred not to be the one to do this, at least not *like* this, but you two forced my hand."

Finally, *finally,* not even the neurotransmitters could hold Devrak up anymore. Not without living tissue. His knees buckled, and his body collapsed out of sight.

Nev couldn't help it, or hold it in any longer; he let loose a wordless cry of rage and horror, veins bulging in his neck.

"*There's* my song," Solara said.

Nev lunged at the feed like I'd wanted to do, as if he could reach her. His sister only smiled back at him, safe across a wide expanse of space.

"Don't," I gasped at Nev. I didn't want her to have the satisfaction, though it was a little late for that.

Solara blinked at me, as if just noticing me. "Qole, dear, what a pleasure to see you again," she said, as if we'd bumped into each other in a palace hall. Her eyes moved over my shoulder. "And you, Arjan. I suggest you board your ship, depart from there, and come join me. I could use you."

Someone with our Shadow affinity, she meant. I doubted we would ever see the outside of a Dracorte laboratory again, if she got her hands on us.

"Not if you were the last person in the systems," Arjan spat.

"Then I'll find you myself. Or"—she shrugged—"you can die there. But it would be a true waste."

"I'll kill you," Nev grated.

"No," Solara said with a slow shake of her head. "You just had your chance, and missed it. *I'm* going to kill *you.*"

I lurched forward and cut the feed then, because she was right. She was distracting us, and that *would* get us killed.

Telu was tapping rapidly at her infopads and listening to her comms at the same time, burying the horror under an avalanche of data. Doing her job, like we all should be. With some effort, I forced the image of Devrak from my mind as she gave a report.

"Like we expected, Solara is sending ahead four destroyers with full complements of starfighters. Not enough to alarm the Treznor-Nirmanas, but enough to blow our fleet to dust."

I took charge, since Nev was still staring, his face ashen, at the now-black vid screen. "Can we delay them?" I asked. "At least long enough for the new fleet here to mobilize?"

Basra's mouth pressed into a line. "Talia and Gavros might have. But it looks like they're running instead. They're activating their Belarius Drives and getting ready to make the jump to light speed from the other side of Valtai. And, yep, they're vanishing from our sensors."

"The Swarm is made up of ground forces," Eton said, before anyone could ask. "We don't have a fleet." It looked like he wanted to say something else, but he held himself back.

"Any other ideas?" Telu asked, then she snapped, "Nev, *wake up.*"

Nev glanced at her, eyes empty. *He* was empty. He looked finished before he was.

With him would go Alaxak. My people.

And yet . . . maybe *I* had to lose a lot, in order to save Alaxak.

327

I suddenly knew what I had to do. The clarity wasn't bright. It was deep, dark, and heavy, like submerging my head into the cold ocean. But it was clarity just the same.

"I think . . . ," I began. "I'm heading for the *Kaitan*."

Telu laughed, and then her smile fell away. "Oh, I thought you were kidding. You're not actually going to go join Solara, right?"

"No. I'm going to stall her."

"Uh," Arjan said. "Didn't you hear the part about the four destroyers and innumerable starfighters?"

I started walking. "Yep."

That finally made Nev blink and look at me. "Qole. No."

I smiled gently at him to take the sting out of my words. "I'm afraid you don't have the right to tell me that."

Nev took a few long strides up to me, reaching for my arm. "You saw what just happened to Devrak," he nearly gasped. "I'm not having another person sacrifice themselves for a doomed cause. I told you, I can't . . . I can't lose you."

Before he could grab me, I lifted my hands to his face and leaned into him. He was shaking, but warm and solid. So real. His eyes widened in surprise.

"We never really had each other, Nev," I murmured. "It was just a fantasy." I had to swallow to continue. "But Alaxak's independence isn't. And you can make it a reality. Please, see it through. For me."

I pulled his face forward and kissed him, sweetly, slowly, savoring this moment for myself, even though we didn't have the time. It was the good-bye I couldn't say, with all the sadness and longing and gratitude I felt. Tears were running down my face when I pulled away.

"Don't try to get in my way," I whispered, my voice still soft. "I'll knock you down if I have to."

Nev, tears in his own eyes, glanced at Eton.

"Don't look at me," Eton said, dragging himself to my side, limping. "I'm going with her. She's going to need someone to shoot those plasma rockets."

"Eton—" I started.

"I've spent too much time trying to keep you safe at his expense." He nodded at Nev. "And that didn't work so well. So maybe I'll try the reverse, and keep him safe at yours," he added, with a humorless chuckle. "Besides . . . if you're making a last stand, there's nothing in all the systems that's going to keep me out of it."

"Or me," Arjan said, stepping up.

"No, Arjan," I said hurriedly. "You have Basra. Stay with him."

He shot a pained look at Basra, whose eyes were wider than usual. "I wish I could. But I'm not leaving you to this. I know what you're planning, and you need me there to . . . to fly, if you can't manage, anymore." He took another step toward me, his voice rising in determination. "This is *our* fate, Qole. Our family's. I've been terrified of it my entire life, but I'm *not* going to let you meet it alone."

Basra threw his hands in the air. "Well, damn it all to hell. I might as well come too. If you fail, I'll just get blown up here, anyway."

"Bas," Arjan said, turning back to him. "You can't come. You have too much to lose. You could take another ship, get out of here. Or we might be able to protect these docks, even if we can't make it ourselves."

Basra marched up to Arjan, seized his face, and dragged it down to his. His kiss was shorter than mine and Nev's, but it made heat rush to my cheeks.

"You're what I have to lose," Basra murmured, as he pulled

away enough to speak, his lips hovering near Arjan's. "So shut up." He pushed past him to come stand behind me.

I turned to the last member of the crew. "Telu . . ." My voice was pleading.

"Don't you even think about it," Telu hissed, stomping right up to me. "You always try to leave me! But there's no way I'm staying behind now while my friends, my *family*, go into a scat-storm without me. Don't. You. *Dare.*"

A laugh burbled out of me, making everyone glance my way. It surprised even me. Telu hadn't unleashed on me like that in a long time, not since I'd become her captain. "Well," I said, clearing my throat and swallowing, "I guess there's not much to say, then."

"Qole—" Nev tried again. "I can—"

"Stay here and lead your fleet," I finished, before he could suggest anything stupid like coming with me. "I love you." *Those* words stopped him dead. "I couldn't tell you because it couldn't work. But now it doesn't matter. I love you, and I'll love you until the end."

His mouth had fallen open. I wished I could kiss it again, but part of me knew if I did, I would never be able to leave.

I heard his stunned words as I walked away, surrounded by family—all except one.

"I . . . I love you too."

━━━

The construction docks were already in orbit, so we didn't even have to leave the atmosphere, only the landing bay.

It also meant that we were way closer to our oncoming destruction. One fishing vessel against four destroyers. One ship between a king and defeat. One ship between a planet, a people, and annihilation. We just had to hold out until Nev joined us with his new fleet.

How we were going to do that . . . I wasn't sure yet.

"We only have ten plasma rockets," Eton reported from the turret. "A lot more photon missiles, but those will only be good against the starfighters."

"I can try to take their communications offline," Telu muttered from her station below my feet. "Scramble their nav-systems. But again, probably only the fighters, at this point. I've already broadcasted Basra's message."

It relayed the offer to come to our side, in exchange for incredibly generous compensation, courtesy of Hersius Kartolus. But so far, nobody serious had bitten.

"I hate to break your hearts," I said, "but I'm not exactly planning on fighting in the traditional sense. How much Shadow in the hold?"

"Full," Arjan said, almost eagerly, from the copilot's station next to me. "What's your plan?"

"Go for the destroyers," I said, my fingers tightening on the throttle. My eyes were locked on the sweeping viewport, where I could just begin to make out the four pale, looming shapes in the distance. The starfighters were still invisible at this point, even though, as the faster ships, they were closer and would reach us first.

"Even if you can fly through those starfighters—which I don't doubt," Eton added, "they'll chew those construction docks to pieces, given enough time. They don't have the heavy artillery of the destroyers, but they can still do damage."

That definitely was a problem to which I had no solution. One on top of a towering pile.

"I'm also putting out a call for any mercenary fleets in the vicinity," Basra said, "with a lucrative job posting."

"This isn't a job," Arjan muttered from the copilot's station next to me. "This is a suicide mission."

"Yes, that's the exact, singular response I've gotten so far," Basra replied tersely.

"Suicide run, huh? Was that what that transmission said?" a voice crackled into the *Kaitan*'s bridge over one of the comms intership. "I think that mercenary captain should retire, or put his diaper back on, because it sounds kinda like a Shadow run, to me."

"Is that . . . ?" My breath caught. I couldn't let myself hope.

"*Yes!*" Eton let out an earsplitting whoop from the turret. "Never thought I'd say this, but thank the Unifier, and you, Jerra. I could kiss you."

"I hope not. You're not my type, and we didn't come for you. You said Qole needed us, and we have our holds filled to bursting with Shadow, just for her."

We. I searched the feeds and there they were, off our starboard side. The Alaxan fleet, or at least every battle-worthy ship with a Belarius Drive. There were hundreds. They would still be outnumbered by the starfighters, but they would be enough, if I could hold off the destroyers.

They had come. With Shadow. With hope. I had to blink tears from my eyes. I opened up a comm channel directly to the turret. "Eton. Thank you. For helping Nev. For this. Everything."

"It's the least I could do."

"Well . . . welcome back."

"Thank you." His voice was rougher than usual. "I said there was nothing in all the systems that could have kept me from this . . . but you could have."

He spoke next over the inter-ship comm channel, his volume masking any unsteadiness in his tone. "Stubborn bastards that you are, I didn't think you'd trust my message. I didn't even tell the captain, because I didn't want her to count on your coming."

Jerra snorted loud enough to vibrate the comm. "She can count on us more than she can you, I think."

I cleared my throat before a bickering match could erupt. "I appreciate this more than I can say, Jerra. And in case you were wondering, this is for Alaxak, not just me."

"We know. That's why we're all here. Well, Hiat's not. He's *taking care* of things in our absence. So let's get back soon, hm?"

Telu made a disgusted noise in her throat.

"I . . . I might not make it," I said, my voice oddly level, given what I was saying. "But if I don't, *you* take care of things for me, Jerra, will you?"

Her voice went soft. "I will. In the meantime, where do you want us?"

"Between the starfighters and the construction docks. Keep them engaged. Take them out if you can, but you're mostly a distraction until Nev's fleet is up and running."

"And when will that be?"

I glanced down at Telu.

"Fifteen minutes," she said grimly, looking up at me through her dark slash of hair.

Jerra whistled through the comm.

"Disengage if you have to," I said hurriedly.

"If you don't, we won't, even if we have to go at those destroyers ourselves. So let's get to it."

There was no other choice. Only seconds later, the starfighters were upon us. All of us in Alaxan ships scattered as the photon blasts began to streak the darkness in a rain of death. The fighters followed, visible as sleek, metallic slashes as they swept by us . . . or tried to.

Our forces dodged and wove, heading them off with a hail of weapon fire that was as varied as our hulls. As with the starfighters in Alaxak's orbit, here too they were caught off guard. They hadn't expected us to be here, nor to be able to maneuver like we could. As for them . . . Truly, they were no more dangerous than a Shadow run, and we all had done that most days—and nights—of our lives.

Even so, there was an overwhelming number of enemy ships. There were a few explosions in the viewport and on the feeds already—Alaxan or otherwise, I didn't know. I hardly spared them a glance. I ducked and rolled through the oncoming fighters as if they were any other asteroid field. Arjan barely had to help me from the copilot's station. The blackness was already completely filming my eyes.

And, through that dark curtain, most of my focus was on the destroyers.

I half wondered if they could even see me, we looked so small in front of them. Of course, they had many other means of detecting us.

A warning alarm whooped.

"Weapon-lock," Eton said. "Plasma missiles."

I pulled up short in the *Kaitan*—simply hovering in front of them. I even let go of the throttle, my hands sliding away as I stood from my captain's chair. I faced the four enormous ships through the viewport.

"Qole, what are you doing?" Arjan asked.

"We stop here." I took a deep breath and lifted my hands, feeling far more than the air around my fingers. "And so do they."

"How—"

The viewport told him how. I felt it through my entire body, the weight of what I gathered. Shadow, pouring from our hold, and the hold of every Alaxan ship, forming glowing rivers through space as it pooled in front of us. Some starfighters didn't know what it was and hit the streams—some no wider than ribbons—immediately bursting into flames and exploding.

More, I thought, and it came. The Shadow spread in front of the *Kaitan,* between us and the destroyers, forming a rippling barrier of brilliant purple-black glittering with white, stretching like colossal arms across space. The edges even looked like hands, fingers clawing toward distant stars.

It was so huge, Valtai could almost certainly see it from the planet's surface. And yet I didn't use it to attack. Something gave me pause. I simply held up my arms and, with them, more Shadow than I had ever touched, along with the weight of everything that mattered to me.

Nev, I thought.

"Yes," his voice responded. "Embrace. That is what we have been trying to tell you."

We? The thought skittered across my mind, but I couldn't hold it. I couldn't try to block out the voice, either. My mind was both as open and occupied as my arms.

And then I felt the impact.

It wasn't the plasma rockets, which were already launching by the dozen from the destroyers and evaporating like snow on a bonfire as they struck the Shadow shielding us. It was a destroyer itself.

Maybe they didn't realize what the barrier was, or they couldn't change course in time, or they thought they could plow right through it. But when they hit it, they knew the truth. Their energy shield, the best the systems had to offer, flared a panicked white against the purple-black. The Shadow only flexed slightly inward, a taut net absorbing their momentum.

Their shields were holding too—but not for long, judging by how they glowed brighter and brighter and began to arc. The destroyer reversed full throttle, thrusters blasting out glowing jets of energy toward their bow as they frantically tried to pull back.

"Don't . . . ," began the voice.

For a moment, I felt like *I,* not the destroyer, was balanced on a knife's edge without fully knowing why.

And then the destroyer slid back, extracting itself from my embrace. Its compromised shield was flickering wildly but still whole, and I felt like I could breathe easier.

"Ancestors," Arjan gasped, his mouth sounding dry. "This is unreal."

I'd almost forgotten that anyone else was nearby, or that there was a pitched battle going on behind us. Eton was busy keeping up a steady stream of fire off our stern, both plasma rockets and photon missiles. Any starfighter that came near us was either devoured by him or picked off by a couple Alaxan ships that were obviously keeping an eye on us.

But eventually, the starfighters stopped trying to approach, veering away to resume their attempt on the construction docks. Even the destroyers, at a standstill on the other side of the curtain of Shadow, ceased launching plasma rockets.

Telu was also busy, fingers flying as she sneaked her way onto the Dracorte channels. The different voices rose and fell in a low, discordant stream, many of which Basra was monitoring, along with the several inaudible comms he held to his ear.

"A command came down the line—telling them to hold fire," Basra said. "Solara must want you alive."

"Of course she does," Arjan murmured. "Especially now that she's seen *this.* Even I'm jealous." There was more awe and fear in his voice than any sort of jealousy. More humor, even, though it was weak.

Telu cursed. "The destroyers are moving—changing position."

My eyes shot back to the viewport, trying to peer through the *two* curtains of Shadow across my visions. I could see, but what was more, I could *feel* it. The very space between us seemed alive, like I was somehow connected to it. It had to be the energy in the Shadow.

Sure enough, the destroyers were trying to angle around my shield.

"They likely want to try to catch you in a tractor beam," Telu said.

Before I could shift the barrier, I realized they were all headed in different directions—an attempt to spread me thin. And it would work. I was already holding the most Shadow I could manage.

Basra lifted his head from one of his comms. "Some good news. Energy shields are now beginning to power up in Nev's new destroyers on the docks. Some have taken damage, but others are able to target and return fire now, even from the docks."

"How much longer until all his ships have shields?" I asked through gritted teeth.

Telu checked one of her many screens. "Five minutes."

My jaw clenched tighter. "Too long." Solara's oncoming destroyers could have those docks in particles in that time.

"Maybe . . . ," Arjan started. "Maybe I could help."

"No," I said. "Don't. You'll need to pilot . . . after this . . ."

"You'll just be tired, right?" he said sharply, alarmed. "You're holding up so far. Don't push it."

But I had to. I had to do something else. Something that would at least give the destroyers pause, make them reconsider their course, at least long enough for Nev to survive.

I had to make one of them into a demonstration, or else we were lost. This was why I was here. I took another deep breath, and my fingers flexed.

One edge of the Shadow barrier curled in response, moving across space fast enough to surprise even me. Lashing like a whip, it struck out . . . and entirely enfolded one of the destroyers.

It was like holding sparks in my grip—tingling, flaring against my palm, in time with the arcing, flickering shield around the ship. And then the Shadow swallowed that too, and I held fire in my hand.

But worse than the fire in my hand was the wail in my head.

It was the voice, raised to an earsplitting shout, but it was too late to heed it. The destroyer was dissolving, flames expanding and curling like solar flares in the darkness. An entire ship crumbling, turning to ash.

The other destroyers changed course yet again, pulling back. As far away from the Shadow as they could get.

I realized my hand was dissolving too. But I had to hold on. I couldn't let go of the barrier, or else this would all be for nothing.

I tried to squeeze tighter, breaking my gaze away from the destruction outside the viewport to look at my hand. My breath rose in panicked gasps when I realized all that was left of it was bone, skeleton fingers clasped around nothing. The flesh of my forearm was flaking away, the horror working its way toward my elbow.

I was dissolving. But I couldn't let go.

"Stop," the voice said.

"No!" I screamed.

Arjan was at my side, a hand on my shoulder. "Qole?" he said, panicked. "What's wrong?"

"Stop." The voice again.

"I can't!" I cried, and then my flesh flew away in strips, all the way up to my shoulder. "Ancestors, please, make it stop!"

But my ancestors weren't answering. There was only the voice. Nev's voice.

"You stop. We stop. You cannot do this. We won't let it happen again."

"Make what stop?" Arjan was holding me. "Qole, you're fine. I'm here. Nothing's wrong with you."

But even as my brother spoke, his own flesh was flying away from his face, and cracks were skittering across the viewport. Before long, Arjan was only a skull, and there were massive fractures splintering the hull with a sound like a frozen lake breaking apart. This was worse than I'd ever seen it. Or heard it. Or felt it.

This was it.

I glanced around in terror and saw a shadowy figure standing on the buckling bridge behind me. I could almost make out a face.

But then everything—me, the *Kaitan,* the entire universe—came apart, and all I could do was scream. That was all there was, all that remained, until I no longer recognized even my own voice.

XVI

I HAD THOUGHT THE SCREAMING WAS THE WORST PART. IT WAS A SOUND no human should have made, one of pure pain and personal disintegration. Hearing it come from Qole made my skin crawl and my heart panic. There was nothing I could do except call her name over and over on her comm, ignoring the looks of those around me.

But now the silence was worse than the screaming.

"Qole," I tried again, almost whispering. I'd said it too many times with no response.

Moments ago, she had accomplished what any reasoned mind would have claimed was impossible: a shield of Shadow that didn't simply slow but stopped ships at full thrust. That was more than remarkable; it was miraculous. And, as though not content with one miracle, Qole had then burned through a destroyer as if her will were the fire and they were the wood.

But it came at a cost, and I didn't know what I would do if the cost was her life. Losing my parents and Devrak was losing home, but losing Qole would undo something inside me, some essential part of myself that would disappear with her.

Telu's voice came online. "Nev."

I spoke before she could continue. "She's alive." It was supposed to be a question, but it came out sounding like an imperative to the universe.

"She's breathing," Telu clarified, subdued. "Basra is taking care of her. Arjan is in her seat."

The words didn't bring relief. Her body might be alive, but I had no way of knowing if Qole, my Qole, was going to return.

On the bridge of the flagship of my new fleet, I was deep in a warren of activity as the crew worked frantically to get us online and battle worthy. It somehow felt more isolating to be surrounded while I was consumed with personal tragedy. Worse, with Qole maybe gone, most of it seemed like some sick game. I could probably save lives by capitulating, if we all just agreed to let Solara have her way.

But I couldn't bring myself to do that just yet.

"Status report," I requested, but was met by uncertain silence. I glanced around the bridge, realizing that in the chaos, I had neglected to appoint my XO. Many of the positions had been assigned beforehand, but I had hardly communicated with the crew around me since boarding.

I frowned. My first five minutes as a commander in chief, and I was making rookie mistakes.

"Fleet is ready in one minute. Shields are at ninety percent." Commander Aris stepped forward, the sharp-faced woman who'd taken part in my Forging and led the operation on the docks.

I nodded, grateful. I would find an appropriate member of the bridge to appoint in a moment, but I had to buy our next few minutes of survival first. "Okay, everyone. Stop charging shields and energy weapons fleet wide. Ready missile ordinance to fire on my command." *It's just another exercise.* As long as I told myself that, the orders came easily. I commed the *Kaitan.* "*Kaitan,* this is Nev. Fall back. *Everyone* fall back."

"You sure about that?" Arjan's voice sounded strained, and I knew that he was being taxed to his limit. It was unsettling to hear him on the line instead of Qole, and I doubted that the irony of us working together was lost on him, either. "Telu says your systems aren't showing you're ready yet. These incoming destroyers will tear you apart."

He wasn't wrong. The Alaxan fleet was creating a diversion of epic proportions, inflicting heavy losses on the fighters, but the destroyers were almost entirely unscathed, aside from the one Qole had disintegrated. We were almost ready, but still docked. If the other three destroyers pursued the Alaxans into the construction docks, we would be sitting targets.

"You've done your job." I managed not to ask him about Qole, but for a wild moment I wanted to beg him to fly away as far as possible, as fast as possible. I pushed the thought away. "May I speak with Eton?"

Eton cleared his throat over the comm. "Already here." I could hear the shriek of his turret as interference, and he swore briefly. "Sorry, had to slag some scrap. What's up? You have a bright idea in that pointy head?"

"Maybe," I said. "My father gave it to me."

"Ugh" was the encouraging reply.

"Yes, yes, but I need to know if you'll be on board. It's going to take some planning."

"Does it involve blowing these guys up?"

"Need you ask?"

Eton chuckled. "I'm all in."

———

As the Alaxan fleet turned and retreated, Solara's advance destroyers gleefully pursued them into the construction yards. I could almost see the pleased smiles on their faces; they had broken the resistance and made it in time to slaughter us unprepared. Their reward from Solara would be unending.

If they had known the grief inside me, felt the hatred it was turning into, they might have been less eager in their pursuit. I reached into the air, twisted to activate the holo-map commands, and brought my fingers to the destroyers on the combat readout. With a flicker, red targeting squares surrounded them. And around them, vulnerable and docked, was my fleet.

Seemingly vulnerable.

"Fire at will," I said as calmly as I could manage.

A thousand pinpricks of light glittered on my viewscreen as every vessel within firing distance unloaded their ordinance. Plasma missiles, photon rockets, and any other weapon type that hadn't required a complete charge on the vessels—thereby giving away our readiness—shot through the vacuum of space.

I steadied my voice again, working to remove the savagery. "Shields and energy weapons to maximum."

The destroyers never even tried to fire back; they pivoted and reversed course with all the speed they could muster.

It was futile. With a ripple of plasma and a shimmer of defenses, missiles connected, the shield on the more compromised destroyer collapsed, and our energy weapons followed close behind. Lasers sliced into the hull, and the destroyer suffered a critical breach. The force of the explosion tore it in two halves, sending them spiraling into its brethren. They followed suit in moments.

My heart pounded in my chest as the crew on the bridge burst into a cheer.

I felt no answering joy. The brief moment of anger had faded away and left me nauseated. I had just been gleeful at the murder of those who had once followed me. As far as they knew, they were putting down a rebellion. I was murdering my own. It was impossible to pretend this was an exercise; the wreckage floating around us, the pinpoint dots that were human bodies floating out of ruptured hulls were all too real. Unbidden, I imagined Qole lifeless.

It made my knees run weak. The last time I had killed, I'd been trying to save Arjan, trying to protect Qole, but now, if she was dead, what was the point? I was a child expected to lead a hastily assembled military force, while the people I cared about were dead or dying. *Dead.* I rubbed my forehead, trying to steady myself, to wrench my thoughts back to the plan I was making while the one thing I wanted to do was curl into a ball somewhere, alone, and escape what was gnawing inside me. I had to plan, rally my troops in the few minutes I had bought us, because I knew Solara wouldn't take this as a defeat. She would unleash the rest of her massive force—the First Dracorte Fleet—in anger, even at the risk of the Treznor-Nirmanas' ire. It would be a gamble, but Valtai had stayed out of it thus far. I knew her; she would take the risk and deal with any consequences later.

But no plan came to me. No simulation had prepared me for this.

My comm chimed, and the wrist feed informed me of a new message from Devrak. My breath caught. *Impossible.* I had seen him die. My throat was still raw from a single scream.

"Hello?" I couldn't bring myself to say his name, in case this was some twisted joke that Solara was playing on me.

"Private video message," a calm synthetic voice informed me. "Please find a secure location to view."

Real or not, this wasn't something I could ignore. With a word to Aris, I ran to my private quarters that adjoined the bridge. I barely registered the absurd luxury of the supposedly military space as, with trembling fingers, I brought a holo-screen to life.

Devrak appeared, in his quarters on the *Kaitan*. He held up a hand, smiling. "Hello, Nevarian. This is a recording. If you're seeing this, my heart has stopped, so odds are, I am dead." He smiled at his own horrible joke, more relaxed than I could ever remember. I couldn't process it, I could only drink in his every motion, every expression, as though that would somehow re-store everything to the way it had been, bring him back to life.

Make it so he hadn't betrayed me.

"Nevarian, your sister is one of the most formidable human beings I have ever met. If anyone is prepared for me, she is." His voice changed, deepening, and he clenched his fists. "But I swore I would never underestimate her again. I will try to kill her, but I know well that I might fail. That's why I have another plan. A way to make her underestimate you. The only way she will believe that you have lost everything, that you've been betrayed, is if you believed it too.

"But you should know better. I told you, if you know someone's nature, you can trust in it. Mine. Hers. Yours. You're strong, Nev. Your parents and I spent our lives trying to cre-ate a better future. They succeeded. Your parents were imper-fect people whose power made their mistakes echo more than most. But so, too, can their successes. You are that echo, Nev. They were so proud, and I . . ." His voice caught.

Tears welled in his eyes, and mine filled in response. I had never seen him cry in my entire life, nor had we discussed how my parents had felt about me. Beliefs, expectations, yes. Feelings, no, and it tore me open.

"To me, you are my son. I leave no family behind but you and Marsius. I love you. I am so sorry to go." He took a deep breath, wiping his face with a smile. "Take care of one another. Believe in a better, impossible future. Don't mourn me more than you must. Everyone has their time. I've had more than I deserve. Besides, I go to join my wife and daughter now." And then, he said what he had the last I'd seen him: "We will speak when this is over, I promise you."

The recording disappeared, and I blinked away tears. All this time I had looked upon Devrak as someone my family adopted, never realizing he had saved me by adopting me into his.

I looked up at the viewport, watching the glowing flares in the ships and docks around me, signaling the lives within. And then I saw steady pinpoints of light among the stars, like a newly born constellation. It was the rest of Solara's fleet, it had to be. She was indeed willing to commit all her forces to snuff me—*us*—out. *This is all so large. Millions of people, systems in the balance.* I looked down at my hands, callused from practice, bloodied from combat. *And I am so very small.*

It wasn't *fair.* I finally let myself think the words, selfish and stupid as they were. I could push them away all I wanted, but at the end, the universe, the Unifier, continued to reach out and extinguish what I loved. Devrak said to believe in an impossible future, but why bother being alive in a world where *impossible future* simply meant being alone, at peace, with the one person who frantically, desperately made me believe in living?

Qole laughed in my head. I could hear her as clearly as though she were there; it was the laugh I knew she would give if I had pleaded for fairness with her. *Get up,* she would say, with the mercilessness borne of familiarity. *It's time to go to work.*

My hands closed slowly into fists. In a world where Qole existed, I would never be able to sit, wallowing in self-pity, when there was work to be done. And every fear, every terror that pressed on my shoulders was lifted by a new thought: to be worthy of a love that expected more of me.

I stood. My dream was that a person like Qole could survive, and I would help create a universe they could believe in. It didn't matter if it was impossible, it was worth fighting for. All I could do was make one more choice.

I made it. It was time to fight.

———

It had not been a king who had entered his quarters, but a young man, bewildered, stricken by grief, and afraid. The person who exited had a job to do, and didn't care what his title was.

The crew stared at me uncertainly, their worry permeating the bridge. Clearly, Solara was betting that the Treznors had their own problems to sort out on the surface, and were waiting to deal with the aftermath. We had precious few minutes to prepare. The First Dracorte Fleet had been undefeated for over a hundred years, and it was heading for us.

"Aris." The woman started when I called her name. "You are now my XO."

"Your Majesty." She looked hesitant. "I'm not qualified. I am primarily trained in ground—"

"Not a question, Commander. I need someone I know I can work with."

She snapped a salute. "Understood. Orders, sire?"

"One moment. Eton?"

"Yes?" he responded.

"Did you tell Devrak the Alaxans were coming? That they would be able buy us time to mobilize in place of Talia and Gavros?" Who likely wouldn't have been able to make it in time, anyway.

"Yeah, but he didn't know for *sure* they would come."

He would have. *The more you understand a person, the more reliable they are. . . .*

I flicked my wrist-comm at Aris, and hers beeped in response. "Get this message to Talia and Gavros immediately, maximum encryption over the QUIN." The network used for interstellar communication. They'd activated their Belarius Drives, after all.

I glanced at the holo-map—Solara's fleet was almost upon us, the red dots that represented her ships spreading out like a wave cresting before hitting the shore. We were officially out of time.

I hit the comm in my ear. "Telu," I said. "See if you can get this next transmission to reach Solara's fleet, in addition to mine." It was hard not asking after Qole, but the best thing I could do for her now was fight a war. And the first salvo of the war had to be fought for the hearts and minds of my crew. There was no better teacher of that than her, and I brought her memory near, channeling her. *Thank you.* I just hoped she would stay alive so I could thank her in person.

When the comm blinked open, I addressed my navy. "Attention. This is your king speaking." I almost stopped, unused to naming myself in that way, but carried on. "You are carrying pieces of a tradition that the Dracorte kingdom has upheld since the Great Collapse, that of fighting to defend those who cannot defend themselves."

My blood hummed in my veins. Father had taught me this was true. Even if his actions had betrayed that in the end, it didn't matter. *I've learned a new lesson. My own.* "Today, we reclaim that tradition from she who would use the Dracorte name for her own gain. We are not pirates, marauders, or tyrants. We are the ones who scatter them."

One by one, the new fleet disengaged from their docks. New hulls gleamed in the light of the Valtai sun, nacelles glowing to life. Cutting-edge design did away with the tri-tine configuration of Treznors' older destroyers, moving the command center and thrusters to the rear like the hilt of a Disruption Blade. Weapons and sensors arrays floated in concentric circles around the hull, their housings moving into position along invisible mag-couplings. Beautiful and deadly, they could dole out hope or despair.

I remembered Eton, the joy of sacrifice written on his face as he fought Suvis, and I thought of Qole, who had given her all to buy us precious minutes. Two sacrifices that would not be in vain. "We are not the plunderers; we are the shield. We will not be made afraid, nor will we hesitate to give our all if we must."

I paused, letting them consider my words. It was, I finally understood, not my parents I had to live up to. Instead, I had to live up to what they should have been.

"But today, I am not asking you to die. I am asking you to draw a line. Solara murdered our king and queen, betrayed the trust of millions, disregarded our law and order, and used the crown for nepotism and dispensing personal vendettas, and she will kill not just us here today, but so many we love in our systems, through direct action and irresponsible rule. Do not fight with me for the glory of my family—that is not why I fight, either. Fight with me because I will fight for you, for *your* family, for everyone you love. Today, give me your all, and I swear to you that I will give you mine."

I turned to my bridge, mouth set in a grim line. "Let us show Solara what it is that preys on the volassa."

As I let my voice fade, I wondered what filled the silence left behind. I hoped it was courage, purpose, and hope—everything that was keeping me standing.

It might not matter. If my sister was a volassa, looking at her ships on the holo-map now made me realize she might be about to unhinge her jaw and swallow us whole. Either she or Faetora had pulled the perfect maneuver, forming a glimmering hemisphere of destroyers and starfighters around the dockyards. It was a colossal display of power, and there would be political repercussions, but there was still no response from the Treznor military. We were on our own. To escape, we would have to either go through the planet or go through her. In reserve, she had kept a force to chase down any concentration of ships and hammer it. It was a smart strategy, particularly with the *Volassa* being part of that force.

Unlike the other destroyers there, the *Volassa* was a ship from a bygone era when the Dracortes still built their own vessels. My family had not favored the colossal carriers of the Belarius family or the battle cruisers that were the backbone of the Treznor military. Composed of long lines and sharp edges that ended in banks upon banks of thrusters, the superdestroyer was almost entirely dedicated to speed and firepower. Energy weapons dominated the prow, and if it brought itself to bear on you, the remainder of your existence would be short and terrifying. With it, Solara had brought the majority of the First

Dracorte Fleet: ten battle carriers, seventy destroyers, and a thousand starfighters.

In other words, her odds were good.

Great speech. Can't wait to see how you deliver. My wrist-comm beeped with the message from Telu, and I wondered how she managed to be both encouraging and dismaying in a few words.

Qole? My fingers danced briefly across the space above my wrist. I wanted to type *Is she better?* or *Tell me everything will be okay,* but Telu's humor didn't fool me. She hadn't gotten in touch to trade sarcastic remarks because things were going well. I wondered if she felt as alone as I did, locked in her station on the *Kaitan,* tied to the comms, fighting back her desire to be at her friend's side.

Breathing, but out of it. The words flashed on my wrist. My heart constricted, a thousand possibilities, each darker than the last, whispering in my head. She had gone crazy. Her brain had failed. She would wake and not be the same.

I forced myself to return to the present before fear and worry tore away at me, looking around the bridge of the newly christened battleship DFS *Devrak.* Viewscreens swept around us, showing the endless construction docks of Valtai and a massive holo-map projecting the battle zone. Both my will and my fingers would direct the lives of many.

Aris was working to filter relevant color-coded information on my holo-map. Immediate staff stood nearby to work on delegated tasks, prioritizing data and commands so I could focus on the larger picture at hand. I had seen it all in war games at the Academy.

It was time to play a different sort of game: *Let's see if Solara reads me as poorly as I read her.*

"Gather the fleet to the rendezvous point." I highlighted

a sector on the holo-map, just outside the docks, putting the structure behind us—between us and the planet. It might have seemed like we were boxing ourselves in, instead of using the docks as a shield between ourselves and Solara, but this way, the rendezvous wasn't far and provided enough space for us to consolidate our forces quickly. Besides, this position benefited us in other ways. "Solara will attack with the goal of keeping us scattered, so order a rearguard to remain at the docks to buy us time." I steeled myself as I said those words. I was ordering part of my fleet to fight an outmatched battle. My forces desperately needed time to regroup from where we had launched, true, but just like that, so soon, I had consigned hundreds to their deaths to save the rest of us. *Must we do this?*

Yes. We must, I replied to myself. Making difficult choices was not a luxury; it was a responsibility, one from which I was done running. "Aris, we're forming battle groups one and two, to either side of the *Devrak,* respectively. I'll take one, you have two. Tie those sectors to your control."

I looked back down at my wrist-comm and my fingers flicked out.

Telu, do you have a line on the drones in-system? If threatened, drones would attempt to stop any military action they saw as a threat to themselves, without allegiance.

This is the Treznor-Nirmana homeworld. They don't let drones interfere with their airspace.

I'd assumed as much, but it bore checking. My family had far and away the best access to what rudimentary drone commands remained, but skilled hackers across the systems, such as Telu, could still influence them. A capital world like Valtai would employ teams around the clock to try to keep them out of their immediate planetary approaches.

Qole?

Same.

My hands reached for the holo-map. This had to be *my* Shadow run.

I had five battle carriers and thirty destroyers to work with, with five hundred starfighters. We didn't lack teeth, but we certainly had fewer.

Solara's crew was composed of the finest naval crew our family had to offer, her commanders plucked from the Royal Academy on Luvos. We were outnumbered and untrained for cutting-edge assault.

But we had other skills. Aaltos was home to the rank and file, to veteran commanders who had dedicated their life to service, not glory. The Alaxans and their ships had shown what determination, skill, and belief could do. I had to hope, pray, that those I led believed in me with the same intensity.

And that I wouldn't fail them.

———

Like new stars, our ships broke free of their docks and streamed to gather around me. Sleek, made with the sharp curves my family preferred, they gleamed with the traditional Dracorte blue. Equipment arrays shifted around them on invisible magnetic couplings, shield generators and weapons looking first like a swarm of insects and then dorsal fins as they floated to where they were needed most. A fleet of daggers, they began to disgorge starfighters, their heavy snub noses and bands of missile launchers in sharp contrast to the older, more elegant starfighters that Solara was leading. I had preferred our older designs, but not now that I was the one wielding the future against the past.

They moved like a wave of blue dots on my holo-map,

trying to escape the incurvate barrier that Solara had put into place as they gathered around the DFS *Devrak*. Her older tri-hull destroyers swooped in, thrusters burning and weapons glowing to life as they discharged their assault. Missiles streamed out first, trailing gold, only to be countered by chaff and miniature EMP bursts opening in balls of coruscating electric energy. Her plasma beams lanced out next, probing, seeking a weakness in the defenses of the ships before them.

Humans all over the universe were capable of perceiving beauty; all it took was the choice to see it. Even in this horrible situation, a useless thought sprang to the forefront of my mind. Taken out of context, there was beauty here: we were painting the space above the planet Valtai with the vivid colors of the strife and anger between two siblings.

I had no part in the heroics of our destroyers and their starfighters that acted as the rearguard, the ones who stayed behind while the rest of us regrouped. Legends were born, men and women performed miracles of courage and strategy in the savage confrontation, and it was thanks to them that the majority of our fleet gathered in a defensive sphere before the construction docks.

It still wasn't a comforting sight. On the holo-map, we were a spot of blue in an ever-shrinking sea of red, as Solara's fighters pinched the space around us shut. When the trap closed, we would be like the last patch of dry land snuffed out in a flood.

I swallowed, tasting acid in my mouth. This was my plan. I had just watched ships burn and disintegrate under my orders, their captains striving to fulfill them to the best of their ability, trusting in me. And one by one, ships winked out of existence as they paid the price for buying us time, the lives of those who had chosen to follow me going with them.

Still online were five battle carriers, twenty destroyers, three hundred fifty starfighters. We'd lost over a quarter of our fleet—all to get time to get into formation.

A holo of Talia flickered to life beside me. "That cost you. But in slightly more positive news, we're in position, as well."

I couldn't help grinning, despite it all. "Good to see you."

"I beg your extreme pardon for letting you believe we'd betrayed you, Your Majesty—"

"You trusted Devrak, and so do I. Let's hope it pays off now. Ready for phase two?"

She nodded, face grim, eyes alight. "Affirmative. We're running on low power and should be escaping notice, especially with the interference, first from the planet, and now the docks passing above us in orbit. Nothing on enemy comms suggests anything other than that we tucked tail and ran while we were on the other side of Valtai."

Rather than scrutinizing their sensors, Solara's forces were likely eavesdropping on our lightly encrypted channels, *not* on the properly secured QUIN we were now using that ships typically only activated over great distances. Besides, Talia and Gavros were off their radar literally *and* figuratively. Solara thought Talia's and Gavros's destroyers had fired up their Belarius Drives and left. They'd done the former, just not the latter, but the effect was the same. Why pay attention to something that was supposedly no longer there?

Gavros didn't bother appearing as a hologram. "This is completely counter to best practices. Your losses were too heavy for such an aggressive move."

"Thank you, Gavros," I said dismissively. I should have been trying to edge away from the planet, allowing myself to retreat wherever I could, using my starfighters to slip around Solara before we were irreversibly surrounded, looking for an avenue of escape. Then I would drive forward, destroyers first, making a larger hole in her fleet for my battle carriers to flee. That would have been a textbook tactic.

But I didn't have the numbers for following the textbook, and my time on the *Kaitan* had made me prefer more . . . daring avenues. I had gathered my ships like a fist near the Valtai construction docks, preparing to strike. My intent was obvious to anyone, desperate, and I didn't care. I was going to fight her head on.

Aris brought up a damage graph without me asking, the number of fighters that were out of play creeping upward in front of my eyes. It was like a slap to the face, and for a second I struggled not to react. I might be eating myself alive inside, but it was the last thing I could show anyone.

"Give the command to execute phase two." I steeled my voice to carry across the comms, trying to sound as aggressive as the maneuver.

As one, thrusters at maximum, my fleet surged to meet Solara's main battlegroup.

I switched to the comm I had used to talk to Solara, hoping she might still be listening. "Let's see if you have the guts to fight me face-to-face, Sol." I had intended for my voice to be neutral, but instead it came out cold and hard.

Solara's voice sounded in my ear alone. "Nev, you do know how grateful I am, don't you? Your naïveté has made all this possible, and now you're letting me wrap it up so neatly. I truly appreciate how cooperative you are."

I swallowed my anger. She wasn't necessarily wrong. I had been her tool since I'd brought Qole to the palace, perfectly executing every step she needed to ascend to power. And it was possible I was being her tool even now, leading us to complete destruction.

But then, all those times, she had also relied on my good-will. She had depended on that as a weakness, exploiting my loved ones against me. Only now, *she* was the one threatening them, and she was about to learn what it meant to be the enemy.

On the holo-map, the blue shapes of my fleet surged forward, starfighters streaming first. We were a laughably small stone being thrown into a crashing red wave, a wave that immediately swarmed to engulf us from behind.

Starfighters engaged in duels. The first missiles began to sprinkle out in the distance ahead, even as Solara's starfighters came in behind us, sweeping through the construction docks to attack our rear.

The construction docks, beneath which the twenty destroyers under the command of Talia and Gavros coasted, signals masked under low power.

They still shouldn't have been impossible to detect, but I had counted on the hubris of my sister—that she'd never considered that Talia and Gavros would go up against such odds, that they hadn't used their Belarius Drives to flee. What vessels Solara's sensors had seen against the structures had been assumed to be part of our mounting casualties.

Our main force swiveled on its axis, yawning wildly to reverse course in the vacuum of space. The blue fist that had just hurtled toward its death now doubled back, careening toward the docks, and closed a trap on the bulk of Solara's fighters coming at us from behind.

Fire lanes came alive as Talia's and Gavros's hidden fleet of destroyers opened fire with razor precision, their placement coming into devastating effect. My own fleet fired from the other side, pinning Solara's fighters between us. They were shredded.

"Four hundred forty-five enemy starfighters out of a thousand remaining," Aris informed me.

That was when the might of Solara's full battlegroup struck.

Between her fleet and a planet, among endless construction docks, we made our stand. Rippling photon fire came in staggered waves, and on the other side of those hulls, crews worked to layer shield types. Laser fire appeared in steady pulses, their dots of energy looking harmless until shields flickered out of life, their generators overloaded and offline. Starfighters corkscrewed and pivoted in mad patterns among wreckage. The Valtai construction docks were our floating armor.

I could only imagine how Makar felt about this. Solara was the one inflicting the most damage, and she was evidently willing to dare the Treznor-Nirmana fleet to engage or stay neutral. But there was no communication from the planet. It was as though the entire population was hushed, watching the horrific light show above with bated breath, while we fought like wild animals.

Solara's specialized EMP destroyers sailed into the battle last, the three-tine design of their hull constructed to unleash powerful bursts of electromagnetic pulses without disabling themselves. We were prepared for that, but these were brand-new ships; we quickly learned that our new Treznor equipment was more sensitive to EMP blasts than the previous generation they'd sold my family. Five of our destroyers immediately flashed as foundering on my screen, and then her destroyers finished them off with rapid fire. Gas leaked out in plumes, missiles exploded in patterns along their shieldless hulls, and escape pods ejected in hope.

My hands moved through the holo-map of their own accord, highlighting targets, drawing fleet maneuvers. Faces flicked in and out of my periphery, people asking questions and updating situations. The expressions of those around me changed as the battle continued, although I couldn't place what it was. I ignored it; there was no time to ponder. I acted.

If our ships had weaknesses, they also had strengths. Our weapons inflicted more damage, their range greater. And Gavros learned those differences with the speed of a lifetime of practice. He countered, coordinating brilliant cross-fire patterns with Talia, annihilating the enemy EMP destroyers while staying out of their range.

In all of this, the *Volassa* hung back. Solara had seen one trap close and wasn't about to let it happen twice. A ship like the *Volassa* had fallen out of favor because of the specialized, directional nature of its weaponry, but to Solara's credit she used it perfectly. She circled the battle, and any time one of my ships strayed too far, the *Volassa* picked them off hungrily, making short work of anything in range. She was waiting for the rest of my fleet to thin sufficiently, for the DFS *Devrak* to founder, so she could move in, mop us up with overwhelming firepower. Because in the end, we were still pinned and trapped.

Or at least, we looked that way as I waited for the last pieces I had on the board to fall into place. Either my entire gambit was about to succeed, or I would simply be a footnote in the history books.

I couldn't resist flipping open the comm once more. "Father did always tell us to beware the unexpected stroke."

Solara laughed sincerely in response. "He was terrible at following his own advice, wasn't he? And this?" The *Volassa* rolled lazily to bring its guns to bear fully on the *Devrak*. "I love surprises, but I'm afraid this isn't one." The line went dead.

"Take us directly at the *Volassa*; try to keep most of her destroyers to our starboard side," I ordered my XO.

Aris looked at me for a moment, her jaw working a little like she was weighing me, figuring out if I'd allow my XO to question me.

But in the end, it seemed I had earned her trust, because she didn't voice the question and instead passed on my command. Energy feeds surging, cores at maximum, the *Devrak* shifted toward the *Volassa*, forward batteries spouting energy and flame. The rest of my fleet followed, but we would face the brunt, leading the charge. As we pulled away from the protection of the ruined docks, Solara's forces took their chance, starfighters flickering across the viewscreen like a meteor storm. The bridge went red; damage reports flashed.

"Sector G shields down!"

Armor peeled away in layers; gouts of oxygen streamed into space like blood. Without regard for our own safety, without places to duck and weave and hide, we took heavier damage, and other ships in the fleet began to go down. Now, including Talia's and Gavros's forces, we had three battle carriers, twenty-six destroyers, two hundred fighters. Still we pressed on toward the *Volassa* like a battering ram, increasing thrust while her destroyers threw everything they had at our broad starboard side, still facing them.

"Life support and weapon systems failing in starboard levels twelve through fourteen," Aris reported.

"Order evacuation or escape pods in those areas," I responded. Three battle carriers, nineteen destroyers, one hundred seventy-two starfighters. The *Devrak* could take it. Our fleet would. We could take it. We had to.

"In the end, you still just want to punch things." Solara sighed in my ear. "Some plan."

No, I replied silently. *This is.* And, as her fleet swarmed us, as we accepted all the damage they could throw, I sent a last encrypted message to the *Kaitan*.

The *Kaitan* hurtled from lower orbit, trailing atmospheric fire as it shot into the battle, skimming up the port side of our fleet, using our ships as cover. Arjan was at the helm, but this was no Shadow run. Accelerating to near maximum speed, far faster than anyone in their right mind would ever dare approach the chaos, Arjan threaded his family's ship through the wreckage of docks, between exploding destroyers, and alongside streamers of plasma following the path we had just cut for him. Like a streak of Shadow itself, the *Kaitan* flowed along the surface of the *Devrak*, skirting the mayhem of the battle, leaping straight for the *Volassa*.

The entire Alaxan fleet followed suit.

We were the shield, but they were the sword. This had been the hardest decision of all, placing Qole, helpless, not just into battle but into the worst of it.

But loving someone didn't mean protecting them. It meant being willing to risk your life for something you believed to be greater. It was a choice we all had made, Qole more than any other, and in such moments I understood the razor balance between sacrifice and love like two edges of the same knife. My father had lost sight of one side, had forgotten—or never known—that to take on the burden of sacrificing others for your belief, it had to come from a place of love.

The *Kaitan* was what we needed; without them, we stood no chance. But my heart, and my hopes, flew with it.

If the Alaxans had been bold enough not to blink at this suicide run, the Swarm seemed eager to prove themselves equally extreme. As the Alaxan vessels swooped in, one could see the Swarm in their battle suits, attached like fleas to the hulls of the ships. As each fishing vessel surged by the *Volassa*, the Swarm launched into space at the last possible second, trailing cables from each ship's Shadow net. They connected with the *Volassa*'s armored hull one after another like a meteor shower, reverse mag-fields in their suits to cushion their landing.

The Swarm was geared for surface combat, so that was what we used them for. Moving with the speed of veterans, they deployed a series of mines—those originally intended to blow up the fleet I was now leading—and then were hoisted away by the attached cable. Left behind were the interlocked charges, blinking merrily.

EMP bursts spread first, disabling systems inside the *Volassa,* and then the thermic blasts fired, with massive explosions followed by billowing gouts of boiling gas across the hull of the *Volassa,* destroying shield emitters and armor.

A different commander would have allowed the ship to absorb the damage, in the hopes that the rest of the fleet would lend aid, or that their superior firepower would win out. But it would be a gamble, and I was betting that Solara was not a gambler with her own life. The Alaxans, Qole's crew, my troops, and I were all willing to lay down our lives for a cause larger than ourselves.

Solara's only interest was herself. The *Volassa*'s engines burned brightly as she engaged maximum thrust, and she fled.

The shock of *Volassa* leaving battle rippled through her forces. Battle carriers diverted, fighter squadrons wheeled to try to catch up. Our forces followed, leaping hungrily on the confused and redeploying forces. Chaos settled into enemy formations as they tried to repel unexpected attacks from multiple quadrants, and conflicting orders sounded. Solara's lines buckled.

And among the chaos, the Swarm feasted. Using the Alaxan ships as launching pads, they attached themselves to wounded or unsuspecting ships and deployed hundreds more charges. In a matter of minutes, three battle carriers and a half-dozen destroyers paid the price for their collapsing order.

I tried not to think about an errant burst obliterating the *Kaitan*. About Qole, unconscious. I had to trust Arjan, trust him to do the right thing by his sister. I had to trust in her to come back. And I had to trust in myself to keep leading if she didn't.

"Now, that's a relief," Aris said by my side.

I nodded with a composure I didn't entirely feel. "Indeed. Now we might actually stand a chance."

POSTLUDE

SOLARA

A MESSAGE BLINKED INSISTENTLY ON MY HOLODESK IN MY OFFICE ON
the *Volassa*. I knew who it was from. It was perfectly timed to
my hour of need, as if coming to my rescue. But I didn't want
to be rescued. I didn't want to be running. I still couldn't believe I *was* running.

If Nev had stood in front of me, I would have torn his guts
out with both hands. And Qole . . .

I didn't know if I wanted to destroy her, or *be* her. The
Shadow, the raw power she had wielded at the start of this encounter, not to mention how she had flown the *Kaitan* since,
had left me awed, jealous, and *quite* unsettled. I did not like
feeling unsettled.

"Your Majesty, shall we engage our Belarius Drive and
signal retreat for the fleet?" The captain of this ship, General
Illia Faetora, came in over a vid comm, her lined, angular face

unmarked by panic or fear, though her tone conveyed a more significant gravity than usual. I had hardly felt the vibrations in here, but my ship had nearly been lost.

"No," I said. "Aren't we just pulling back to reassess the situation?"

The message light still blinked at me, as if waving for attention. I tried to ignore it. The lights of the intense firefight going on in space between Nev's and my forces, flaring on my feed, was somehow less of a distraction, and Devrak's corpse still at my feet—I would have to wait for Suvis to return to take care of it, to limit the questions—was the least of my concerns.

"But it may be best to have a contingency plan in place, in case—"

"We are not retreating," I snapped. "Do I need to make that an order?"

"No, Your Majesty. Copy that. I'll reposition the fleet, allowing for our current losses."

"Yes, yes." I threw myself back in my chair as I closed the comm line. *Repositioning.* That was all this was. Maneuvering for a better angle at Nev's jugular vein.

But part of me knew better. This was a turning point in the battle, and it might have just turned the wrong way for me.

I told myself not to look at the waiting message, but I did anyway. The light winked at me, its gaze warm, not hostile. That was worse. With a sigh that was a half-snarl low in my throat, I finally clicked it open. It was a video message, which my holodesk translated into a three-dimensional image of Heathran.

Heathran *kneeling.* Normally, the sight would have filled me with pleasure: king of kings, head of a galactic empire, on his knees before me . . . but I knew what this was. And that, if I yielded, I would be the one kneeling to him.

"Solara, queen of my heart," Heathran began, and I suppressed a grimace. He couldn't see me, since it was only a recording, but I was in the habit. "There is nowhere I would rather be than at your side, especially during your time of greatest need. Politics forbids it, but there is a way for me to take your side and the systems couldn't question it."

Here we go.

Heathran's eyes seemed to meet mine, even though the time lag made that impossible. "Marry me. Be my wife, and I will defend you and your family to the death. Because then your family will be mine, and mine yours. Belarius-Dracorte would be an alliance—no, a union—to surpass any other in the history of our systems."

To surpass Treznor-Nirmana, he meant. I noticed that he didn't put the Dracorte name first, as Treznor had. The most powerful, dominant family would of course come first. The kneeling, on my part, would begin.

And so would the weakening of our line.

"In a breath, in a single word," he continued, as if sensing my resistance—though he could never have imaged the extent, "you could turn your entire civil war into a minor annoyance, the childish tantrum of an upstart sibling. With Belarius behind your half of the Dracorte family, we will render your brother insignificant."

With me, he was saying, *you will be significant.* As if I weren't already, without him. I relaxed my jaw when I felt my teeth grinding together.

"Marry me," he repeated, "and I will make all your problems vanish. Together, we will remake the systems how we see fit."

I didn't want *him* to make all my problems vanish. I wanted to reduce them to ash on my own. I wanted to remake the systems as *I* saw fit, starting with my family.

Not that a subtler approach would be foolish. Conserving resources by abandoning this war would certainly be the wiser choice for me . . . but far less satisfying. And perhaps not wise *or* satisfying if the only way for me to do so was through Heathran.

He still wasn't finished, and took a deep breath. "To prove my devotion to you and the ideal of us, I'll show you something that no one outside my innermost circle of advisors has seen, and certainly no one on the King's Council."

That succeeded in gaining my full attention, like he knew it would. I had always rather liked being on the inside of secrets, and Heathran was perceptive enough to recognize that. I blinked and sat up straighter, while Heathran, without standing, waved his hand—probably over an infopad out of sight on the floor beside him. A holographic image sprang into the air nearby. I was seeing a holograph of a holograph, but the picture was still clear.

It was a planet, dark gray with a cracked and cratered surface. It looked lifeless and cold—no planet I could recall seeing before.

"This is Nexral, at the edge of our system, which is in turn at the edge of the galaxy. It is extremely isolated, uninhabited, and, without extreme terraforming, unable to support life. It was largely ignored by my family . . . until recently."

At a gesture from him, our view of the planet's surface grew large. There, I saw signs of human contact, construction . . . excavation.

"As part of a routine search for new and valuable minerals to mine, samples were drilled from Nexral, and therein we found what we at first couldn't believe." Heathran leaned closer, urgent. "It is Shadow, Solara, but like none we've ever seen. It's refined, plentiful, and completely tied to the planet's organic composition, but in such a concentrated state that it would take us an age to exhaust it all . . . an age that, for the systems, could be revolutionary. It doesn't need to be to bound to biomatter like algae to be usable—it already is—and it contains five times the energy of an equivalent amount of raw Shadow."

He held up a hand, as if to forestall the fury bubbling and burning under my skin. "I do not wish to compete with your production of Shadow as a usable fuel. Rather than rivalry, I see cooperation between our families, a combination of resources that could create untold growth for both of us. It would take us years before we could invent the technology to utilize our discovery. I just want you to know that Alaxak doesn't have to be your only source of Shadow—you can leave Nevarian his frozen rock. My family is most concerned with creating the new engines that would be powered by your new fuel, or this more refined form of Shadow that we've found. Together, our families—our *family,* if you so desire—could secure our place as the preeminent leader of the systems without question or rival for *many* ages to come."

And then came Heathran's finishing blow—or what he supposed would be, for the person he supposed I was. He held out a ring.

It was a pretty thing, I had to admit, gold and silver intertwining in such an intricate way that was almost obscene coming from a Belarius—catering to Dracorte taste. Gold was the dominant of the pairing, while the silver for the Dracorte name was more decoration than structural, if lovely. Attention to every detail, reinforcing hierarchy even in jewelry. The metals twisted around each other until they met in the middle, cradling a huge, multifaceted stone that was the deepest gray, and yet somehow managed to shine with its own silvery light.

A golden shackle.

"It's a stone unique to Nexral and unequaled in the systems," he carried on, assuming my rapt attention, "infused with this new, never-before-seen form of Shadow. I assure you, it's safe . . . and that no one has worn the like. You will be the first, if you will have me. It represents something never done before, that can only be admired but never emulated. A symbol for the union of our families in everlasting glory."

Now he was sounding downright grandiose. Even so, for a moment the temptation was almost too much to resist.

Almost.

"No," I hissed between my teeth. I didn't go so far as to pound my desk, even though I nearly indulged in the outburst. One thought pounded through my head, unchecked: *No, no, no.*

"I await your response like my lungs await air to breathe. I have never before wanted something so desperately. Please say yes, Solara. My love." He'd never been so flowery. They were words to match the overwrought ring—what he assumed I wanted to hear, no doubt. And with that, the image of him, kneeling suspended over my holodesk, winked out.

No, no, no. I wanted to grip my head in my hands. Because, as much as I didn't want to admit it, as much as I was actively denying it, saying yes would certainly be the easiest alternative to my current situation.

Easy in some ways. In others, it would be the hardest thing I would ever have to do. How could I just hand myself and the Dracorte name over to Heathran for safekeeping, and let him hand me victory, prestige, and power in return? Those were things I should have been able to earn on my own, in my own name, without selling myself. If I'd wanted to marry him, I could have arranged it ages ago. The trick was supposed to be securing his loyalty and support *without* giving anything in return. Marrying would be failing.

I did not want to be my mother, another queen relegated to being a king's wife. The Belarius family was supposedly more egalitarian concerning the sexes and leadership, but I didn't want to share a throne with anyone, not even equally. More importantly, I didn't want the Dracorte name to come second to anyone's.

There had to be another way out of this. I had to find a way. I leaned into my desk, my eyes focusing on my feeds, searching.

I will.

It was only a short time later that the drones began to attack.

XVII

QOLE

I WAS FLOATING ON A DARK SEA. MAYBE I *WAS* THE DARK SEA, OR dissolved into it. Nearly. The current flowed through me like breath, and any limbs or skin I might have once had drifted loosely, farther and farther from me. It was so peaceful I wanted to let myself go. To disperse, dissolve, dissipate.

But an insistent voice wouldn't let me. "No, you cannot."

It was Nev's voice, but not. And yet, who was Nev again, and why was that important? I almost wanted the voice to quiet. I was tired—too tired to think or remember, or even to hold on to this little bit of me that was left, whoever I was. I wanted this darkness to entirely become me, or for me to become the darkness. To be free.

"We need you. You are the first listener in so long. All we have been able to do is scream, but you can hear us. Through you, we have words again. You cannot let go. Not yet."

The words, so crisp and clear, felt like strange, sharp objects lodging in my mind. Did I even have much of a mind, anymore?

"Yes. And ... we are sorry, if our words are not ..." I saw, *felt,* flashes of slipping into warm water, of arms coming around me, of soft fur. *Comfortable,* maybe? "We are still learning your language," the voice added. "It is ... difficult, after so long alone. So long in the darkness." Even though the words were clearer this time, they flickered, almost shimmering with meaning that I couldn't quite see the depths of, like reflected stars highlighting only the surface ripples of deep, black water. I could sense the strain and struggle—the reaching and groping and never finding. It was as difficult as trying to find a way through a maze without light.

"But here, like this, it is easier. Here there is not so much in the way. No pain, no screaming." The darkness undulated around me, emphasizing that there wasn't even my body between me and the voice anymore.

Where are we? I asked. Not with lips or tongue. It was a thought that floated up through me like a bubble in the oceanic darkness.

"Inside you. When you are not like this, though, we still try ... try to talk to you."

When I wasn't like this ...? Did the voice mean when I was awake? Walking around and talking like normal, with arms and legs and eyes and mouth?

"Before, we could only scream. Only hurt. But then, you embraced us, despite the pain. And so we remembered words. And then you listened."

It had definitely been trying to talk to me. And I'd been ignoring it, because it was a figment of my strained imagination—a sign of that stress, a crack in my sanity, like the hallucinations. I'd touched something like this place once before, when I'd used too much Shadow. When I'd nearly lost myself. I couldn't remember the incident well, but I knew that much. Maybe this was the final descent. My fated destination.

Maybe this was insanity.

"No."

Sparks popped in the distance—however far that was, and whatever *distance* meant in a place of endless oblivion—like the white glimmers in the middle of the deepest Shadow. Then they began to gather, floating closer like lamps at night, like the lights of Gamut—Gamut?—as I taxied over the waves. I would have thought it was a trick of my eyes, if I'd had eyes.

And then I felt the vague sensation of my eyelids, warm, as the lights glowed upon them, like dawn before waking. Reminding me that my eyes were there. And that maybe the rest of me was out there, somewhere, ready to be brought to light, to wake, to remember.

But I wasn't ready. Not yet, maybe not ever.

The lights changed shape, like water filling an empty vessel, swirling and flowing into something new. Something recognizable. A bright figure filled my strange vision—a familiar one. A perfect, beautiful face to match the voice, somehow even more perfect in this glowing form.

It wasn't him. Just like the voice wasn't his. It wasn't that it was impossible for it to be him—though it was—but I knew him, even if I didn't remember precisely why or how, and although it looked and sounded exactly like Nev, it wasn't.

Who are you? came my thought.

"We are . . . different. So close, and so far." Each word was a drop of water now, rippling the depths of meaning.

Deep down, I saw it glimmering in the darkness. I felt it, the truth. There was only one thing it could be: Shadow. Was this *actually* Shadow speaking to me? Or was this it—I'd finally gone mad?

Don't, I thought. *Don't look like that.*

"Why?" those perfect lips said.

Because you're not him.

"You care about this face, and we want you to care about us. You listen only sometimes. We want you to hear us always."

My thoughts flowed freely, uninhibited by any of the usual filters: *I don't care about you, whoever you are. I hate you, if you did this to me. I hate you for looking like him when you're not him.*

"No. No hate." The glowing visage didn't change. The features only softened into something resembling concern. "We never meant to hurt you. Not like this."

You don't mean to hurt me by driving me mad? By making me see and feel these things? Hurt is an understatement.

"We couldn't help it, at first. We have tried to talk to you, to those like you, for so long. But we . . . we were broken by pain, ourselves. All we could do was scream, and that hurt you, and others." I felt, more than saw, a flash of skin peeling away from flesh. Exposed muscle and bone. If I could have recoiled, I would have. "But you are strong. You listened through our screams, heard us, and embraced us. You taught us words again." The voice paused, as if considering its way forward, each word a step on a path, leading me toward understanding. "But strength is not always right. It can be wrong. Like *the* Wrong. That is what made us forget our shape and the sound of words. *You* can be wrong. When you do not hear, we show. Sometimes screams are more powerful than words."

The hallucinations, I thought. *You mean . . . that's you trying to communicate?*

"Communicate. Yes. At first, it was an accident, like we said." An accident. The madness that had driven my family, my *people* mad, for hundreds of years. A miscommunication. I almost wanted to laugh. To scream. "Now it is to warn you, but not to hurt *you*." Sadness creased that face. I'd seen actors on the vids before, and it was like that—the perfect expression of sorrow on Nev's face.

Maybe that was why it didn't quite pass as Nev. It was *too* perfect, even for him. Unreal. Inhuman.

What do you mean, the Wrong? I thought.

"The tearing-apart. The destruction."

You try to make me see the damage I do, the pain I inflict?

"Yes. So you understand wrong."

My body, flayed, unraveling, disintegrating—it wasn't pointless, tortured madness, at least not anymore, but a message. A lesson. That it was one of empathy didn't make me feel grateful, exactly. But this Shadow creature, whatever it was, whether real or imaginary, was right that what it "showed" me was probably what I'd done to hundreds of others. The vaporized guards in Dracorva. The fiery *Luvos Sunrise*. The disintegrating "peace" platform. The exploding destroyer that had sent me here.

But the visions didn't only touch me when I was using Shadow as a deadly weapon, so what it was saying didn't entirely make sense. Sometimes the hallucinations came when I reached for Shadow, period, without using it, or sometimes not at all.

"We are not always perfect in our communication. Sometimes we get scared easily, and want to . . . scream. Sometimes we talk to you like that when you feel wrong, and when you cannot hear our words. Or when you *refuse* to."

Or whenever I most tried to block out the madness, hold it at bay. Part of me knew that was only holding off the inevitable, only making it worse, but this was a side of it I'd never considered before. The visions were indeed like a voice raised to a scream.

But what do you mean, when I feel wrong and I haven't even done anything? That's not exactly fair.

"You cannot be like them."

Like who?

The face grimaced, this time so exact a mirror of Nev's anguish that I almost wanted to gasp. The thing was learning— learning what had the best effect upon me. Then it shuddered, shivered, and darkness coiled like a living creature in the background, forming vague shapes. Hints of claw and teeth.

"We cannot show you. It is too . . . difficult, too wrong. But you cannot . . . hate. Consume. Extinguish."

With the words, too many things moved too quickly in the darkness to focus on for long. Fire, but deep silvery gray, cold rather than warm, spreading across space like an unstoppable avalanche. Entire planets enveloped. Portals swallowed by it, the gateways severed as if by teeth.

I gasped, realizing it was showing me the story of the Great Collapse, only laced with this cold gray . . . presence.

The purple-black of Shadow felt right, good, compared to this. This gray fire was hunger, bottomless, something that would consume for the sake of consuming, inevitable, unrelenting. It was unlike anything I had ever seen, and I wanted to do more than recoil. I wanted to scream. I wanted to run. I wanted to never, ever face it.

And if the visions were right, *this thing* was what had destroyed society and cut our systems off from the rest of the universe. *This* had caused the Great Collapse. And *this* was what had driven Shadow mad, causing those who could hear its screaming to follow suit, for centuries.

Like who? I repeated.

"You will know them. You will see now. You are learning too. You have met one like them already."

A man's face flickered in the darkness. Rubion. Nev's uncle, who had tortured Arjan to learn what he could from our Shadow affinity. I was remembering more and more, coming back to myself despite how I might have wanted to drift. Except, now, when I imagined Rubion's face—or when Shadow showed it to me—his eyes glowed a dull gray like the sickly, terrifying light I was seeing.

Before Basra had killed Rubion to save my brother, Nev's uncle had told us something immense, almost too huge to contemplate. . . .

The portals. The myth was that Shadow had caused the intergalactic portals to collapse just over four hundred years ago. These portals had once interlinked, through instantaneous transport, other entire *galaxies*. They were now lost to us, too far away for even a faster-than-light ship to reach in human lifetimes.

But then, contrary to myth, Rubion had told us Shadow hadn't destroyed the portals, but *powered* the portals, and that Shadow—wielded by someone like me—could reopen them. He'd been right that reopening the portals would revolutionize society by putting us back in touch with the rest of civilization—with unimaginable planets, resources, and technology. But he'd wanted to get to the portals first, to control the pathways to the rest of the universe, to accumulate terrifying power. And he'd been planning on using me to do it.

"The Wrong . . . the Wrong hides. Waiting. Hungry. Hating. You cannot be this. You have to know it. Find it. Reveal it."

How? I'm not even entirely sure what it *is.*

"We will help you. You will be able to recognize it. And

we will heal you now, not hurt you, so that you can help us. We need you."

I didn't quite understand. *To do what?*

"To be our . . . link. Our eyes and hands and voice. Our weapon, but not used for wrong. To open and embrace. You need to stop it."

I would be Shadow's tool instead of Rubion's. But if whatever evil I'd seen had been responsible for the madness that had plagued Alaxak for centuries, and shut down the portals in order for people like Rubion to regain control of them, then I didn't mind. They, *it,* definitely had to be stopped. But how? Was *I* supposed to open the portals first?

But if sometimes I'm wrong, like it, *why do you trust me to stop it? How can I?*

"Love makes you right. Hate makes you wrong. Remember that." Light flared, and the not-Nev moved forward. Glowing hands touched my cheeks, and I felt the rest of my face. The bright visage smiled—so sweet and brilliant that tears sprang into my eyes.

I had eyes again. Ears to hear. A mouth to speak. A body to move. The light—*Shadow*—was saving me. Pulling me back together. Returning me to myself. And when the words came again, they were as audible as if spoken to my face.

"With your strength returned, it will be difficult to speak this clearly again. But we are here. We are in you. Do not forget."

Then my eyes truly opened.

———

I awoke to chaos. I awoke to *drones.*

They were everywhere. In the feeds and through the *Kai-*

tan's viewport, as huge and deadly as a nightmare, as real and tangible as the naked eye could see. Feeds, viewport, and drones were all visible from where I lay on a bench on the bridge, held down by both a cocoon of blankets and safety belts designed to keep loose objects from getting thrown around during flight.

Squinting closer, I spotted scratches on my shoulder that looked like they had come from fingernails. I rubbed the tips of my fingers together under the blankets; I couldn't inspect them, but they were sore.

Perhaps I was tied down as protection from myself, not just from momentum and abrupt changes in direction. Without the straps, the inside of the ship would have pulverized me far sooner than I could have torn myself to pieces.

Arjan was in my captain's chair, cursing and maneuvering the *Kaitan* with equal deftness and violence. The violence, at least, was necessary. There were dozens of drones, rending starfighters wing from wing, tailing other midsized vessels like they were tethered to them, and even latching on to destroyers and digging into them with both tentacled arms and giant lasers. It took everything Arjan had to keep us away from them—and everything in Eton's arsenal, by the reverberations I felt through the ship.

I opened my mouth to say something, and all that came out was a dry rasp, inaudible over the noise of the comms and Eton's fire. Right, I'd been screaming. A lot. The hallucinations had been so intense, blotting out sight and reason. Now I was seeing and processing everything as clearly as the battle outside—I could remember everything that had happened, both before and after I'd blacked out, but it was like I was viewing it all from a different, sharper perspective.

A *sane* perspective. Or at least, it felt like it.

And yet I knew for a fact Shadow had been talking to me. That Shadow, in a word, was sentient.

Alive.

And that didn't sound very sane.

None of that would matter, however, if drones tore us to scraps first. I had to figure out what was happening with them before I could make sense of what I'd experienced with Shadow.

"Arjan," I wheezed. It came out as barely a whisper, and good thing, because I realized I shouldn't distract him. I also realized I still had my ear-comm in. The last time I had used it, I'd been talking directly to . . . "Telu?" I said, after mashing my ear against my shoulder with the hope I would hit the activation button. My voice wasn't much louder, but it reached its intended target.

"*Qole?*" Telu nearly shrieked in my ear.

"Telu, I'm awake, and I'm fine, but—"

"Oh, thank the ancestors! Let me comm Nev."

Nev. My stomach twisted with something between happy anticipation and dread. He must have been thinking I'd gone completely insane. I wanted him to know I wasn't, but that wouldn't exactly help our situation, either with the drones or with his being a king. "Wait, doesn't he need to focus on—?"

She interrupted me again. "Trust me, this will help him focus."

And then his voice cut in over the comm. "Qole?" Breathless. Desperate. Filled with such a potent mix of hope and anguish that tears flooded my eyes. It was the same feeling that roiled through me.

He loved me, like I loved him, and there wasn't really anything we could do about it.

"Nev ... Nev, I'm okay. Right now I just need ..." It was sort of embarrassing to say.

"What? What do you need?" He asked as if he would drop everything, never mind the drones outside or that he was commanding a fleet, to give it to me, whatever it was.

"Well, I sort of just need to get off this bench that I'm strapped to. And then I would prefer it if my ship didn't get shredded by drones," I added.

"Oh, *sorry!*" Telu said, for my strapped-down state, probably not the ship. "But I'm a little busy. Basra?" And then there were more voices on the line, each one shouting my name in relief. Their responses were real things, heavy, squeezing my chest just like Nev's had. Arjan even turned around in his seat to glance at me with a wild, triumphant look, but he went right back to piloting.

A second later, he managed to level us out long enough for Basra to slip up onto the bridge, place a cool, comforting hand on my cheek, undo my buckles, and then hurry back down to his station below. I shakily hauled myself over to the copilot's chair and strapped myself in.

And none too soon. The next second, Arjan executed a jarring maneuver that threw me sideways in my seat.

"We can switch, if you want," he murmured out of the side of his mouth.

I felt short of breath just from moving that far. "Give me a second. Looks like you're doing fine, anyway." His smile was brief, pleased. I hit the comm. "Now does anyone want to tell me what the hell is going on?"

Nev spoke first. "I never imagined even *she* could try to use the drones for warfare. They can't tell friend from foe."

Solara. This was her work, then? But if I was seeing

clearly—and I was pretty sure I was, in spite of the unrealness of it all—the drones were attacking *both* sides. "They can't. They're going after her ships, too."

Eton's voice growled from the weapons turret. "Did she do this just to cause mass confusion, with the hope of coming out ahead? Because I think it's working."

"It's not," Arjan said. And he was right. By the looks of it, Solara's forces were getting hammered at least as bad as Nev's. A burst of pride warmed me for a moment when I saw that the Alaxan fleet was way better than anyone at maneuvering. And instead of bothering to fight back against the drones—which was futile at best, deadly at worst, as more and more drones responded to the distress signals—the little fleet of fishermen were picking off Solara's forces in the chaos. They were tipping the scales.

"And ... um ..." Telu's voice, uncertain. "I don't think she's doing this, either."

"What?" Nev's response was incredulous.

"I'm hacking their programming to try to redirect their orders, and ..." She hesitated again. "This is really damn creepy, but I'm not seeing any orders. It seems like they're just doing this on their own."

"Malfunctioning," Nev said, putting such a practical label on something that made the hair stand up on my arms. "There have been increasing reports of the drones acting up."

"Sure," Telu said. "Call it what you want. I'm going to call it really, really *wrong*."

Wrong. The word echoed in my head—I'd just heard a different voice, an inhuman one, saying it so many times, after all. *Wrong.* It echoed, and then clicked into place, like a gear that sent other thoughts whirling.

The Wrong.

Telu likely didn't mean it in the same way, but that was what made me think of it. My focus suddenly shifted. I stared out at the drones, trying to see something *else*. My eyes blurred. I used that sixth sense, my Shadow sense, to reach out. All the while being very, very careful not to have a hateful or angry thought in my head.

It was still surprising that nothing shivered or cracked or broke apart. No dizziness or disorientation struck me as blackness coated my vision. No disorientation other than that caused by seeing, *feeling* in a way that almost no one else could.

There was only the suggestion of a whisper in my ear. "Yes."

Maybe it was giving me the hint that, for once, I was doing this Shadow-thing right.

What I saw made me gasp. Against the darkness in my eyes and the blackness of space, I didn't spot any normal Shadow beyond the residue that remained in the holds of a few Alaxan vessels. I'd used up most of our stores.

No, what I saw glimmered silvery-dull, not bright purple-black, in a web that streaked and morphed in my vision, clearer than the swarm of ships outside. It stretched between all the drones, connecting them.

Rather, it ran *through* the drones, like veins in a circulatory system. It was their blood.

Tentatively, I stretched my senses toward it. Touching the gray web sent a wave of nausea rippling through me, and I pulled away immediately. I still felt sticky, stained.

This was what the Shadow, *my* Shadow, had been trying to warn me about. This new substance was almost like Shadow, except it was just . . . *wrong.*

Images flashed in my mind—razor teeth, hungry maws, sickly fire, dissolving flesh, collapsing portals, and destruction,

destruction above all. I didn't know if it was the Shadow inside me, reminding me, or my own memories.

I gasped, recoiling and shuddering in my seat. "It's in the drones."

"What is?" Arjan glanced at me. "Are you all right, Qole?"

Nev's voice came over the comm. "What's wrong? She's not . . . she's okay, right?"

"It's not me," I said quickly. "I'm fine. It's the drones. *They're* wrong. Something is controlling them, something really bad, and I can sense it."

"Some*thing*?" Basra spoke up, sounding dubious. "Not some*one*?"

"I told you, no one is controlling these things," Telu cut in, and then she murmured almost too low for me to hear her over the comm. "No one human, at any rate."

"Um, okay," Nev said. He must have heard Telu, too. "So you're saying . . ."

When he didn't finish, Eton chimed in. "What the hell *are* you saying? I'm getting the creeps up here."

But I wasn't listening, because there was another voice speaking in my head, sounding clearer, rather than muted, through the veil of Shadow. It sounded a lot like the other voice on the comm, the real Nev. But it wasn't.

"Find the Wrong. Reveal it. Stop it."

Stop it. With those words, I suddenly knew what to do. This *Wrong* . . . whatever it was . . . was close enough to Shadow that it probably had similar qualities. Shadow was volatile, and I could set it off, like touching fire to an explosive substance.

"Everyone just be quiet for a second," I said. "I'm going to try something."

Chatter died. "Let me know if I can do anything to help

you," Nev said. "And, uh, I don't mean to rush you, but the faster the better. We're taking heavy losses."

"Wait," I said, as it occurred to me. "You *can* help. Solara is taking heavy losses, too, right?"

"Correct. She's being decimated."

"Stop the Wrong. Now," the voice repeated with more urgency.

I took a deep breath, ignoring it and hoping I wouldn't pay for it in a second. My intentions still had to do with stopping wrongness, after all—just two-for-one. And I wouldn't even be killing anyone. I would be saving lives.

"Tell your sister I'll call off the drones if she surrenders and retreats immediately. If she doesn't, we'll let them finish her."

"But won't we be letting them finish us too? And *can* you even call them off? That would be—"

I didn't have time to explain. "Nev, just trust me!"

Without hesitating, he said, "Affirmative. I'm comming Solara."

I couldn't help holding my breath, my heart in my throat, my guts threatening to sink out of me. *Please, let this work.* Through the viewport, in the time that it took Nev to get back on our comm line, I saw three more ships go down by drones. Two were Solara's. *Please, please.*

"She agrees." Nev's words were like air, making me light-headed. "She'll surrender. In fact, she's trying to retreat now. We . . . we might consider trying to do the same."

"After this," I breathed, "we might not have to."

Blackness flooded my vision, making the dark-gray web spring into sharp relief through the viewport again. It was like a net, connecting all the drones.

Good thing I was a fisherwoman. A net could also be used as a trap.

This time, when I touched the substance with my senses, I didn't recoil. I let the repulsiveness slide over my consciousness like dipping my arm in a vat of rancid oil. I drew strength from the Shadow inside me until I burned with it. My touch was like a spark to a fuse. Rather, the entire web, the whole pulsating system, diseased veins that led to sickly mechanical hearts, was one giant, interwoven fuse. And it reached straight into every drone in the vicinity. *I* reached into them. Dozens upon dozens.

With a spark of Shadow—good Shadow—I set it all alight.

And so it was dozens upon dozens of drones that suddenly froze, or jackknifed, or spiraled in flight. Cleansing fire was in their systems now, and I forced it to their cores, clenching my fists against the pressure, the resistance I felt. Nothing could hold me back for long. Every drone I could see through the viewport glowed like molten steel, from the inside out. And then they exploded spectacularly, raining flame and chunks of metal across space with glowing tails like comets. For a moment, we were all in the middle of an intense meteor shower.

I guessed I should have thought of that. Arjan managed to dodge and weave, though others weren't so lucky, becoming small meteor showers of their own.

But at least, when it was all over, there was quiet. No drones. There were no distress signals for them to broadcast, once they were taken down from the inside out. For a second, silence reigned. And then crying and cheers and shouting erupted over the comms. It was chaos nearly to match what had come before. Except this was a good kind of chaos.

Arjan pounded me on the back, seized my head in his hands, and planted a massive kiss in my hair.

Nev was shouting at me. "You did it! Unifier's sake, you did it, Qole!"

"I . . . I guess I did." My voice was stunned, shaky. But not from anything other than shock and exhaustion. For only the second time in what had felt like ages, I'd used Shadow and hadn't felt the side effects.

Or maybe Shadow had used me, and that was the difference.

I still had no idea what the Wrong was, the substance that seemed to run the drones. The one that the Shadow inside me was almost afraid of. The one that I apparently had to stop. But at least I understood a few more things than I had before.

Not that it would be easy to explain to anyone else.

"How, Qole?" Nev gasped. He sounded on the verge of tears, and I remembered what he'd had at stake today. "How did you do that? How did you even *know* to do that?"

The words came out, almost numb, before I could stop them. "Shadow told me."

Silence fell again over the *Kaitan*'s comms, if not everywhere else. Arjan stared at me as he practically fell back into the captain's chair.

"Uh, it *told* you?" Eton said. "Is this a figure of speech or a metaphor or something?"

I grimaced, wishing I could take back the words. "I don't know how else to say this, but you should be the first to know. You're my family. All of you."

"Yes, yes, we love you too," Telu said, impatient, "but back to Eton's question . . ."

I took a deep breath, looking out at space through the viewport instead of meeting Arjan's incredulous gaze. Solara's forces, what was left of them, were indeed retreating. Nearly gone. Ours were ragged and battered, but still here, in holding patterns among the shattered remains of drones and the

Treznor-Nirmana construction docks. So much damage. So much to rebuild.

But at the very least, my crew, my family . . . *Nev* . . . they were all alive. The *Kaitan* was whole. *I* was whole.

And I only had Shadow to thank for that. And I already knew what it wanted in return.

A voice. *My* voice.

"Open. Embrace," it said.

There was nothing else for it. *In for a reentry, in for a freefall,* I thought dryly.

"Yes," it responded.

Maybe Shadow liked idioms.

Before I could stall any longer, I said, loud and clear, "Shadow has been talking to me. I know that sounds crazy, but I promise you all that this is the sanest I've ever been."

"What?" At least four people said it at once, voices rising in unison over the comms. Arjan, at least, only continued to stare at me, his mouth open.

"Yeah, so, I thought you should know. . . ," I said as conversationally as I could manage. "Shadow is alive."

XVIII

NEV

"SO THAT'S SETTLED."

I studied her face in the holofeed. I knew it so well, but the new details I now saw unnerved me. On Alaxak, I had seen ice glint in the sunlight: beautiful, friendly, inviting exploration. But sometimes the twinkling of an ice crystal hid a dangerous crevasse. An experienced eye would learn to discern those glimmers of darkness, know that they gave way to awful depths.

I had learned how to pick out those treacherous signs with Qole's help, and without intending to, she had taught me to see honesty in the eyes of someone else. So I saw the depths in Solara's, and I saw the lie.

It turned my stomach to treat with her, and I doubted she was any happier about it. But having fought ourselves to a bloody standstill, we both needed something from the other: peace.

I nodded, working hard to keep my expression neutral. "It is. In exchange for the listed subsystems and all their respective holdings, we declare a truce to all hostilities, effective immediately." It was a higher number of planets than the ones who had immediately declared their support for me. With their associated defense fleets, we would be a respectable power.

"In return," I continued, the word turning bitter in my mouth, "you retain the rights to all other subsystems belonging to the Dracorte system."

Solara's eyes bored into mine. "Including Luvos."

She was making me say it, relishing it, and I hated her for it. "Including Luvos."

That meant she kept the primary source of family revenue: the raw materials from the drones. Of course, it also meant she had to deal with whatever was making them run rogue, and I didn't envy her that.

But she didn't get Alaxak. Or the Shadow grounds.

"Then that is indeed it," I said. "Our advisors will finish the formalities." All in all, we had both gambled everything in our showdown outside Valtai, and ultimately, I had come out ahead. I quelled a rebellious smile at the thought and prepared to end the transmission. *Be an adult,* I reminded myself. "Solara, I'm sorry for whatever part I played in bringing you here. Take good care of Luvos."

"Nev, what brought me here is people like you assuming they can direct my life. Just ask Devrak." Solara's cheeks dimpled in a smile. "And I will use Luvos as it should be. I always did want to host an engagement party where Mother had hers."

I blinked, surprised. "You're getting married."

"She is." Heathran Belarius stepped into the holo, dressed in the dark suit that fit his imposing frame well. Solara held her hand out to him, which he took almost reverently. "The long friendship between the Dracorte and Belarius families has now reached its pinnacle," he continued. "We have become one." He opened his mouth to say more, but Solara spoke first.

"Heathran and I have a great many plans to make. Needless to say, you won't be invited."

Heathran was always something of an inscrutable brick, but he and I had been on friendlier terms than most. Now I could find nothing on his face but distaste. Somehow, Solara had convinced him of my regicide, and merged her fortunes with his. This meant her position was nearly unassailable, and if it hadn't been for my alliance with Makar, who had already regained control of the Treznor-Nirmana family, my forces would be crushed by Belarius might.

But now that I saw she had Heathran on her side, I didn't understand why she had surrendered so much, when she could have pressed for more—for Alaxak. It made me nervous, rather than grateful.

"Congratulations are in order, then." Qole stepped in by my side. "But I'm sorry you won't be able to attend the ceremonies."

When it came to allies, I doubted anyone could begin to imagine mine.

Solara's face went blank, and Heathran's brow furrowed. "Ceremonies?"

Qole's eyes flashed. "Nevarian's official coronation as the *true* Dracorte king, and the declaration of Alaxak as an independent system."

Solara raised an eyebrow all too similar to mine. "What a mighty power that shall be. I wish you the best of luck."

"We don't need luck." Qole held out her hand. With an implosion of light and darkness, Shadow flared to life above her palm. Silence fell as we all stared at the tendrils of purple fire licking the air. For once, Solara's emotion was plain to see—overpowering hunger.

Qole snapped her fist shut, the flame vanished, and the spell was broken. She grinned. "I wish you all the happiness you deserve."

I didn't feel I could really add to that, so I smiled, waved, and killed the transmission.

"Childish," Basra commented.

I shrugged. "What do you expect? She's my sister."

We were just off the bridge of the DFS *Devrak,* in my private chambers, which were fully equipped and ready for almost any royal need. The entire crew of the *Kaitan* was with me; I had insisted on bringing Qole aboard, knowing full well the rest would be with her. They were a package deal, and I didn't mind at all. With no regard for my privacy, they had set about ransacking the place and reorganizing the furniture into a more congenial arrangement.

Telu collapsed backward on the armchair that had been intended for me to sit in and look royal during meetings. "Ancestors, is it over then? Give me drones running amok over hours of *subsection twelve, paragraph Q* on interstellar trade agreements."

"It was paragraph B," Basra observed mildly. "Paragraph Q was on industrial lane setbacks."

Telu looked up at him in horror. "You remember that? How can you remember that? *Why* would you remember that?"

Arjan wrapped an arm around Basra's slim shoulders, his

face splitting in a grin. "It's how Basra unwinds. The more boring the facts, the more relaxed he is. It's like a stiff drink."

He had forgiven Basra for any deception about his identity, that much was clear. But Arjan wouldn't tell anyone the details of how he had led the unbelievable assault on Solara's forces. While he'd always been a phenomenal pilot, everyone knew he had struggled to match his previous heights with one eye, and after the battle, he had remained withdrawn in his quarters for some time. But he did not emerge more sullen; rather, his demeanor had signaled a new change. For the first time in a long time, he had started to joke and laugh again.

I sat down myself, hardly believing the banter I was hearing. Everything had been a blur since leaving Valtai, and now that we had returned to Aaltos, it was finally sinking in that we had all survived. We were okay.

And Qole, especially Qole. The first time I had seen her after the battle, her eyes had been sunken and she had appeared ready to drop. And yet she was calmer than she had been at any point since my parents had arrived outside Alaxak. Possibly calmer than I had ever seen her. Something had lifted. I wasn't sure what it was, but I had to guess it was related to her disturbing revelation about Shadow and the spectacular destruction of the drones. Another impossible feat, but this one hadn't put her into a coma. I wanted to ask her, find out how she was feeling, what she was thinking, but there hadn't been a second to be alone.

Eton appeared over my shoulder, distributing bright orange drinks. "Whoever stocked this place did a good job," he said. "Good selection, allowed for improvisation."

Qole experimentally rattled the ice in her glass with a straw. "Probably courtesy of King Makar." She looked up at me, and the smile on her face did more to ease the aches in my body than all the painkillers in the world. "Did you have someone test your food for surveillance chips or broken glass?"

"No one would ruin ingredients of this quality," Eton said stuffily, settling himself on a sofa that creaked in protest. He took a sip. "I know the mark of someone with taste when I see it, even if it's someone like Makar."

"Yeah, a taste for delicious, delicious blackmail, that ends with him dissolving his own family council and using us as allies against Belarius." Telu burped, putting down an empty glass. "What's next?"

What's next is that I need to talk to Qole. Things were looking better, but I still felt something constrict in my chest every time I thought about her. She and I hadn't had a proper conversation since we'd left for Valtai, and that hadn't ended so well.

I turned to her, opening my mouth, but it was Basra who spoke.

"What's next is that we need to talk about Shadow."

Judging by the quiet that settled on the room, we had all been avoiding the topic as carefully as the next person. Even Qole.

She regarded us ruefully. "I'm honestly not sure I can explain."

"Try." Basra laced his slender fingers together. "You said it was alive. Do you mean the way we've always referred to it, as fishing—or something else?"

"Something else. Well, at least I think." Qole frowned. "It *said* it was alive, and since it could do that, I'm inclined to believe it."

I had been wrong. The room hadn't been quiet before; it had been a noisy bustle of breathing and movement. Now it was truly, deathly still. *It said?* I had been hoping that perhaps that part of the story had changed since we'd left Valtai.

"Everyone says they hear voices before . . . before they stop making sense," Arjan said eventually, staring at the floor. He looked up. "But you seem fine. More than fine, actually. You're better."

"I am." Qole's face softened. "You seem better, too." In that moment, the conversation was between brother and sister, and we were the outsiders.

Arjan nodded. "I had to dip down into Shadow real deep for that last run. I don't know what it's like for you, but at first, it was pretty swift. I didn't even need eyes. I just . . . felt the ships, knew how they were going to move. But when I started fighting . . ." He trailed off and rubbed his forearms.

Qole winced. "Things started to fall apart."

"Yeah. I kept it together for a while. Not really sure how, just did. But then after it was all over, I passed out."

"He was unconscious." Basra was relaying it as a fact, but there was an edge to his words. "Which is why I've asked him not to use it, and to do something about his eye. But he refuses."

"Sorry, Bas," Arjan said, sounding sincere. "Thank you for what you've offered, but I just . . . I can't take you up on it. I would feel like I was betraying myself, to gladly accept what no one else on Alaxak has access to." He brushed Basra's arm. "It's not an insult to you."

"Just because you *do* have access to Shadow doesn't mean it's the better alternative. What other option do you have, other than to give up piloting when you stop using it? Because you *are* going to stop, right?"

Arjan winced at the very idea. "I honestly can't help using it—I couldn't even before I lost my eye. None of us can, if we have the affinity. It just sort of sneaks in. Telu, I bet it happens to you too, hey?"

The hacker shifted uncomfortably. "Yeah. But that's why you don't catch me piloting. The less I find myself using Shadow, the longer I'll live, and the happier I am." She glanced sideways at Qole. "Nothing to do with you. Whatever you've got going on, that's a whole different thing, I think."

"But maybe it's something I can learn too," Arjan said, also looking at Qole.

She stood and paced to the window, then turned around and paced back.

"Just spit it out," Telu said, not unkindly. "Talk to us."

She sat down, leaning forward, her eyes fixed on her brother. "You said it yourself, Arjan; it feels good, right, up until a certain point?" Arjan nodded. "That's because if you try to bend something out of its nature, it fights back. Blocking the destroyers, I was fine. I felt . . . all-powerful." Qole shook her head. "But when I attacked the one, I thought I was going to die, because I was fighting it. It didn't *want* me to attack. I know that sounds crazy, and yet it seems so obvious to me now. When it stopped me, kept me from forcing it to do what I wanted, and I just listened . . . that was when it talked to me."

"What did it say?" Everyone looked at me, and I spread my hands. "What? That seems to be the interesting part to me."

"It said it wanted to communicate." Qole paused, uncertain. "That it doesn't want me to use it for destruction anymore, and that the hallucinations are a lesson to teach me this. They weren't always a lesson. Shadow couldn't always talk, at least not for a long time. It could only scream, accidentally drive humans mad, until apparently I . . . did something that let me hear it. It says I should keep being . . . open. That something bad is headed our way, and that we—I—have to stop it."

"We," Eton reasserted, stirring to life for the first time. "And what is it? What's this 'bad thing'?"

"I'm not sure. It's a substance, sort of like Shadow, but . . . not. Worse. I couldn't make sense of it, but it looked like it was related to the collapse of the portals. Maybe what caused the Great Collapse, instead of Shadow. And Rubion was all tied up with it somehow." Qole and Basra exchanged glances.

"Rubion seemed to think he could open the portals again, using Shadow, and now Shadow is telling you to be open," Basra mused. "That would be an altogether incredible thing. The systems would unite to see it happen. I can certainly imagine something worse than Shadow causing their collapse in the first place, and *someone* worse, the Rubions of the systems, wanting to hoard or ransom the secret of their reopening."

"I'm not sure if that's it, but I *do* know that it's what's in the drones," Qole said, meeting my eyes levelly. "That's how I was able to stop them. Stop *it,* whatever it is, like Shadow wanted me to."

We were silent, again, each one of us trying to process everything Qole had just told us. For me, as a ruler, there was a great deal of unsettling thoughts involved. The drones were a very real problem, but anything to do with the portals was near myth at this point. And yet if they did somehow come into play, they might lead to a power struggle not seen since the formation of the Belarius empire—a problem worse even than drones. If Shadow was sentient on top of all that and had an opinion on the matter . . . then the paradigm for everything changed so much that I wasn't sure I had the tools to process it. Or that I even wanted to try, in case I uncovered a simpler truth—that Qole was simply, quietly unstable.

But I trusted her and, at the very least, it seemed clear that Qole felt she had reached a true, lasting sort of equilibrium with Shadow, something I barely dared to hope for. The rest we would have to take a step at a time, deal with when we knew more. For now, Qole had spent her entire life under the threat of insanity; the possibility that that might be gone gave me hope I couldn't quite describe.

Hope for what? The knot in my chest tightened.

I opened my mouth to speak when Basra beat me to it, looking at Arjan in much the same way I was looking at Qole. "A discovery even better than the key to the portals would be a means for everyone to use Shadow safely." And he meant it. Qole had told me how he'd given up learning the secret of the portals from Rubion simply to rescue Arjan. "And if you can't use it to fight"—he shrugged—"well then, that would keep you even safer, now wouldn't it?"

Arjan smiled back at him lopsidedly, the peace back in his expression. I realized Qole must have already spoken to him of the possibilities for them both, while I'd been busy.

My wrist-comm beeped, reminding me I was *still* too busy. I looked down at the message and sighed. "I'll need to pick this up with you later. Looks like it's time to get ready for a coronation."

———

There was no light. I walked in complete darkness, trusting that I would maintain a straight line and not collide with the people I could hear shifting beside me. I counted my steps in the same way I had with Solara the night we ran across a light-less hangar on Luvos, when she was trying to help me save Qole. It interrupted my count for a moment. Not matter how different I thought we were, we kept making choices that led us to the same place.

Maybe the difference between my coronation and hers was knowing I was surrounded by people who wanted to help each other, not themselves.

I found my count again and, at the last step, avoided tripping on the stairs that let me mount the dais. I stood, waiting, silent in the dark.

A gentle light washed down around me. The simple circular crown glowed to incandescent life, and the Priestess of Truth lowered it onto my head slowly. After the darkness, the light of it on my brow almost eclipsed my vision. I blinked, trying to see.

A dozen bows touched their strings, and the notes broke pure and urgent, the light slowly rising with them. A mass of people materialized as the light expanded, the music racing, reaching a crescendo that spread into a fanfare of horns. Light exploded everywhere.

The ballroom in Luvos was designed to show every planet in the Dracorte system. But here, in the chamber of ceremonies on Aaltos, those who had fallen in war were represented in bursts of glory, shooting stars flaring across the space above us. My eyes watered from the blinding light, but I forced myself to watch them, to accept the pain of those I had sent to their deaths and who had sacrificed themselves before me.

Rows of nobility, dignitaries, and commanders stretched to every corner of the grand hall. Makar, our new ally, stood near the front, black-and-platinum suit shining, managing to look simultaneously bored and pleased. Rava and Marsius were resplendent next to him, almost beside themselves with excitement, and I felt a smile crack the edge of my mouth. If we were in a world where Marsius could be happy, despite it all, some things had to be okay.

The priestess stepped in front of me, solemn as she raised

a hand in benediction. "May you be guided by the Unifier to bring us together, whole, in peace and wisdom." She repeated this twice more, and then, turning to the assembled multitude, she spread her hands. "Nobles, leaders, friends, family—those without power and those who are mighty—behold, Nevarian Thelarus Axandar Rubion Dracorte, the true Dracorte king."

I knew what was coming next. Everyone present, who loved me, hated me, or was indifferent, would bow.

But I had spotted Qole, and I could not imagine her bowing to anyone. I wasn't her king, and I didn't want her to have one. I didn't want her to kneel; I didn't want anyone kneeling. Because I wasn't a person to be knelt to. I was young man, a child, who was muddling his way through, with the lives of millions in the balance.

So I fell to my knees first.

I could hear the inhalation of breath ripple through the giant space, a movement of uncertainty and confusion.

"I am yours," I said. I was quiet, but I knew my voice would carry to every corner of the room, to every vid on every media channel that was broadcasting across the systems. It would be recorded, discussed, and dissected. *Good.*

I raised my head, my eyes searching out those of the people around me. I wanted everyone who could see to understand that my sincerity was absolute.

"I am not here to keep anyone safe by making them my slave. I am here to wield power so that each person can make their own choices, free of fear." *Free of fear.* I didn't know if such a thing was possible. Living in fear of torture, theft, and exploitation was more real, more pervasive than I ever imagined even a few months ago. The very foundations of the power I now wielded were built on fear. Using that power to undo the very things that had created it seemed like twisted logic, a path to chaos. *Or just to an attempt on my life. Again.*

I didn't care. I hadn't passed through fire and brimstone, sent thousands to their deaths, to start playing it safe. People like Qole and her crew didn't have that kind of luxury. It might be chaos, or it might be change.

"Our beliefs and traditions, our ability to live up to them, are what set us apart from another megalomaniac with delusions of grandeur." I clenched my fists. "So let this serve as both encouragement and warning. I am King Nevarian Dracorte, and I serve a centuries-old creed, the impossible belief of my family: that power can, must, be wielded for the betterment of others. I will pursue it at any cost." I found myself angry. I hadn't expected it, but I could already see the fight ahead of me. The agonizing bureaucracy that would drag that down. The promises, the compromises required to succeed at anything. The slight chances of me keeping my values when every long-term goal required their short-term debasement.

But I had a secret weapon.

Everyone was cheering their obligatory cheers when I lifted my hand again, raising my voice. "When my ancestor, Velus Dracorte, was crowned our first king, he named his good friend, Belarius the First, *heartkin*. Family that is adopted after birth. To attack them is to attack us, and their interests are ours. Today, meet *my* heartkin. Rise, crew of the *Kaitan Heritage*."

And so, Qole and her crew walked down the aisle toward me to the voice of a thousand drums, the choir of a thousand chants. They were dressed not in formal wear, in dresses and suits, but the new uniform of the Alaxan navy.

Heartkin was an honor bestowed only upon people who were not part of the Dracorte systems and thus supposedly already part of the family. So as much as this was a ceremony, it was also an announcement to the systems: *Alaxak is rising.*

This was their grand introduction, and they owned it. There was Eton, a landmass all his own, military training resulting in perfect posture and precision of movement. Basra, crest of curls trimmed to compliment the cut of the uniform, was tranquil but focused on something more distant than us, seeming almost otherworldly. Telu, hair tucked back to reveal the sharp tattoo around her eye, held her chin up, eyes glittering with an intensity bordering on madness. She had to be terrified, but instead she came across as a beam of pure intelligence, ready to dismantle any problem. In front of them was Arjan, the swagger of his walk, the faintest of smiles on his lips—a far cry from the Arjan who had entered the Dracorte palace months ago. His eye boldly swept the room, and he winked at Marsius as he passed by.

But it was Qole who led them. Walking with straight, sure strides, she kept her gaze level. She wasn't relaxed like Basra, or possessed of any bravado like her brother. She was contained within herself, and her purpose.

She was the person, the thought, that would keep me honest. My father had had my mother, but they had been too alike, too focused on the greatness of the family. Qole didn't lie to herself, or to anyone else. And to her, an excuse was tantamount to a lie. As long as I held Qole close to my heart, I felt I could always work at turning my responsibilities toward something good.

But keeping the thought of Qole close was not keeping Qole herself close. And as they flanked me on either side, as we formed a wall to the rest of the world, as the seals of friendship were placed around their necks, her glance connected briefly with mine. I couldn't read what was there, and a knot in my chest grew tighter.

———

After the ceremony, I kept peering over heads to spy on the crew of the *Kaitan,* sticking together like a small island in a choppy sea of royal revelers. As king, it turned out to be no faster for me to move across a crowded ballroom than it had been as a prince. Some of the distractions were welcome, like talking with Marsius about how he was enjoying Valtai in Rava's company—immensely—and exchanging handshakes and even back-pounding embraces with both Gavros and Talia. Still, half my attention was elsewhere.

Many excuse-laden minutes later, I arrived at the Alaxan party where they had, again, assembled a collection of furniture they deemed comfortable in a large swath of sunlight slanting in from a wall of ceiling-high windows. But instead of greeting me, they stared over my shoulder, each with their own distinct variation of a carefully neutral face.

"Your Majesty," a voice said behind me, approaching as I did. "Congratulations on your coronation and your victory."

I turned and cursed inwardly. This was not the ideal pairing of social groups; in fact, it was the worst. Daiyen, the Xiaolan princess I had promised to court, was part of the complicated knot writhing inside me. Two narrow straps ran down from her shoulders to the dress that started in a straight cut just above her chest. The green dress fit without a wrinkle to her knees, where it relaxed into an asymmetrical tail. Glimmers of Dracorte blue traced their way in a spiral design along one hip, a subtle tribute to my family.

"Allow me to introduce Her Royal Highness, Princess Daiyen, of the Xiaolan family," I managed to say with the brightest voice I could muster. "Daiyen, I'm honored to introduce you to Captain Qole Uvgamut and her crew: Arjan, co-pilot and engineering; Eton, weapons master; Basra, accounting and trading—also known as Hersius Kartolus the Thirteenth," I added, with an attempt at dryness, "though we like to keep that quiet—and last but not least, Telu, hacker. As you know, I would have never survived if it weren't for them."

Everyone stood, and you could have cut the air with a Disruption Blade. If I'd had one with me, I would have tried, just to relieve the tension. They all must have known about Daiyen.

But then Daiyen smiled warmly and dipped down in respect. "I'm honored. And congratulations on your victory, as well. I understand you led the Alaxan forces with distinction. Nevarian is a friend, and I thank you for any part you had in keeping his hot head on his shoulders."

Qole, her expression grave, bowed in return. "Your Highness, a pleasure. To meet you, that is. Trying to keep a prince alive despite himself is one experience I'll be avoiding in the future."

Daiyen stared for a moment, then burst out laughing. With a basso rumble, Eton followed suit. Then everyone else, except for me. I scowled.

"I see how it is. I'm worth keeping alive unless it's inconvenient. See if I invite anyone to my next coronation." I hadn't known how this was going to go, but out of all possible scenarios, this was the least expected, but the most welcome. The tension inside me didn't go away, but for a brief moment, I allowed myself to imagine a future where being at court didn't mean I had to worry that my Alaxan friends were shunned or feared.

"May we not have need for any more coronations for a very long time," Daiyen said, growing more serious. "And may drones stop going rogue. Speaking of which, will they?"

The question didn't surprise me. Daiyen was the closest thing I had to a friend in royal circles, but we were still royals. And the drones were a problem worth worrying about.

Qole caught my gaze, and I gave her the faintest of nods. If sharing some of what we knew predisposed Daiyen toward Qole, and therefore Alaxak, that would only be valuable. I left it up to Qole how much to tell her. There was the little we had actually proven, and then there were Qole's claims with impossibly huge ramifications, for which we just had to take her word.

But there would be many who wouldn't listen. Who would call her mad.

Qole shrugged lightly. "The short answer is that we don't know." My shoulders relaxed imperceptibly. "Telu may be in a better position to explain."

"Hmm?" Telu, who had sat back down, tried to nervously fold her legs under herself before she remembered where she was and straightened out with an exasperated sigh. "For the amount of money in these places, you sure would think someone would want to buy comfortable furniture," she complained. "There's not much I can explain. I've been hacking around inside those damn drones most of my life, and in the past week I've been comparing notes with the Dracorte hackers. Every accessible log we pull doesn't show Solara tampering with them in any way other than trying to get them to stop attacking. Whatever happened to them was happening at a higher level, one no one has access to."

"That," Daiyen said slowly, "is probably the last thing I wanted to hear."

"You and everyone else," I said. "But . . ." I looked at Qole again.

"I can stop them," she finished for me. "But I might be the only one, and there are thousands of drones in the systems. I'll do what I can to help friends and allies, but that's all I can do."

The word *allies* didn't escape Daiyen's notice, and her focus on Qole grew keener.

"The fact is, I'm determined to get to the bottom of what has been causing drone malfunctions," I continued, "even though the bulk of the drone hubs now lie in Solara's domain. Because it's a problem that concerns all of us now. This is the first time they've turned on vessels and settlements in such numbers, without any evidence of provocation."

Never mind that they *might* be running on a substance that even Shadow feared. And that Shadow was sentient enough to be *able* to fear it. Merely considering it made my head hurt.

Daiyen nodded thoughtfully. "Thank you for sharing this much with me. Let me know if we can be of assistance. In the meantime, if you'll excuse me, I might let Mother know we should steer well clear of any drones." She paused, looking at all of us. "Incidentally, I don't know if we can consider each other allies, at least not yet, but I, for one, will never be able to repay you for beating that monster."

Her words made me blink in surprise. Her mouth formed a smile, but her eyes showed something else. They burned with anger and hatred for Solara, and she wanted me—*us*—to know it. She curtsied again, and was gone.

Even though the animosity between my sister and me was clear, in the world of royals everyone was supposed to stay neutral, unless they were an officially declared ally of one side or another. Daiyen's words, even if spoken in confidence, didn't exhibit the neutrality that a Xiaolan usually adopted. Her passion was unexpected; it felt personal, whatever was between her and Solara.

At least I didn't think it was because of whatever was between her and *me*.

Basra sipped his drink speculatively as he watched her go. "She's formidable."

Qole sat down and propped her boots up on another chair, eyes on me, her own voice decidedly neutral. "She's nice."

I suppressed a wince.

"Very nice, for a royal," agreed Arjan blithely, also settling himself back down. "Then again, the last time I met a nice royal I got chopped up."

"Right now, all you're doing is chopping up my furniture," I replied irritably. "Is that your plan every time? *Hey, we're visiting Nev, let's build a fort from priceless antiques?*"

"We're honorary family now," Arjan replied loftily.

"That's right!" Telu nodded. "So really, this is my chair."

Standing in the last rays of the setting sun, all I wanted was to join them. Make fun of them, find out how they felt, or what they were planning. To simply sit next to Qole as though we belonged together, and spend time with people I wanted as friends.

But while they were finally experiencing the Dracorte hospitality I had promised them at our first meeting, a rapidly approaching gaggle of officials made it clear that it wasn't my job to share it with them.

——

The next time I saw Qole was on Alaxak. After the coronation, the number of details in organizing a new government bureaucracy was overwhelming in itself, and Qole and the other Alaxans could most certainly relate.

"We have come to a decision." Hiat stood at the top of a hill where a new meeting hall stood half-constructed, a short way outside of the wreckage that was Chorda. Only the smooth girders of the new structure arched above us, leaving the sky open. Here, along the equator, the sweep of the land crept out from under a glacier, turned to rolling grassland hemmed by trees, and then leveled off into an endless ice-scattered ocean. Flecks of white flowers bobbed in the grass from a steady breeze, mimicking the waves crawling toward shore in the distance. The chill of the glacier made everyone in the Dracorte delegation shiver.

Everyone but me. The only shiver I had to suppress was from dealing with Hiat, chosen by the newly formed Alaxan System Relations Council as their spokesman, because of his breadth of experience in hogging the spotlight. Telu shifted uncomfortably out of the corner of my eye, and I felt bad that she had to witness this. I took some solace in the fact that Jerra had been elected as the head chairperson of the council, after Qole had refused it. Qole, herself, had assumed a lesser seat as the regional representative of Gamut.

"King Nevarian Dracorte." Hiat extended his hand to me. "The people have decided to cease being part of the Dracorte family system, establish our independence, and conduct our own inter-system diplomatic relations. As a person who once claimed to make decisions for the people of Alaxak, you have been invited here to respond."

I stepped forward, squaring my shoulders. The assembled crowd was even larger than the one in Chorda, where all this had begun. Some were dressed in festive clothing, others in fresh new uniforms, still others in their standard fishing gear. The crowd surrounded us, a few seated in whatever chairs could be gathered in the unfinished structure, most standing, an endless array of variety.

I felt I was entering a palace grander than any I had been in. The clouds had broken, and the sun lit the whitecaps of the waves. The crowd was silent, but their energy rolled over me. I took a deep breath, a strange joy fighting to flower inside me. For the first time, I felt I was being given an honor that had nothing to do with my station, that wouldn't even be seen as an honor by many, but it was one I had earned with blood, sweat, and tears.

"Thank you for the opportunity to speak." I pitched my voice to carry, and stopped. Many of my new advisors had urged me to find some way to strike a compromise; make them a protectorate, insist that independence was a path to self-destruction.

But it was out of my hands, and I knew, come what may, that was as it should be. I had an entire speech prepared to tell them of their new glorious future, but what role, really, would I play in shaping that? It wasn't for me to say, and it never had been. It was time for me to get out of the way.

"I extend the hand of friendship," I said simply. "Call on us if you are in need." I reached my hand out and took Hiat's.

His was surprisingly warm in the cold air, the grip firm, if possessing the softness of someone who had avoided physical labor in recent years. Looking into his eyes, I could see resolve, experience, and the calculating look I had learned to associate with politicians. This time, Telu didn't stir; she stared at him as if she would kill him if he made one false move.

If the fate of a people was in Hiat's hands, it was hard to

know where it would go. But as I released him and stepped back to the cheers of everyone around me, I swept the crowd with my eyes. There was Qole, Arjan, Telu, Jerra. Their fate was in their own hands, not in any one person's, and so they all stood a better chance than anyone I knew.

The cheering swept through the crowd as Jerra wheeled out into the center of the human circle I had just been in. She was grinning ear to ear, and gave me a salute as she passed by.

"Friends!" she shouted. "We are here because of Qole Uvgamut. She was the spark, the fuel, the Shadow fire that started this insane run. In addition to her role as regional representative, what do you say we name her our ambassador to the systems?"

She turned, inclining her head to Qole. "Presuming you are willing, Qole. I know you'd rather fish in peace. We all would. But considering you've proven yourself unable to stay out of the thick of it, we might as well make it official."

Qole grimaced and shook her head, but the crowd was not to be denied. They began to chant her name, and with a helpless shrug to her crew, she walked out into the center of the circle.

Only at times could I see how young Qole truly was. In many families, she would be a child, considered incapable of coping with the world on her own. Here, she had been nominated to represent a planet to empires.

A silence fell over the crowd, and only the whisper of the wind sounded for several long moments. Qole stood quietly, thinking.

"My dream was to simply live my way of life in peace," she began. "It took watching other people sacrifice everything to make me realize there is more than that." Her eyes flicked to me. "So many of us have died. Ships, friends, ways of life destroyed in battle. My brother, the last of my family, was almost taken from me.

"But we have endured worse. We live where others won't; we love a way of life others are too weak to survive. I used to think our survival was because of our traditions, and it is, but now I understand that one of our traditions has been to adapt. The roots of the plant exist only to bring new life."

She turned a circle, and her voice grew stronger with the wind. "It's time for new life. We have lived through the winter, and now we are the spring. There is no room for fear in a Shadow run; there is only the goal. I call on you to not fear the future, only to focus on our goal: a better life on Alaxak, a free life, independent from our enemies and close to our friends."

A wild emotion hammered in my heart while Qole spoke, something that was almost out of my control, as though I were one with the crowd that pressed around us. I knew I had seen a movement born when Qole had spoken of fighting for Alaxak before. Now I had the strange sensation that I had seen Qole's future. She would never again live the life of a simple Shadow fisherwoman and, along with Alaxak, her future was almost infinite in possibility.

I didn't know if that would make her happy, or end well for her. I didn't know how it involved me, if at all. But as celebration spread, as great things continued to happen, her life was changing rapidly, and the urgency with which I needed to speak to her only grew.

As night fell, the Alaxans lit a flare for each person who had died fighting for their independence. Thousands of flickering lights heated paper rockets that floated into the night air. The breeze caught them almost immediately, creating an ever-widening exodus of fire from the shore over the ocean.

Driftwood had been dragged into place to construct giant

bonfires. Their heat and noise warmed one half of me, while the other froze, exposed to the elements. It was strangely comforting. Meat sizzled on makeshift grills, drinks were handed out with abandon, and the only sense of social strata existed in the groups that gathered and dispersed for food, dance, or conversation. I couldn't help but smile as the discomfiture of the Dracorte delegation was slowly eroded, and they one by one joined the others around a bonfire, laughing and joking.

Telu settled herself on a log next to me, looking subdued, if peaceful. She'd had to watch her uncle smile and politick alongside the ruins of Chorda, just as she'd watched him smile and chat with her father over her bruised and blackened eyes as a child.

"Are you okay?" I asked her without preamble.

She raised an eyebrow at me, as if to mock the suggestion that she wouldn't be, and then she frowned, taking the question seriously. "I think so. Hiat is a piece of scrap, but I work for Qole, not him. He can hobnob or burn, for all I care." She leaned forward to warm her hands by the fire. "Now this," she said with a pleased sigh, "feels perfect."

She wanted to change the subject, so I helped her. "Oh, so a log is more comfortable than my furniture?" It was my turn to arch an eyebrow.

"Nope," Telu said. "So I appreciate any comfort it provides. I don't appreciate your furniture, since it supposedly exists for comfort and yet it's pretty much on par with this." She patted the log.

"What she's saying," said Basra, materializing behind me, "is that you have to adjust your expectations."

I jumped. "Great, then I'll start with the expectation that you'll constantly appear behind me like a ghost. Preferably so I don't leap out of my skin every time."

Basra didn't change his expression, but managed to project pleasure nonetheless. "I would say that's exactly what I do, yes."

I looked around. "Where's Arjan?"

This time Basra truly smiled. "He's off by himself, to practice using Shadow." The thought of a loved one toying with such a dangerous substance by himself shouldn't have warranted that reaction, but I understood. Arjan was using it safely, away from anyone he might hurt.

I opened my mouth to reply when I spotted Qole talking with several other people at another fire. She laughed. It was, I reflected, a completely wonderful sight. The knot inside me churned. For once, everything was going perfectly. And yet.

A large weight settled onto my shoulder, a literal one, and I startled again.

"For Unifier's sake!" I said. "First Basra and now you."

Eton flipped a coin over to Basra, who caught it neatly. "Just a bet I had."

I snorted, and we sat side by side for a moment, staring at the fire and listening to the logs pop.

"What happened to you after Devrak's family died?" I hadn't expected to ask the question, but it had formed between us before I could think better of it. Tonight was becoming a time for hard questions and truths.

Eton was silent for so long I thought he wasn't going to reply. But then he cleared his throat. "I didn't know Devrak that well. He was mostly away. But I did like him. His daughter more. She was a good person."

I had been right about Zenaria and Eton. "And someone killed her to get at Devrak? You were blamed?"

"No." Eton's voice had sunk to the rumble of two stones grating on one another. "She wasn't even the target. But Devrak wasn't there, and I wasn't either. I came too late. Finished it."

I felt a shiver run down my spine at the chill that had crept into his voice.

"I didn't leave anyone standing, so there weren't any witnesses," Eton continued. "Which made it easy to frame me. Royals found that easier than facing what one of their own could do." He looked down at his hands. "Devrak said he knew I didn't do it, but I don't see how he could have. After, I wandered for a while, joined the Swarm. I don't think I was a very nice person. I lost myself. Killed a girl. She could have been someone like Zenaria, for all I knew. When I quit, I wanted to get as far away as possible."

"Alaxak sure fits that description."

"Yes," agreed Eton. "And the first time I saw Qole she reminded me of the girl I'd killed and also . . . I was reminded what a good person was like. She was what I both loved about myself and hated. She was how I could make amends, maybe."

That definitely explained Eton's hatred of me when he had learned who I was, and the lengths to which he was willing to go to protect Qole. She had given him a home, and he had dedicated himself to her—his chance at redemption.

"I thought I had to keep her safe at any price," Eton continued, as if following my line of thought. "Didn't realize I was trying to pay the price with *her* happiness, not just yours." He looked at me. "Sorry about that, by the way."

Forgiving him, so hard at first, had made my anger disappear more completely than I could have imagined. "It's space behind the thrusters, and all that."

Eton looked over to where Qole was standing. "Sure. And if you don't stop gazing longingly at her instead of talking to her, I'm going to want to kill you again. Take it from me, staring doesn't accomplish much with women."

I looked up at him in surprise, then back at her, shame

suddenly setting in. I had spent the past few weeks constantly hoping for a chance to speak to Qole, when I was the person who had to create it. There was no comfortable time for what might be an uncomfortable conversation.

Some leader I am. I can't even arrange a conversation.

But Eton was right, and I nodded. *Hard questions and truths.* Without another word, I stood from the log and headed right for her.

"Excuse me," I said. Everyone standing with her started, giving the stupid part of my brain some pleasure, since I had been sneaked up on all night. "Ambassador Qole, when you have a moment, I need to have a word in private. At your convenience, of course."

She raised both eyebrows. "Really? Well, King Nevarian, lead the way."

I couldn't explain what it was, but something about how she said it made my heart pound in my chest. I nodded, mouth suddenly dry, and felt even more stupid. "You might possibly know the area better than I do."

"Possibly."

Qole led me down the gravel beach, outside the ring of light from the fires. We rounded a cove of trees so scraggly they could have been bushes, and she stopped on the lee side, where the wind died down to merely a whisper.

She turned and crossed her arms. "Well?"

I knew I might be in trouble, and I tried to sort through my words. *Talk, damn it, say anything.* "I'm sorry we haven't spoken in the past few weeks."

She shrugged. "You've been busy. I've been busy."

"I know. It's just ..." I paused, the knot in my chest even tighter. I was sick of it. "That's kind of a rotten excuse. I was just afraid to talk to you, and I wasn't really sure what to say. I wasn't really sure what I was doing with any of *this,* honestly." I gestured at the space between us, which, as usual, seemed too great. "I just knew I had to . . . keep you close. So I kept avoiding the problem."

In the darkness, Qole's lips quirked. "In for a reentry, in for a freefall."

No kidding. "Qole, I love you."

She was silent, staring at me.

"It would probably be better for both of us if I didn't. But I do. Every decision I make is different because of you. You're part of me, and there's no getting away from it."

"Nev . . . ," Qole started, but I raised my hand slightly to stave off her words.

"Honestly, I'm not sure exactly how you feel right now, but the absurd thing is, I think you maybe feel like I do. And it's almost unbelievable that both of these things happened at the same time. It's a miracle, frankly. There's just one problem."

"You need to marry Daiyen. I know," Qole said, sounding tired.

I exhaled. I felt like I was picking at the knot inside me, finally, but it was stubborn, impossible to undo. I had to do something, do it right, to get everything to work.

I had to stop pretending I hadn't made certain choices.

"I promised the military tribunal I would, yes. Not just because it was the only way they would support me, but also because, at the time, we needed an alliance to survive. But that was before Makar—before Marsius and Rava. Before the battle."

Qole went very still. "What are you saying?"

"I'm saying that if our position is strong enough, I might be able to avoid that marriage. Makar is psychotic, but he's a powerful psycho on our side. At this point, if I stabilize our system, there's a real chance the generals will agree to drop the demand."

"I already told you, I don't peddle in fantasy." Qole was trying to keep her voice down, but anger infused it. "I'm not going to—"

"No, you're not," I said quickly. "And I was wrong to ever suggest we should live with that kind of hope. It's not fair to you, and that's why I'm telling you right now: we can't be together. But if I'm going to be honest in that way, then I also need to be honest in this one: I won't ever stop fighting for us. The only person I'm interested in marrying, Qole Uvgamut, is you. So right now, you live your life as you see fit. But if I can get free, then you should know that I'm coming back for you. There are very few certainties in the systems, Captain, but I promise you, this is one. I will hope for you, I will fight for you, till my last breath."

The knot dissipated. All it had taken was the truth.

The wind rustled in the leaves, and the ocean retreated down the gravel, gathering itself for another wave. I could hear the celebration behind me, and now that my eyes adjusted to the dark, I could see Qole's face more clearly. In the faint firelight, there was the glint of tears.

She smiled to hide it. "Well, that's the most romantic thing you've said in a while."

"Gaaaaaah." She was joking, obviously, but at least she *could* joke and smile. I clutched at my hair and sat down suddenly. What I wanted to do was hold her close, kiss her, but I had just effectively riveted that door closed. A retractable rivet, I hoped, but a rivet nevertheless. "You don't hate me, at least?"

She sat down next to me and laughed shakily. "Not anymore. That doesn't mean I'm any happier than you are about this, but I understand, better than ever before, the weight of your responsibility, and I don't blame you for it. We're both at a point where we are making choices to get things done, not to make ourselves happy."

I sighed. "That's for sure."

She leaned over to bump me with her shoulder. "But if you want to stabilize your system, you need to figure out why the drones seem to have minds of their own. And I think you'll need help."

I stared at her, hope rising once again in my chest. "Really?"

She nodded. "Obviously, it's a big problem for us too. In my new position, I've been asked to help investigate, especially since I believe what's going on with them has everything to do with what's going on with me—and with Shadow. I might have suggested this in vaguer terms to the council."

The thought of continuing to work with Qole . . . that she had helped *arrange* it . . . I shook my head. "Unifier, but I love you."

Her dark eyes burned into mine, warmth blossoming inside me as she smiled. "Same."

It was as inevitable as the wave that hit the shore. I kissed her.

Her lips were warm, full, against mine. I thought I would explode at the moment they touched, that my chest would shatter with happiness. I wrapped my arms around her waist and pulled her to me as her fingers found my hair. She molded against me as though we had been made to fit perfectly, and our kiss became hungrier, more urgent. I lost my balance as I hitched her closer, falling backward, and she fell on top of me, laughing, hands cupping my face. We kissed again, as I relished the feel of her, the weight of her body against mine.

Then laughter overtook us both, and I simply held her as we rocked back and forth at the absurdity of it all.

After a little while, that died down too, and she lay on top of me, hair spilling across my chest and cheek.

I ran my fingers through it, looking at the moonlit caps of the waves, and at the last of the flickering rockets in the sky. Like those lights, this moment would be gone in a few more minutes. But if life was making a choice, again and again, then right now I was choosing to be here, and happy.

"I guess we're not so good at staying away from each other," Qole whispered.

"I know," I whispered back. "That's what gives me hope."

ACKNOWLEDGMENTS

Book twos are hard to write, and that's before having to write acknowledgments for them, so bear with us. This book was more of a grueling marathon than a sprint, and many people helped us along the way.

Thanks firstly to our incredible support team at Delacorte Press—our editor, Kate Sullivan; her assistant, Alexandra Hightower; our publicist, Aisha Cloud; and all the amazing people behind the scenes—for helping to make our imaginary galaxy a glowing reality. We still can't believe you put up with two weird Alaskans like us. Thanks also to David Moench, who's not even at our imprint but is a publicist for Del Rey, for treating us like one of his own.

Thanks to our agent extraordinaire, Kirsten Carleton, for being our champion, the voice of reason, and our favorite critic. Nobody can nerd out on our manuscripts like you can, and we love you for it.

Thanks to our critique partners and beta readers (aka guinea pigs), most notably Jodie Gilbert, Chelsea Pitcher, Logan Bean, and AdriAnne's mom, Deanna Birdsall, who is made of illimitable patience because she read and proofed every draft. You should be sainted, seriously. And as always, thanks to our spouses, Lukas Strickland and Margaret Adsit, for reading and critiquing our books with an unbiased eye (even though you probably could have been nicer and less useful but we're-kidding-thank-you).

To our amazing community in Alaska, especially in Palmer: thank you so much for showing up for us when you might not give two craps about space operas. We feel the love. And thank you specifically to David Cheezem, owner of our beloved Fireside Books. Your enthusiasm has been like starship fuel to us.

Our online community is just as amazing, and we'd especially like to thank Nicole Brinkley, Julie Daly, and Rachel Strolle for shouting about our books and for just being stellar people. Also, author friends such as Richard Kadrey have made this journey less arduous, and we're grateful to have met you along the way—even if, sadly, you prefer bourbon to scotch. Thank you for the advice and good company.

Thanks to our behind-the-scenes support teams at home, as well, including our spouses (yes, again), and Michael's new addition, his darling baby daughter, Lilia, for making our lives rich and beautiful even if we're depleted husks of human beings. Michael can't thank Margaret enough for carrying Lilia inside her in the hundred-degree Uruguayan nights while he obsessed over space battles. Thanks to Pam and Dan Strickland for being two pillars that support AdriAnne's chaotic life—she couldn't have begged the fates for better parents-in-law. Last but not least, thank you to Odin, AdriAnne's pug, without whom she couldn't have kept her sanity this year.

As always, Michael owes gratitude to God, and AdriAnne to beer—and also scotch, this time. (Didn't we say this book was hard?)

ABOUT THE AUTHORS

Michael Miller and AdriAnne Strickland met in their home-town of Palmer, Alaska, where they agreed on books 99 percent of the time and thus decided to write together. They grew up on Lord of the Rings, Russian folktales, the Ender Quartet, the Little House on the Prairie books, and *The X-Files*. Michael grew up off the grid on a homestead in Alaska and ironically now works very much on the grid in IT and Web develop-ment. AdriAnne grew up in Nevada and now spends her sum-mers as a commercial fisherwoman in Bristol Bay, Alaska, and the rest of her year writing. This is the sequel to *Shadow Run* and their second book together.